William Brodrick was an Augustinian friar before leaving the order to become a practising barrister. His previous novels, *The Sixth Lamentation* and *The Gardens of the Dead*, are available in Abacus paperback.

Praise for *A Whispered Name*

'Impressive . . . Brodrick captures brilliantly the sickening nature of the soldiers' task in having to execute one of their own . . . He uses this emotive material to its full potential, spinning out an interior drama that is every bit as gripping as the events themselves . . . Brodrick tells his story skilfully, pacing it well, building up the tension and revealing just enough to keep the pages turning . . . There are some brilliantly evocative and poignant descriptions of the trenches . . . A passionately human story about a most inhuman moment in history' *Irish Times*

'Sensitively wrought . . . Brodrick's exploratory novels are refreshing and restorative, his style is thoughtful and precise; his integrity powerful. You feel better for having read them. Maybe you are' *Spectator*

'The horrors of Passchendaele in 1917 run through this exquisite novel. Just how much can a man take before he must simply walk away? And what kind of strength enables one man to lay down his life for another?' Matthew Lewin, *Guardian*

'Brodrick writes very well about inner movements of tension and realisation. This is an ambitious book in the way that it balances these profound questions with an intricate and pacy plot, and in its scope, tracing lives spanning nearly a century' *Scotsman*

'A powerful addition to the ranks of memorable World War One fiction' *Metro*

'Brodrick is undoubtedly a fine storyteller . . . [Father Anselm] is a compelling protagonist' Matt Thorne, *Sunday Telegraph*

Also by William Brodrick

The Sixth Lamentation
The Gardens of the Dead

A Whispered Name

A novel by

William Brodrick

ABACUS

First published in Great Britain in 2008 by Little, Brown
This paperback edition published in 2009 by Abacus

A CIP catalogue record for this book
is available from the British Library.

ISBN 978-0-349-12129-1

Typeset in Bembo by Palimpsest Book Production Limited
Grangemouth, Stirlingshire
Printed and bound in Great Britain by
Clays Ltd, St Ives plc

Papers used by Abacus are natural, renewable and recyclable products sourced from well-managed forests and certified in accordance with the rules of the Forest Stewardship Council.

Abacus
An imprint of
Little, Brown Book Group
100 Victoria Embankment
London EC4Y 0DY

An Hachette UK Company
www.hachette.co.uk

www.littlebrown.co.uk

For Anne

He lifts his fingers toward the skies
Where holy brightness breaks in flame;
Radiance reflected in his eyes,
And on his lips a whispered name.

'How To Die', Siegfried Sassoon

Part One

Chapter One

The Prior, in his wisdom, had made Anselm the beekeeper of Larkwood. As with many decisions made by Authority, the architecture of the 'Why?' remained obscure. Anselm's relationship with bees had never got past the sting issue. He'd made that clear when the Prior first raised the matter. But neither zeal nor aversion for a pending task had ever carried much weight for the Prior – his asking what you thought was simply another factor, as much a warning as an inquiry. 'The hives of Larkwood have been silent for too long,' he'd said, summoning the poetry of the Gilbertines. By that route, Anselm attended a beginner's course in Martlesham on apiculture; he bought the simplest how-to manual he could find (as he'd done with law in former times); and he duly took up the title and craft that had passed from Larkwood's life with the demise of Brother Peter who had loathed the taste of honey.

The hives were not well situated, according to Chapter One of the manual. But the choice of location had nothing to do with maximising productivity. Charm had been the deciding factor. Larkwood's cemetery was situated – literally – in a grove of aspens. At the eastern corner the trees thickened, rising on a gentle incline to a clearing. Here, among ferns, nettles and wild flowers, eight hives had been arranged in a circle. To each of these Anselm had given the name of a saint. For his own comfort, he'd secured a spot for himself, dumping an old pew between Thérèse de Lisieux and Augustine of Hippo. Memorising who was where among the rest had not been an easy task. Anselm only succeeded after Sylvester, the Gatekeeper, gave him a Christmas present after midnight mass: oblong labels cut from a worn leather apron. Upon these, in India ink, the old watchman had inscribed a name in glorious copperplate. Within the hour they'd baptised the hives.

It was summer and the time of harvest was fast approaching. The sun, low upon the Suffolk dales, cast long, lazy shadows. Now and again a breath of wind sent the aspens into a tinkling shiver. Anselm heard nothing. He sat legs crossed on his pew reading Chapter Seven on how to remove the main honey crop. Turning a page, he glanced up and saw a woman in a long black coat threading her way between the trees and white monastic crosses. She was in her fifties. Auburn hair, drawn into a bunch, fell behind her shoulders, giving contrast to her pale face. At intervals she paused to read an inscription like someone checking an address. Anselm's attention crept on, behind her . . . to a large, hunched figure with a rugged white beard. An old man had come to a sudden halt at the edge of the copse, leaving his escort to advance as though he dared not enter this strange place of graves. His capped head slowly fell and moments later his shoulders began to shake, like the leaves around him. His hands, one flat on top of the other, rested upon the bulb of a crooked stick. Anselm's eyes flicked back to the woman. She, too, had come to a halt; she, too, had lowered her gaze. Evidently, she'd found what she was looking for. Sunlight slipped through the branches, settling a reddish mist upon her head. Anselm laid his book on the pew and took off his glasses. Gingerly, the skin on his back prickling, he left the safety of the hives.

'Good afternoon,' he said, quietly. 'Can I help you?'

The woman raised her face and fixed Anselm with a look of unconcealed disappointment. Her features were cleanly drawn, with care lines around the eyes and mouth. A scattering of freckles patterned her nose and cheeks.

'Unfortunately, no,' she replied, a natural smile vanishing as she spoke. The Irish intonation was unmistakable, as was the hint of irony. 'The only person who could assist us lies buried here' – she arched a faint eyebrow – 'in quiet extraordinary peace.'

Anselm blinked at the cross between them. The paint was flaking and the work of roots had levered it to one side. A small plaque revealed the essential details of a monk's life: his name, birth, profession and death:

Father Herbert J Moore
1893 – 1925 – 1985

Anselm had first met Herbert at the outset of his own journey towards Larkwood. He'd stumbled upon the elderly monk in a remote part of the enclosure. There, sitting in a stranded car, Herbert had dropped some chance remarks about the monastic life that Anselm had never forgotten. They'd foamed in his mind like yeast. Upon joining the community Anselm had looked to him as friend and guide, though death was to take Herbert far too soon.

'We came here to see Father Moore,' resumed the woman. Delicate fingers reached for a necklace of shining black beads. 'I'd hoped against the odds that he might still be alive. I would so very much like to have met him . . . to have asked him so many questions.'

Her diction was exquisite. There was a fatigue around the mouth that would have looked like sorrow if it were not for the narrowed, unyielding eyes. Behind her, the old man had taken out a handkerchief and was dabbing his beard. A suit of tweed, too heavy for the season, blended naturally with the soft greens and blues of the landscape. It was like camouflage. He pulled down the nib of his wide cap, shuffling his bulk out of Anselm's line of vision.

'I knew him,' ventured Anselm, 'are you sure there isn't something I can say on his behalf?'

He was acutely aware of the gentleman who would not approach Herbert's grave. Though out of sight now, his distress had charged the air between the three of them.

'You knew him well?' The woman appraised Anselm with what seemed to be a last look of hope.

'Yes.' But not well enough, he thought. Not as much as I would have liked.

'Did you know that Father Moore had been an officer in the Northumberland Light Infantry during the First World War?'

Her eyes searched Anselm's face, knowing already the response.

'I'm afraid I didn't.'

She sighed, and her voice fell. 'Then you won't know that he was a member of a court martial that tried an Irish volunteer, Private Joseph Flanagan.'

Regretfully, Anselm shook his head.

'And that is the pity of it,' she said, 'no one does. Neither you, nor anyone over there.' A tilt of the head brought Larkwood into the conversation, and Herbert's decades of close community living; the people who'd lived alongside him not knowing a part of his personal history.

Anselm was genuinely surprised to learn of Herbert's military career. He couldn't easily picture the man he'd known in uniform. He couldn't see him saluting or barking an order or holding a weapon of any kind. Herbert had been, if anything, a man wholly associated with peace and reconciliation. But the not knowing was hardly out of the ordinary. The Gilbertine value on silence tended to pare down both trivia and facts of substance. For this reason everyone was a surprise, at Larkwood. All it took was a loose question to prise out the most astounding personal details. What troubled Anselm, however, was the manifest importance of Herbert's past for this woman, or perhaps more particularly, the old man who'd blended into the trees. Without being able to justify his impression, Anselm sensed an ambience of blame; the suggestion of a wrong in which Herbert had played a part. He felt a sharp confusion in his spirit – to understand the aggrieved but also to defend the memory of a very special man.

'Was the court martial a matter of consequence?' Anselm blenched at the awkwardness of the question; but he could think of no other way to open up the central issue. And he sensed that the woman was ready to pull away, that this visit to Herbert's grave had run its course.

'For Joseph, I'd say so,' she replied, with her natural smile. 'The army sometimes shot a deserter.'

The old man cleared his throat. It was a gruff plea to leave in haste, to stop answering the monk's questions.

'This was no ordinary trial, Father,' she whispered with sudden feeling. 'It had a meaning, a special meaning among so much that was meaningless.' She fastened her disappointment on Herbert's cross. 'I'd hoped he would explain it to me . . . and bring an old man some peace before he died.'

Anselm fiddled with his belt, arranging the fall of his scapular. He was out of his depth, now, as much through ignorance as incomprehension. At such times he held his tongue.

'I must go,' she said, holding out her hand. 'Forgive me, I haven't even introduced myself. I'm Kate . . . Kate Seymour.'

She turned and stooped under a branch. All at once she slowed and said, over her shoulder, 'What does the middle date on the cross mean?'

'That's the year a man took his final vows.'

'I see,' she murmured, one arm resting on a branch. 'Over sixty years a monk and not a word to a soul.' Her voice was low and drained of colour. 'You know, Father, I get the impression this trial was almost as significant for him as it was for the man with his back to the wall. To keep quiet about something so important . . . well, it's almost a lie, wouldn't you say?'

Ms Seymour didn't elaborate. She tiptoed out of the shaded copse into a flush of sunlight leaving Anselm helpless, his arms swinging at his side, as though the activity might pump something sensible out of his mouth. Moments later he watched the two visitors on the track that led to a hotchpotch of red-tiled roofs huddling round a bell tower. They moved slowly, arm in arm, while the old man's stick rose and fell like a steady oar. They moved with the closeness of family.

Presently, Anselm was alone. Frowning, he went back to the hives and tried to enter the mysterious world of bees. He turned the pages of his manual, forcing himself to examine the funny diagrams and the bullet points in bold; but he kept seeing the judder in an old man's shoulders and the sunken head. There is nothing quite so painful to witness as the tears of the elderly, he thought. They accuse the natural order of things. Old age was a time for nodding by the fire, not hiding behind trees. Anselm tossed the book to one side, chewing his lower lip. He sensed again the vague atmosphere of wrong-doing; the hint of blame. Herbert had been one of the founding fathers of Larkwood, revered as much as loved – for his simplicity, as for the largeness of his heart. He was part of the Priory's ambience, a tonality that attracted believer and non-believer alike. The idea that someone could look on his grave and speak of a lie – in however abstract a fashion – was inconceivable. Inwardly, Anselm groaned. He sensed a movement beneath the trimmed lawn of what was familiar and securely established in his understanding of things. 'Those moles are at it again,' he murmured. They turned up every so often, leaving little heaps of disappointment and excavations that couldn't be filled in. Herbert's face seemed to rise before him: fine bleach-white hair, meandering veins around the temples, hollowed cheeks, a mouth open as if ready to cry or laugh. The image dissolved. Soberly, Anselm eyed the labels on his hives. He liked to have his saints, he thought, without the stain of things he need not know.

Chapter Two

1

Anselm's disturbance at the meeting among the aspens did not abate as the day drew on. By early evening he was restive, haunted by the old man's weeping and the disillusionment of the woman at Herbert's graveside. Up until that moment no one had ever sought Herbert's company without looking up to him. No one had ever looked down, detached from and unmoved by his reputation. Preoccupied, Anselm wandered into the common room, not quite thinking where he was going. There, on the far side of the room, occupying a niche built into the stone wall, sat Sylvester – the monk Anselm most wanted to see. He'd been Herbert's oldest and closest friend. Together, with others, they had literally rebuilt Larkwood upon a heap of thirteenth-century ruins.

Sylvester was forever in his nineties, his cranium covered with a gossamer down clipped so short that the shadows on his bones carried the stronger colour. A length of orange plastic twine served as a belt around his thin waist. With the aid of a large magnifying glass he was checking the football results in a newspaper.

'Bristol Rovers one, Burnley nil . . . Chesterfield two, York City—'

'You knew Herbert better than anyone, didn't you?' said Anselm, brusquely. He dropped on to a footstool, arms resting on his knees.

Sylvester lowered the paper to his lap and minutely examined his younger brother through the glass. 'We first met in the summer of nineteen twenty-five,' he declared at last, one large eye fixed upon Anselm. 'I count it one of the greater blessings of my life.' He paused and lowered the lens, his memory wandering into the past. 'At the time I was a thatcher. I'd come to mend a roof . . . shortly after meeting Baden-Powell in London. Shook his hand, you know. We talked privately of the South African war and the siege of—'

'Sylvester,' interrupted Anselm, snatching the newspaper and the glass and placing them on a side table, 'did Herbert serve on the Western Front?'

The Gatekeeper tucked his thumbs into his string belt and said, 'Why do you ask?'

'Well, I met a woman today . . . near the hives . . . she was standing over Herbert's grave. She looked upon him with such . . . I can't quite put my finger on it, but it was something like disillusionment . . . and blame.' Anselm wanted the wisdom and sense that only the aged can give; he wanted Larkwood's night watchman to tell him there were no wolves within the city walls to threaten his memory and understanding. 'She said he'd judged a man . . . for a capital offence . . . that he knew the *meaning* of a trial.'

Sylvester's watery blue eyes studied Anselm with an old fondness. He smiled, gently, and winked. 'I met her, too,' he confided. 'She's made a mistake, that's all.'

'Really?'

'Oh yes' – Sylvester flapped a bony hand at something and nothing – 'I met her at reception. Full of questions. All about Herbert, before he came to Larkwood. Had he left any letters, notes, sermons – Lord, you name it – anything at all to do with a court martial. Had he said *this*, had he said *that*? We had tea, you know. And I'll tell *you* what I told *her*. I knew Herbert for well over half a century. He was my Prior. He was my friend. When his mother died, he told me first. Same with his father. And may these listening walls bear witness – and they've heard a lot over the years – I never heard him mention the Great War once.' He slapped Anselm's knee. 'It was a long, long time ago. The young lass has made a mistake, trust me.'

That was typical of Sylvester. Anyone younger than seventy was a mere whippet. But Anselm wasn't altogether convinced. 'She seemed pretty sure to me.'

'That's the nature of a mistake, my boy.'

'The point is, she didn't come alone.'

'Really?'

'No. There was an old man . . . old by your standards . . . and he must have been sure of something because he just stood beyond the trees, weeping. It was awful. I felt helpless.'

The disclosure landed heavily on Sylvester's confidence. He wrapped a trailing end of orange twine around one hand, as though he'd use it to climb up a wall. 'Weeping?'

'Yes.'

The watchman coloured slightly. Dropping the twine, his hands rummaged in his pockets. Then his lips formed as though to whistle. To reach him, for he seemed to be drifting away, Anselm slapped the Gatekeeper's knee. 'But you should know, Bearer of the Lantern. There must be some mistake. Has to be.'

'Yes, of course . . .'

'Another Herbert, that's all.'

'Aye.'

'A different Moore.'

Sylvester groaned and reached for his paper and magnifying glass. He was not the same man who'd been lodged contentedly in his niche. Another troubled fellow had slipped into his skin. Moving the lens across the page, he said, uncertainly, 'Now . . . where was I?'

'Burnley nil, I think,' mumbled Anselm.

2

On waking the next day Anselm's first thought was upon the obvious: Kate Seymour had come to the reception alone; the old man had remained outside the monastery, just as he'd kept back from the graveyard. It was a compelling image of shame, remorse or respect – Anselm couldn't tie it down, but its force sent him to the Prior's door.

'I'm worried about something,' said Anselm, taking a seat by a window on to the cloister garth.

'Let's be quiet for a moment,' the Prior replied, closing his eyes briefly.

Despite living most of his life in a Suffolk monastery, the Prior's Glaswegian accent remained untarnished. His hair was very short, silvered and spiked. Thick eyebrows, also silver and sharp, pressed against round, cheap spectacles. His eyes were smouldering and dark, and so deep that they seemed to lack any specific colour.

'Now, go to the end of your concerns,' he said, intensely present to Anselm's disquiet.

Ordinarily when listening, the Prior communicated very little save this defining concentration that threatened to absorb the speaker. But no sooner had Anselm mentioned the visitors to Herbert's grave than his eyes moved with a kind of fearful recognition.

'Sylvester believes they've made a monumental mistake,' said Anselm, 'but I'm not so sure. I was present at a terribly private moment for that old man, whoever he might be. It was as though something had happened in his life that reaches right into Herbert's . . . identity. The woman said as much.'

The Prior nodded and then lapsed into thought, his eyes on the Garth.

'There's no mistake,' he said reluctantly, after a while. 'I know the name of the man who kept his distance. Herbert longed to meet him. He lived much of his life hoping and waiting that one day the man you saw might come to Larkwood.' The Prior went to a cupboard in the corner of the room and withdrew a cardboard box. Placing it squarely on the table between them, he said, ceremonially, 'Anselm, I'm going to tell you Herbert's secret. Though he's dead, he needs our help. And so, it seems, does Joseph Flanagan.'

Outside a light wind found the Lark's valley and the old oaks lost their poise. Listening to the Prior, Anselm placed himself in the common room, years and years ago – long before he'd ever thought of a life as a monk – imagining he was present when Herbert Moore had wrecked a bit of fun on Christmas Day.

The festivities were over and evening had fallen. Everyone had gathered before a dangerously large fire. Long flames licked the back wall of the hearth, devouring sweet wrappers and a few stale cupcakes. Someone suggested a diversion whereby each monk would reveal whom he'd like to meet most, and what he'd say if he got the chance. Since Larkwood was a sort of upside-down place, another monk tipped the idea on its head: you had to state *who* might want to see *you*, and disclose what *he* or *she* might have to say. The room for embarrassment was colossal, so everyone eagerly approved the bespoke version. Lots of outlandish encounters were duly revealed, until it came to Herbert's turn. Despite the laughter, his head had fallen on his chest, as though he were asleep. After a nudge and some bawdy cheering, he looked up, his face drawn, his mouth slightly open. Someone egged him on, repeating the rules. Herbert scanned the community anxiously, as though he were searching for a face in a foreign crowd. With a wavering hand, he drew the Prior towards him and mumbled that he was tired. An awkward silence extinguished the banter and the old man shuffled between the chairs towards the arched door that led to the night stairs. Fretting, the Prior followed his steps, for Herbert had also whispered, 'I must speak to you . . . *now.*'

Herbert propped his sticks against the table in his cell and began talking immediately. 'I've always wondered where he might be now, and what he'd made of his life, but I had no way of finding him, not after I became a monk.'

'Who?' asked the Prior, pulling over a stool.

Herbert slumped in a chair. 'There is so much I'd like to say to him . . . but it never occurred to me, not until tonight, that one day *he* might want to see *me*. There's a chance . . . a slim chance.' As always, Herbert's large eyes swam with affection, amusement, tragedy and hope – everyone commented on them; and now they were bright with a plea. 'Can I take over reception?'

'Yes,' replied the Prior gently, appreciating that the Gatekeeper was the first point of contact with any visitor.

'Should he turn up after I'm dead,' pursued Herbert, 'tell him this: he must banish any remorse. There's no room for guilt. He must lead a full and happy life. Have you got that? Full and happy.'

The Prior patted Herbert's arm, assuring him that he'd do as he was asked.

'And give him these . . .' Fumbling with animation, Herbert reached behind his collar and tugged on a leather string. Shortly he pulled free two circular bits of metal, one red, one green. 'They're army tags. They represent the two of us, him and me.'

'Of course.'

Herbert smuggled the discs back against his skin. 'Thank you, Andrew. You're not that bad as a Prior.' He closed his eyes and he seemed to have slipped off, though his lips were moving, as they often did in prayer.

The Prior coughed. 'Who is it?'

Slowly Herbert opened his eyes. His features were fixed, the expression filled with emotion. 'Joseph Flanagan.'

In this way Herbert became Gatekeeper at seventy-five. For fifteen years he sat in reception, greeting all and sundry, waiting with his message and his two gifts. Towards the end of his life he yielded the front door to Sylvester, his understudy. Unambiguous instructions came with the responsibility: that contact details were to be recorded of anyone making a substantive enquiry about any member of the community. No one ever came for Herbert, not until Kate Seymour arrived too late with her many questions.

'He died without that last wish being fulfilled,' said the Prior.

Anselm had slipped into a trance. As a postulant he'd seen Herbert at close quarters every day, often guiding him to the parlour for yet another impromptu consultation with a stranger who'd sought his guidance. The elder had never once mentioned the army, a trial, or the man who might have finally come to see him: the one person for whom he was waiting. Anselm remembered the low ringing of the bell after Herbert had died, that distinctive toll that told everyone to down tools and assemble in the Chapter Room. Dropping a garden rake, he'd joined the hushed crowd. The Prior had been unable to speak through his tears. He'd used the old sign language instead.

'As usual, I collected together Herbert's belongings,' sighed the Prior, reaching into the box. 'This is what I found in his left breast pocket.'

The Prior passed an envelope to Anselm. The writing on the

front was large and slanted, addressed to Private Harold Shaw of The Lambeth Rifles, British Expeditionary Force, France. Anselm took out the letter. A glance told him of a life left behind: of Uncle George's pigeons, family bowling on a Sunday, and a proud mother whose prayers for her son were constant. It was dated May 1916.

'I've no idea who Harold Shaw might be,' volunteered the Prior, 'or why the letter was so important to Herbert that he wore it by his heart.'

Anselm put the note to one side, for the Prior had produced a thick red tome with several coffee or tea rings on the cover. 'This book was in his cell.'

The flysheet announced the *Manual of Military Law*, published by the War Office in 1914. In the top right-hand corner was a signature in faded blue ink: H. J. Moore. Anselm read the title and autograph several times, unable to picture the book in Herbert's hands, still abstracted by those Christmas Day revelations. He flicked through the pages, squinting at the tiny print. His attention fell upon the International Declaration Prohibiting the Discharge of Projectiles and Explosives from Balloons, signed at The Hague on 18th October 1907. The Hague, he mused, anchoring himself to the present moment. So much was sorted out at The Hague . . . even the misuse of a balloon. Cautiously, and mindful of the subsequent ingenuity for killing, he placed the book beside the letter.

'However, it's what I found on the body that surprised me most.'

All Gilbertine Priors prepare their dead for burial. It was a Larkwood custom that the local undertakers couldn't quite comprehend. During the washing down, Father Andrew had lifted Herbert's right arm and found traces of a most peculiar wound. A scar ran from the elbow, round on to the forearm, across the wrist, bending into the flat of the hand. 'As far as I know Herbert had never hurt himself like that in all his years at Larkwood.'

'A war injury, then?'

'So it seems.'

The Prior nudged his glasses high on to his nose. 'Of course I kept the tags. Here, take a look.'

They were round and well worn, like game tokens. Anselm made a start: he'd expected to read a name he recognised. Instead, each tag had been stamped 6890 Private Owen Doyle. 'Who the hell is Doyle?'

'God knows,' replied the Prior.

A letter, a book, a scar, and some tags. Anselm's mind began to float away once more. These relics didn't really belong to the prayerful man who'd slept during Compline. What did they all mean? Part of his intelligence set to work without him, for he heard himself say, 'You can still fulfil Herbert's request. Kate Seymour must have given her address to Sylvester.'

The Prior promptly left the room and returned ten minutes later, carefully snipping the door into place.

'She left a business card,' began the Prior, back by the Garth. With a fingernail he tightened the paperclip repair on his glasses. 'Unfortunately, our man at the Gate can't find it.'

Anselm closed his eyes. There was always a risk with Sylvester. His memory was half shot, finding greatest accuracy in his youth, when the horse had given way to the engine. His dislike of all contraptions without cogs or springs – especially the telephone – meant that reported conversations were often garbled; and written messages frequently vanished, though they usually turned up after a while. This lapse, then, was no real surprise. And, in a way, it was the Prior's fault for having kept him at reception. But he would have none other in his place. Sylvester, he frequently argued, was the face of the Gilbertines. He carried the community with him. He was the right monk to first meet any traveller.

'So what do we do now?' asked Anselm.

'What we always do,' replied the Prior, supremely undisturbed. 'We wait. It is always good to wait.'

Anselm began his descent from the Prior's study, negotiating the narrow spiral stairs. He had a strange feeling of interlude, as before a great awakening; as when the sky is bruised before dawn. All will be laid bare, he thought, seeing again that old man in tears by the aspens. The fields will lose their shadows. It was a matter of necessity. Anselm's thoughts, however, soon turned in the opposite direction, away from what must come to pass, towards the contingent; to the small accidents that had helped change the direction of his life.

Chapter Three

1

It was chance that first brought Anselm to Larkwood Priory. Aged eighteen he signed up for a school retreat in order to avoid an otherwise compulsory geography trip. However a glance at a vocations leaflet on the last day left him subtly changed, for the words slipped deep into the housing of his mind and heart. In the years to come they rattled the bolts between the two and tapped insistently upon the more obscurely located windows. He learned in due course that Herbert had written them:

> We can't promise happiness,
> but if God has called you to be here
> you will taste a peace this world cannot give.

This pledge tracked Anselm from schools in England and France to university at Durham and a career at the London Bar. And so did its geography: Larkwood itself had touched his life, leaving a sort of wound that would not heal. While progressing in the law from hit and miss performances in the Bow Street Magistrates' Court to the occasional scintillating triumph at the Old Bailey, his inner eye remained upon a folding of low hills, thick trees and a mishmash of pink and russet tiles. The clumsy chimes from the bell tower floated over the Suffolk dales, the M11, and a maze of London's streets, to reach a spacious flat in Finsbury Park, where they reminded Anselm that peace might yet be his. A special kind of peace. The words on the leaflet were like a voice by his ear.

Being a lawyer, Anselm examined the main clause. Peace was

on offer 'if God has called you to be here'. There was, unfortunately, no room for argument. There could be no wrangling towards an acceptable compromise. It was only when a tourist from a distant land snapped his photograph outside the Royal Courts of Justice that Anselm recognised the enormity of the problem: the fellow had gone away with the wrong picture; the man in wig and gown was not truly Anselm. Defeated but profoundly unsure, Anselm decided to return to the place of his undoing. He was thirty. It had taken him twelve years to act on what he'd read.

At first he kept his distance. There was a charming B&B in the village and from there Anselm made discreet excursions into the monastic enclosure. But once upon its tangle of aimless lanes his longing grew intense, even painful. This place was home, though he didn't know anyone who lived there, though he'd never been inside the cloister. Weakened and miserable, he'd drive back to his flat and untie the red tape on the papers of another trial. This is real life, he'd say: defending the possibly innocent or the probably guilty. But he didn't believe his own rhetoric. After a few weeks of terrible homesickness he reserved the same room in the same B&B. The owners thought he just loved the homemade Suffolk dumplings (known as 'swimmers' because they floated).

At length Anselm left the lanes and bushes behind and entered the chapel. He sat at the back, eyes on a glimmer in the sanctuary, stunned by the silent celebration within himself. Distantly and calmly he recognised that there *were* questions to be answered at some point, but that there was no urgency, no haste in finding the answers: Why does my restlessness speak of God? What are these cowled men doing here? How can a chance reading of a promise so dismantle one's life? These mind-benders, and more, were all rather remote, because for that one brief moment he felt he was dancing in the waters of life. Thereafter Anselm abandoned the 'swimmers' and always stayed in the guesthouse. To no one did he confide his growing desire to cross the gravelled lane marked 'Private', the narrow lane that led to the monastery door.

It was at this moment in his life, when the questions were well formed – ripe, one might say – that Anselm came across an old monk called Herbert.

2

At the precise time of the meeting Anselm was wrestling with a problem which even to his own mind was of superficial importance. When not in court or wondering how to separate God's voice from his own (in a forensic sort of way), Anselm's passion was jazz. The earlier stuff, mainly: Louis, Bix, Bunny . . . Fats, Teddy Wilson, Earl Hines. Art Tatum. He'd been thinking (wrongly, as it turned out) that these wild cats would have to be caged if he became a monk. Troubled by the notion of no more foot tapping, he'd ambled without purpose to the limits of the enclosure where, to his complete astonishment, he saw a battered green Cortina stuck in a ditch. It had no number plates and the headlights had been smashed long ago. The stranded driver was very old and obviously a Gilbertine because he was dressed in the distinctive black habit and long white scapular. He was laughing to himself. Anselm tapped on the window.

'Do you want a lift?' said the monk, mischievously.

Fifteen minutes later, after jamming a branch under the back wheels – a method he'd seen in a film about commandos in the Burmese jungle – Anselm was sprayed in mud, but the vehicle had been salvaged. He sat in the passenger seat and the monk started asking questions, as if he'd known Anselm since childhood but had a lot to catch up on. There they sat, not moving in the middle of the road, surrounded by oaks and chestnuts. It was November. Every now and then a copper leaf floated down, swooping right and left. The path ahead was covered in acorns and split conker shells. Everything fascinated the old man. It was as though the commonplace details of someone else's life were further proof that existence was wonderful. When Anselm revealed his profession, however, he groaned.

'Ah, the Lord wasn't that fond of lawyers.'

Anselm glanced sideways. The old monk's hair was white and ruffled, and he grimaced. 'Law and love, it's not always a happy marriage.'

Somewhat defensively, Anselm volunteered another analysis, that love without law would be licentious, and law without love would be ruthless. The monk liked that one. He thought it through, moving his mouth round the idea as if it were a gobstopper. Anselm was about to turn the tables and ask the old man what *he* had done before coming to Larkwood, when, to his own surprise, Anselm's sights shifted target. 'Father, what do you do here?'

The question sprang from Anselm's longing to understand. He didn't really care about previous employment histories. He'd watched the monks shuffle to their stalls, their heads shaved and bowed, their robes long and slightly ill fitting; and he wanted to join them, though he didn't fully know why.

The old monk seemed to be watching a memory out of the car window. His face became quite serene, though his lips trembled. Suddenly wistful and frail, he said, 'We tend a fire that won't go out.'

Anselm would have liked an extensive exegesis upon that remark, but he was already learning: Gilbertines often lapsed into silence. As if he'd left out something of importance, however, the monk added cheerily, 'I'm Herbert by the way.'

He turned on the engine and revved with such force that the car shook and birds fled from the neighbouring trees. He rattled the gear stick and they lurched forward with a terrifying bang. Herbert was enjoying himself immensely. The car swung off the track and bounced through a field. It slid and the wheels span, and Anselm at once understood how the car had ended up in a ditch in the first place. By the time they reached the Priory Anselm was rattled by fear. With forced calm he said, 'I came across you by accident. What would you have done if I hadn't turned up?'

The monk thought for a moment and said, 'Nothing happens by accident.'

3

In retrospect – though one can never be sure of these things – Anselm considered himself altered by that meeting with Herbert. The following morning he woke to a certain brightness in the room; on rising, he felt well-toned and athletic, though he was a man who looked darkly upon strenuous exercise; throughout the following months his mind seemed well aired and, for once, simply furnished. While cross-examining a belligerent policeman he realised that his own private questions no longer stood as riddles above the door to monastic life. Which is not to say that they'd been answered. In meeting Herbert Anselm now understood that it is faith which seeks to understand, not understanding that seeks faith.

Confidently and freely, like a man leaving his house wide open, never intending to return, he decided to become a Gilbertine monk. As a first step towards asceticism he put all his jazz collection in a crate by the bin. There was no more serious gesture of which he was capable. He said goodbye to Bix and all the other tigers.

Unfortunately the powers-that-be at Larkwood didn't immediately share Anselm's enthusiasm. The novice master suggested he dwell upon Isaiah, Chapter 11, verses one–ten, a passage which Anselm later read with horror, because it laid out the wondrous qualities of a good judge. The community was pushing him away, he thought, back to the law, to the misery that would desiccate the marrow in his bones. Of course it was wise counsel: they had to be sure; and he had to clearly appreciate what he might leave behind. But Anselm refused to be discouraged. For two years he knocked tenaciously upon a heavy door that only opened ever so slowly, ever so cautiously. He looked through the gap, seeing more and more; and the community looked back like puzzled badgers in their set. In fairness, each side blinked once or twice, wondering what they might be letting themselves in for, but each eventually formed the sort of merciful judgement described by Isaiah. Aged thirty-four, jazz records in his bag, Anselm's feet finally crunched upon the gravel of a lane marked 'Private'. The door was already open and he stepped into the silence he'd first discovered in the woods nearby, when he'd been lost to the world, when he'd not yet found himself.

It is a monastic practice that a junior member of the community is given the task of helping an old monk – literally someone for the elder to lean on. The junior helps him manage the night stairs, brings him tea laced with illicit Scotch, steals the newspaper from the library, or takes him out for a breather when it's not too cold. While these and other mundane tasks are carried out, the elder – in return – usually comes to share his understanding of the silent life. It is a kind of deep teaching by default.

Since coming to Larkwood Anselm had had few dealings with Herbert. The old man was just another shaved head on the far side of the chapel, where he often fell asleep. When awake, he'd sometimes wink across the nave, as if to say that mischief lay at the heart of mystery. So it came as a welcome surprise when, in the sixth month of his postulancy, the Prior appointed Anselm as Herbert's assistant. Of course there was no knowing at the time, but Herbert was to die within a year. Fortunately Anselm had already concluded that the man he would assist was of a rare order. He entered upon his duties with wide, attentive eyes; with, as the Rule advised, the ear of his heart inclined to the Master.

Which was all well and good. But Herbert wasn't the kind of man to volunteer guidance. His strength lay in *who* he was. Even his bending down to pick up a dropped match had become a recollected activity. Simply to watch him move was inspiring. As a result, Herbert didn't really utter anything of spellbinding consequence to Anselm. It was as though he'd said all he had to say out there beneath the trees in the stranded Cortina. He talked, rather, of his childhood, often touchingly. His mother's sandwiches had enjoyed a legendary reputation . . . his father had loved the pebble beach by Derwent Water . . . these were the kind of disclosures that punctuated a stroll by Our Lady's Lake or the grove of aspens that surrounded the hives. They were like small flowers gathered from his infancy, their fragrance known only to him. To an extent he was a secret man. He never once touched upon his role in the history of the Priory. Anselm learned that from the other monks.

Herbert had joined a Gilbertine community in Belgium: Notre-Dame des Ramiers (popularly known as Les Ramiers). That in itself was not remarkable, since those called to monastic life are always drawn to a specific *place*. Herbert, however, was asked to help establish a new foundation in Suffolk, which duly brought him and a number of others to a heap of dilapidated buildings by the Lark, which they restored – apparently (and this taxed the imagination) with the help of Sylvester. At the age of forty, Herbert was elected Prior, a remarkable event because he'd only been professed for eight years. But such was the appeal of the man. His reputation spread. People came from all over to seek his advice, for he seemed to understand in advance any situation, however vexed, however much blame and innocence were muddled into a crisis. His eyes revealed an inexplicable fusion of joy and sorrow. He cried easily – happily, or in shared sadness. By the time Anselm came upon the battered Cortina, Herbert had been at Larkwood for fifty-six years. The car – a sort of motorised wheelchair – had been the object with which he was universally and fondly identified.

This was the community's memory. And it became Anselm's experience.

Almost every week someone arrived at reception asking to see Herbert. They were from all walks of life and often complete strangers. By their manner and questions some were evidently unfamiliar with, or unenthusiastic about, religious institutions. Not a few were distressed. With his arm like a rail, Anselm would lead Herbert to the parlour. On entering, the old man would sigh with delight and raise his arms, his fingers characteristically spread out, as if his limbs were straining to give effect to the warmth and extent of his welcome. Anselm would withdraw, wanting desperately to stay and listen: he was quite sure that Herbert said nothing about extravagant picnics or the fall of light upon Derwent Water.

When Herbert died, Anselm was all but overwhelmed with sadness. Despite the privilege of his position, he'd never really got to know the man who'd drawn him into Larkwood. Over the following years he listened attentively whenever Herbert's name was mentioned. Through passing, affectionate conversations he learned more about the man who'd gone, what he'd said and what he'd done. It took time for a peculiar truth to emerge in Anselm's mind. But it dawned on him nonetheless: to none of these others, Sylvester included, had Herbert ever spoken of fidelity to a sacred fire or the want of accidents.

Chapter Four

1

Kate Seymour's business card did not 'turn up', despite an extensive search of reception and each of Sylvester's many crammed pockets. That she was the daughter of the old man was a fair assumption shared by the entire community; that he was Joseph Flanagan and had made a first and last pilgrimage to Larkwood was virtually certain. For once, the mislaying wasn't only tiresome; it was serious, for nothing could be done to effect Herbert's wishes until it surfaced. In the meantime, Sylvester condemned himself in silence, forgetting to shave for the first time in seventy years. His stubble, in patches and rather like moulting fluff, aged him dramatically. In choir he padded to his stall, reminding Anselm of those forlorn sheep with half their coat trailing on the ground. The community was again of one mind: the Gatekeeper was distressed as much by what he'd done as the discovery of Herbert's selective trust.

Only the Prior was untroubled, being content to let matters take their course. He did, however, have several conferences with Brother Bede, who was responsible for the archives. Bede was always red in the face as if he'd washed his loins in liniment. It made him look awfully wounded and serious. With the Prior's attention resting on his expertise, he'd acquired a further rash of blistering importance which Anselm found almost impossible to look upon. Anselm's direct engagement with recent events and the memory of Kate Seymour's disappointment in a man special to his memory had implicated Anselm in a personal way with the resolution of the crisis – at least as far as he was concerned. But the Prior had simply stepped around him . . . to raise the temperature on Bede's self-esteem.

It was with a cluster of such prickling thoughts that Anselm went to his hives, pausing among the aspens to ponder on Herbert's role in Joseph's ordeal. *Law and love*, he'd said . . . *it's not always a happy marriage* . . . was that part of the meaning of the trial? Before Anselm could develop the thought he heard footfalls behind him on the path. He turned to see the Prior.

'Can the bees spare you for a moment?' he enquired, coming level.

Anselm led him through the leaning crosses to the bench among saints.

'Bede has checked the archives,' began the Prior, without preamble. 'He found nothing whatsoever of relevance. But while digging out the boxes he had an idea. A good idea. He suggested contacting the Public Records Office – the PRO – at Kew Gardens in London.'

'To what end?'

'It holds the national archives . . . and millions of documents from the old War Office, including the transcripts of First World War courts martial.'

While the Prior possessed Herbert's message and the tags, what he did not have was an understanding of *the trial*. And that was the central issue, he stressed, even to Mr Flanagan himself. On this matter neither the Prior nor anyone else could say anything – as Herbert would surely have wished – because Herbert had never shared his thoughts on the matter. Not holding out much hope of success, the Prior had rung the PRO and had eventually been referred to a Military Specialist called Martin Reid. 'A Scot,' added the Prior with approval. 'And he's familiar with "The Flanagan file". So much so that he knew the names of the court's members.' Herbert was indeed one of the three – a knowledge of detail that struck Anselm as extraordinary – but the Prior had moved on, saying that the trial was a complete anomaly.

'Only the papers relating to *executed* soldiers were kept by the War Office. The rest were destroyed . . . which means that, in principle, Private Joseph Flanagan was shot by a firing squad in September nineteen seventeen.'

Anselm looked towards the aspens, to a spot well beyond Herbert's grave. The old man's shoulders had moved horribly, like an injured child's.

'I said nothing to Mr Reid about our visitors, or Herbert's message,' said the Prior. He, like Anselm, had sensed a very private purpose in their coming to Larkwood. 'And that makes his next remarks all the more fascinating. Joseph Flanagan's trial is anomalous in that no one knows what actually happened – either through the court process or afterwards. There's no record of the outcome; no record that he returned to the ranks; no record of imprisonment; no record of death; no record of burial; he was never discharged; his name does not occur upon a single monument or memorial. It's as though he vanished into thin air.'

And vanished he did, thought Anselm, until last week. 'What's held at the national archives?'

'A complete transcript of the evidence.'

'Anything else?'

'I didn't ask. He suggested I come and read the file for myself. It's a public document.' The Prior's eyes wandered over the hives, a slow swing from right to left, squinting at the names of saints and sinners. 'Even if I had Kate Seymour's business card, I wouldn't call her, not just yet. As I say, it's always good to wait. Especially when there's something else to be done.' He waved away a bee, his prickly concentration falling at last upon Anselm. 'I'd like you to study this file. Read it warily. See if you can feel the heat of *meaning*. Something that even now might bring life to Joseph Flanagan.'

Anselm nodded, humbled, for the Prior was far more capable of carrying out that particular task than himself. He made a text live. On occasion, his sermons could be exhilarating, something to make you run outside and drag people in from the byways.

'There seems little doubt that Herbert's hope has not been fulfilled.' The Prior's voice had changed, the warmth of tone revealing his own attachment to Herbert; and at that moment Anselm noticed that at no point in their discussions had the Prior rehearsed a single private memory of Herbert in relation to *himself* . . . which at once outlined their depth and significance. 'We can't simply give the man you saw some tags and a message, as if Herbert had left a scrap of paper with Sylvester. First and foremost, we need to understand what happened between these two men in nineteen seventeen. One found peace, the other did not. And if things follow their usual course, Kate Seymour's address will turn up just when we need it most.'

'But why me?'

Of course Anselm recognised his own qualifications: as a lawyer he'd had appropriate training and he understood French, which might assist with any ancillary documents. But he was quite sure these were not the Prior's reasons.

'Long before you revealed your desire to be a monk, Herbert said that one day you'd come to Larkwood.'

'Really?' Anselm recalled again their long conversation in the battered Cortina. He'd said nothing of his intentions.

'He also said that you reminded him of himself, from the days when he'd been lost.' The Prior put a hand on Anselm's shoulder. 'That's why I want you to go and find him.'

2

It was thus with a sense of Herbert's deep imprint on his own history, and that of Larkwood, that Anselm prepared for his trip to London. Increasingly he was struck that while old soldiers might keep quiet about their experiences, it was nonetheless extraordinary that Herbert had said nothing to Sylvester about his time in the army. They'd met when memories were fresh and raw; it would have been difficult if not impossible to avoid reference to the war and how it might have touched them. But then a cog clicked in Anselm's mind: *Sylvester* never spoke about it either. He'd lived through the trauma and its aftermath, and yet he was permanently locked into the Boer conflict of the previous century. After that, it was as though the world had been saved by Baden-Powell and boy scouts armed with sheath knives and balls of string. He'd leapfrogged one of the defining catastrophes of the twentieth century. With this incongruity scratching at his mind, Anselm rang Martin Reid at the national archives to arrange a meeting.

The Military Specialist was a natural conversationalist, the sort of man you'd invite to animate a potentially subdued dinner party. Quite how they got on to the subject of personal histories passed Anselm by, but he learned that Martin had been in the 'Silent Service' of the Royal Navy (submarines) until a degree in war studies brought him out of uniform and into the service of the national archive. His primary academic field was First World War Naval Operations, but an interest in military discipline had led him to other troubled waters. His voice was wonderfully smooth, leading Anselm to suspect that the Scots accent had been pressed through a sieve at Dartmouth.

'The Flanagan file stands out in several respects,' said Martin. 'But the first clue to its significance is the timing.'

The court martial took place during a lull in the battle for Passchendaele, the name of a village that would henceforth be associated with carnage and unimaginable suffering. Herbert's unit had just carried out a costly attack east of Langemarck. His regiment, and several others, had withdrawn to Oostbeke, near Poperinghe. For the next two weeks – between 2 and 17 September 1917 – they prepared intensively for an engagement on the Menin Road.

'Private Flanagan's trial took place on the first. This is interesting because the court martial was evidently arranged at the earliest opportunity, a matter of days after the offence, which might suggest that the army command wanted to find an *example*' – he paused, letting the sharpness of the word cut its meaning – 'so if the Commander-in-Chief felt that an execution was required to firm up resolve, then the time to give the order was *before* the troops went back into the line on the seventeenth. No one knows what happened. But the timing is not propitious. As I said to your Prior, it's unfortunate that Father Moore didn't leave a diary or testament of some kind, just a line to clear up the confusion left in this little corner of history.'

In something of a daze Anselm set about organising the remaining practicalities. He booked a room in a B&B near the Public Record Office, though he hardly listened to the directions. He was too distracted, his mind returning to the long conversation that had developed with Martin about the Great War. What had once been seared into the heart of a generation now required an exposition, like Hastings or Waterloo. Martin described how for fifteen miles the Western Front looped around the battered city of Ypres, creating a tongue of land that projected into the German defences. It was called 'the Salient'. The high water table coupled with a fragile drainage system meant that the terrain was a kind of moist putty. Constant bombing since 1914 had shattered not only Ypres, but also the land. When it rained, the ground became a swamp. This was the place that Herbert had never spoken about.

Hesitantly, Anselm knocked on the Cellarer's door to obtain the means for travel and subsistence. Cyril always behaved as if necessary expenditure was somehow profligate and that by releasing funds he was being forced to participate in a dubious enterprise. An industrial accident had left him with one arm, overloading the other with gestures to support his remonstrations. Reluctantly he counted out the bare minimum, slammed the money box lid and dismissed Anselm with a curt demand for receipts. On leaving his office Anselm bumped into an atmosphere as solid as the man.

'Is it true?' challenged Bede. 'Are you off to the PRO?'

Responsibilities are sharply defined in a monastery. The kitchens, the laundry, the guesthouse, the sacristy . . . the archives . . . all of them have a monk in charge, and generally speaking people get very hot under the collar if someone treads on to their patch. It's to do with efficiency. But trespass can also ignite the jealousies that give an edge to community living.

'I'd have thought this was an archival matter,' he panted.

'The Prior wants a legal angle.'

'Did you volunteer your services?' Sweat had gathered above his brows.

Anselm didn't even reply.

Ordinarily these last two encounters would have vexed him, but now they were utterly inconsequential. Among old soldiers (said Martin, mingling anecdote with fact) the Salient was called Immortal because of its strategic importance, and for the vast numbers of dead it claimed. At this small spot the hopes of the opposing sides had collided in increasingly desperate attempts to break the deadlock, to make the static war a mobile conflict. No price had been deemed too high. For whoever broke through could launch a sweeping movement inland to win the war. But it never happened. By 1917, he said, there were bodies in the Salient reflecting the age of the conflict.

Anselm had grimaced – not so much at the idea, but because Martin had used an archaeologist's phrase to illuminate the past. It was an unavoidable technique when all that remained of the bloodshed was an archive. The very exercise, however, revealed the acute nature of Herbert's problem. His silence wasn't a species of lie. He'd *seen* the geology of death and it had left him speechless. Confronted now by Bede's wounded feelings, Anselm couldn't quite summon the sympathy. Any more than he could now understand Kate Seymour's disappointment.

Even as he knelt upon the floor of the nave to receive the Prior's blessing and commission – always given before a journey of any kind – Anselm sifted his concerns, trying to shake off the chaff. By the time he dozed on the train as it rattled across the gentle hills of Suffolk towards London, he was sure of his objectives: what had happened to Joseph Flanagan? Why was a letter to Harold Shaw in Herbert's pocket? Who was Owen Doyle? Why were his identity tags around Herbert's neck? Why give the tags to someone called Flanagan? And, of central importance, what was the event that bound these people together? The meaning of the trial had to lie within these markers.

In fact, Anselm had listed the questions in five minutes. The issue that had preoccupied him most was of a personal nature and quite incidental to his mission. He approached it with something like reverence and fear: what had happened to Herbert out there, in the fight for Passchendaele – an experience so powerful that he should forever keep it secret?

Anselm slept fitfully. Occasionally, he slipped into the depths, where he saw a kind, wise face lined with happiness and pain. Even in slumber he knew that Herbert's secret was the key to Herbert the man – the man Anselm had found stranded in a battered green Cortina: a monk who didn't believe in accidents or the charms of luck.

Part Two

Chapter Five

Execution

1

On the evening of the 25th of August 1917 Captain Herbert Moore woke on the slope of a shell hole. He'd hardly felt the blast. It had torn the sleeves off his raincoat, and part of his jacket and shirt. He'd been crouching just behind Alistair . . . Major Brewitt, the Company commander, a solicitor from Morpeth . . . who must have taken the brunt. After the wallop, Herbert found himself prostrate with his face against the dirt, vaguely aware that time had passed, that water was creeping upon him; that he would have to move or he'd drown. It had been early morning when the coal-box had whistled towards them . . . but now the light was fading. He was alone on the edge of a black pool with oily swirls of red and green. Rain chopped its surface and battered his face and arms. Explosions thundered continuously, masking their personality, though nothing landed anywhere near him. The German gunners behind Passchendaele Ridge must have tweaked the gradient of fire, he thought, keeping pace with their enemy's advance. Herbert slid through a sludge of intestines and grit, hauling himself into the open. Staring across the beaten land, he tried to gain his bearings . . . he couldn't see anyone else from the regiment. Abruptly, like the coming of an unforeseen mercy, he fainted.

He opened his eyes to the sound of a hoarse struggle. It was barely light. Rain still pounded all around him, though the crump of explosions had reduced. Crawling on all fours, Herbert made for a voice. In places his legs sank to his thighs but he pulled himself free, leaning on bodies or shattered limbers, as if he was getting out of the swimming pool in Keswick. The voice cried out to God and Herbert came upon a mangled track of half sunk duckboards, recently laid, he guessed. A team of engineers following the advance must have run out of planking or caught a shell with their numbers on it. Herbert, still on his hands and knees, peered ahead at a creamy quagmire and the face of Company Quartermaster Sergeant Jimmy Tetlow. He was up to his waist in mud behind a jerking mule whose bray had become a whimper. The two of them were slowly sinking. Just beyond, some twenty yards away, the Zenderbeek river had collapsed.

'What are you up to, Quarters?' said Herbert. 'This is no time for fooling around.'

'Very good to see you, Sir.' His face was spattered with dirt but the skin around his eyes was almost clean, giving him the look of a man who'd lost his goggles.

They'd last seen each other before zero hour. Quarters' job was to bring up rations for the lads. The plan had been to meet on the Green Line, the battalion's third objective. Neither of them had made it. Dead animals and scattered panniers revealed that the team had probably been hit by another coal-box. They usually came in fours. One man and one animal had survived. Herbert's temples began to beat. Quarters was about two yards away, both arms hooked over the flank of the beast. Terror lit his eyes. Foam and mucus spurted from the mule. All three of them were panting. Looking around him, Herbert saw a tangle of barbed wire, weapons, cloth and limbs. He grabbed a rifle by the barrel and reached out towards the drowning man . . . but the animal subsided slightly, taking them both fractionally away. Herbert stepped into the morass and instantly sank to his knee, falling to one side. By the time he'd dragged himself on to the firmer heap the mule's mouth was thrashing against the mud, and Quarters was up to his chest.

'Shoot him, Sir,' spat Quarters. 'Don't let him go down alive . . .'

Herbert aimed at the head, swore, and dropped the rifle: there was a man to be saved. He tried to yank free a section of duckboard, but it wouldn't budge . . . he grabbed an arm on a torso, but it came away like a wing on an overcooked chicken . . . in a panic, he grasped a length of barbed wire, shook it loose from the heap and threw it across the short divide. Quarters' hands flapped, his fingers spread incredibly wide, but he got a hold. Herbert wound the wire around his right arm and took a grip with his left hand. With all his strength he pulled. His head arched back and he roared through his teeth. This man was not going to die like a brute.

'It's no use, I'm done for . . . oh, God help me . . . oh, Mum . . .' cried Quarters.

'Just hold on,' Herbert muttered, his arms hot but painless.

The mule jerked violently, snorting and spitting as its head slowly sank, the mud oozing into the open jaws. Quarters still had one hand wrapped in wire. The other was out of sight, on the submerged flank of the drowning mule. He tried desperately to raise himself but he just went further down, jerking with the spasms of the beast. Herbert thrust out his jaw and yanked hard but the force made him spin and slide. The wire fell slack and Quarters slumped . . . his chin dropping on to the face of the swamp.

'Shoot me,' he spluttered. 'Don't let me drown . . . shoot me . . .'

With the wire still embedded in his arm, Herbert picked up the rifle and aimed at Quarters, his finger on the trigger.

'Shoot straight, sir.' He snarled, baring his teeth like the animal that had drowned.

But Herbert's hand wouldn't move. His fingers were paralysed. He blinked and spat and began to pant and heave. The barrel first wavered and then began to swing from side to side. The light had almost gone now. A faint glamour lingered on the dirt. Jimmy Tetlow's pale skin around the eyes was eerily bright. The fall of the rain was like applause.

'Shoot.' The voice was weak now, and pleading like a child.

'Forgive me, Quarters,' said Herbert in a faltering parade ground tone.

All that stamping of the feet – the ritual of extended order drill, the barked commands to 'left wheel' and 'right wheel' – it helped you stamp on your own sensibility. He lowered his aim into the mud beneath the chin and pulled the trigger. Quarters took the thump without a sound. Mud and water splashed over his face, blanking the patches round the eyes. He sighed and his mouth fell open. Herbert watched . . . waiting for him to descend into the Salient. But he didn't move. He'd come to a halt. Herbert licked the dirt on his lips and dropped the rifle. His right arm and left hand began to burn. He raised them as if they belonged to someone else and saw the wire embedded in his flesh . . . it linked him to Jimmy Tetlow's clenched fist. At once he felt cold and wet and shivered.

'Go down, Jimmy,' he pleaded, teeth chattering. 'In the name of God, go down.'

But deep in the morass Quarters had found firmer ground, perhaps a tree stump, a heap of sand bags, a vein of bodies from '15, who could tell. Herbert stared at the open mouth. Normally the food rations were brought up on limbers, but Quarters had organised a mule pack because of the wet ground. He'd said, 'See you on the Green Line.' Nothing would have stopped him. Before the war he'd been a fisherman with his own boat. He'd sailed out of North Shields on the Tyne. Twice he'd been thrown overboard. Herbert didn't know much else. That's what it was like . . . you picked up potted histories of life before enlistment. Everyone became the snappy outline of a life on hold.

'Please go down, Quarters . . .'

The rain grew heavier, drilling into the ragged land. Herbert fell back, trying to face-off the sky but he couldn't keep his eyes open. His arm and hand throbbed but deep inside, deep in the numb place beyond the reach of the war, where finer feeling had found a refuge, where the killing and the brawling was still somehow strange, he felt a stab of pain, like a nail in the pulp of a tooth. He shuddered with a most terrible agony. Herbert moaned and tried to crawl away but the wire in his arm tugged at Tetlow's grip. With a scream of pain he tore himself free and span to one side . . . and his flying limb struck part of the litter of no-man's-land, a revolver. He sat upright, wiping the weapon on his torn trousers. Licking his lips, feeling a kind of smoke billowing in his mind, he placed the barrel against his head and pulled the trigger. The hammer scraped back and . . . jammed. Herbert stared at the gun as if the cartridge had just fired. He felt nothing . . . he noticed his own breathing but inside he was dead; as dead as Alistair Brewitt from Morpeth or Quarters from North Shields.

From somewhere behind – among the shadows, the rain and dismemberment – Herbert heard splashing and the low grunts of a working party. The engineers were back, laying the route to Passchendaele.

2

Still on his hands and knees, Herbert followed some stretcher-bearers back to the old front line. He pushed and slopped his way through the grid of communication trenches jammed with bulky shadows clinking and steaming like cattle. At the reserve trenches he made for the RAP – Regimental Aid Post – a dugout covered by an oily canvas flap. Outside the entrance a length of Wilson canvas had been hitched between the parapet and the parados, creating an improvised corridor. The entire trench was jammed with the wounded. Blood spouted black and shiny into the faces of the helpers, their hands flapping as though a fire raged out of control. The whimpering, the cries, the gurgling and the swearing filled the horrendous gaps between each explosion. Grinding his teeth, Herbert slumped to the ground and entered oblivion, a pit so very different from sleep.

He woke to the stab of a hypodermic needle. Somehow he'd been moved under the shelter and dumped upon a crate. The artillery had died down. Captain Oliver Tindall, the Regimental Medical Officer, was mumbling to the RC Chaplain from Brigade, Father Maguire.

'. . . but I always wanted to be a vet,' said Tindall, resentfully. 'My father pushed me to become a doctor. Said it was more worthwhile.' He'd become the unit's RMO six months earlier, freshly qualified from medical school. At the time, his predecessor had lain freshly dead in a crater, along with the then Anglican chaplain, who was yet to be replaced. With a steady hand, the priest held a lantern over the wounds while Tindall fiddled roughly with a bandage.

'It's the same job.' Herbert heard his own voice. There was a pause, as if he'd interrupted a confession.

'No, it isn't,' objected Tindall.

'What's the difference?' asked Herbert, looking up.

The medic's mouth tightened. A firm nose descended from a prominent brow. The chin had a deep cleft in the centre. He glanced at the priest as if for support. Embarrassed he said, 'You've got a soul.'

'Ah,' said Herbert, stupidly. His head dropped and his eyes glazed at the mud lit by the lantern, at the caked puttees wrapped around his shins.

Tindall groaned. He'd forgotten to bring a safety pin. His feet splattered into the darkness and, after a moment, Herbert felt a hand on his neck. It stayed there, warm and heavy. He wouldn't look up: he'd shot a man who didn't drown: he wouldn't face a priest, now or ever again. Shadows jigged and the roof flapped in a freezing swell. When Tindall returned empty-handed he did what his predecessor would have done in the first place: tear the bandage and tie a bow. Once the left hand had been treated Herbert was sent to the Advanced Dressing Station further back from the line; there he'd be registered again and sent further away, to a Casualty Clearing Station. He didn't see the need, but the system had kicked in: he'd been tagged by the RMO and a form had been filled out. If he left the tramlines thereafter, it was called desertion. Everyone knew the rules of the game and what happened when you broke them.

When Herbert splashed out of the corridor, a thin shimmer of light had given shape to the low seeping cloud. Suddenly shells whooshed and whined overhead, aimed a mile or so away to shake up the reinforcements, but Herbert's stomach still lurched to one side. In front of him, a thin figure grovelled against the trench wall, a crimson dressing held with both hands against his eyes. He was sobbing.

'Don't worry,' said Herbert, watching the shoulders heave, 'you're out of it now. You're going home.'

He reached over but the soldier recoiled at the first pat. Herbert dredged up some pity from the obscurity of his soul, for the collar bone had felt small and flimsy, even through the weight of his uniform: and while all bones were flimsy and ready to splinter, that sudden sensation of a bone still growing had stirred a recollection in Herbert . . . of playing fields and bruises to the shin. He looked at the shorn head, and the shadow above the vertebrae where it joined the skull. That terrible awareness of what men were made of – brains, lungs, a stomach, jelly – revealed itself, yet again, as a blasphemy. These were things no man was ever meant to see. Again Herbert stared at the nape of the soldier's neck. What are we doing bringing our youth to a place where it is better to be blind?

Just then Father Maguire trudged into the open with his arm around a stooped Private. The soldier was speaking in a strange tongue . . . it was a musical, racing hum, with the syllables dragged out at the end of each sentence. For a brief moment Herbert forgot where he was, so foreign was the sound. He watched the rapid movement of the lips as if they were an instrument, grateful for this short reprieve, hardly noticing the man's humourless smile or the priest's panic. Father Maguire's head was bent, his breath misting as he listened. With a groan, he splashed over to the boy and pulled out his identity tags. After a quick check of the name he said, 'Come on, son.'

A doctor who wanted to be a vet, and a priest who talked of his children: everything is upside down, thought Herbert. Absolutely nothing makes sense. With that observation he set off for the Advanced Dressing Station where, amid the chaos of emergency amputations, screams and final sighs (like a rapture), his larger cuts were stitched and he heard that half his regiment had been wiped out.

Chapter Six

The Summons

1

Herbert's wound was a 'Blighty', one that would take him back to England, if only for a few weeks. Herbert, however, refused the opportunity and went instead by train from Abeele to Étaples, far, far away from the guns, and then hitched the remaining thirty kilometres to Boulogne. The rain continued to fall, thinning to a heavy drizzle. Weak sunshine raised a low mist that shrouded the endless columns of troops marching to the Salient. In the town he popped into the Officers' Club, leaving his contact details on the notice board. Then he took a room in a hotel by the sea – the room he always took when he was on leave. He didn't open the door, save to go downstairs and eat. For hours on end he stared out at the twinkling waves, his mind drifting to the North East coast, to the sands of Beadnell and the looming Castle at Bamburgh. Betweentimes he twice wrote a letter to Quarters' mother, Mrs Tetlow, and twice he threw it in the bin. Finally, he wrote to Mrs Brewitt, who'd married Alistair last May when he'd been on leave. In a way the Major had saved his life, and Herbert said so with imagined feeling, for he wasn't sure of any gratitude. When he was drained of emotion, he wrote to his parents.

Dear Mother and Father,
We've come out of the line for a spell and I'm having a few days' well-earned rest in Boulogne. Lovely view of the sea and, best of all, I can get up when I want to! Well, what can

I tell you about the war from our end? I'll let you into a secret: even out in the sticks, dinner is a good show; and we only have two pots and a frying pan. Seriously, though, most of the men are cheery and keen as punch to do their bit. There are grousers, of course, but not many, and we egg them along – sometimes a little unkindly! Everyone leans their shoulder to the wheel without asking too many questions. That's not our place. It is, as you well know, Father, the only way. When one looks at the sheer size of the army, and the sophistication required to direct it purposefully in a state of war, one cannot reasonably form a judgment on tactical or strategic matters. So while we in the trenches may not know what the overall thinking might be, I can assure you we remain determined to see the business through to the end, come what may. As usual, Mother is right: it means doing as one is told!

I'm now a Captain, by the way.

Your loving son,

Herbert

Every word was true. In a way he was writing to himself, repeating an important credo. But his parents needed to hear it also, along with those friends who gathered in the sitting room in Alwinton. Herbert's mother, Constance, would read it out loud. The atmosphere would no doubt be hushed and slightly tense. But everyone's spirits would be bucked up by the end, by the rallying call; as were Herbert's, now. He wrote much the same thing whenever he put pen to paper. He padded out his testament with snippets of daily routine, never referring to gas or bones or the guts upon the wire. Not because it was forbidden by the censors, but because the censors were right: it wouldn't help anyone.

Though an officer in the 8th (Service) Battalion, Northumberland Light Infantry, Herbert and his family hailed from Keswick in Cumberland. Upon his own estimation, Herbert had been blithely content until his eleventh year. At that young age he'd put his foot down about Stonyhurst in particular and boarding school in general. He wouldn't go and, much to his surprise, his parents failed to demur. Consequently Herbert went to the local school in Keswick and was generally miserable. His hands were a bit too soft for the farming lads. As though it was an object lesson in life, his parents would not let him revoke that initial decision. Upon completing his education Herbert did the family thing and joined the regiment – the 22nd Lancers. He'd just been gazetted a Second-Lieutenant when an Archduke was shot in Bosnia. The papers said the Serbs were involved. 'Who in blazes are they?' muttered Ernest, Herbert's father. He was outraged at the assassination. The done thing was a clean fight. In Keswick the shooting was simply table talk about barbaric people and distant places. 'That would never happen in England,' said Constance, checking the index of her atlas, not for one moment anticipating an eruption that within weeks would shake the surface of Derwent Water. She'd barely paid homage to Herbert's uniform when he joined the British Expeditionary Force that sailed to France in August 1914. The boys were expected home for Christmas but events sent another ripple across the lake. Herbert was back by September. According to Colonel Maude, his Commanding Officer, Herbert 'had failed to demonstrate the qualities of character that had secured the renown of the regiment'.

'Let's not talk of it, darling,' said his mother in the drawing room that overlooked a pebble beach that skirted the water's edge.

She was shattered but would never say so; and, not being prepared to say so, she couldn't touch on the subject at all. Her hair was wonderfully sculpted, matching the fulsome contours of a white lace blouse with endless buttons on the front. Herbert marvelled that his father ever managed to get past them. To do so required the resolve that had held the line at Mons. And even that brave stand was a prologue to retreat.

'Maude should never have been commissioned,' grumbled Ernest, swishing the decanter. He was an understanding man with heavy whiskers upon each cheek. But he was shattered, too. The Moore men had served in the Lancers for three generations. Only the buttons and braid had changed. 'He was my staff captain in South Africa. Couldn't tie his own damned laces.'

The Moores, on the other hand, knew a thing or two about laces and buttons and brass. Without any reference to Herbert, a pow-wow was organised by his parents. Herbert only knew of it when Sir Ralph arrived, a long-standing family friend and military colleague of his father. General Sir Ralph Spencer Osbourne VC cut a short, compact figure. His lower jaw was slightly advanced; a pencil moustache gave emphasis to his upper lip; hair parted in the centre confirmed an air of precision not vanity. He stood in the drawing room, hands behind his back, not facing Herbert.

'I'm the first in the family to break regimental crockery,' said Herbert evenly, accepting another level of shame.

'Least said, soonest mended.' Sir Ralph kept his eyes on the lake, his fingers lightly slapping each other.

Into the ensuing silence was ushered another visitor dressed in a morning coat. A man with a sallow face and the quiet step of an undertaker.

'He's what your father calls the Loss Adjuster,' explained Constance outside, while the men talked. 'We're going to show Mr Maude what this family is made of.'

The matter was never referred to again.

One day, over tea, Constance announced that she'd found a magnificent property in the North East: Whiteland Manor, near Alwinton. An estate, she explained, with meadows banking the river Coquet. 'Altogether beautiful,' she concluded. 'And yielding a reasonable rent, too.' Though it was four in the afternoon, Ernest reached for the decanter. He loved Keswick and the beach of stones by the lake.

So the family moved to Northumberland. Within three months of settling into the huge, grey-stoned manor, the Moore family had shown Colonel Maude their substance and mettle. In a daze, Herbert went to the tailors in Alnwick where he was measured for a uniform befitting a Second-Lieutenant of the Northumberland Light Infantry. 'Forget the Lancers,' whispered his mother, once more blushing with pride. 'You can start a new tradition.'

Over the years that followed, Herbert often wondered if Colonel Maude had cast his eye over the London Gazette, checking for unusual promotions. He'd have been disgusted.

* * *

On the third day of Herbert's convalescence, when the rain finally stopped, there was a knock at the door. A sergeant from the military police swung a slow, model salute and handed over a small folded sheet of paper.

'A signal, Sir. It is addressed to you.' He took one ceremonial step back, stamped his foot and said, 'I understand the contents are of an urgent nature.'

All three disclosures struck Herbert as completely obvious. But he was used to it. The army had a special ritual for the obvious. With comparable gravity he opened the folded paper and read:

Report to Battalion HQ on 31st August instant.
FGCM. Third officer required.
Confirm receipt.
E. Chamberlayne (Capt & Adjt.)

After the sergeant had left, Herbert walked to the window and gazed across the water. He could have gone home. But he'd stayed . . . because of a private vow to remain with his unit for the duration . . . to keep that life over there free from the corruption of this one over here. He sighed and opened the signal once more, his mind dwelling on one phrase: 'Third officer required'.

At 4.00 a.m. on the 31st August Herbert began the return journey towards the guns, scrounging first a lift on a charabanc to Étaples. At Abeele he obtained a horse and rode to Oostbeke, a small village northwest of Poperinghe where his and several other regiments from the same division had been billeted after leaving the front line. All the way he brooded upon the words dictated to Chamberlayne by their CO: 'Third officer required'. In itself that was a statement of the obvious, worthy of the sergeant in the military police: a Field General Court Martial had to comprise at least three officers unless the convening officer (usually the Brigade commander) dispensed with the obligation for operational reasons. As Herbert cantered down a lane of puddles between fields of cabbage or hops draped on wooden scaffolds, he remembered that two officers had limited sentencing powers . . . the worst they could dish out was Field Punishment or

Imprisonment. After a mile or so Herbert came upon the rows of bell tents and wooden huts, smoke smudging the sky above the troop kitchens. In the distance, near the artillery lines, three observation balloons floated high like fat maggots feeding on the clouds. It was obvious, really: without a third officer, there could be no death sentence.

2

Herbert's billet was an old shed that housed various items of agricultural machinery. They were like instruments of torture – rows of spikes or claws on wheels – and he couldn't for the life of him imagine how they might be used on the land. When he'd settled in, he tracked down Lieutenant Colonel 'Duggie' Hammond to a low farmhouse with a small courtyard occupied by three chickens. His room overlooked their manoeuvres. He was sitting on his bed, arms folded while his dog, Angus, slept twitching at his feet.

'I'm told we lost half the regiment,' said Herbert, sitting on a wooden stool.

Duggie shook his head. 'There is no regiment.'

'What do you mean?'

'We're down to fifteen per cent.' His hair was ruffled. Blood spots from lice covered his face. He had a permanent frown, revealing temperance and a reluctant gentleness. He was a regular soldier though he looked like a man who would have preferred the quiet of marking books, his severity confined to solecisms of grammar and bad spelling. He glanced at Herbert's arm and hand. 'How are you getting along?'

'Fine, Sir. Just some big scratches.'

'You didn't go home?'

'No, Sir.'

Constance and Ernest knew of their son's decision and thought he was going too far, but they'd been quietly awed by his resolve to stay on the field of battle. They let it slip to the locals, and Constance told friends back in Cumberland, hoping they'd tell someone in the Lancers.

Offensive operations had been brought to a halt, explained Duggie, 'Just as the damned rain stopped.' The next move was planned for the 20th of September – though that was secret – with an attack on the Menin Road. The broader objective: strong points on the Gheluvelt Plateau. If that could be taken, along with the Passchendaele Ridge, a glorious charge could be made for the coastal ports of Belgium: it would be a routing of the foe. A mile away was a mock battlefield, the terrain resembling the ground to be attacked. The regiment was to be urgently reconstructed with two Companies from the 10th Battalion in reserve, along with a batch of individual battle casualty relacements. With those added numbers, they could just about continue to fight. Rehearsals would begin in two days, on the 2nd. After the court martial.

'One of our boys was picked up behind the lines,' said Duggie, as if there was nothing else to say. 'An Irishman from B Company. Flanagan. Do you know him?'

'No.'

'He vanished during the show. After the arrest some bright spark told Division who rang up Brigade. It's out of my hands. They want the matter dealt with quickly, before we go back into action, so the court martial sits tomorrow. I'm sorry to have called you back. It's a nasty responsibility.' Duggie's arm folded tighter, as if he were cold. 'Brigade's been twitching –' he tilted his head as if the next echelon of power was brooding upstairs – 'Pemberton says we have to keep our nerve, especially after what's happened . . . he tells me the boys have to know where their duty lies.'

Brigadier General Anthony Pemberton. He'd brought the remains of his four battalions out of the line and his first contact with Division had been about a desertion. They'd leaned on him immediately. As if following the same motion, he'd leaned on Duggie, the relevant CO; and Duggie, albeit reluctantly, had then tipped the accumulated weight of authority's expectations on to Herbert – not any of the other available officers, but *Herbert*.

They watched the hens scratching for seeds among puddles of water.

'I'm a regular soldier,' said Duggie, remotely. 'I know what I signed up for. But these volunteers, yes, they wear the same boots and uniform but they're not the same as us. And all the rules in the King's Regulations can't make that one important distinction.' Turning to Herbert, he said, 'I'm sure you remember, but it bears repeating: the military law we serve under was born in Wellington's time. It was meant to restrain the mob. With a bit of tweaking it met the needs of an empire's professional army . . . it wasn't meant for *this*?' He tilted his head towards the chickens, and the farmyard gate, and the troops beyond eating bacon in the fields.

The court martial was set to take place in an old school, a mile down the road. Herbert was to present himself at nine-thirty the next morning. At the door, Duggie said, 'The boys know their duty well enough.' He paused to find Herbert's eye. 'Just do yours.'

3

Herbert ambled down the lane, turning over this last remark in his mind. In saying the boys knew their duty, Duggie seemed to be taking issue with Pemberton: the boys needed to be reminded of nothing; the one man who had to address his mind to duty's call was Herbert. In some peculiar way, Duggie was relying upon him. He'd picked him out. Nothing else needed to be said. As if waking, Herbert stalled, his attention caught by a strange kind of singing.

Turning to his left he saw a chipped brick wall and, behind it, a rather short steeple. Herbert had been so absorbed with his thoughts that he hadn't paid any attention to where he was going, so much so that he hadn't even seen the church. It was as though the place had just appeared. A wooden plaque read 'Notre Dame des Ramiers'. A gate was ajar, without a bolt or a lock. Herbert pushed it open and walked down a long stone corridor, open to the sky. Ahead was a white arched door. The singing grew louder as he drew nearer upon a path of cracked flagstones. He stood outside, disturbed by the rising chant. The sound echoed as if from a very distant place. He didn't understand the language but he recognised a sort of pleading matched to a wholly foreign spirit of confidence. The melody was unbearably beautiful . . . it spiralled into the very place where Herbert's soul grovelled when the shells came screaming towards him. Without deciding to do so, Herbert fled from a new kind of fear, back to the world he hated and understood. By the time he reached the lane, the singing had stopped. Herbert looked right, towards the tents and huts. On either side were the ordered dispositions of three brigades. There were officers galore, but Duggie had called on Herbert. He'd brought him back from Boulogne to 'do his duty'.

Chapter Seven

Far from being the depot of Anselm's imagination, the Public Record Office was a modern structure rather like one of those pillboxes in Normandy, only it was immense with a plentiful distribution of tinted glass. A great weeping willow by a lake bruised Anselm's sensibility. The branches hung so low that the fronds trailed in the water like an act of veneration. At the reception desk Anselm asked for Martin Reid. Presently, approaching quietly from behind, Anselm heard a soft Scottish voice. 'Good morning, Father. Welcome on board.'

The joke was more self-conscious than clumsy. While Martin had been a confident, even commanding, presence on the telephone, face to face he was somewhat shy. Anselm placed him in his late forties. He was immaculately turned out: polished black shoes, pressed grey trousers and a blue blazer with silver buttons – an appearance wholly fitting a man who'd served under a naval ensign. It was a uniform of sorts, the only delinquent attribute being the open-necked checked shirt, though Anselm suspected a tie bearing a dolphin motif was neatly folded in one pocket. His eyes were dark brown, showing reserve, absorption and a friendliness more easily expressed from a distance. On entering his office, Anselm smiled. The room was in savage contrast to the character of its occupant. Books and papers were heaped on his desk among photographs in various garish frames. Four children smiled out with the exuberance – Anselm presumed – of their mother.

'Remember, I was a submariner,' said Martin, scratching his head as if someone else had wrecked the room while he was out. 'After you've lived in a bicycle pump you don't quite know where to put things once you get the space.'

The disorder was entirely superficial, Anselm was sure. A controlled reaction to the extraordinary discipline of his former professional life. His attire, tone and manner communicated his defining qualities: seriousness of purpose, respect for the subject of his work, and the utmost reliability.

'Given the nature of your enquiries, I've managed to secure some special arrangements: a room of your own, quick access to a photocopier and a telephone if you need help. You mustn't hesitate. Just dial forty-eight.'

Anselm took a facing chair, quite certain that Martin was at least fascinated by his presence. He was, after all, a link to the past, however slender; a thread into a troubling court martial that had escaped any simple classification.

'I hope you can find a clue to the meaning of this trial,' said Martin. He rested his square jaw between cupped hands, letting his pessimism drift across the room. 'For it has a meaning, of that I'm sure. I just have no idea of what it might be.'

Anselm blinked as if a shaft of light had shot through the canopy of aspens over Larkwood's cemetery. Those phrases belonged to Kate Seymour. She'd been here. She'd dialled 48 from a private room. That's how Martin had discovered that Herbert had been a member of the court martial.

'I can't make any promises,' admitted Anselm. He waited politely to see if Martin would confirm the intuition but they were both observing the same discretion: respect for another's confidentiality. But Anselm wasn't really bound. He'd been told no secrets. And an open conversation, now, about Kate Seymour, could only help her and the man she represented. 'Meaning?' He smiled, ingenuously, seeing Martin gauge the temptation to share what he knew. 'Forgive me . . . but how can a trial have a *meaning*?'

Twiddling all three silver buttons on the cuff of one sleeve, Martin nodded at the puzzle. He was unflappable. Which wasn't surprising, given that he could fire an intercontinental ballistic missile if the right person asked him to. When he was ready he asked, innocently, 'Do you understand how military law operated in the field?'

'No.'

'May I explain?'

'Please do.'

Somehow the cluttered table had turned. The shadow of Kate Seymour receded and Martin, very much on his own patch, settled back into the chair of a researcher with a client. He spoke with the one-step-back authority he'd brought to the geology of the Salient. He was not going to discuss the troubles of Kate Seymour.

If a FGCM – a Field General Court Martial – passed a death sentence, he said, hands falling open, the trial bundle hopped up the ladder of military authority: from Brigade to Division to Corps to Army. (A finger counted out the rungs.) At each stage different commanders appended their view on the *character* of the soldier . . . the *evidence* . . . and whether the *death penalty* should be carried out. All this paper finally landed on a lawyer's desk at GHQ who checked the transcript for any procedural errors. Assuming everything was in order, the case went before the Commander-in-Chief. He alone decided if a condemned man was reprieved or not. (Martin's hand came down the ladder, as if it held the order.)

'When you open the Flanagan file you will see that several crucial documents are missing.' Martin pulled a cuff into view. 'Most important of all, there should be a blue Army Form A three. Ordinarily, the C-in-C wrote his decision on the back page. If the man was shot, the officer commanding the firing squad added his own endorsement confirming date and time of execution. In this case, that form has vanished. With it went the doctor's death certificate . . . if there was one.'

'But gaps in the narrative don't add up to a meaning,' objected Anselm, judicially, recalling that he'd often had to handle interjections of that kind at the Bar. They vouchsafed a percipience to the Bench that was not, in fact, there.

'No, they don't. But a *pattern* emerges if we take a wider trawl of the records . . . a pattern that cannot be explained by accidental loss.'

Other types of document ought to have been filled in. Registers of Field General Court Martial; an AF B103 Casualty Form; Regimental, Company and Field Conduct Sheets . . . and Flanagan's name was nowhere to be seen.

'And as I explained to your Prior, the puzzle doesn't end with the trial,' pursued Martin, leaning back in a kind of controlled slouch. 'There's no reference to Flanagan resuming active service, he's not listed as a casualty, and his name was never carved on a monument. In the twenties, civil servants drew up lists of executed soldiers and memoranda for ministers facing post-war flak . . . and again Joseph Flanagan is never mentioned. In terms of a paper trail, he literally vanished in September nineteen seventeen.'

Listening to the succession of truancy, Anselm found himself looking back to where it all began, to the primary source – the file he would shortly examine. 'Assuming that the original court martial papers formed the basis for the later registers and memos –' Martin nodded, tapping the edge of his desk as if it were a piano – 'doesn't that suggest that the file was weeded by someone in the *army* . . . back in nineteen seventeen?'

'Absolutely.'

'And that whoever did it knew that anyone looking at what was left would be mystified?'

'Yes.'

'But no one would sabotage a file for the sake of a man who'd been shot.'

'I agree.'

'It might make sense if he'd lived.'

'And he almost certainly didn't.'

Martin leaned forward, smuggling his elbows into the available space among his books and papers and the photos of his children. 'This is why I talk of a meaning. We're not dealing with a glitch in the administrative apparatus. It was an attack. A deliberate wrecking of the machine to leave an enigma. But as to *who* attacked the file and *why* . . . I'm sorry, but I don't think we'll ever find the answers. My guess is that Father Moore could have told us a tale to bend our ears.' His deep brown eyes found Anselm and didn't waver. 'Maybe you'll uncover his secret. Should you do so, I wouldn't be alone in thanking you.'

That was the nearest Martin would go to admitting that Kate Seymour had come to the PRO; and that he knew she'd gone to

Larkwood as a last hope. His propriety was inspiring but slightly incongruous. Kate Seymour had not revealed the one secret that mattered: Joseph Flanagan was still alive.

Martin became 'at ease in his trainers' as the French say, showing Anselm 'the Donk Shop' (submarine jargon for the engine room) with a mystifying relish. It housed two photocopiers, a computer terminal and a stack of redundant fax machines. In a kind of delirium, Anselm pressed a button that would guarantee the instantaneous annihilation of Moscow. We've come a long way from throwing projectiles from a balloon, he mused, following Martin into the room secured for his research.

An old oak desk faced a window overlooking the lake and the great, weeping tree. Posters of past exhibitions coloured the walls. The focus belonged, however, to a sort of exile standing forlorn in the corner.

'It's a friendship plant,' said Martin, scratching his head. 'Everybody hates it. Remember, just dial forty-eight if you think I can help.'

Anselm pulled back the chair and sat down.

A beige file marked 'Private Flanagan WO 71/001A' lay on the table beside a telephone. Written in pencil on a faded green sticker was the instruction 'Closed until 1992'. Anselm opened the cover. The first item that caught his eye was a yellow slip of paper with his name on it – a computer generated ticket showing who was in possession of the nation's heritage. The second item was far more interesting: another file, labelled 'Private Owen Doyle', the soldier whose tags had been worn by Captain Herbert Moore.

Chapter Eight

The Court Convenes

1

After a desultory breakfast Herbert left his billet and walked down the misty lane towards the old village school of Oostbeke. He passed the monastery, glancing through the open gate in the wall at the cracked flagstones that led to the white door. Pressing on, he came to a low barn on his right that was open on one side, its back to the direction of the wind. A burly carpenter was hammering together two pieces of wood. The mallet fell like percussion as he sang a song from *The Mikado*. 'The flowers that bloom in the spring' – whack-whack – 'breathe promise of merry sunshine' – whack-whack – 'As we merrily dance and we sing' – whack-whack – 'we welcome the hope that they bring' whack-whack – 'of a summer of roses and wine.' Whack. Whack. Whack. Behind the carpenter was a pile of crosses, neatly stacked. To one side an assistant crouched on one knee, slopping white paint on the finished article.

The school was set back from the road with a playground in front. Morning sunshine lit the haze around the square brick structure. White shutters, damp with dew, seemed to float upon the walls. A framed air vent at ground level glimmered with an oily light. The prisoner was in the cellar, it seemed. Herbert thought of the Tommy, locked up and trapped. So vivid was his evocation of the damp concrete walls, the window of morning mist, the sound of the sentry's stamping feet behind the bolted door, that he suffered a wave of nausea. He didn't want to weigh another man's worth; to judge the performance of his fibre, as though he were cloth. No one wanted to sit on a court martial, though none would admit why: it brought you close to your own fears, your own weakness, your own capricious nerve – one day strong, another weak. All soldiers feared the incidence of a bad day when, for once, backbone really mattered. If you failed the test, well, no matter who you were, you ended up in a cellar by an oil lamp. He breathed deeply, nodded at the guard and pushed open the heavy door.

To the left Herbert saw a room lined with benches, beneath which were hooks fixed no higher than his chest. Two greatcoats had been laid out, each with their sleeves joined as though they were carved knights upon a sarcophagus. Herbert brushed against one and it slid to the floor, revealing a book in the inside pocket. The title was visible: *Military Law Made Easy*. Herbert knew it well. A lifesaver, written by Lieutenant Colonel S.T. Banning. There were exam papers at the back, with answers. Briskly, hardening his mind, Herbert strode down the tiled corridor towards the hum of modulated voices.

Herbert didn't know any of the other officers, save the prosecutor – Edward Chamberlayne, the adjutant of his battalion and Duggie's administrative Captain. He'd been thrown out of Oxford for indolence, a distinction that he wore like a decoration. His eyes were strikingly clear surrounded by a dark line of shadow, a feature that suggested he was a minor principal in an amateur operatic society. He introduced the other members of the court: Major Robert Glanville, the President, and Lieutenant Graham Oakley, the junior officer. They were gathered by a window which, incredibly, still had net curtains. Through the grey lace Herbert could just make out a stretch of distant woodland. Far away the guns thumped like a racing heart.

'Before we settle down to work,' said Glanville, 'I'll just remind you of some basic drill. I'm pure Yorkshire and I'll make myself plain.'

Square-faced with a large moustache, the major towered over everyone in the room, his uniform bulging across the arms and chest. There was a far away kindness in his expressions, as though he might announce the founding of a public library or the donation of brass instruments to form a band. For all the Yorkshire credentials, his accent had the smoothness of a Sandhurst alumnus.

'Have either of you sat on a court martial before?' asked Glanville.

Oakley and Herbert shook their heads.

'A pity. Have you seen an execution?'

Another joint shake of the head.

'Good. Now put that out of your mind.'

Herbert had of course seen a firing party from another regiment heading off in the half-light before dawn. He'd stood beside Duggie several times when Routine Orders were read out by Chamberlayne to the four companies of the battalion, informing them that a court martial had taken place and that the sentence had been 'duly carried out'. The words always unsettled Herbert. All the details were given: name, rank, regiment, offence, place of trial, date of execution and, worst of all, the exact time – to the minute. It evoked the picture of an officer with a stopwatch and notepad. After each public reading Duggie had said a death sentence would be imposed on anyone who committed a like misdemeanour. The major was wise to have sensed these unspoken memories, and to have named them at the outset.

'First things first,' said Glanville, hands on hips. 'This lad will be undefended. It's our job to make sure he gets a fair crack of the whip. If he has a defence it's up to us to ferret it out. Understood?'

Oakley and Herbert nodded.

'Second, the assumption of innocence doesn't apply. He's deemed to have deserted his unit. It's a General Routine Order. Correct, Chamberlayne?'

'Almost, Sir.' The Adjutant made a bow with his head, as he'd probably done to his tutor at Oxford. 'As a court, you are bound to assume that the accused intended the natural and probable consequences of his actions. If the accused absented himself to avoid a special or dangerous duty, that act raises a presumption of intention to so avoid. You are entitled to act on that presumption unless the accused can prove otherwise.'

'That's what I said,' replied Glanville, 'only in a more memorable fashion.'

'Of course, Sir.'

'Third,' resumed Glanville, 'a couple of years back, a lad pleaded guilty to desertion and was promptly shot the following week. Since then we take a not guilty plea whether the accused holds his hands up or not.'

As Herbert tried to reconcile the implications of these last two decrees, Oakley said, 'I'm sorry, Sir . . . you mean we presume that he's guilty, make him enter a not guilty plea, and then see if we can find a defence to undermine our own presumption?'

'I do.' He examined Oakley with a smile – the remote smile, Herbert thought, of a professional soldier faced with the mystification of a volunteer. 'There's a logic to it, Lieutenant, if you think about it long enough.'

Oakley looked like he'd only recently come out of the firing line, perhaps the night before – it left a mark on a soldier for several days: a kind of pallor and exhaustion of spirit. He had a broad forehead and his mouth sloped down slightly at the sides. Not having a neck of any significant length, his head seemed to be balanced on his shoulders.

'I hope you don't mind my asking, Sir,' continued the Lieutenant, 'but why is there no Prisoner's Friend for the defence?'

'The lad doesn't want one,' replied Glanville.

'And a CMO . . . a Court Martial Officer?'

'There aren't enough to go round.' Glanville smiled again, remoter still to the disquiet of the civilian mind. In a soothing tone – or perhaps he was lightly mocking his own masters – he said, 'Fortunately, we've got Mr Chamberlayne to keep us on the straight and narrow.'

The prosecutor made another bow with his head. (As far as Herbert knew, prior to his expulsion from Oxford, he'd been reading Greats.)

Herbert strongly suspected that Oakley's questions were derived from a hasty reading of Lieutenant Colonel S.T. Banning. That showed diligence, at least. But it also demonstrated one of the realities in this endless war: most of the college-trained officers had been killed, very early on, in fact; the volunteers or conscripts who filled their place had little if any idea of military law or procedure. But what did that matter? Desertion was a terribly *simple* offence.

'A final word of advice . . . and some encouragement,' said Glanville. 'The advice: remember what I said earlier; don't think about the ultimate sanction. That's none of your concern. Your job is straightforward: find out what happened according to the evidence. Parliament wrote the law; all you have to do is see if the lad fits the bill. Now the encouragement: if the offence is proved, then there will be a sentence, like day follows night – and if it's death, then it's someone else's job to decide whether it's the right thing to do or not. Your hands are clean either way. It's nothing to do with you. For what it's worth, most of them get reprieved. Now, let's do our duty.'

Chamberlayne opened a pair of double doors and they all passed into the improvised court.

2

A table for the court had been placed centrally between two windows. Upon it was a pile of paper, a pencil, a large red book (the *Manual of Military Law*) and a small black book (the Bible). To one side was a smaller table for Chamberlayne. The room was high and airy with a fireplace in the corner. Wood panelling shaped like a Greek temple rose from the mantelpiece to frame a cracked mirror. School desks lined a wall as if they were seats for the jury. A chair had been placed in the centre for the accused. At a signal from Glanville, an escort of two soldiers marched Private Joseph Flanagan into the room.

He was a slight man of average height. Sandy hair with a gentle wave had been neatly parted, revealing a high, smooth forehead. His fine mouth gave the hint of a natural smile, suggesting approachability and an easy temper. Raised eyebrows disclosed the vulnerability of the trapped. To Herbert, he looked vaguely familiar, though he couldn't place any specific meeting. The soldier's eyes flicked over the officers that would try him with an expression of knowing dread . . . like Herbert had seen upon the face of Quarters. With that thought he felt again the kick of the rifle, deep in his shoulder. A flash of mud blanked out the sockets and his mind escaped into darkness.

'I'm Major Robert Glanville. On my right is Captain Herbert Moore. On my left is Lieutenant Graham Oakley. Do you have any objection to being tried by any one among our number?'

Flanagan made no response. Glanville repeated his question.

'None, Sir,' said Flanagan. The Irish accent was very strong, the intonation musical. 'Thank you, Sir.'

'Private,' said Glanville, 'it's not your fault, but you are wearing a belt. That is against King's Regulations during a court martial. I let the matter pass, but it is the only irregularity I will countenance.'

His authority on procedure thus stamped, Glanville thumbed through the red book till he found the relevant passage. He placed his right hand on the black book and, in a low monotone, eyes on the red book, he swore to try the accused according to the evidence, without partiality, favour or affection, to never divulge the sentence until it was confirmed, and to never disclose the vote or opinion of another member, unless required in due course by the law, 'So help me, God.'

Glanville passed the books to his right and Herbert made the same oath, hardening his voice to hide the fear. His heart was beating out of step. He felt queasy again. The books moved left and Oakley, like a man on the touchline, almost bellowed his promise. He, too, was afraid.

Glanville then stared at Flanagan, rumpling his nose and upper lip as if his moustache were itching a nostril. The pause gave density to the three yards between the accused and his tribunal. Peering down at a small sheet of paper torn from an exercise book, Glanville read out, 'Four-eight-eight-eight Private Joseph Flanagan, eighth Service Battalion, Northumberland Light Infantry . . . you're charged with . . . when on active service, deserting His Majesty's Service in that you, on the twenty-sixth of August nineteen seventeen, absented yourself from the said eighth Battalion until apprehended at Elverdinghe on the twenty-seventh of August nineteen seventeen.' He crumpled his moustache again. 'Do you understand what I've just said?'

'I do.'

While the charge was being read out, Flanagan had looked slightly over Herbert's right shoulder. His gaze had become fixed. Gradually the expression of dread had been replaced by a striking image of resignation, immobility and attentiveness, as one might find on an ancient icon. His skin had acquired the same subdued patina.

'Please record a plea of "Not Guilty" on the schedule to Army Form A three,' said Glanville.

He then squared off the pile of paper in front of him. The top sheet already carried the date, names and regimental details of everyone present (in Chamberlayne's hand). After a glance at his pocket watch, Glanville licked the point of his pencil and added at the top of the page: 10.04 a.m.

'When you're ready, Mr Chamberlayne,' he said.

Chapter Nine

According to a scrap of paper hanging from a frayed piece of string, 6890 Private Doyle's papers were to be lodged with those of 4888 Private Flanagan, 'pending resolution of the latter'. A resolution that had never taken place. The Doyle file contained an uncoordinated assortment of memos, telegrams and letters between different administrative and active units within the army. Doyle's inglorious life was pretty much covered from enlistment onwards. Anselm began by isolating material relevant to Flanagan's trial.

In short order, Owen Doyle was a Private in the 1/29 (City of London) Battalion, London Regiment (Lambeth Rifles). On the 26th August his regiment was waiting to join the attack on the Passchendaele Ridge. At or about 1.00 a.m. Doyle's section leader reported his absence. Shortly afterwards, at 3.49 a.m., Doyle was registered as *injured* at another regiment's Aid Post – the regiment to which Flanagan and Herbert belonged, the Northumberland Light Infantry. It seemed that Doyle had simply drifted across an inter-battalion boundary. That assumption was short-lived, because thirteen hours later two soldiers were stopped by the military police at Étaples on the French coast. One was Joseph Flanagan, the other was Owen Doyle. Both men escaped 'after a brief altercation'.

It was at this point that Anselm was obliged to shuffle the papers and check the dates and times, because a most peculiar resolution of the affair took place. Flanagan was eventually arrested at a village named Elverdinghe. A lawyer of some kind at Division HQ subsequently provided the following advice:

The two military policemen who apprehended 6890 Pte Doyle

> and/or 4888 Pte Flanagan have provided unreliable evidence as to identity. Proceed therefore with Pte Flanagan's court martial without reliance on the Étaples material. The charge should simply cover the period of absence from 26.8.17 until his arrest at Elverdinghe on 27.8.17. We understand, in any event, that Flanagan denies being in Étaples at the alleged time. It is recognised that the exclusion of the incident from the trial is a boon for this soldier, but there is no way around the matter.

So much for Flanagan. He'd run, he'd been caught and he'd been tried. Not so for Doyle. According to a letter from Brigade HQ, Doyle was killed in action on the 15th September northwest of Glencorse Wood. In other words, Doyle had somehow rejoined his unit, escaping the legal process that had crashed into Flanagan. He would die within weeks, in the very manner he'd sought to avoid.

How did you get hold of Doyle's tags, Herbert? thought Anselm, climbing back into the battered Cortina. Dead leaves fell like feathers in his mind. *Why did you wear them?*

There were so many names and places and ranks in the file that Anselm couldn't impose any order on the material. Abruptly, he picked up the telephone and dialled 48.

'Martin, I need some tools.'

'Go on.'

'First, a map covering Étaples to Ypres showing the position of each man's unit on the night of the twenty-sixth August nineteen seventeen.'

'That won't take long.'

'Second, it would help if I could see how the key players and their regiments were related to one another in the army . . . a sort of family tree.'

'That is to hand.'

Prepared for Kate Seymour, thought Anselm, but he said, 'Finally, I'd like to explore Joseph Flanagan's war experience prior to his desertion . . . something that would give me a handle on to why he might commit a capital offence?'

'The best place to look would be his battalion War Diary. This records the day-to-day activities of the unit. I'd also check the War Diary of the Adjutant and Quartermaster General for his Division. It covers disciplinary matters. I'll get them for you now.'

Anselm put the telephone down, asking himself whether Martin had made those last suggestions once before. He wasn't sure. And he didn't have time to dwell on the matter because the door opened and Martin stepped inside, holding out a sheet of paper. As Anselm tried to take it, Martin held on to his end, causing a slight tug between them.

'This is simply a bare diagram,' he said, with a note of warning. 'It shows where each man stood in the army of August nineteen seventeen. You wouldn't know that Major Glanville's brother had been killed in the battle Flanagan tried to avoid. Or that Father Moore's regiment had all but ceased to exist. Or that the average age in the court was twenty-six. Or that no one was a lawyer. In fact, that's about all we do know. The full picture is out of reach, now, and has been since the war: with the exception of Moore and Chamberlayne, none of the men involved in the trial survived longer than six weeks. Neither witnesses nor members. They were all dead by mid October.' He let go of the paper. 'It probably wasn't the most impartial tribunal. But this was war and everyone was a bit too busy. I'll get to work on that map.'

Anselm could have easily argued about the basic requirements for justice, either in a field or a temple built for the purpose. Instead his mind went numb and he felt a surge of melancholy in his stomach. He experienced it sometimes at the funerals of people he did not know, or when examining a photograph of someone he'd never met, wondering at the familiar pain in the face. He stared at the papers spread across the table. They were like messages from a graveyard.

Look for something that even now might bring life to Joseph Flanagan, the Prior had urged. *Read warily.*

Anselm studied Martin's diagram, prepared in all probability for Kate Seymour. He'd asked for it because he'd hoped – no doubt like Kate – that it might add some detail to the context of the trial. And it did, as Martin well knew. Every member of the court martial was in the same division as Flanagan. Not one of the officers was an outsider. The honour of the family was to be judged by three men who were already guardians of its reputation. They'd seen monumental casualties only the week before; and they were each of them wounded in so many ways, ways beyond the skill of any Medical Officer. On 1st September 1917 Joseph Flanagan's chances of acquittal were almost non-existent.

Read warily.

Anselm picked up the transcript of the evidence. Closing his eyes he tried to picture 4888 Private Joseph Flanagan before a court in Flanders but no face would grace his imagination.

Chapter Ten

The Case for the Prosecution

Captain Chamberlayne stood behind his small table, hands behind his back. For some reason he addressed himself to Herbert. 'The case, I submit, is straightforward. The accused, four-eight-eight-eight Private Joseph Flanagan of the eighth Service Battalion, Northumberland Light Infantry, absconded on the twenty-sixth of August. He was arrested the next day. Between times his unit was engaged in a special or dangerous duty. I will argue that the accused deserted His Majesty's Service contrary to Section twelve-one-a of the Army Act eighteen eighty-one, as amended.'

'Thank you, Mr Chamberlayne,' said Glanville with a slow nod of the eyelids. 'Call your evidence.'

Bile touched Herbert's throat as a sentry by the door marched outside, his boots ringing on the flags. He came back moments later followed by a short, square-faced Regimental Sergeant Major. Stamping his way forward, the witness came to a louder halt, facing the prosecutor, midway between Flanagan and the three members of the court. Chamberlayne retrieved the black book from Glanville and held it before the witness. The RSM duly swore to tell the truth, the whole truth and nothing but the truth, 'So help me God.'

'Your name?' asked Chamberlayne, returning to his place.

'Three-four-three-four Regimental Sergeant Major Francis Joyce, Sir.' He rattled off his unit details. His voice was unnaturally subdued, as though he were alert to a drastic change in his ordinary circumstances, such that he couldn't shout and curse.

'Where were you on the twenty-sixth of August?'

'The battalion was in action near Black Eye Corner.' He stood to attention, his face expressionless, his battledress limp and stained. 'I was with a section that included Private Flanagan. We'd settled into a captured German bunker for the night, Sir.'

'Did you have reason to speak to the accused?'

'I did, Sir.'

'What did you say?'

'Major Dunne, the Company Commander, had been seriously injured, Sir. He'd lost his nose and eyes in the same shell blast that'd killed Mr Agnew, the leader of Flanagan's platoon. I'd put a couple of field dressings on the Major's face and told Private Flanagan to take him back to the Regimental Aid Post . . . I know it wasn't the done thing, Sir, but no stretcher-bearers had been seen for hours and what with the major's eyes all gone, I was worried he might lose too much blood, and anyway we'd have to leave him if the fighting heated up—'

'No one's questioning that decision,' said Glanville.

Listening to the narrative had calmed Herbert, though he seemed to be floating apart from his own heavy guts. Blood throbbed in his veins but he was detached from the pulse.

'Thank you, Sir,' said Joyce. 'Well, it was dark and the guns had quietened down a bit, so I thought Flanagan had a fair chance of making it and getting back before dawn, Sir.'

'What exactly did you say?'

'Something like, "Take Mr Dunne to the RAP." I confess, I swore a bit, Sir.'

'I'm sure you did. And then?'

'Flanagan piled his kit in a corner and put his arm under the Major's' – he demonstrated, suddenly hunching himself to take an imagined weight – 'and off they went, Sir.'

'What time was this?'

'Shortly after midnight, Sir.'

'Which would be the morning of the twenty-sixth?'

'Yes, Sir.'

'How long would you expect the journey to take?'

'Well, Sir, the weather was grim, but in our sector a track had just been laid by the engineers . . . so I'd have said about an hour or two, because Major Dunne could walk.'

With a nod of thanks Chamberlayne sat down.

Neither Herbert nor Oakley could think of a question. Mr Glanville, however, glanced over his transcript and said, 'Please repeat the exact order you gave to the accused, along with the verbs and adjectives you have so kindly suppressed.'

'Sorry, Sir?'

'The swear words.'

'Ah.'

The RSM obliged and the president checked each word he'd written with an ostentatious tap of the pencil. 'Quite novel, and remarkably clear if I may say so. He was to come back immediately. That was the gist?' Quietly, he added, 'Please remember your oath.'

Joyce blinked, his chiselled face livid and suffused with emotion. The temerity and respect had been swamped. Flanagan's life hung on the reply. All Joyce had to do was lie, but his sunken eyes sought out the black book on Chamberlayne's table. 'I think so, Sir. Yes. But there was still some noise . . . shells . . .'

'Thank you.' For everything, Glanville seemed to say: for your loyalty to your regiment and your vagueness to the court. Appraising the accused, he added, 'Private Flanagan, do you wish to question the witness?'

'No, Sir.'

'Be very careful,' said Glanville. He spoke with suppressed tension, with the same false calm used to encourage the boys before the whistles blew. 'You heard Joyce. If you disagree with anything he said, now is your time to tell us.'

'He's a good man, is the RSM, Sir.'

Flanagan kept his eyes fixed on the spot somewhere over Herbert's right shoulder. He remained mysteriously calm and detached from the proceedings, as if he were watching another drama of greater significance. The more Herbert examined his simple, clean features, the more he was sure that they'd met . . . maybe just once.

The next witness was 3939 Private Frederick Elliot. His face had burns across one cheek. Out of deference to the court, he'd shaved the other side. After being sworn he explained that he was in the same platoon as Flanagan, but not the same section. He'd been injured and was waiting for treatment at the RAP. In this way he saw the accused with a mug of Oxo while talking to one of the chaplains, Father Maguire. This would have been about 1.45 a.m. on the 26th. 'After the MO, Mr Tindall, had bandaged up the Major, he told the accused to guide him back to the stretcher-bearers, and then get back to his unit. He gave Joe a couple of field dressings, and off they went, Sir.'

'Who, might I ask, is Joe?' asked Glanville, his lips thinned and white. He was a big man and became threatening simply through the intake of a breath.

'Sorry . . . Sir, I mean the accused.'

Quickly, Chamberlayne tossed the witness a closing question. He, too, had felt the heat. 'What time was it when you saw him leave?'

'About two o'clock in the morning, Sir.'

Glanville wrote the words down, his head lowered. He stared at them as if they were of immense importance, but his eyes didn't move, because he wasn't reading. Various emotions played with his mouth and eyes, the minute movements revealing a struggle between rage – presumably towards Flanagan – and . . . Herbert thought it might be a very private anguish. Gradually Glanville's features became still. He breathed out slowly and said, apologetically, 'Thank you very much, Private. You've been a great help.'

Chamberlayne sat down and Flanagan shook his head, indicating that he had nothing to say. At Glanville's invitation, Herbert then spoke. 'How were you injured, Private?'

'With a flare, Sir.'

'One of ours or one of theirs?'

'Ours, Sir.'

'That was unfortunate.'

'Yes, Sir.'

'How did one of our flares strike your cheek?'

'Mr Hoskins fired it, Sir. I was crouched in front, Sir, and I stood up, Sir, and . . . it grazed me, Sir.' Sweat above the burns made Elliot's skin shine.

'That was unwise, wasn't it?'

'It was an accident, Sir.'

'Did the medical officer discuss with you the mechanism of this accident? The how and why?'

Herbert already knew the answer. Tindall had recounted the incident while dealing with Herbert's arm. The MO had been most unhappy about the affair because it didn't appear to be the usual kind of self-inflicted injury: 'Sounds more like he was trying to finish himself off. What a way to try, though.' Duggie decided to let the matter drop.

'I told him what happened, Sir,' said Elliot.

'Private, has anyone suggested that you injured yourself on purpose?'

'No, Sir.' Elliot seemed to sink beneath some waves in his mind.

'Well, let me. Did you?'

After a pause Elliot whispered, his face suddenly dark, 'No, Sir, I did not.'

'You are sure of that?'

'Yes, Sir.'

'As sure of a Medical Officer's order sending this man back to the front?'

'Yes, Sir.'

Glanville's pencil scratched on the paper as he mouthed Elliot's reply. Looking up, he observed, 'Dismiss, Private.' The dismissal was wholly polite, as might announce an exile.

Herbert knew that this attack had been brutal and probably futile. But Elliot was the last witness to see the accused: he'd heard the order sending Flanagan back to his unit. If his evidence could be muddied in any way, it might help this strangely distant man who, so far, had done nothing but support the witnesses brought against him. But Herbert still felt aged and soiled, for he pitied Elliot's desperation, only he couldn't say so . . . he could never say so . . .

The door clicked shut and Chamberlayne said, 'My last witness is Captain Maurice Sheridan.'

The sentry marched out of the room and returned with the officer moments later. His uniform was clean, his buttons shining. Herbert knew that the captain's batman had spent a day getting his master's gear into this condition. Similar measures had been taken for Herbert, Oakley and Glanville. The filthiness of war went very deep, though; and Herbert felt dirty. He was a greased cog in a machine that couldn't stop, because he was part of a force that moved while being moved. This was military duty: to go through the motions without thinking. And Herbert did not want to think. What did he want? To be back in Keswick as a boy, long before the move to Northumberland; long before failure had a claim upon him. The days of kites and Dandelion and Burdock.

After taking the oath and identifying himself, Sheridan said, 'On the twenty-seventh August I was on horseback, riding from Brielen to Elverdinghe. To my left I saw a local . . . a peasant or something . . . a farmer waving his arms in the air. I couldn't follow a word the fellow was saying, but he was frantic and kept winking.' In one hand Sheridan held a pair of thin leather gloves. While he spoke he lightly tapped his trouser leg. 'I told him to pull himself together and he pointed towards a barn. I dismounted, withdrew my revolver and approached the building, and all the while this farmer fellow was whispering and jerking his thumb towards his mouth as though the hand were a jug. The next thing I know the accused is there before me, standing in the open gate. He was soaking wet and covered in slurry. He had no kit whatsoever, Sir.'

'Did you say anything?'

'I asked his name, which he revealed, along with his army number and unit details, Sir.'

'Go on.'

'I then asked him why he wasn't with his Company, Sir.'

'And his reply?'

'He said he'd brought a wounded officer back to the reserve trenches and had then set off to rejoin "his people" – I think that was the phrase. However, because of the rain and the dark and the shells, he'd got lost. He'd wandered all night until he'd found shelter, Sir.'

'What time was this, please?'

'Approximately five p.m. in the evening, Sir.'

'Did you notice anything about the accused's demeanour?'

'Yes. He smelled strongly of alcohol. To be precise, wine. I found two empty bottles in the barn and a third half consumed, Sir.' The tone suggested weary contempt, a familiarity with the grubby doings of people who always wore the same pair of shoes.

'And then?'

'I checked his pockets, confiscated a penknife and placed him under arrest, Sir.'

'Thank you, Captain.'

Glanville jotted down each word, his lips thin and white once more. He sat high in his seat, elongating his neck as though to get a better view of the evidence. Drunkenness was a common feature in courts martial. All Divisions kept a keen eye on its prevalence – along with sloppy saluting and VD.

Oakley coughed and said, 'Did he have any field dressings with him?'

'No,' replied the Captain, mystified. 'As I said, he had no kit, which is why I searched the barn in the first place, Sir.'

Glanville smiled indulgently, as if Oakley had managed to stay on a bicycle for the first time. Looking left and right, he invited further clarification from the court before leaning forward to say, 'Do you wish to cross-examine this witness, Private Flanagan?'

'No thank you, Sir.' His gaze remained firmly held by that other drama behind Herbert's shoulder. While apparently impassive, his breathing began to stagger. *We have met*, thought Herbert. *In the rain . . .*

'That concludes the case for the prosecution,' said Chamberlayne, sitting down.

There was a long pause. Far off the guns boomed and clacked. In that strange quiet captured by a classroom without children, Herbert understood that Flanagan was windy – Herbert knew the feeling; it was awful; you never got used to it – but he'd taken a grip on his terror: it was a decision. Flanagan was smiling at an open grave. Herbert could just make out the whisper of air being drawn and pushed through his teeth.

Chapter Eleven

The Case for the Defence

'Do you wish to call any evidence in your defence?' asked Glanville after he'd found a clean sheet of paper.

The heavy sound of marching floated on the air. A battalion was on the move, heading out of the village. Maybe they were going to relieve the Lancashire Fusiliers, thought Herbert. They were due out of the line and the Lambton Cup was up for grabs. Flanagan's staggered breathing seemed to enact the fear that bound them all together.

'Evidence,' repeated Glanville, kindly. 'Do you wish to call any?'

'No, Sir, I don't.'

'Do you wish to give evidence yourself?'

'I'll just make a statement, Sir.'

Flanagan let his eyes drop from the vision behind Herbert, from whatever it was that had drawn him away while the evidence was being marshalled against him. His head remained bowed.

'On oath?' asked Glanville in the same kind tone.

'I think not, Sir.'

Flanagan stood up, his arms loose by his sides. His clear eyes slowly followed some phantom pattern on the floor, moving closer and closer to the table where Herbert sat. They rose deliberately towards him. When their eyes met Herbert's stomach pitched as if he'd been kicked.

I saw you with Father Maguire . . . the day I shot Quarters . . .

Herbert felt faint. His eyes rolled as purple spots popped like fireworks in his brain. Flanagan's stare was remorseless. To escape him, Herbert focused on the faded wallpaper: a repeated pattern of roses, bunch after bunch surrounded by golden tendrils. His mother would have loved it. She'd loved his uniform, too. *You can start a new tradition*, she'd whispered. He breathed out to disperse the smoke of nausea. It was like that first, sickening cigarette.

'Everything said here today is true, Sir,' said Flanagan, his breathing suddenly normal. That's what it was like, when the whistles screamed at zero hour. The anguish could even turn into ecstasy when you stepped into the open, into the shrapnel and the whining. 'After I'd handed Major Dunne to the stretcher-bearers I set off for the front line. It was terrible dark . . . raining like it did back home, when a load comes off the sea, after weeks of the gathering. The sky and the waves would join up, so –' he slowly brought his hands together, frowning – 'and then for days it would pour, or rather . . . everything returned to water. The land was part of the sea.' His eyes were wide and heavy with suffering, and Herbert recoiled from this man's very private memory. 'That was home, so . . . and that's what it was like after I said goodbye to Major Dunne, and I got lost. I didn't know my left from my right. I came upon this barn . . . just like you heard . . . and in it I found some drink. I was upset from the bombing and the death of Mr Agnew. And cold I was and wet. I drank myself under, Sir. And when I woke I drank some more.' He paused to lick his lips, his calmness run dry. Herbert, however, had latched on to Flanagan's speech pattern. It wasn't quite English. Here and there the word order was striking, almost poetic, but not deliberately so. *And cold I was and wet*. The peculiar phrase unsettled Herbert: it named with refinement his own experience of abandonment.

You spoke to Father Maguire in another language . . . a kind of music . . . foreign to the filth and the dying . . .

'I came to France in nineteen fifteen,' continued Flanagan, his mouth clacking for lack of spit. 'I've always done my best, Sir, and I'm sorry for getting drunk this once. If I'd left the bottle alone, I'd have probably found my Section . . . I hadn't run off, Sir. It won't happen again, Sir.'

Flanagan sat down, arms on his thighs, the hands slack between his legs. Remembering himself, he straightened his back and knitted his fingers; his eyes swiftly returned to that refuge over Herbert's right shoulder. Throughout the statement Glanville's pencil had squeaked, oddly louder than the erratic grumbling of the guns. After he'd checked his spelling he said, 'Thank you. Since the statement was not taken on oath, there will be no questions, am I right?'

Chamberlayne gave one of his nods.

'Given what's been said, there's no need for a closing address – either from you or Private Flanagan, and we will not require a summary of the evidence. The court will now retire.' Glanville checked his pocket watch and noted the time: 10.28 a.m.

The sentry, sullen-faced throughout the trial, marched forward and escorted Flanagan from the room. Boots crashed upon the tiles, the outside steps, and the flags of the playground, and Herbert (with his ears) followed the accused down more steps to the cellar beneath.

. . . and Father Maguire looked after that poor kid . . .

'We'll go next door,' said Glanville to Chamberlayne, implying that he could stay put. He shuffled his papers into a neat pile and plopped them on the red book.

Silencing the voices in his head, Herbert went down the room, to the chair used by the accused. Turning on his heel, he looked to the place he himself had occupied. To the left (over what had been Herbert's right shoulder) was the cracked mirror in the Greek temple frame. Glanville and Oakley both appraised him as though he'd lost his senses. But Herbert was gazing elsewhere. The cracked mirror was angled such that he could see through a window whose lace curtain was missing. Herbert's eyes watered with a longing for a world that had passed away. A reflection of its loveliness remained as a most awful reminder: between the Doric pillars he picked out a low bank of distant trees, a blue sky and scudding pink clouds. The morning mist had completely disappeared, burned away by the one sun that had illuminated his childhood and left Quarters astride a mule.

Chapter Twelve

1

Anselm read the evidence of the trial in ten minutes. He'd studied it in fifteen. It had been delivered – according to the record – in twenty-four. That was some going. He'd felt like he was leaning over someone's shoulder because the transcript, written in pencil, had been scored here and there with brown and red crayon. These, he assumed, had been added by two different people involved in the review process – perhaps the lawyer (brown) checking for irregularities, and the Commander-in-Chief (red) who would make a decision on sentence. Each colour was like a window on to a different level of indignation. The most excited effort had been reserved for 'alcohol', 'wine' and 'drunk'. Each word had been underlined twice, each time in red.

And indignation settled upon Anselm.

Flanagan was on trial for his life, unrepresented, before amateurs. Decent folk with the awesome powers of a king. That had last happened in the Middle Ages. The prosecution evidence wasn't tested: no defence witnesses were called; no plea of substance was made for leniency. The only cross-examination of any force was Herbert's questioning of Private Elliot, the person who'd last seen Flanagan in the reserve trenches. And that was a waste of time, because while the account was inadmissible anyway (repeating the order of the Medical Officer that sent Flanagan back to his unit) Flanagan cured the irregularity by accepting what had been said – and that demolished whatever value might have been attached to Herbert's assault.

Testily, Anselm reached for the additional documents ordered by Martin and strode to the Donk Shop. Phrases from the trial whirled through his mind. One in particular baffled him: *And cold I was and wet.* It was a strange way to talk . . .

Beginning with the Battalion War Diary, Anselm photocopied every entry between January and September 1917, hoping that within the pages he'd find a route into Flanagan's mind. It was while leafing through the War Diary of the Adjutant and Quartermaster General, however, that Anselm came to a surprised halt, knowing that he must have stumbled upon something of significance. There, on the 17th September 1917, like a bookmarker, was a yellow ticket. This one had Kate Seymour's name printed on it. She'd left it behind by accident.

Anselm studied the page with growing confusion.

A post-war censor had cut a square hole beneath the title '113. Courts Martial – Desertion.' Written in the margin was a tiny word: 'weeded'. There was literally nothing to be seen. Frowning, he copied it, along with a few subsequent pages. He was trying to guess why Kate Seymour had come to examine this material when the telephone rang.

'The map is ready.'

They laid it on the table overlooking the lake and the weeping willow.

Ypres occupied a central position, roughly ten kilometres from Poperinghe. The Salient had been drawn in red, curling to the right, round the city, and then turning back again. Three small stickers – blue, yellow and green – had been added, labelled respectively M, F and D.

'I've marked the positions of Moore, Flanagan and Doyle on the night of the twenty-sixth August,' said Martin, his finger tapping each letter. 'You'll see that Doyle was beside the other two, separated by a brigade boundary. His unit was due to move forward in support.'

Anselm looked at F and D. They were bunched together on the map, whereas on the ground they'd been world's apart. Somehow they'd met up.

'Where was the Regimental Aid Post for the Northumberland Light Infantry?' Anselm misted his glasses and polished them on his scapular.

'Here, in the reserve trenches,' said Martin, pointing behind M and F.

'If someone left the Salient for Étaples on the coast,' continued Anselm, 'what route would he take . . . to get there and back again within a day or so?'

Martin didn't answer that question for a long while. This was a fresh angle. He took off his jacket and threw it on the chair. After tweaking each cuff he tapped a confluence of lines south of Poperinghe. 'There was a railway depot here . . . at Abeele . . . that's one route. This was quite a busy area.' He stubbed the map, louder than before. 'There was an airfield . . . and a number of Casualty Clearing Stations.'

'What were they?'

'Field Hospitals,' replied Martin, thrusting his hands into his pockets. A look of gathering comprehension sharpened his smooth face. 'Serious casualties were moved from a Regimental Aid Post to an Advanced Dressing Station and then to a Casualty Clearing Station. At the time of a battle the system all but collapsed. It was mayhem.' He glanced sideways. 'But it was a sure route away from the front.'

'Where's Elverdinghe?' asked Anselm, checking the coast around Étaples.

Martin pointed elsewhere, to a village not far from Ypres . . . not that far from the reserve trenches of the Northumberland Light Infantry.

Well, well. You came back, thought Anselm, with an intake of breath. You went to the coast, but *you came back*. You were arrested a couple of miles from the front.

'Can I just rehearse the evidence?' enquired Anselm, wrinkling his face. He needed to hear his own voice, to thresh his impressions, to spit out the husks.

There was a Gilbertine quality to Martin, the man who lived deep inside himself. He spoke mainly when it was necessary, and now he gave no reply.

Anselm wasn't going to dwell on the trial's flaws, and God knows there were many: from inadmissible evidence to an abject failure by the Prosecution to call the relevant witnesses (Father Maguire, Lieutenant Tindall, the stretcher-bearers – those who'd spoken to Flanagan and had been the last to see him). No, Anselm wouldn't focus on these defects because none of them mattered. Flanagan, defending himself, had admitted everything and questioned no one. Anselm's energy lay rather with the undisputed facts.

'What bothers me is the shape of the evidence without reference to the Étaples material,' began Anselm, nudging his glasses. 'It's neat. Too neat for a partial record of what actually happened. There should be ragged edges. Tears that show some facts are missing. There aren't any. Save, perhaps, the field dressings which are not accounted for and the phenomenon of wine in a barn.'

'The wine?'

'Yes, it's too good to be true.' He wafted away the notion impatiently. 'It's *convenient*. Anyway, the French keep wine in a cellar. I imagine the Belgians are no different.'

Anselm's finger plotted a crow's flight upon the map, moving ponderously from Black Eye Corner, to Abeele, to Étaples, before coming back to Elverdinghe. It was a kind of round trip. 'Let's just add the Étaples material to the evidence given to the court. Let's just see what sort of picture emerges.'

Hands hidden behind his scapular and hooked into his belt, Anselm ambled round the room. On occasion he kicked imaginary conkers, as if he were in the woods at Larkwood. Every so often his gaze moved to Martin for confirmation when he was unsure of a detail. He spoke rather quietly.

Flanagan leaves his unit after midnight on the morning of the 26th August (said Anselm). By 1.45 a.m. he reaches the Regimental Aid Post. He's last seen at 2.00 a.m. Doyle then makes an appearance before the same MO at 3.49 a.m. and at that point he enters the system of tagging and treatment. 'An eye injury, apparently,' recalled Anselm. Martin nodded. Doyle *and Flanagan* are then accosted thirteen hours later in Étaples, sixty odd miles away. 'From which we conclude that the two men must have met some time after 2.00 a.m. The where, when and how is anybody's guess.' By the evening of next day, Flanagan – alone once more – is back near Ypres with three bottles of wine.

Anselm leaned over the map.

'To make that long journey in that short time, Flanagan must have caught a train.' Anselm ran a finger along the railway line between Étaples and Abeele.

'And if that's right,' conceded Martin, 'he must have walked or hitched a lift to Elverdinghe . . . some twelve miles north-west.'

'He wasn't going to Elverdinghe,' corrected Anselm reluctantly, for he didn't like playing the front runner. 'That is where Flanagan was *caught*. If you carry on the trajectory, he was heading here . . . back to Black Eye Corner.'

'But he got drunk.'

'Which is far too convenient,' insisted Anselm, repeating his earlier point. He'd glimpsed what may have happened. 'He brought the bottles with him.'

'Where from?'

'Étaples . . . I'm not sure,' suggested Anselm. 'But he didn't find them in a barn.'

'Why bring alcohol halfway across Flanders?'

'Because it gave him an excuse. Something to say when the army finally caught him. Because he could use a hangover to hide the time he'd spent with Doyle. I mean it's almost convincing –' Anselm became earnest, giving substance to a speech he didn't believe – 'Flanagan had ploughed through the mud and hail to save an officer's life; he'd snapped under the strain of the noise and the death of his leader – that was a nice touch – and then he'd got lost and drunk in the howling night.' Anselm shrugged his shoulders. 'Flanagan came back knowing he'd get caught. He was banking on a merciful court.'

Martin slipped his jacket back on. He checked the buttons at the cuffs and squared his shoulders. 'So what is the picture that emerges?' he asked, humbly. 'Why are you troubled by the evidence . . . the neat story given to the court?'

'Because it reads like something planned,' said Anselm. 'Because I think that Joseph Flanagan was in control of that trial. That's the picture I see.'

2

Evening came and Anselm wandered back to his B&B feeling like one of those students of mysticism who inhabit a charnel house. Everywhere he'd looked, everything he'd touched, concerned the dead. He'd bought three books on the Battle for Passchendaele. A quick glance had revealed only two points of agreement: the maps and the immense scale of the slaughter. The dispute was restricted to blame and merit. In the late afternoon Anselm had sought Martin's advice once more.

'Why have two identity tags?'

'One remained on the body and the other went to records. Sometimes you couldn't bury the dead. Sometimes they were laid in a common pit, so . . .'

Anselm had guessed the rest. The tag gave a name to the remains: to help the War Graves Commission, to warn a farmer in the years to come.

'. . . and, in fact, they still turn up.'

How did you get both of them, Herbert? Anselm had thought, letting the receiver drop. *Why wear them? Why offer them to a man called Flanagan?*

Anselm simply could not escape the shadow thrown by the past, even now, when he entered a corner shop stacked high with bright magazines, cheap toys, brown fruit and endless tins. Despite a strong attempt, he failed to engage with the headlines and the cheap abundance, or the banter of the man propped by the till. A capital trial was loud in his mind like a play on the radio. He came out of the shop empty-handed, pondering Flanagan's last words to the court. 'I didn't run off,' he'd said.

Then what did you do?

The question remained with Anselm, even as he sat in the dark of his room, mumbling the psalms for Compline, only vaguely conscious that his brothers in Larkwood were chanting the same ancient words. During the Great Silence, that deep monastic quiet that Anselm carried within himself, he tried to imagine everyone from Major Glanville, who'd been grieving for his brother, to Private Elliot who'd burned his cheek . . . those faceless names on the page, a convocation of the damned with six weeks left to live. But he thought most of Herbert, a monk who'd often slept through Compline, whose Great Silence filtered through to the morning light, when he'd rise, and smile with quiet gratitude for his life. How had this advocate of the heartbroken ever sat as a judge in the kingdom of death?

Chapter Thirteen

Judgement

1

The memory of the pink nimbus in the mirror wounded Herbert's mind. Another kind of cloud seemed to settle upon him, violently contrasting with the strips of sunlight upon the tiled floor. For a while he couldn't engage properly with Glanville's admonitions. The president repeated everything he'd said at the beginning, including the Army's decision that the assumption of innocence would not apply, only this time, mid-sentence, Chamberlayne appeared with a copy of the actual text. Oakley studied it with a grimace and Herbert turned away, drawn to the lingering beauty in his mind. He sought the window for another torturing glimpse. A cough from Glanville came like a reprimand.

'It's time to do our duty,' he said, full of Yorkshire frankness.

The last word drove Herbert further into himself. Going through the motions he sat on one of the three school desks that had been arranged in a triangle. The others took their place in front of him. Their boots faced inward, inches apart. They looked at each other foolishly. Everyone looked their age – twenty-something and boyish. Pretenders in an adult game. Herbert felt even younger. He thought of his first day in the playground among the mute sons of Cumberland farmers. Herbert was from the big house down the road, an outsider. As he was now.

'Leaving aside the time spent guiding Major Dunne to the RAP,' said Glanville, 'this soldier was absent for thirty-nine hours while his comrades were in action. He was found three miles behind his own lines. His defence is that he got lost.'

They looked from one to the other. Herbert's expression was forced, his apparent concentration a kind of mime. He'd been slipping away, back to the trench and the gore of the Regimental Aid Post. Flanagan had been there too, moments before his desertion. Herbert had seen him . . .

'I'm unsure of Elliot,' said Oakley, dutifully. He looked at Herbert, showing he didn't quite understand why this witness's evidence might be important.

'He was the last to see him,' said Herbert, as if that mattered.

'You can ignore the RSM, Elliot and Mr Sheridan, if you want to,' said Glanville, cutting through the trees to show up the wood. 'Flanagan's statement is all we need.'

Oakley nodded, satisfied, and Herbert acquiesced: he'd seen the point coming even before his attempt to discredit Elliot, while Flanagan had been confirming the evidence brought against him. The trial was just a public airing of the reasons for the verdict.

'To avoid anyone being influenced by the opinion of his superior officer,' said Glanville, a hand on each knee, 'the junior member goes first, finishing with the president.'

Herbert noted the rose wallpaper, the scratched wood panelling to waist height, and he wondered why the floor was laid with long strips of timber when the hall was tiled. The family home in Keswick had similar tiling, though it wasn't black and white, as here, but varied like a mosaic. Red, blue, green and white, all waxed by a retired farmer with bad knees. His grandson had been one of the gloomy lads in the schoolyard.

'Guilty,' said Oakley, obviously.

'Guilty,' said Herbert, tasting ash.

'Guilty,' said Glanville, fishing out his pocket watch. A ruby flashed on the chain. He flicked open the cover with his thumb and started counting the minutes.

'We can't go back in . . . not yet,' said Oakley, reading the memorandum once more. His decency was as strong as his sense of duty. 'It wouldn't look right.'

'I'm inclined to agree,' said Glanville, snapping the lid closed. With a stamp of his boots he rose, stretching his long legs. Standing squarely at the window, his broad back blocked the sun sending a huge shadow across the floor. How had he survived? The tall ones always got shot sooner or later. In the head. Snipers got them after breakfast when their prey stood up in the shallower trenches, forgetting that they had to crouch just that little bit more than everyone else. It was called being 'clipped'. The confusion within Herbert's skull rolled heavily as though it had substance. This man will die, he thought, casually. A clipper will get him.

For the next twenty minutes they talked about the show they'd all been a part of – mainly in terms of the weather, because that is how a British soldier handles tragedy.

'God left a tap running,' said Glanville, swinging one leg on to the other. 'It rained almost every day last month.'

'All but three,' confirmed Oakley.

'Just like home,' said Herbert, on cue.

No one mentioned the massive casualties. That would have been indecent. And the raising of their memory would have been stained by the purpose of this assembly at Oostbeke – to judge the one that had got away. After a glance at his watch again, Glanville sharpened his pencil with a pocket-knife. Out of the blue he began to reminisce about the day his little brother let a bath overrun.

'The downpour destroyed a seventeenth-century ceiling in the room beneath.'

He sighed, noted the time on his record of evidence and wrote GUILTY in the third column of Army Form A3. Examining his writing on the pale blue paper, he said, 'Come on, let's get on with it.'

2

When the members were seated once more, the sentry marched the convicted man back into court. If Flanagan had retained any hope, Glanville snuffed it out by calling for evidence of character. It was the Army way: you weren't told the finding of the court. Herbert couldn't remember why. Banning's lifesaver hadn't dealt with that one because it didn't turn up in the exams. But if the members took further evidence, you'd obviously been convicted.

'Here is the relevant conduct sheet,' said Chamberlayne. Herbert sensed contempt in the courtesy. The dark rings around the prosecutor's eyes grew still darker. 'It is without any endorsement of significance.'

Glanville examined the columns with a degree of surprise. Apart from four days confined to barracks for dumb insolence, his record was clean.

'You'll appreciate that this soldier saved the life of his Company Commander,' said Chamberlayne with a hint of irony. He nodded as he might have done when the Dean of his college threw him out. 'That individual is now in England. You will remember that this soldier's platoon commander – Mr Agnew – is dead. As a consequence there is no one left to speak upon this man's character, save a second lieutenant who is currently hospitalised. He has provided this brief statement.'

'Please read it out loud,' said Glanville. The genuine interest struck Herbert as farcical. It wouldn't really affect the sentence . . . and that thought swirled his consciousness and he blinked as if sand had struck his eyes.

Chamberlayne angled a scrap of paper towards the light. '"I have been with the battalion for six weeks. I'm reliably informed that Private Flanagan's behaviour has always been commendable. He has been with the battalion since nineteen fifteen. As a fighting man he is of average worth. He fulfils his duties without particular distinction. In April he reported to the MO regarding his nerves, though the battalion was out of the line. He made a similar complaint in June. He has never caused concern under fire." It is signed by Lieutenant Alan Caldwell.'

'Thank you, Captain,' said Glanville.

Pointedly, Chamberlayne handed the testimonial to Herbert who, in a show of diligence, studied it with a puckered brow. The handwriting was slanted and neat with two mistakes, one of punctuation and the other of spelling. A flush of nerves in spring and summer, thought Herbert, trying to understand its significance. And a trial in autumn. He passed it to Glanville who licked his pencil and wrote 'Exhibit A' in the top right-hand corner. Fastidiously he made a reference on his notes, glancing between the two.

'Have you anything to say, Private, beyond what you've told us already.'

Flanagan didn't reply. He was among clouds that were losing their colour, above a low tree-line of vivid green, a congestion of living colour, so unlike the desolation of the front, of the torn and shattered land, the endless brown of exhumed soil and the white chalky mud. 'No,' he said, staring directly at Glanville. Unintentionally, he'd dropped the 'Sir.' And in that one error he showed himself to be, in the smallest possible way, beyond the authority of the proceedings.

Glanville closed the court and the sentry stamped forward. Herbert hardly saw Flanagan swivel on the heel, but he heard the confusion of boots on the tiles and the gritty flags outside.

'Gentlemen,' said Glanville rising. His open hand was pointing in invitation to the double doors as though it were time for port and a cigar, and perhaps a measured game of billiards; time for honourable men to talk seriously.

3

Oakley flicked through the *Manual of Military Law*. Finally he settled on the offence. Shortly he moved to the index and then to several other places. Herbert watched, hearing Glanville's voice from across the room. The big man was facing the window, blocking the light once more. He'd been repeating his already repeated admonitions. Herbert let the words flow over his head. The pages of the manual brushed against Oakley's sleeve as he turned here and there like a man trying to find directions to a secret way out, a passage he thought had to be there, something he'd read once, unless he'd been mistaken. Suddenly Herbert's attention shifted to Glanville's baritone, for he'd gone off script and was saying something new.

'. . . is their concern and not yours. Mercy is not in our gift. Division has made it clear that morale can slip through want of proper discipline. And we can't afford to slip in this weather.'

Glanville turned away from the window and sunlight struck Herbert like a silent explosion. He screwed his eyelids, seeing pink and purple, and the vague outline of the big man. A staff officer at

Division had leaned on Glanville – very gently, of course – and Pemberton at Brigade had leaned on Duggie, who'd leaned on Herbert . . . or had he? Duggie had been ambiguous. All at once Herbert thought of a rugby scrum, when eight men gripped each other in a ferocious bind, ready to push in one direction. He'd been a flanker, a man on the outside edge, the one whose job it was to break away if the ball was lost.

Glanville sat on a desk lid and made a reflective humph. 'You know, there was a time when we branded and flogged our boys. And after branding was abolished, flogging increased. But now flogging has gone, thanks to our enlightened reformers.' He folded his arms, as if to say, But what's left to us now? In fact, he said, 'As before the lowest rank gives his decision first, free from fear or favour.'

Oakley sniffed and flicked through the pages more quickly, returning to the index several times. Glanville watched him with a tremendous pity in his tired, grieving face. Grieving for what? So much, thought Herbert. The grating of the charabancs, the platoons in rowdy chorus, the short journeys up the line, and the all too brief companionship. Oakley let the book cover fall and close.

'Death,' he said, with a cough. His head, low on the shoulders, threatened to topple and fall to the floor among their boots. 'He may have saved an officer's life, but he took advantage of the trust that had been placed in him.' His eyes moved boldly on to Herbert. A frightened glare acknowledged that he'd showed his hand and that the stakes were high.

Instantly, Herbert saw everything with stunning clarity: the room, the three desks, his two brother officers. He heard the scrape of the sentry's rifle as he leant it on the wall, the shoulder strap jingling like a harness. A match struck and someone laughed. Some birds crashed through the fat leaves of a lime tree. And Herbert realised among all these acute sensations – almost painful to receive – that Flanagan's life lay in his hands. When his turn came, Glanville would say, 'Death': Herbert knew it. Oakley had committed himself. The outcome belonged to Herbert. *FGCM. Third officer required.*

He paused, breathing heavily, sweat gathering across his back. Duggie had picked him out; he'd recalled him from the seaside. He'd told him to do his duty . . . as if it were a kind of punishment. Duggie had decided to test Herbert's metal: by asking him to do what he did not want to do. A rite of initiation. A chance to demonstrate his utter commitment to the regiment and the Army's law. He wouldn't do it. Not in this way . . . he *couldn't*. Herbert wanted to scream, and his throat contracted at the idea that he must speak. Like Oakley running through the manual for a way out, Herbert summoned the face of Major Brewitt from Morpeth and the weeping boy waiting for the RMO. He called them together, along with the greater part of his vanished regiment: he formed a crowd of the righteous behind his closed eyes to bear witness to his coming betrayal, to ask their forgiveness, for he was going to spare this man. And then, as if lit by the strike of a match, Herbert saw Quarters staring out of the blackness of his mind. He was waiting for the shot, eyes wide with terror. Herbert hesitated . . . as he'd done in the rain when the rifle wavered side to side. Taking a breath, he lunged for a phrase of Glanville's, that most of them were reprieved. Holding on to that assurance, he squeezed a finger. 'Death with a recommendation to mercy.'

'Can we do that?' jabbered Oakley. 'If we can, well, I follow suit. God, I didn't know we had the right.'

Glanville raised a calming hand and said, quietly, 'Death.' He leafed through his notes until he found Army Form A3. Turning to the schedule he carefully wrote DEATH beneath the word GUILTY. Leaning back to get an overall impression of the document, as if to judge its neatness, he said, 'I'll add the recommendation suggested by Mr Moore.'

Eleven minutes had elapsed. For a long while they sat in silence, then Glanville explained that his little brother had once let a kettle boil until it melted on the stove.

4

The trial was over. Joyce and Elliot were released. Sheridan stood in the playground smoking. Flanagan was left in the cellar. For completeness, Glanville added the court's decisions to his own notes, duplicating the entries on Army Form A3. The military urge to think in triplicate made him hesitate. Frustrated, he then signed every page of the record, checking his watch as if a train might depart at any moment. His fastidious attention to the passage of time struck Herbert as suddenly heart-rending, for it contained an acknowledgement that his remaining days were few, that they were precious, even here, in this terrible place of terrible duties.

Chamberlayne banked his papers and books and left without saying anything to Herbert, though they shook hands – part of the ritual that had begun with the other members of the court. Silence lay in the room where the two greatcoats lay upon the low benches beneath the rows of hooks. Glanville and Oakley stood at different windows, each straining to see nothing in particular. Herbert was between them, feeling helpless and adrift. Oakley was the next to leave. He gripped the collar of his coat and threw it over his shoulder. Another shake of hands all round, and then Glanville was left facing Herbert.

'You didn't waver, old man,' he said, placing a huge hand upon Herbert's shoulder.

Herbert thought he might sob, that tears of protest and remorse might fall, but he kept his lips hard across his teeth. Father Maguire had done much the same; his hand had touched Herbert's neck with a scalding pity.

'I didn't warn you that it's always worst for the number two,' said Glanville. 'You were the pig in the middle, in this animal business of keeping the pack in order.'

Herbert nodded.

'I'm sorry,' said Glanville, checking that his chest buttons were seated properly, with the regimental emblem upright. 'Those liberal reformers left in place the one penalty that really mattered, and promoted its significance and use. But, you know, there really is no other way. Not until this bloody awful war is over.'

The big man blocked the doorway, shrugging his greatcoat into a comfortable position. When he turned to accept Herbert's salute, the bulge of the book in his inner pocket was barely noticeable. *Military Law Made Easy*. Herbert's father was on familiar terms with the author: Lieutenant Colonel S.T. Banning. They'd been at Sandhurst together in balmier days.

Chapter Fourteen

Anselm rose at 8.00 a.m., a full two hours later than his brothers at Larkwood. He found a high-street café and ordered eggs and bacon, relishing the temporary abandonment of monastic routine. He read a tabloid and listened to a radio blaring from the kitchen. It was just wonderful, if ultimately unsatisfying. After two cups of boiled coffee he walked briskly to Kew Gardens. Within fifteen minutes of his arrival the Flanagan file was back on the desk that overlooked a lake and a weeping tree.

The court deliberated for forty-two minutes, almost twice as long as they'd spent listening to the evidence, concluding that Flanagan was 'GUILTY'. The subsequent sentencing procedure occupied a similar period: thirty-nine minutes. In all the trial had lasted one hour and forty-five minutes. The hand with the brown crayon had drawn a magisterial line through the entire evidence of Lieutenant Alan Caldwell, the officer who'd given evidence on Flanagan's character. In the margin it was noted: 'This is hearsay upon hearsay and should never have been admitted before the court!!!' He was right: Alan Caldwell had *never met* Flanagan; he couldn't know, for himself, about Flanagan's nerve problems in April and June. Despite the angry brown line the red crayon had underlined the word 'nerves' twice and corrected two errors, one of orthography, the other of punctuation. The red had ignored the brown, thought Anselm, dwelling upon their respective functions, fearing the power of that last hand.

Turning to the final page of Major Glanville's notes, Anselm paused. There, under the heading 'Sentence', was the all important phrase: 'DEATH – with a recommendation to mercy'.

Herbert had said the decisive word, along with Major Glanville and Lieutenant Oakley. Anselm read it several times, as he'd once read Herbert's signature on the flyleaf of the Manual of Military Law: almost in a daze, feeling now that something he valued had slipped away from him: the simplicity of his memory of Herbert. Anselm quickly averted his mind from the painful thought, not wanting to acknowledge it, hoping it might disappear if he looked elsewhere. He opened the manual at the sentencing section. It actually *began* with 'death' before descending to penalties for the living. This was a severe code for a severe time, he assured himself. Herbert and his companions had been trapped by an arcane law and a war that hadn't ended by Christmas three years earlier.

But Herbert had said the Word, and the Word had an effect.

That much was clear from the remaining documents in the file: there was a sequence of memoranda from the commanders at Brigade, Division, Corps and Army, each commenting on whether 'the extreme penalty' might be carried out. But, as Martin had observed, it seemed that any document that might reveal the outcome of the trial, explicitly or by implication, had been deftly removed.

The review process would have begun at battalion level with Flanagan's Commanding Officer, Lt. Colonel D. Hammond. That first recommendation was missing. Anselm therefore moved to the next level, Brigade, and the opinion of Brigadier General Anthony Pemberton who, on the 3rd of September concluded:

> I am doubtful if the evidence is sufficient for a conviction on desertion, but an example is required to show that no soldier in the British Army can abandon his comrades when they are in action.

The heavy red crayon had got to work again. Decisive factors were being isolated in the mind of this ultimate judge: so far, he'd marked out 'alcohol', 'wine', 'drunk' and (inadmissible) 'nerves'. Now he'd underlined 'example is required'. He didn't seem troubled by the

Brigadier's opening doubts on sufficiency. Anselm tried to visualise the moral undergrowth that needed to be cleared before one could move from inadequate proof to exemplary justice. For the Brigadier – and the judge – it was manifestly wide open. Couldn't see a blade of grass, never mind a tree.

The next day, on the 4th September, Major General Boyle at Division had expressed a similarly unencumbered view: 'I do not know this man but I think he should be shot.' Anselm almost laughed with horror.

The papers, with their gathered weight, then landed on the desk of Lieutenant General Cooke at Corps HQ. An underling of sorts had typed up a chit: 'I recommend that the sentence of Death in the case of No 4888 Private J. Flanagan, 8th Batt. N.L.I. . . .' and the commander had added, with admirable economy, '. . . be carried out.' No reasons, no head scratching. Just decisive leadership.

Anselm was beginning to sense the life behind the structure. He pictured a rider or driver taking the bundle to the next echelon of authority, General Osborne, commander of the Ninth Army. Perhaps it was the altitude of his importance, but the general was not a man to be influenced by the unanimous judgement of his subordinates. On a large sheet of paper he'd written, neatly and in the centre of the page, 'The sentence of death can reasonably be commuted to five years imprisonment, to be suspended. This man has a clean record. The plea of mercy has merit.'

And at this point, on the 10th of September 1917, the trail went cold . . . or coldish: for while there was no text recording the actual decision of the Commander-in-Chief, no order from Division to Brigade requiring a firing party, no certificate from Dr Tindall, RMO, confirming death upon execution, there remained a single but monumental clue.

The final document in the Flanagan file was dated the 11th September 1917. After checking the denotation of the acronym, Anselm realised that it was an internal request from one lawyer to another at GHQ . . . in the department where the file had come to rest, complete with five recommendations. It read:

> Please assess and provide an argued response to Lt. Col. Hammond's comments. If you concur with the point on intention, the court should be reassembled to consider *de novo* the charge of desertion and, if necessary, the question of sentence.

It took Anselm a few minutes to penetrate the implications of this text. Lt. Colonel Hammond had raised a technical objection. He'd been concerned about Flanagan's state of mind. That point had been tacitly acknowledged by the Brigade commander who nonetheless wanted 'an example'. But the argument had found a lawyer's ear . . . perhaps the angry man with the brown crayon.

A sudden turn, then, had come to pass in the fortunes of Joseph Flanagan. And while the papers were ultimately ambiguous on the upshot, a tantalising possibility remained: it was just possible that the court had reconvened and had either acquitted Flanagan or reduced his sentence.

Anselm closed the file.

How did you survive? he thought, dreamily, his eyes on the great weeping tree.

He'd been a bent figure, treading slowly away from the aspens on a path that led to the monastery. It was an abiding image for Anselm; and after lunch it sent him on to the path of Kate Seymour's research. They'd probably moved in step, so far. But she'd ended up in a place where Anselm was yet to venture: the War Diary of the Adjutant and Quartermaster General for Flanagan's Division. She'd left behind a yellow ticket by accident. Like a bookmark.

Anselm quickly found the entry dated 17th September 1917. The hole was beneath a title: <u>Courts Martial – Desertion.</u> Turning the page Anselm found a reference to the event that had been suppressed:

> AS OTHER CASES SIMILAR TO THE ABOVE HAVE OCCURRED, MEN ARE TO BE WARNED THAT DRUNKENNESS IS NO EXCUSE FOR CRIME, AND IF A MAN GETS DRUNK AND DELIBERATELY ABSENTS HIMSELF FROM AN IMPORTANT DUTY

HE RENDERS HIMSELF LIABLE ON CONVICTION TO THE FULL PENALTY FOR DESERTION.

The attention of all ranks is to be drawn to this order.

Anselm returned to the hole. A man had got drunk. He'd been executed. His name had been cut out. Even as an 'example' he'd ceased to exist. 'The matter is sensitive.' Anselm could hear the censor's confiding tone, he could feel the pity-come-lately. 'Fellow has a family, damn it.'

Whatever happened as a result of Lt. Colonel Hammond's intervention, death had brushed Flanagan by: he'd been one of the 'other cases'. But what had happened to him next? Once more Anselm turned to the Attorney General for guidance. Immediately beneath the warning on drunkenness he found this notice:

> It may be of use to Officers to know that 'Burberrys' have established a Depot at: L. Chavatte, 10, Grande Place, Armentières.

This, then, was where the trail into Joseph Flanagan's secret history came to a halt: with the appearance of the quintessential English raincoat.

Chapter Fifteen

A Jaunt to Margate

1

Herbert walked away from the school knowing, with a punishing certainty, that he would never forget the steps up to the main door, the white shutters on the chipped brick walls, the black and white tiles, the parquet flooring, the rose wallpaper, the cracked mirror between the columns, and the waxy yellow light a foot or so above the ground.

Ahead, marching on the lane from the encampment, was a column of troops. Three mounted officers led the way. Flanks of chestnut, black and grey glistened in the sunlight. Occasionally, the horses shook or tossed their heads, and light flashed from the dripping bits. Straps jingled. Behind, like a monstrous khaki centipede, came the men. They were heading up the line towards the artillery. Steam shot from their nostrils.

Herbert stumbled to the verge. He let them pass, not looking at their faces. But there, at his feet, he saw Quarters above the mule. Closing his eyes he listened to the stamp of feet knowing that, further on, the road would break down, that they would reach the track of sinking sleepers, and then the duck-boards, and finally the market-place that would claim the greater part of them – without reference to the quality of their lives, to the allocation of what had been decent and what had been foul. The want of discrimination was almost a release for Herbert: the dying would continue; blood would drop like water through Glanville's ceiling; maybe Flanagan was just another splash; maybe Herbert would join him, with Glanville and his pocket watch. Merit had no place in this mêlée.

The carpenter wasn't in singing mood. Herbert glanced inside the barn. Head bent low, the craftsman carefully joined the mortise and tenon and then hammered together another cross. A pile of sallow timber lay stacked against one wall. Turning aside, Herbert's eye caught on the wooden plaque of 'Notre Dame des Ramiers'. He slowed, remembering the unutterable beauty of the chant. After a moment's hesitation, Herbert pushed open the gate and walked towards the white door.

The abbey was cool and deeply silent. Beeswax filled the air. Despite the long clear windows, the light was dim. A tiny red flame flickered like a beacon on a distant headland. Way ahead, like guardians of the sanctuary, stood two large wooden statues: on the left a man, to the right a woman, each with joined hands. Stopping between them, Herbert thought of his parents. They'd mocked Colonel Maude rather than show their disappointment. Within the monastery a door banged and shuffling feet made a soft echo. And from a direction utterly tangential to Herbert's frame of mind – like the breaking of a window in an adjoining property – came an intuitive certainty: what had happened that morning at the Oostbeke school was gravely wrong.

2

When Herbert reached Duggie's billet he paused at the window. The CO was sitting at a small card table, furiously writing, watched by his dog, Angus. To one side lay the *Manual of Military Law*, propped open with a stone. Spread out on the floor were the trial papers. After knocking, Herbert entered and hovered by the empty hearth. He chewed his lip while the ink pen scratched and scraped. When he'd finished, Duggie held up the paper and blew upon it as though to revive a dying flame.

'Why did you call me back from Boulogne?' said Herbert, his voice dead and low. Both hands gripped the sides of his trousers. He felt like he was back before that sanctuary, flanked by his parents.

'Because I thought there was a chance you might see things differently,' said Duggie, without turning around. With rapid finger movements he screwed the lid on to his pen and placed it on the green baize, perfectly parallel to the table's edge.

Herbert had only spoken to Duggie on one occasion about his departure from the 22nd Lancers. Since then, the CO had never referred to it once. Sweat broke on Herbert's upper lip: that sensitivity was about to be compromised. Barely audible, he said, 'What do you mean, see things differently?'

Duggie swivelled round on his stool. 'I thought with your experience of . . . let me use the word kindly . . . failure . . . you might have been circumspect about the demands we place on our men. But you showed great courage. You faced up squarely to the demands of duty.'

There was no sarcasm in Duggie's compliment. Only a certain sadness that one he thought was weak had turned out to be strong. He'd taken a chance and lost. Herbert was stunned. Duggie had warned the battalion almost every month that the 'full penalty' of the law would be exacted for desertion, but now it transpired he'd tried to circumvent the machinery of a court martial by placing Herbert in a crucial position of responsibility.

'I don't blame you, Herbert,' he continued, 'because you've done nothing wrong – any more than I have. No one's to blame for anything. That's what I find so disheartening. As I've got older –' the phrase showed how a sense of life span was reduced, for Duggie was in his mid-thirties – 'I've come to notice that with the great wrongs there's rarely a scalp to hand. There's never a sinner when you want one.'

Duggie was a typical and well-loved CO. Tough but fair. He'd much prefer to wash regimental linen in private, but in this case Division had found out; and they'd told Brigade. And thus a trial on a capital charge had become inevitable. Still, while Duggie would, if possible, support one of his boys, the attempt to save a deserter was almost incredible. Herbert didn't have to wait long to find out why.

'You won't know this,' said Duggie, 'but after Flanagan left Mr Tindall he went to Étaples.'

It sounded as though he'd gone to Margate for an ice cream. Herbert dropped on to the edge of Duggie's bed, his mouth open.

'He denies it,' protested Duggie, 'and it wouldn't have done him any favours if he'd owned up . . . but it looks very likely that he got to the coast and back again in pretty sharp order.'

'What the hell for?'

'I don't know. It seems he teamed up with a Paddy from another brigade, buggered off and then changed his mind.'

Herbert studied the frown among the speckled sores. 'You don't believe that.'

'No, I don't.'

'Why?'

'Because the whole story doesn't hang together,' he admitted. 'Prior to this fling, Flanagan had never touched a drop of booze in his life. He's a Pioneer . . . some Catholic thing. Maguire, the chaplain, is one of 'em too. They pledge to stay dry for life. Can't imagine it, frankly. Not my sort of God. The point is, this lad sees action at Aubers Ridge, the Somme and Arras and it's only now he needs a stiff drink with another son of Erin. Doesn't make sense.'

'You mean he lied?'

'I mean he hid the truth.'

Herbert let his chin sink to his chest. He wanted to shout, as he'd done in the abbey. A jaunt to Margate? This parallel narrative, if genuine, would have removed the slim defence implied by Flanagan's statement – that he'd got lost. And yet, ironically, this was Duggie's reason for attempting to upset the court martial.

'If we're going to shoot him before breakfast,' explained Duggie, 'we ought to do it for the right reason.'

With a low groan Herbert covered his face. Through spread fingers he watched Duggie on all fours, grunting as he gathered the trial papers. He couldn't bring himself to help, to get down there on the boards. When Duggie was upright he tied the bundle securely with a length of white cotton tape. Later in the day Chamberlayne would collect it, and off the case would go, first stop Brigade. It was as though some great, unknown truth would shortly slip away, never to be understood. Duggie made a tilt with his head and they went outside into the courtyard, followed by Angus.

The sun was high and warmed their necks. It was crazy: after all that rain, they were heading for a drought. For a while they talked of football and the Lambton Cup. The regiment had struggled through the early stages of the competition but had managed to secure a place in the final against the Lancashire Fusiliers. While the team had always suffered 'injuries,' this time none of the team had survived August.

'I'm conceding the match,' said Duggie. 'I couldn't look at that cup if we won it.'

Angus whimpered, his tongue wet and horribly long. He'd been 'a parting gift' from a General and was a familiar figure to the men, almost a mascot. Though he had his own gas mask, he stayed behind moaning when the battalion went into the line.

'By the way,' resumed Duggie, 'I've just written my recommendation. It's a bit cheeky, really.' He drew a pipe from his top pocket and pressed the shank into the corner of his mouth. 'It's important not to do things directly, so I've advocated imprisonment, but observed, in passing, that when intention is of the essence of a crime –' he struck a match, puffed and squinted – 'drunkenness may justify the court taking a lenient view of an otherwise serious offence. And on that basis, I've floated the idea that our boy should've been found guilty of "absence without leave", despite the charge of desertion.' He examined the chewed mouthpiece. 'If some legal bod picks up the ball the court might be reassembled . . . which would open the door to the lesser offence, and a different sentence.'

'I'm sorry,' said Herbert, hot at his own failure to dodge and weave; angry that he and Glanville should have worked harder at Sandhurst; irritated that Oakley hadn't been the one who'd sat the exam, 'I don't quite follow.'

'"Intention" is the key,' said Duggie, jamming the pipe back in the corner of his mouth. 'If a steady, respectful soldier absents himself through a drunken frolic, the court can reasonably conclude that he did not really *intend* to desert. It's in the manual. Page twenty-three.'

Herbert's face showed the accusation: why not tell me this beforehand? And Duggie's silence demonstrated the CO's own uncomfortable position: he'd done Pemberton's bidding: he'd passed on to Herbert the subtle pressure for a conviction. Duggie scratched on a blood spot on his cheek, as if to flatten the louse responsible. 'First, it would have been wrong for me to coach you, though I do so now; second, I thought you already knew; and third – and at least I was right in this one respect – I didn't expect you to think in a legal way.' His disappointment surfaced again, only this time he made a grin. 'I thought you'd disgrace yourself and my regiment.'

For the first time since he'd joined the 8th (Service) Battalion, Northumberland Light Infantry, Herbert cast a smile upon his past. Angus seemed to laugh, too.

Chapter Sixteen

1

The young man's ingenuity was admirable. But not as pitiful as his limitations, his desperation and his incompetence. His lack of inner resources was evident on every page.

Anselm had decided to revisit all the Doyle material because he was, from one perspective, the central figure in the drama. His relationship with Flanagan was the key to the trial. His tags were the key to Herbert's message.

6890 Private Owen Doyle enlisted in 1915 at the age of eighteen. He'd joined a London regiment based in the East End. His Battalion came to France in the spring of 1916, when he was deployed behind the lines in various non-combat maintenance operations. He deserted after two weeks but was caught three days later dressed as a farmer. A Field General Court Martial condemned him to death, the sentence being enthusiastically endorsed at every level of command, until it hit the desk of the C-in-C who finally determined upon a term of imprisonment to be suspended for the duration of the hostilities. Returned to his unit, he then saw action on the Somme – although not for long, because he deserted once more, this time reaching Boulogne with a forged pass. Once again he was caught, convicted, condemned to death and reprieved, a second suspended sentence being imposed with the heavy implication that lenience had run its course. Whatever else, Doyle was a resourceful young man, for upon this his second arrest he'd been found on the docks wearing a stolen naval hat and greatcoat. He'd been very close indeed to stowing away and reaching home. His third desertion had, in one sense, been successful. Warned for the front, he had vanished the night before his unit advanced into action – the 26th August 1917. There was no record of him being caught or reprimanded in any way. The gap in the facts was enormous: somehow Doyle was back with his unit by September, meeting his death near Glencorse Wood on the 15th at the age of twenty.

It had been a pinched life: the greater part of three years spent scratching behind the skirting boards of France and Belgium. He'd been a forger, a thief and a mannequin in someone else's uniform. To quote a tart line from one of his commanding officers, he'd been a 'worthless soldier and a worthless man'.

A man who was central to the trial of Joseph Flanagan.

Anselm simply could not imagine what had bound such different men together in a mortally dangerous enterprise – an enterprise that appeared to be senseless: they'd both come back. And that conclusion placed the trial back under scrutiny. If Anselm had one certainty it was that Flanagan had returned to the front expecting to be tried by Field General Court Martial.

How, then, had he escaped, given the mounting odds against him?

With that question in mind Anselm sought Martin's company.

'It's an odd trial, and it must have been odd at the time,' began Anselm, sitting down on a chair surrounded by cardboard boxes, books and research papers laid out on the floor like stepping stones.

Martin had changed his kit but it was still a uniform. A camel jacket. No buttons at the sleeve. A crisp pink shirt. He reached between two piles of books for a bunch of index cards held by a paperclip.

'I'm thinking of those people outside the review process, those not called at the trial, the people who actually spoke to Flanagan on the night of the twenty-sixth. If the trial was strange for them, as it is for me, then maybe they wrote something down . . . a memoir, some letters—'

'Or a sermon,' Martin slipped in.

He wasn't being rude. He was sending Anselm a warning signal, an oblique reference to Herbert who had been unable to speak of his experience.

After a scratch to the silvered hair around the temples, Martin removed the paperclip and laid it on a pillar of books. 'You mean Father Maguire, Captain Chamberlayne, Lieutenant Tindall . . . ?' His hand rolled out the rest of the names in silence.

There was no point, Anselm now realised. Kate Seymour's done the journey. Her last stop was Herbert Moore.

'I'll start with Chamberlayne,' said Martin to the first card in the pile. 'He came back to England in nineteen nineteen and then vanished. Could have thrown himself into the Thames. Could have emigrated. Who knows? Sent his medals to the War Office without a stamp. No address given. His brother was a legal officer at Division. He died in nineteen thirty-seven.'

He flipped the card on to the table, tapped the rest and resumed the litany. 'Father Maguire. Applied for a change in Division in October nineteen seventeen. Killed two weeks later while giving the Last Rites in full view of the enemy. Posthumous MC. Should've been a VC. University College Dublin has a handful of letters. No mention of Flanagan.'

Anselm let the words wash over him. He'd ceased to listen attentively. *The waves of history*, he extemporised silently, *how they crashed and fell . . .*

'Tindall was killed in nineteen eighteen . . . an only son . . . Lieutenant Colonel Hammond bequeathed three diaries to the Imperial War Museum . . . no reference to . . .'

. . . *and now the sands of time hide our calamity*, thought Anselm, completing his invention. It was bad Tennyson. Or worse early Brooke. When war was made glorious by a cadence.

'On the other hand . . .' Martin's voice had risen. He drew out the last word, letting it reach an acceptable peak of friendly reproach.

'Yes?' apologised Anselm, despondently.

'General Osborne left a vast collection of papers, all of which are retained by the family. His great-great-granddaughter, Sarah, is currently writing his biography.' Martin stood up. He brushed close to the wall, avoiding a crate of ring-binders. 'I'm sure she'd like to meet you. I'll make an appointment.' At the edge of his desk he paused, unsure of where to go next. 'Father, can I ask you a question of real importance . . . something I've wanted to raise since we met?'

'Of course,' replied Anselm, a little worried.

'Do you like beer?' Martin shrugged inside his jacket. 'You know . . . proper bitter? Roasted peanuts? Crisps? That sort of thing.'

'Lead, kindly light,' murmured Anselm. 'Lead thou me on.'

2

'How many were shot altogether?' asked Anselm in the back room of The Wheat Sheaf, after he'd asked for the Friendship Plant. The timber floor was stripped and smooth. Paint peeled off the walls around large etched mirrors. It was a last stand against the uniformity of plush seats, new brass fittings and beer by franchise. The only concession was a one-armed bandit. A youth in his late teens stood over it, yanking the arm. He wanted a big win.

'For military offences, three hundred and twenty-one,' replied Martin. 'Most of them for desertion.'

'How many were condemned in the first place?'

The youth pushed in more coins. He drew back the lever and the fruit span.

'Over three thousand. So nine out of ten had their sentence commuted.' It was a complex subject with no easy summary, his face seemed to add. 'How the unlucky one got picked we just don't know. Prejudice. Class. Eugenics. Contemporary fairness. Who knows? Maybe the state of the war. During the Somme, for example, the number of executions rose . . . same with Passchendaele.' He sipped his beer. 'In fact, executions soared during September nineteen seventeen and fell dramatically afterwards.'

The very month when Flanagan's case was under consideration, implied Martin with a tightening of the mouth. He was telling Anselm, gently, to give up this search for the missing pieces that would lead, inexorably, to a dead man. Martin was as compassionate as he was efficient.

Lights flashed and the youth slapped the side of the machine as if it were stupid.

For an instant, Anselm fell into a reverie. Herbert had refused to view existence as the play of chance. When the fruit had stopped spinning, Herbert had looked beyond the bandit and the disappointment. Was that simply naked faith? Or had it also been informed by an *experience*. Was this the significance of Joseph Flanagan's story? Anselm's mind blurred. He broke the reverie by returning to the central enigma: statistics had been against the Irishman, as well as the timing, the warning on drunkenness, and the hole in the page . . . and yet he'd escaped. But how? Kate Seymour, of course, knew the answer. Anselm drained his glass and said, 'I found a yellow ticket with a woman's name on it.'

Gently, coaxing now, the youth pulled the lever. He looked like Bede when he sought the Prior's permission to travel somewhere.

'I can't discuss other users of the archive,' Martin declared, with the bogus finality of a man who realises that the matter is far from over.

'And I wouldn't want you to,' said Anselm, untruthfully. 'Look . . . we both know that Kate Seymour came to Larkwood. You've guessed it was a waste of time. You're wrong. What you don't appreciate – and neither does she – is that Herbert left a message for a man called Joseph Flanagan.'

Martin showed mild surprise, but Anselm was quite sure that he'd been stunned.

'Yes,' pursued Anselm. 'I didn't know until she'd gone. Unfortunately she left her contact details with a monk whose mental powers are antithetical to those of the elephant, which is to say he can't remember where he put them.' Anselm appealed to Martin with a helpless sigh. 'I want to fathom the trial of the man who came with her. A man I saw weeping.'

Martin raised an eyebrow. He'd thought the surprises had ended with the leaving of a message, not the arrival of the beneficiary.

'But at some point I will have to find her . . . and him.'

To the sound of a whoop, coins poured from the mouth of the bandit. The player had beaten the odds.

Martin raised his glass. 'I'll get the admin people to call up her details.'

They watched the youth pocket his winnings. He was a bit

embarrassed now that all the noise was over. And Anselm felt remotely sad. Other gamblers had once been shot when they lost.

3

A monk needs his monastery, regardless of the tensions and occasional anguish of close living. And Anselm had been away long enough to make him restless for the nave, the bluebell path, the track by Our Lady's lake, his hives – all the secret places that gave him sustenance. On the train back home, rattling away from cafés, tabloid colour, tinned food and the national archives, Anselm began to doze. In a dream he saw Herbert in a cold room, though Anselm did not recognise him. He heard him say 'Death' while guns boomed in the distance. There were others present, all of them standing solemnly, none of them moving, each with a bloodless face. The only person Anselm knew was Flanagan . . . he'd known him all his life. His skin and clothes were vibrant with colour and life. Upon seeing him, a word chafed against Anselm's consciousness and he woke.

Nerves.

The word had chafed the man with the red crayon. It occurred twice in the inadmissible evidence of Lieutenant Alan Caldwell. Flanagan had suffered an attack of nerves in April, when the unit was away from the firing line, and later in June. Anselm rummaged in his bag for the photocopied excerpts taken from the War Diary of the 8th (Service) Battalion, Northumberland Light Infantry.

The page was organised into five columns: place, date, hour, summary of events and remarks. Anselm gleaned that Flanagan's unit had been camped by 'Dead Pig Farm'. For the month of April 1917 the 'event' column noted a route march between two villages, a football practice, company 'training and preparations for move to forward area', divine service, a visit from the Corps Commander, the first round match for the Lambton Cup . . . and then, at the bottom of the page: 'Total number of dead soldiers (English and German) buried by members of B Company was 2314'.

Anselm checked the family tree prepared by Martin. Flanagan was in B Company. The 'event' took four days . . . which meant – he did some maths in the margin – five hundred and seventy-eight burials per day; seventy-two per hour in an eight-hour shift.

Anselm next checked the month of June. The battalion was evidently in the firing line because there were lists of casualties and the factual entries were brief. One, however, caught his eye: 'Mines detonated at Messines. Extraordinary sight. German front line completely vanished.'

Anselm tired suddenly. He packed away his papers and leaned his head against the window, letting the ra-ta-ta-ta, ra-ta-ta-ta soothe him. Without knowing why, he felt he'd stumbled upon something important. The question that framed itself was not, however, of an investigative character. It was anthropological: what would it do to a man to handle so much death in spring?

Part Three

Chapter Seventeen

The Family Silver

1

After the trial Seosamh Ó Flannagáin (as Joseph understood himself) was taken back to the cellar. '*Go hifreann leat*,' he muttered as the bolt went home – 'To hell with you'. Joseph thought in Gaelic, he dreamed in Gaelic, his world was Gaelic; but English was his tongue, now, making him a man distant from himself and from the land for which he hungered; a land whose worth he hadn't grasped until he'd left it far, far behind.

He'd been condemned, he knew it. If you were convicted, they asked about your character and if they didn't call you back after the recess . . . well . . . it was death, that quietest of words. In Gaelic: bás. That was the last you knew of the affair, until one fine day on parade you were told whether the Big Fella had 'commuted' your sentence to 'field punishment' or 'penal servitude'. Those strange expressions had never reached the tiny school on Inisdúr. There was no music to them.

When all the voices up top had died away the sentry rattled the lock and Corporal Mackie stuck his head around the door. 'C'mon, out, you Irish . . .' He couldn't find the word, so he threw Flanagan his cap (removed before the trial) and, feeling very silly, they marched from the school to the battalion's billet a mile or so down the road. They passed the carpenter clouting wood with a mallet and the abbey where Father Maguire said his prayers.

'Your only chance is drink,' the chaplain had said in Gaelic, with an oath that would have shocked Flanagan's mother. 'If anything goes wrong, get drunk.'

And things had gone wrong, badly so. That's why he'd come back with three bottles of wine. Lisette had brought them up from the cellar. But one sniff had turned him against the chaplain's counsel: instead, he'd poured the stuff all over, head to foot, and what an awful stink it had raised. The bite in the air had reminded him of the French fishermen who, from time to time, had called into the small harbour back home, huge lads from Brittany who wouldn't touch a drop of porter. A strange lot they were. They played football barefoot with a cabbage.

'If you get caught, you'll be tried,' Father Maguire had said, leaning close in the trench, the smell of tobacco strong on his breath, 'and if you're tried then it's death, unless you can give mercy a decent yoke. So get drunk, son.'

His Gaelic was like an islander's, though he was a mainland clod, from Dingle. He'd learned the tongue on An Blascaod Mór, among the weavers, before he'd heard the Voice.

The chaplain had stalled to ponder his own advice, turning his face to the rain. 'The thing is, you're Irish.' He'd muttered that to himself in English, as though it was a problem all of its own, as though it was a dark water that lapped against Flanagan's chances.

Corporal Mackie didn't speak. They marched in silence past hundreds of faces, pale among the steaming tents. Occasionally men stared, some with pity, others with disgust. The sounds of drill – hollering and the thud of feet – came from a trampled field beside a barricade of hop frames. Mackie stomped right, then left, then right again, his arms swinging stiff like bits of driftwood, old spars off the beach. He stopped at a low farmhouse with a courtyard and a few crazed chickens. As if a bell had been rung Lieutenant Colonel Hammond appeared from a doorway. He led Flanagan away from Mackie towards the corner of the courtyard, where a dog lay panting.

'How are you?' asked Duggie. Everyone called him that, but behind his back, of course.

'Not so bad, Sir, considering.'

'Yes, considering.'

They fell silent. The dog's tail flapped on the dirt, its breathing uncommonly loud.

'I can't help you if you won't help me,' said Duggie, lighting his pipe.

Flanagan's father used to say the same thing, sitting in the exhausted light by the fire. But his father had been talking of the farm and the fishing, the breaking of rocks to make the walls, the burning of the kelp to make iodine. And Flanagan had wanted to escape the harness of life on the island, to taste air without salt, to walk for miles without sight of the sea.

'I said I need your help,' repeated Duggie, striking another match.

'I don't know what you mean, Sir,' he lied.

'Let me help you. How did you get to Étaples and back again without a pass?'

'Hah, I'm sorry, Sir, I am.' He shook his head, as did the dog. 'I told you before, it wasn't me. The police must have stopped some other fella. There's—'

'—Flanagans aplenty in the army,' recited Duggie.

'Aye, there is, Sir.'

'A tot of rum?' Duggie asked, playfully, reaching for a pocket flask.

'I won't, thank you, Sir.'

'Thought not. Drink isn't your thing, is it?' The CO sighed and scratched his cheek. 'You'll be kept under close arrest. However – he picked a shred off his tongue and flicked it away – 'between the hours of four and six, you'll polish the weapons of the regimental band. I'm told there are twenty-six instruments in all. Do them carefully, please. And do bear in mind . . . there's no rush.'

Flanagan had expected to be locked up day and night until the Commander-in-Chief had decided what to do with him. But the CO had a way of startling you in moments of crisis by a quiet word or, as now, a kind decision. Something to show that the individual soldier was as important to him as the battalion itself. There was another reason, though, for why Flanagan liked his CO: he served the army like his father had served the land. Both of them saw further than their own horizons, both of them would never say so. Yet both of them understood someone who did, for they looked on to the world from their own regret, from a field they would not leave.

2

Later that day, when the rest of the battalion was being screamed at while they marched, Corporal Mackie escorted Flanagan from the cellar to an abandoned house on the roadside between the abbey and the school. Thin orange bricks framed sections of beige cement stamped with imprints like a cat's paws. Mackie unlocked the door and pushed Flanagan inside.

'If I was in charge,' he whispered, 'I'd have shot you by now, you worthless bastard.'

The door banged shut and Flanagan entered the sitting room. Most of the instruments were stored upon shelves along one wall. On the floor were two big drums and a tuba on its bell. He sat on a stool and opened a bottle of Goddard's Silver Polish. Mindful of Mackie's bitterness, and the many others who felt the same, he began to think of Owen Doyle. He, too, had been worthless . . . from one angle.

After Flanagan had taken Major Dunne to the stretcher-bearers, he began the return trip to Joyce and the boys. Out there, among the craters and rain, he literally crawled upon Doyle. The heap moaned and hit out, an arm rising from the dirt that smacked Flanagan straight in the teeth.

'Calm down, ye brute,' he snapped. 'I'm on your side.'

The soldier remained crouched, each hand over the back of his head, face down in the muck, whimpering.

'Are you injured, so?'

The heap wouldn't speak. It rocked from side to side as if it were a mole trying to get its nose under the earth. Sitting upright, Flanagan patted its back. He did that for a long time, as his father had done on the farm, helping a beast push out a calf. Pat, pat, pat. And all around the rain thumped into the soft land. Finally, the soldier raised his head, his hands kneading the mud. He sat upright, like Flanagan. They looked at each other, each unseeing, each etched against the darkness, rain thundering down upon them. This other man had no gun, no bandolier and no helmet.

'Where's your people?' Flanagan asked. The figure just rocked from side to side, humming on a monotone. He wasn't one of Flanagan's pack, that was for sure. He was from another battalion. He'd crossed a boundary. He was on the run.

'What's your name, so?'

'I want to go home,' he wailed, answering neither question.

'And where might that be?'

The voice answered, this time aggressive and through bared teeth. 'I don't have one, but it's Blighty. Not this hole. This cemetery.'

Hah, the fear. It could split the lining of the lungs if you let it loose. The impulse to avoid death rose from a pit, from somewhere deeper than any thought or idea.

'Aye,' he said. 'But you'll likely as not get caught.'

The hunched figure rocked and hummed under the beating rain. Flanagan could imagine the running nose, the tears, the juddering lip, and that terrible relaxation in the limbs, so like exhaustion and helplessness. He'd heard about an execution, once, when on leave. The poor wretch couldn't hold his limbs. He'd flopped in the guardhouse and kept apologising. They'd had to drag him out and strap him to a chair, and all the while he was saying, 'I'm sorry, lads.'

'I can't go back,' whispered the shape. 'They'll shoot me.'

'Tell me your name.'

'Owen Doyle.'

There in the rain, soaking up the mud, they talked. In the dreadful, low, unquiet between explosions. Or rather Doyle did, of home and the cobbled streets of Bolton in Lancashire. He'd come to London and taken the King's shilling, and now he wanted to give it back, without interest. Flanagan's eyes misted. There were no cobbled streets on Inisdúr . . . just tracks across grassland that had been worn through to the strong rock beneath, a rock that wouldn't yield. As Doyle spoke of the cotton mills with their tall, thin chimneys, the tight terraced houses, and the gas light halos at night time, Flanagan remembered the fields of seaweed and sand, and the white gable ends of low houses huddled in the lee. This gathering of flesh and stone he'd left behind. He'd sailed away, leaving a crowd at the slip.

Hardly listening to Doyle's moaning, Flanagan made the greatest decision of his life, though it appeared more as an instinctive reaction than a rational choice. In truth, the thinking had been completed long ago.

It had begun with that spate of burials last spring. For three days Flanagan manhandled his own future. He smelled it on his fingers. It made his trousers tacky. Afterwards, he was told to count the identity tags that had been collected in a pannier taken from a mule. There were two thousand, three hundred and fourteen discs of different shapes and sizes, like coins . . . all sorts of strange currency, crudely stamped with number, name and religion. The essentials. He'd remembered a winter's morning on Inisdúr when, as a boy, he'd heard an explosion of wings and seen thousands of birds in flight at once. The discs became heavy in his hands. On the fourth day, and shivering, he told the new MO that his mind was sick. 'The faces of the dead hang around me like a crowd,' he said. So the doctor checked his tongue and shone a torch in his ears and snapped, 'You're normal.' Flanagan had been relieved. He'd thought maybe it'd been too much sun and not enough water. But then, in June, the mines were blown at Messines. A million tons of TNT, they'd said. The German positions just disappeared in a great belch of hot wind. Bás. Flanagan had never seen anything like it, awake or in his dreams. After he saw the crater, he couldn't speak. The MO shone a torch in his throat and muttered, as if it were a threat, 'You're normal, just like me.' But Flanagan knew he wasn't. That he'd changed. That he wanted a death with *meaning*.

Not death from a whizz-bang. Not death from a coal-box. Not death from bullets scything out of nowhere. Not death from suicide, or accident, or a hideous, screaming brawl with another man-beast. The capricious butchering had almost driven him mad. Only one sanity remained: if he must, he would *choose* the manner of his dying. He'd reached the point of serenity where 'thinking' was no longer necessary.

And then, like a bitter gift, he crawled upon Owen Doyle. At a very deep level, without being able to fully appreciate the workings of his own decision, or track the velocity of the insight, Flanagan knew that in finding this unhappy boy he'd received the opportunity he was looking for: to die in a meaningful way.

His mind blank, his emotions numbed, Flanagan dipped a field dressing into a pool of bloody water and thrust it against Doyle's face. The brat fought back, howling with terror, but Flanagan had the strength of a God. He'd made a decision that set him above this arbitrary universe. He dragged Doyle, weeping and deranged, all the way back to the RAP, where he told Father Maguire what had happened out there in the rain. For a few, flashing seconds they argued about the right word to describe it. They quickly settled on *nochtadh* – a disclosure. Either way, Flanagan had made up his mind. He was going to Lisette Papinau's. 'Just do as I ask,' he begged. The chaplain splashed off into the shadows to get Doyle's number. When he came back, ill with worry, he listed the lad as injured. 'But not me,' hissed Flanagan. 'Just him. That's important.' It was then, on hearing the sketch of Flanagan's plan, that the mainlander muttered, 'Listen, man, your only chance is drink.' Hastily and shivering, Flanagan wrapped his arm with the second field dressing. As the familiar words came out of the darkness, he bowed his head.

'*Nár lagaí Dia do lámh.*' May God not weaken your hand.

It lacked the whack of the original.

Within half an hour Flanagan and Doyle joined the utter chaos of injured troops moving away from the front towards an Advanced Dressing Station.

Protected by the crowds and madness, they smuggled themselves into a Red Cross ambulance which took them through the rain to a Casualty Clearing Station at Abeele – an awful, eight-hour rattling journey among cries and the silence of dying. There, at Flanagan's request, a nurse procured two clean uniforms. In the late morning, washed and presentable, they slipped away to find a train. As usual it pulled in bursting with troops for the Salient, the coach windows glazed with body heat. More chaos, as the shining faces disembarked. And while the NCOs shouted and stamped their ground, Flanagan and Doyle clambered on to a goods carriage and hid among some crates.

As they trundled towards the coast, Flanagan made a greater escape into memory. He talked of Inisdúr and the sharp smell of the tide, the steaming rocks, and the labour of Muiris, his father. In a mist of longing he saw Róisín, his mother. She was proud, holding Brendan's little hand. Flanagan gasped his explanations. It was like he was going home, at last.

Flanagan pressed a valve on the tuba, reflecting that it was only on the train that he'd got a chance to study the face of his accomplice. The talk of the island had sent Doyle to sleep. Flanagan looked on the slumped head, slightly fearful, wondering if he'd picked the wrong man.

Side on, Doyle was boyish with an upturned nose and a top lip that curved gently outwards, as if he was one of those Christmas angels or the bronze lad of so many fountains – the tyke with the arched back, passing water into a marble basin filled with pennies.

But Doyle had stirred. His head had turned and his eyelids had opened for a moment. And Flanagan had seen someone else. The brow was heavy, the eyes mature and disconcerting: one was narrowed and vigilant, the other dull and unfeeling, as if it could watch terrible things without rolling over. That impish nose showed itself squat above uneven lips . . . all in all, a face that had been hit once too often. Perhaps by hands like his own, with tattooed dots on each knuckle.

He was, as Flanagan's mother would have said, contrary. 'Be careful, Seosamh, that one can go either way.'

Taking a soft cloth he set to work on the bell, bringing up the shine till he saw his own face across the trademark of Boosey and Company, makers, 295 Regent Street, London. His features were so distorted that he saw the man within: not a shape but an assembly of attitudes: fear, determination, abandonment and hope: all gathered into the grimace of someone who'd found a way out of senseless dying.

Chapter Eighteen

Mutiny

1

'There's unrest in the regiment,' said Duggie, carelessly.

'What kind?' Herbert felt queasy.

They were in battalion HQ – the back room of a blacksmith's forge, the enterprise rendered useless upon the demise of the owner and his four sons at Verdun. The widow and her only daughter now crept about in black, tending to the cares of the British Army by the careful management of vegetables grown where the horses used to wait. Chamberlayne had insisted on peacetime comforts, and to that end had filched a desk from the post office, securing for Duggie a more imposing specimen from a blown-out bank.

'Among whom?' pursued Herbert.

Chamberlayne typed laboriously with one finger, not looking up. 'Those who remain.' He span the roller three times, pulled out the document, and signed it through a quite awful hush.

Herbert had already suffered the stony salutes of the RSM and Private Elliot. There was a ruthless obedience among the NCOs and men: no muttering or undertones of complaint, just brute compliance with his orders. Flanagan's conviction was common knowledge among 'those who remained' and it had struck a nerve.

Chamberlayne fed another sheet of paper into his typewriter. 'A court martial subsequent to the decimation of an entire regiment in twelve hours has not been received with universal understanding by the rank and file,' he observed, turning the roller slowly to align the page. 'But that is not the problem to which our Commanding Officer refers. Do I address this one to Division, Sir?'

Duggie nodded and Chamberlayne set about the usual preliminaries, hitting each key with a jab of calculated uncertainty.

Herbert's stomach rolled as if he were at sea. The animosity had become personal, focusing on himself. It was not unknown for men to finish off a hated officer in no-man's-land, among the litter of bodies. It could never be proved. He'd once heard a tale of some rough nuts sticking a Mills bomb down the trousers of a Second Lieutenant who thought he was Hannibal.

'Joyce came to see me this morning,' said Duggie, sitting on the edge of Chamberlayne's desk. One leg began to swing. 'He's overheard some strong talk.'

'Yes?' Herbert squared himself.

'Apparently, the men will be buggered before they'll hand a win to the Lancashire Fusiliers.'

'What?'

'They want to pull a team together for the Lambton Cup. They want to win it for the old team.'

Herbert flashed his rage at Chamberlayne for leading him on. The adjutant gave a servant's nod of gratitude and hit a full stop with a stiff index finger.

'The final will take place on the sixteenth,' said Duggie. 'That gives us two weeks to field a team that can't be beaten. I'd like you to sort out the players. There's some new boys from Blighty, but four of them come from Flanagan's old section. Gibbons, Pickering, Nugent, and Hudson. These are the ones he left near Black Eye Corner. In fact, I'm transferring them to your Company. Along with Elliot. Joyce will be there, too. He says he's a robust defender.'

'Yes, Sir,' said Herbert, understanding at once the breadth of Duggie's intentions.

'I think it would do you good to mingle with the men.'

Any hostility thrown up by the trial had to be dealt with, but not on the level of ideas and explanations. As ever, with the army, it was a matter of solidarity and mutual respect. And Duggie was sure that Joyce understood Herbert's position, just as Elliot understood that of Joyce, just as the rank and file understood that of Elliot. The place to re-establish the bond between officer and soldier was not the parade ground but the field of play.

The CO gave Herbert the document that Chamberlayne had prepared. It was a memo setting out the members of the squad and the practice times. Fourteen names were listed, the last of whom was Joseph Flanagan.

'Flanagan?'

'Edward's idea.'

Chamberlayne nodded, accepting the praise. But the CO's decision was nonetheless remarkable. It meant that Flanagan, for a certain time, would be released from imprisonment . . . a condition that had already been relaxed through his polishing of the regiment's instruments. At that instant, Herbert realised that Duggie had subtly changed. Something had broken inside him after the annihilation of the battalion in August. The CO wanted to save his men . . . even from a court material and its consequences.

Duggie slid off the desk and led Herbert outside on to the road. In the distance the guns rumbled, forever erratic and monotonous. To the right another battalion was marching to the front; to the left, in the distance, charabancs lined the verge. They'd brought fresh batches of men from Poperinghe and Abeele for the rehearsals that would begin in earnest later that morning. It was as though Herbert and Duggie were at a still point between this coming and going.

'Division is pushing this one through,' said Duggie, referring to Flanagan's case. 'He was tried within three days of being caught. They'll decide his fate in the same breath. We'll know before we go up the line. That gives you time to find out what really happened with Doyle in Étaples.'

'But why me?'

'Because I think you might thank me for it in the years to come.'

2

Herbert spent the morning in a nearby village, attending a lecture for officers on the coming operation. A severe Brigade Major called

Tomlinson pointed with a long cane at a model of the battlefield made of plaster-of-Paris. It had been painted a muddy brown, and there were various bright flags on cocktail sticks identifying key objectives. Red, yellow, blue, green. It reminded Herbert of a golf course. The attack would take place along an eight-mile front. The sector relevant to Herbert was at the Menin Road, where the 8th and other units would provide flanking fire to an Australian division.

'This is a four-step operation,' said Tomlinson, uttering each word with exaggerated clarity. 'Between each stage there will be three days of consolidation and three days of preparation. That constitutes a six-day interval.'

It sounded so very easy.

'We anticipate subdued resistance,' he continued, rocking on his heels. 'The bombardment will be colossal. Three and a half million shells have been set aside. It will open on the thirteenth. It will increase in density with each successive day. It will inch across the German defence territory removing machine-gun emplacements and wire. It will—'

'Tell Jerry that we're coming,' chipped in an Australian Colonel.

Everyone laughed, including Tomlinson. It was an old joke. But, as Tomlinson observed, the old ones were always the best.

They're a rebellious lot, the Aussies, thought Herbert. Even the officers.

3

In the late afternoon, when the men were enjoying Extended Order drill, Herbert went to collect Flanagan. His plan was to walk to the field of play before the rest of the team arrived. Corporal Mackie was standing like a statue at the door. As soon as Herbert stood among the gleaming silver, he coughed and said, 'Do you play football?'

Herbert had expected resentment – masked, of course – but discernible nonetheless, as it was with Joyce and the rest. But Flanagan showed nothing more than the customary reserve borne from their difference in rank and station.

'Well, now, Sir, I played it once with a cabbage.'

'A cabbage?'

'Yes, Sir. It's a French thing, Sir.'

'Ah.'

Herbert explained that, notwithstanding such novel tuition, Lieutenant-Colonel Hammond expected Flanagan to make a sterling contribution to the winning of the Lambton Cup for the battalion. Bemused, as one might expect from a man sentenced to death, Flanagan pledged his enthusiasm, if not his talent, to the objective. On that understanding, Herbert led the prisoner into the lane. Having dismissed Mackie, they were alone.

Throughout Tomlinson's lecture Herbert had been unable to conjure up a conversation that might approach the Étaples incident. Instead, he began with a question he'd often thrown at a new face, to welcome them to his Company. 'Where are you from, Private?'

'The plains of Banba,' said Flanagan, 'Ireland.'

Banba. The reference surprised Herbert. It revealed learning. Uncertain of himself, and who he was dealing with, Herbert escorted Flanagan towards the clump of trees that had been visible from the schoolroom. The football pitch had been laid out in a nearby field.

'Whereabouts in Banba?' asked Herbert, his voice as detached as Major Tomlinson's.

'An island, Sir . . . on the west coast.'

'When did you last see it?'

'An age ago, Sir.'

'Really?' said Herbert. 'Didn't you see its reflection in a cracked mirror?'

The skin around Flanagan's eyes creased slightly.

'Tell me about home,' said Herbert, no longer distant like Tomlinson. 'I could do with a tale of a faraway place.'

Strangely, Flanagan described Inisdúr from the sea, seen as he was leaving it. He'd stood at the stern of a hooker looking back at the misty rocks. Shadows thrown by the cloud hid the coves and the tiny fields – neat compartments framed with chunks of stone, marvellously laid. The dark wrangled with the light, as they struck the white gables and the fissures on the flat expanses of rock. The speckling of green and ochre glowed and died. As Flanagan drew further away, the island itself seemed to move west, trails of smoke rising from the houses as though they were a fleet of tiny boats, a whole community leaving him to his chosen future.

Flanagan's parents had a farm near the slip – a small harbour in a cove where the men of a morning landed their lobster pots and the catch of the night. He had a brother, little Brendan, a tyke with chestnut hair and blue-green eyes, like the sea. He'd come late to the family, when Flanagan was too old to be a true companion. Brendan would follow him around, though, looking for approval, just as he followed the men as they trod to the shore, their currachs shouldered as if they were huge, black beetles. Flanagan had been the same. All the boys wanted to carry their own boat, and to find their true place in the island's hierarchy. There, on the slip, among tradesmen from the mainland, Flanagan had picked up his first phrases of English.

Muiris, Flanagan's father, had only left Inisdúr twice, and on each occasion it was to visit Inismín, where he met Róisín. Over twenty years he'd made the three fields that surrounded the family home, their soil made from sand, smashed rock and seaweed. That was the history of the island, said Flanagan. Men and women, on their hands and knees, had slowly made the ground fertile. They were bound together: man and woman and earth.

Herbert drifted into something like a trance. It was the way Flanagan talked of the land. His respect was almost fearful. While speaking, he occasionally stretched out both arms, his fingers spread wide, as though to approach something that had to be felt to be understood: a blaze in the ground.

'Róisín, my mother, was famed for her quilts,' said Flanagan. (He'd begun to relax, forgetting – as Herbert had hoped – that he was talking to an officer.) 'She'd scrub her hands in the pail, to wash off the milch cow, and then she'd set to work, sewing by the light of the fire . . . a marvellous thing it was, of blue and yellow and green and brown, the pigments of the island. Without a clock or a timer, she knew when to pause for the bread that was baking beneath the sods –' he glanced aside, adding by way of explanation – 'back home,

Sir, you can bake with a peat fire, if you know how.'

This was Flanagan's inheritance. He loved it. Whole lives were played out to the sound of the wind and the sea. He wanted no other future. But then a school was built in nineteen hundred and one, and a teacher came from the mainland.

'I learned my letters and numbers fast enough,' he said. 'A Blasket poet became my companion, Piaras Feiritéar –' he waved a hand – 'sure, it was all desolation and dismay, you know, but it works up the blood like nothing else. War, distant horizons, love. What else do you want?'

The teacher, Mr Drennan, was a travelled man from Cork with a water butt for a chest and bruises round the eyes from the porter. His short legs had been to America, to England, to France. He told stories of Boston high society, where he'd tutored, and of painters among the slatterns of Marseilles, where he'd played. Flanagan listened in awe. He wanted to walk those streets and hear those other voices. But by aligning himself with the teacher, Flanagan was risking the suspicion of his elders. 'Island folk dwelled in the shelter of each other, as we say in Gaelic, and books – the notion of writing itself – somehow ruptured the scheme of things. For many of them, the teacher was a kind of necromancer . . . a *draíodóir*. They didn't trust his spells, which was crazy, because they're a poetic people –' he paused at the thought – 'you know, some of the older folk, they speak as many would like to write, without a trace of planning, just off they go, peeling the language. Putting phrases on paper . . . well, it's against the telling, the oratory, the freshness of the word . . . do you follow?'

Herbert nodded. He'd withdrawn into himself, fearing Flanagan slightly, as he'd feared the singing in the abbey. There was a kind of heat in the soldier, a crackling in the air around him.

'Now, Mr Drennan had loads of books, piled this high –' Flanagan raised a hand level to his smooth chin – 'all over his cottage. Books to stop the door, books to jam the window open, books to level the floor under the table. And they were all in English. "There are wide fields out there," he once said, "and people rare, but unfortunately they don't have the tongue –" he meant Gaelic, and he'd pointed to a huge map pegged to the wall – "look, Boy, it's an English-speaking world; look at the spread of Empire pink."' Flanagan gazed at Canada, India, Australia . . . little Ireland, and Inisdúr.

For Mr Drennan it was a history lesson about oppression, 'the politics of tenure'. But for Flanagan it was an invitation to break loose. So one night he went by stealth to the teacher's cottage (there was no need, he could just as easily have walked down the road in broad daylight, but he wanted to clamber through fields as though he were a fugitive). Little Brendan followed him and Flanagan sent him back home with a playful clip to the ear. When he was out of sight, Flanagan took a first step towards the island's harbour: he asked Mr Drennan to teach him the profane language of the subdued nations.

They met every evening, when Flanagan should have been learning the knack of those long oars, when he should have been out at sea with the others and, like them, attuning himself to the moods of the wind, and the meaning of a sudden wave – that other *instinctive* manner of living. But his mind had lifted like one of those gulls over the slip.

'In a way,' said Flanagan, 'it was a betrayal without treachery. A turning away from my father's soil to those pink lands beyond the cliffs. But, you know, it wasn't an *empire* I saw. Sure, I don't know what it was . . . more land, I suppose.'

Flanagan stopped talking but Herbert was left with the drift of his own thoughts. He, too, had come from a close-knit community: each side of the family had worn a uniform for the empire. Military service had been followed up by civic responsibility, at home or in India. His father's connections ran to the fringes of government, his mother's to those titled by birth. Herbert had not rebelled; he'd just failed at the first hurdle . . .

The sound of a bouncing ball on the road behind them brought the conversation to an untidy end. It was as though a bubble of soap had popped. They were back in Flanders, not far from Ypres; and the guns, which had seemed subdued, rumbled louder with something like scorn.

Chapter Nineteen

1

'My, oh my,' said Father Andrew, the Prior, with a shake of the head.

He ran a finger down the column of offences endorsed on the regimental crime sheet of Owen Doyle, covering infractions between the date of his enlistment in 1915 and his voluntary departure two years later.

'Unshaven on parade, improper conduct, losing by neglect his trench waders . . . the list is endless.' He frowned. 'With a little imagination, those would apply to Sylvester. But he soon gets into gear . . . insubordination, absent without leave – eight times – drunkenness, malingering, insolence to an NCO . . . it just goes on and on . . . until he's court-martialled for desertion . . . twice . . . then he gets drunk again.' He looked up and showed his pity. 'Not bad for a man of, what, twenty?'

Anselm nodded. He leaned against the window that looked on to the cloister garth below. When it rained, Herbert had liked to sit down there, wrapped in a blanket beneath an arch, simply watching the rain spill from the loaded guttering. Anselm sighed and turned away. He wasn't quite with the Prior, though not because of Herbert. Since returning from London his meditations had drifted endlessly over the mass burials of spring 1917 and Joseph Flanagan's way of talking. His way of describing the land and the sea. His disquieting admission to the court: *And cold I was and wet.* The collision between reality and language was so dramatic that Anselm could not forget it. Flanagan's nerves had been shot, without a gun being fired . . .

The Prior, not getting a full response, buried himself again in the paginated bundle. Anselm had prepared it. On the front sheet he'd set out three central issues: the relationship between Flanagan and

Doyle; the outcome of Flanagan's review process (as a door to his disappearance); and the link between these questions and Herbert. 'Solve these,' Anselm had said, feeling very tall, 'and we find the meaning of the trial.'

The Prior turned back a page.

'With two reprieved death sentences to his name,' he said, smoothing an eyebrow, 'this fellow would have been shot . . . had he been caught. "Absent at Ypres. Age twenty, height five feet six inches, dark brown hair, clean-shaven, rather brown complexion, blue dot tattoos across each knuckle. Believed to have taken Field ambulance to Abeele."'

Anselm recognised the description. It was from a roster of absentees reported to the Provost Marshal and annexed to the War Diary of that office, a copy having been placed in the Doyle file. Two other documents were attached to it with a rusted staple: the first, a curt memo dated November 1917, revealing that pursuant to the King's Regulations the same details had been sent to Scotland Yard on Army Form B 124 for publication in the Police Gazette; the second, dated September 1917, rendered the first a total waste of time: a letter from Doyle's Brigade HQ reported the soldier killed in action on the 15th of that month. The system had obviously fallen out of step: the right hand did not know what the left hand was doing.

'His offending began as soon as he joined the Army,' resumed the Prior, 'but I'm not persuaded his behaviour can be explained by that fact alone . . .' Anselm had always thought the Prior would have made an awful judge, though admired in certain quarters. He always looked *outside* the evidence, for something to *explain* the evidence. The Court of Appeal would have pulled their hair out, faced with his extramural fairness.

'His wrongdoing is too widespread . . . it adds up to an unhappy youth; to a manhood charged with vague grievances and specific antagonisms. Someone very difficult to live with.' The Prior whistled, as though thinking of one or two names close to home. 'I'd be interested to know if he'd troubled the magistrates before he troubled his King.'

The idea had not occurred to Anselm but he nodded again, to affirm that their minds were, as ever, one.

'Herbert said Doyle's tags *represented* who he was,' went on the Prior, pronouncing each word slowly. 'Can you make any sense of that?'

'None whatsoever.'

The Prior was at Anselm's side. Beyond the monastery wall, they could make out the bluish path that hugged the Lark. It veered away towards a copse of aspens, the hives, and Herbert's white, slanting cross.

By Anselm's judgement, he'd got nowhere at the Public Record Office, though Martin did not agree. The idea that Flanagan had been in control of his own trial was both novel and persuasive. Only a lawyer would have seen that, he'd said by way of compliment. Sipping more beer in The Wheat Sheaf, he'd added, 'I'd assumed Doyle led Flanagan astray. Now I'm not so sure.' It was an inference, a next step in the thinking process, that Anselm had not in fact taken, but it made sense. If Flanagan had run the trial, so to speak, then it would be odd if Doyle had run the offence.

Maybe the Prior had been tracing similar territory in his silence, because he picked up Anselm's own line of reflection. 'Something momentous happened between these two soldiers.' Then he made a squint and mumbled as if he'd found himself on the wrong track, puzzled because the trees on either side looked so very familiar. 'Both of them came back. That's the trick. And, you know, Anselm, it doesn't feel right.'

2

Anselm had stepped into the nettles of community living within minutes of his return to Larkwood. No jubilation at the return of the prodigal, and so on. No fatted calf and minstrels in the gallery. 'Receipts?' snapped Cyril, as if it were an obscure kind of greeting. 'A gift,' Anselm snapped back, putting the Friendship Plant on the table.

Bede made a point of being very busy. He was desperate to know what Anselm had learned at the PRO, but he wouldn't ask. More, he wouldn't show his interest. He aped indifference. He wanted Anselm to seek him out in the archives, to knock on the door and subordinate himself to an office of importance. Perhaps it was a small thing to ask, but Anselm wouldn't play ball. His real and abiding concern was for Sylvester. He'd been to see him before taking off his coat, his bag still in hand, his papers yet to be bundled and paginated. For days afterwards Anselm ran the scene in his head, wondering what had gone wrong:

'Hullo, Old Timer.'

The gatekeeper raised a wavering hand in salute. 'Your trip to London was fruitful?'

'Yes and no. The trial's out of reach. Too long ago.'

'Water under the bridge.'

'Exactly.'

'Let the dead bury their dead.'

To build up tension for the coming release, Anselm decided to say nothing for a while. He rustled in his pigeon hole for letters. Finally he began with hesitation, 'Have you found Kate Seymour's address?'

Sylvester's eyes seeped regret and Anselm reproached himself harshly for not having spoken out at once. Quickly, wanting to bestow peace on the scamp's venerable head, he said, 'Rejoice, Keeper of the Gate. Her details are held at the Public Record Office. I've sent on a message. *She* can contact *me*.'

Sylvester hooked his thumbs behind the orange twine that served as a belt. He slumped back as if beaten by a straight flush and, with a scowl, threw down his disappointment. 'Bully for you.' And with another wave of the hand, curt this time, he dismissed Anselm from the room.

No amount of repeated viewing helped Anselm understand what had taken place. It belonged on the cutting room floor, because there was no need for Sylvester's continued depression. The address was to hand. But, like Bede, he was unreachable. And Anselm knocked on his door but Sylvester would not answer. He could only look on while the Gatekeeper limped around reception. His feet were fine but he was bowed. A weight was pressing down his shoulders. His eyes seemed bruised and he moaned about the cold. Entanglements of memory, worse than usual, left him miffed. Irritation fused with sudden flights of humour that were difficult for everyone to gauge. Worse, the pensioner who'd never drawn down his years had finally become an old man.

3

Anselm was filling a bucket with hot water in the scullery when the telephone call came through. At a shout from Bruno, the cook, he went into the kitchen and took the receiver.

'I've good news and bad,' came Martin's fine voice. 'First the bad. When Kate Seymour left the PRO she insisted that her details be removed from the database. It's her right.'

'Blast.'

Martin was again the loquacious host that Anselm had first encountered on the telephone. It must be all that close-up living, he mused. You withdraw inside and then pour out familiarity through a mouthpiece. It's safer that way. He'd moved on to the good news. An appointment had been made with Sarah, the great-great-granddaughter of Ralph Osborne, the general who'd recommended clemency for Flanagan. 'Her father, David, will be there too. They're chalk and cheese, oil and water . . .' The character sketches, while opposing, described a close family with a deep and personal interest in military history. Anselm jotted down the Cambridgeshire address and returned the receiver to its cradle.

Confused and irresolute, Anselm returned to the scullery.

Now that Kate Seymour was out of reach once more, the onus fell back on Sylvester to find that little business card. Perhaps he'd wanted to find the wretched thing himself. Maybe he'll feel better if the ball bounces high, back in his court, so he can whack it down a tramline to the astonishment of the whole community. Do I tell him, now that he's stopped looking?

Decisively, Anselm clattered into the refectory with the bucket and mop. It was his turn to clean the floor. And he recalled the Prior's own, inimitable strategy. If things follow their usual course, he'd said, Kate Seymour's address will turn up just when we need it most.

Chapter Twenty

The Company of Strangers

1

Flanagan felt no resentment against Mr Moore, not because he'd taken those swipes at poor old Elliot – who'd nearly killed himself – but because Flanagan had noticed that the Captain stared at the wallpaper as he, Flanagan, had stared at the mirror. Both of them were strangers in some way. Islanders can sense these things, for they know what it is to belong and to be excluded. And that aside, Flanagan had chosen to put himself in that court: he could hardly blame the people who were obliged to jump through the hoops afterwards.

The football practice nearly reduced Flanagan to tears. True, the off-side rule was baffling, but it wasn't the laws of the game that unsettled him, it was the lads of his old section. He hadn't seen them since the advance near Black Eye Corner. Pickles, Stan, Tommy and Chips. And the RSM. He'd expected a rebuff, but while no word had been spent on the trial, they'd passed him the ball, they'd tidied up his many mistakes. He'd wanted to tell them all, 'Fellas, I didn't leave you, it's more involved, so,' but he couldn't – Mr Moore was there with his whistle, banging on about the off-side rule.

That night, Flanagan lay locked in the cellar, his limbs aching as they'd done as a boy when he'd helped his father make the fields. He couldn't sleep because the sounds of Inisdúr were all around him: the conversation with Mr Moore had released the many prisoners in his memory. No one had asked him about home – not since the Rising of 1916, when the Republicans had made a bid for power in a Post Office (as one English officer put it). Now, like birds uncaged, they swooped wildly in the darkness, seeking a window to freedom. Mr Drennan was one of the heavier gulls. What had become of him? Had he left the island to shoulder the Cause in Dublin? Or was he teaching little Brendan that yawn of an elegy by Feiritéar? Fifty-seven verses of desolation and woe written for a pal who'd died in Flanders. Mr Drennan had considered Piaras Feiritéar to be a symbol of Irish history, a guide to its past and a light to the future. A Norman-Irish Lord, respected in England and Ireland, he'd finally sided with the Irish when it came to rebellion. He'd been court-martialled and executed by Cromwell's boys. Flanagan could still remember some of the verses. Reciting them made him drowsy, and as he slipped away to the sound of Mr Drennan's heavy incantation – he'd always joined in, stamping his foot in time – Flanagan thought of . . . Lisette, whose thick hair he'd only ever touched once.

She, too, had been a stranger among her people.

2

Flanagan had first met Madame Lisette Papinau in early 1916. He'd been on five days' leave with High-Pockets O'Brien and a group of lads from their platoon. One of them said, 'We have to go to Pap's'. Flanagan had often heard talk of the place, though he'd never passed through the front door. The boys loved the proprietor. She looks after you, they all said. She just cleans up the mess. Never throws you out, never calls in the redcaps, never makes you pay for a broken glass. She understands the war. She understands soldiers. She's wonderful, is Pap. Flanagan had thought she must be a woman who's punishing herself, one of those unhappy angels that appear near a battlefield.

And so, one night, Flanagan and his pals joined the rowdy boozers quaffing cheap white wine, only Flanagan didn't drink, so he'd asked for tea. 'Tea?' repeated the mistress of the house with wide, astonished eyes. Though in her mid-thirties, she possessed the dazzling gravity that comes with grief. A frightful brew she made him, but he banked it with sugar and sipped it slowly while the boys got singing drunk, some of them staggering in the dark hours to spew in the toilet, to disgorge the war from themselves. All the while, Flanagan sipped tea on tea and those sorrowful eyes kept flashing in his direction. He was the only sober man in the house. For three nights he drank tea and as the darkness grew outside, she watched him from afar, until, finally, she called him over to her table – it was more of a plant stand covered in receipts and napkins – and among that riot of self-cleansing, chants and sickness, they talked, easily: him of Inisdúr, her of Brittany. She, too, had learned the King's English.

Madame Papinau had a fine nose, sharp without suggesting brittleness of temper. Her eyebrows were high and her lips were sad. Thick hair was tied back with a black ribbon. Widowed at twenty-one after three years of marriage, she'd left the salt flats of Guérande in 1902, and come east with her only child, to start afresh in Étaples. A girl who knew the sea, its many smells and sounds, she'd simply found another coastal town. That night, at closing time, High-Pockets and the boys waddled off, singing in the street, but Flanagan stayed behind. He made a wood fire in the parlour while she carved slices of boiled bacon from a hock. Striking a match on his boot he told himself he'd been right: this woman accuses herself. He felt it in the shared silence while he ate with contentment and while she watched with pain. And Flanagan perceived something tragic in this ritual: she'd been at her plant stand sipping water, watching soldiers and cleaning up since 1914.

'Let me sing my kind of song,' he declared, putting his plate on the table.

His voice began uncertainly, but he closed his eyes and thought of a lost love he'd never known – Mr Drennan always said it gave edge to an air. '*Siúl, siúl, siúl, a rún, Siúl go socair agus siúl go ciúin* . . .' 'Come, come, come, my love, Quickly come to me, softly move . . .'

Like one of the elders back home, he leaned one hand on his knee and sang to the reluctant flames. It was the plea of a young woman, begging her soldier boy to stay at home and not to go to France. When he'd finished, Lisette did the decent thing; like an islander, she wept.

'You must call me Lisette,' she said, wiping her eyes. But the tears kept falling. She covered her face with long fingers and gently shook her head.

'I'm Seosamh,' he replied, abashed, aware that something had gone wrong. 'Joseph.'

Flanagan left Pap's that night with an uneasy step. The song had been a Drennanesque lurch towards sentimentality, brought on by the bacon, but like an invocation it had summoned feeling – in Lisette and himself. And feeling – that immeasurable range of subtle responses from joy to sorrow – had, for Flanagan, been a brutally reduced universe. With the exception of High-Pockets, all the lads who'd joined up from the shipyard were dead. Flanagan's heart had become numb. It had become a muscle that pumped heat when he was scared. But another kind of warmth had returned . . . so he walked briskly down the street, away from that fire in the parlour. Away, too, from Lisette, and the warmth in her tears. In the barrack room, surrounded by the frightened moans of sleeping men, Flanagan felt something dangerous had happened, for him and Lisette; dangerous for their survival of the war. Each of them for different reasons couldn't afford to feel anything. But Flanagan tingled with the thrill of being alive, and it kept him awake.

The next morning High-Pockets winked, making a bawdy remark – the ordinary stuff of soldiers – but Flanagan suffered a flash of feeling, so intense he saw stars. He shouted him down, rebuking the filth in his mouth. And then, in the stunned silence, Flanagan laughed and roared. He giggled, even. But then tears blurred his vision. He fought them back and staggered to the toilet where he was sick. The war was in him too.

Flanagan made his peace with High-Pockets. On their last evening of leave, he went again to Pap's, but with a profound detachment to his manner: he imitated his mother's reserve for the mainland priest. And Lisette did something similar, appearing to be bruised by some unmentioned slight. But they talked while the boys got drunk. And later, though it was reckless, Flanagan again lingered past the locking of the doors. After they'd cleared up the mess in the toilets, they sat in the empty café talking of dead lives that each of them had lost: she, the raking of salt in Guérande; he, the making of fields on Inisdúr.

Both of them were wary, but unable to avoid the fascination of the living; each of them was quickened by the return of banished emotions. They were coming back in all their varieties. They were as fresh as fear.

Thereafter, whenever Flanagan had some home leave, he came to Étaples and stayed in a first-floor bedroom at Pap's as though he were a paying lodger in a Dublin boarding house. Without being asked, he did odd jobs. He made a drawer run smoothly and opened a jammed window. He changed the washer in a tap that had dripped since 1911. One glorious October – the only one, in fact – they picked apples together in the small walled garden at the rear of the premises. After they'd cleared the fruit within reach, Lisette climbed one tree and Flanagan climbed another. While reaching dangerously, Flanagan stalled, his hand left stretching out. Lisette was looking at him. She was quite still, in a very particular way, as though her portrait might be taken at any moment. Her eyes were full and dark, frightened of the coming flash. They seemed so very far apart. Two people in two trees, surrounded by heavy fruitfulness.

No matter what they did, or where they were, she called him Joseph and never Seosamh. It was artificial, but the formula allowed each of them to return to their duties, though at every sound of that distant label he felt pain, a pain so very different from all the other injuries of war. He saw the same wound in the returned glances of Lisette. And whenever Flanagan left her to return to his unit, his mind swirled with confusion because he didn't know where this strange friendship might lead. His consolation – and it explained why he would never cross the room and touch her – was that after leaving he would probably not return. He'd lasted a long time at the front, had Flanagan. His number was coming up, as the superstitious liked to say.

Apart from the time he'd sung by the fire, Flanagan never went into the parlour again, save once, when Lisette made a confession. And on that night Flanagan learned why this woman he would love watched the troops and waited upon them, and why she would always accuse herself. Without realising it at the time, her words went very deep into his memory – perhaps because by then he was lost to her. They came to the fore of his mind in the strongest possible way when, in August 1917, Flanagan came across that crumpled, condemned heap in no-man's-land. His mind fled to Lisette, whose only boy, Louis, had joined the French army in 1915. Everyone who went to Pap's had heard of the boy. He was at the front, fighting for France.

Chapter Twenty-One

At Madame Papinau's

When Doyle woke he offered Flanagan a cigarette. They smoked in the heavy silence that lies between conspirators.

'Give me your tags,' said Flanagan, removing his own.

'Wot fo'?'

'Because if we're stopped we'll need to confuse the redcaps. We swap pocket books and we hide our tags. If we're unlucky, you show my book because I'm not listed injured or missing.'

Flanagan hid the tags inside the bandage on his arm, smarting at his own stupidity. What was he going to do if *he* were stopped and questioned? He could hardly show them Doyle's book. He soothed himself with the probability that Doyle's desertion hadn't yet filtered through to Étaples, that the injured lists should slow the drip. And anyway, the trading of books and tags was just a ruse, part of a wider ploy that served Flanagan's purposes: for, unlike Feiritéar, when it came to noble acts he preferred anonymity.

The train pulled into Étaples at five in the afternoon. Ten minutes later their luck struck a hitch after all. While ambling down the main street, two bulky MPs motioned them against a wall. Sweat broke out on Flanagan's chest and Doyle swore under his breath.

'We're on leave,' said Flanagan as Doyle handed over the pocket book.

The policeman rumpled his pocked face, squinting at the one-line description. Fortunately such entries were often so brief as to be useless, unless you had an identifying feature . . . like tattoos. *Damnú,* thought Flanagan, I'd forgotten about those blue dots. *Damnú air.*

'And yours,' said the second policeman to Flanagan. His eyes were hidden by the low nib of a cap that was far too small for his head.

Flanagan produced Doyle's book. Seconds later the eyes appeared from a head lifted high – hard blue eyes above a slit for a mouth. 'Hold out your hand. I want to see your knuckles.'

Flanagan's resistance drained away. He was about to throw in the towel when, on the far side of the road, a shining black door opened. A group of women dressed in black stepped into the street, comforting the eldest of their number, a bent and huddled figure leaning on a stick. They were all dabbing their cheeks with white handkerchiefs while the men looked on, coming from the darkness behind . . . out of a Pompes Funèbres: a funeral parlour. Before Flanagan could clock what was happening, Doyle whistled through two fingers and pointed further up the street: 'Oy, Fitzy.' The two policemen's heads turned as one, and at that moment Doyle dashed across the street, towards the crying and the open black door. Without thinking, Flanagan followed Doyle's example. To a great hollering, he crashed through the stained faces into the dim interior, knocking over a table, two chairs, a little man with a waxed moustache; on he went, arms flailing, past an open coffin with a god-awful yoke inside with whiskers sticking out of his ears like a shaving brush, across a back yard, among three lads smoking by a couple of horses, and into a narrow back lane lit by breathtaking sunshine. Flanagan was laughing out loud – a reaction that would have traumatised his mother, had she seen him, but not Mr Drennan . . . not that great traveller. 'Go, boy,' he heard him splutter, and with the spirit of that old Fenian roaring joy in his ears, Flanagan grabbed Doyle's collar and tumbled down an alleyway, into a warren of left and rights, until the only sound was the quick fall of their own feet. Panting and dragging Doyle as if he were the milch cow, Flanagan cautiously made his way to the back door of Madame Papinau's *estaminet*, widely known as Pap's.

Flanagan lifted the latch, his other hand on Doyle's arm. Beyond the scullery and the lounge he could hear the rush of army voices and the clink of bottles and glasses. They entered and Flanagan motioned Doyle to sit on a stool by the sink. 'Peel those spuds,' he said, heading towards the clatter.

In a dim corridor that led to the main room he spoke urgently to a dark, lowered brow. He'd brought a deserter with him, he said, a rough and ready sort who'd surely be shot if he were caught. Her eyes shone as she glanced towards the kitchen's light. That profile, seen of a sudden, stabbed Flanagan's soul: he longed to touch her hair, that was all; to feel if only for once the softness of her hair. With the turn of her head, a shadow claimed back her face and she said, 'Take him to the cellar, Joseph.'

The cellar where Flanagan had stored the apples picked in an October long gone. 'Compote for the boys, Joseph,' she'd said. The formality had flayed him.

At midnight, Flanagan, Lisette and Doyle assembled in the lounge, their three faces lit by a single candle. Flanagan pressed the raised edge, releasing the small pool of hot wax from around the wick. As it ran down the neck and dried, he said, 'This lady may be able to help us. If she does, it's at considerable risk to herself. She must have reason to do it. She knows my tale already. Tell her yours, so, the tale you told me in the rain.'

Doyle told another story altogether – far worse than the earlier account – beginning at his birth and ending in a borstal. Even Flanagan was rapt. For in this, his second testament, Doyle accused himself as much as the conditions of his infancy.

'You can both hide here,' said Madame Papinau in a faint voice. Her eyes brushed over Flanagan with desperate happiness, not quite believing its arrival. 'I'll write to my cousin in Boulogne. He works on the harbour. When the time is right, he'll help you find a boat.' She faced Doyle. 'Tonight you sleep upstairs; from tomorrow it will be the cellar for you both.'

Lisette stood up, as did Doyle, and the light from the candle made their features grotesque.

'Thank you,' muttered Doyle, tugging nervously at his belt. He looked reduced and ashamed.

'Don't thank me,' she replied, the pitch of her voice dropping. 'Thank my son, Louis. You'll have the use of his bed.'

Alone by the candle, Flanagan calculated he'd been away from his unit for twenty-two hours. But for a nap on the train he'd been awake for over two days. A terrible desire to sleep came upon him, and it would have seized him if he hadn't seen Lisette's haunting face. She was crouched by his chair. 'Is it true . . . will you stay?' she whispered, knowing in the uttering that she'd been mistaken. 'Won't you run to me, Seosamh?'

Chapter Twenty-Two

Disobedience

1

Chamberlayne was not the sort of man to show much emotion. He needed irony and sarcasm to transmit what, for another, would be a rush of passion. Consequently, it was with an air of apparent indifference that he said to Herbert on the afternoon of the 10th September: 'Duggie has received a telegram from a legal mind at GHQ regarding the Flanagan matter. I don't know what it says because he's been summoned to a pow-wow with Pemberton. Who knows, Captain, perhaps your judicial skills are to be required once more.'

Chamberlayne meant that there might be a retrial and a fresh sentencing process. If Duggie's argument had found a sympathetic ear, then that was a potential outcome. Herbert could not linger for Duggie's return to find out. But it was with a lightness of foot that he led his Company in a mock attack upon the mock battlefield. Coloured tape had been fixed to the ground to guide his men forward. They flapped in the breeze, catching the sunlight. The entire setting was like a gigantic board game. 'Snakes and Ladders, Sir,' whispered Joyce, making his peace with Herbert.

During a break in rehearsals, Herbert heard a rumour. Rioting had broken out in Étaples. Major Tomlinson filled out the detail. 'We're not using the word "mutiny",' he said, enunciating each word precisely. 'Rowdy troops are roaming the streets at the base camp. An MP was obliged to discharge a firearm. Measures to restore law and order are under way.'

To Herbert, that sounded like mutiny.

'Obviously,' confided Tomlinson, as if the German High Command must never find out, 'Senior officers at GHQ are rattled.'

The very officers who would decide the fate of Joseph Flanagan. They would open the file and think, instantly, 'Another instance of drunkenness in place of duty.' Herbert's optimism disappeared. His preoccupation endured for the entirety of the afternoon and was still present when, after supper, he walked past the abbey and the carpenter's shed to supervise another kind of practice. Detached, he observed the team as they planned manoeuvres to outwit the Lancashire Fusiliers. Only Elliot was more introverted. He kicked stones out of the ground, his hands in his pockets. Herbert left him be, not knowing what to say, for he was the one who'd stripped him bare.

After training, Joyce joked some more (about Tomlinson); Pickles Pickering headed the ball non-stop for eighty-four strikes (until Stan Gibbons pulled his trousers down); and Flanagan listened to Father Maguire explain the off-side rule in Gaelic. Herbert edged towards the Irishman and the priest, his unease growing. They huddled together, as if it were raining. It was a musical, memorable language; and Herbert had heard it before. The chaplain had looked as agitated then as he did now. The more Herbert listened – and Father Maguire was beginning to lose his cool so the dramatic inflections were rising – the more Herbert wanted to press Flanagan with a question that had taken root throughout the afternoon, when the assault brigades had rehearsed their moves under the watchful eyes of Tomlinson and his companions. When the team left the field, Herbert called Flanagan to one side. As the others went down the lane, Herbert set off in the opposite direction, towards the woods. When Flanagan came alongside, Herbert asked his question. He'd forgotten all about that night in the reserve trench, Étaples and Elverdinghe.

'How in the name of God did you ever come to join the British Army?'

2

An airplane had droned low over the island, Flanagan explained. In a fright, the people ran from their cottages, their faces turned to the sky, towards a burst of leaflets. Flanagan tore one into strips to use as markers in his copy of *The King's English* by the Fowler brothers. As he'd ripped the paper he'd read the call to join Kitchener's Army.

'No one took any heed,' said Flanagan, 'and neither did I. No, if there's a reason for my coming to France, it's the doing of my old teacher Mr Drennan, though he'd be flabbergasted if he ever knew.'

Mr Drennan was a devout nationalist. Or, rather, having travelled wide and far, he'd discovered Ireland – as an abstract heaven – which, to his vexation, he'd been unable to locate with any precision on his return to Cork. He'd woken up to an appalling personal conviction: the Ireland beloved in the Diaspora, the Ireland of merry wars and sad songs, had never quite existed in the first place, at least not in living memory. It was a hope rooted in the might-have-beens of history, if subjugation and hunger hadn't dispersed a nation's children. He'd felt a fool, because he'd said that more than once before leaving for Boston, only he hadn't appreciated the scale of the tragedy. Bruised but unbowed, he'd finally come west to Inisdúr in search of Celtic purity. There, on the salt-bitten grass, eyes glazed, he'd condemned Dublin Castle and the British Rule of Law.

'"Disobedience" was his favourite word,' said Flanagan. 'The Irish had to disobey if they were to find their true identity. Defiance was their destiny –' he laughed softly – 'and their duty. He'd belt this stuff out while we loaded up the currachs with kelp. The elders just leaned on the wall chewing their pipes. They'd never paid rent or rates in their lives. They'd once stoned the boat of a collector when he'd dared approach the island. That was the last we saw of him. Home Rule? Sure, we had it.'

Perhaps that was why Flanagan had never been able to get worked up about British domination. Island folk didn't even think in terms of being Irish, not in Mr Drennan's sense. There was the mainland. There was the sea. And there was Inisdúr. That was it. The people's relationship with their rock and beaches was at odds with nationalist thinking, precisely because it was 'thinking'. An islander was part of his island. There was no link, as with a chain. Man and soil were one. When he'd said that to Mr Drennan, the table banging started all over. 'That's why you're free, damn you. You're Irish and you don't know it.'

Flanagan, however, did learn something from Mr Drennan that he may not have wanted to teach: that freedom is always purchased by disobedience. This wasn't about the 'politics of tenure'. It was about personal identity. And Flanagan wanted to break from the island's ways, if only for a while. He'd seen a map – a guide to other places than the one beneath your feet. It had spoken to him in a way that Lord Kitchener's appeal had not.

The moment of decision was not chosen. It presented itself.

'The fields were hemmed in with walls,' said Flanagan. 'My father built them to some strange design from his dreams. It was carefully done, balancing the large with the small, arranging the weight in such a way as to bring beauty from strength. They were patterned, like my mother's quilts, but in stone. When the third field had been enclosed, when the last stone had been laid, my father turned to me and said, "And now we make a fourth field, for Brendan." I took a breath. For Brendan? He can make the yoke himself, that's what I thought.'

At that moment, opposite his father's exultation, Flanagan decided to leave Inisdúr, though of course it had nothing to do with the making of another field. After supper, in the simple way of an islander, without preliminaries or ornament, he told his parents he would leave for England in a week. Brendan had been sent outside but he was listening at the window. 'I want to stretch my legs,' Flanagan had said. There was labouring to be done over there, what with the shortage of men away at the war. 'I'll be back in six months or so,' he'd pleaded, as his father, in the way of an islander, stomped from the room.

Word went around the low, granite houses: 'Seosamh is going away.' No one believed that he'd come back. It was Drennan's fault, some said. He'd given the boy ideas. There was a kind of fear in their silence towards him. One woman gave it voice. She lived alone on the far side of the island. Her husband had been taken by the sea. Meg was her name.

'The house was alone in a cove surrounded by cliffs,' said Flanagan. 'The inside walls were black from the soot. Her clothes were black and smelled of the fire. Even her skin was black, from years of tending the turf in the grate. Sure, she was half gone.' He tapped his head and winked. 'Well, there I was, on the beach. The tide was out and I was gathering shells, something to take with me to England, when I felt this hand grip my elbow. I hadn't heard her coming. God, she was a sight: all bent over and black and dribbling. "Seosamh," she said, "don't go." She pulled me down to her level. "Don't leave the land." Dear God, what's she been eating, I thought . . . I told her to calm herself and have some tea. But that night . . . that night I dreamt of Meg. And it was so . . . so real. I was back on that beach, running away, and her voice bounced off the cliffs, "The fields will die." The shells were sucking at my feet. "If you leave the land, Seosamh, death will claim you." I woke up with a cry, panting and covered with sweat. My mother was there, by the bed, holding my hand. "I'm not *leaving*, Ma," I cried, "It's six months, a fling, nothing more."'

He was calm by the time they reached the woods.

Herbert wasn't. Agitation had entered his blood. He felt accused: by Flanagan's story and his own. They'd come to a halt. On their left was a long, low barn. To their right a track ran into the shadows towards a clearing. A mix of trees crowded the verge. For a moment they stared into the leafy space, at the grass, the sifted light, and a speckling of tiny mauve and yellow flowers at the mouth of the path. Abruptly Herbert turned around and, though he walked, he was fleeing the colour, as he'd once run from the chant. He'd no senses left that were fit to receive beauty; what he had was contaminated. He'd been stirred, too, by Flanagan's mutiny. It had been deeper than the poetry of his teacher, deeper than the nationalist thought-out politics of self-determination, but what had Herbert done? Had he ever reached that moment of necessary, liberating disobedience?

'The night before I left,' resumed Flanagan, when Herbert dropped back, 'I went to see Mr Drennan. Again I went by the fields, avoiding the road. He was expecting me. Normally he drank porter or poitín from his own still but this time on the table was a neat white cloth. In the middle were a bottle of burgundy wine and two glasses. I told him I'd taken the pledge, and he gave the table a whack and he fairly flew off the handle: "This is not some cheap forbidden froth. 'Tis a sacred drink, boy. Take the glass and honour our parting."'

Herbert's parents had done much the same thing when he took his commission with the Lancers. His father had opened a bottle given to him by his own father for such a moment. When decanted it was found to be corked.

'I said I couldn't, that I'd made a vow.' Flanagan was almost laughing. 'So Mr Drennan paced around, muttering and swearing, and finally he said, "A vow be damned. Sit yourself down, so, and you can watch." So I did. Slowly he poured the wine, into his glass and into mine, and he said in a drone, "I'll drink this one now. The other I shall save for your homecoming, however bitter the grape might turn." He drained his glass in complete silence and he put mine on a shelf and covered it with a writing slate.'

Herbert's father had poured the old vintage down the sink and opened something young and fresh. They'd toasted youth and the coming of age and responsibility. Herbert had been very happy. Time seemed to stop, and Herbert suffered once more the joy of that last night in the dining room, when the road from the front door was clearly marked.

For some reason, explained Flanagan, with another laugh, labour in England was not a heresy against the Drennan canons of Irish orthodoxy. The teacher had many friends over there. When Flanagan left the cottage, he carried a letter of introduction to a good man in Tyneside who ran a gang of boys on the shipyards. A foreman with the power to hire and fire, a bad Gaelic speaker. The next morning Flanagan left Inisdúr.

'There was a track from the slip to our farm,' said Flanagan. 'It wound through the scatter of houses. As I walked away, my mother watched from the window. My father was alone, looking over the fields. Every now and then folk came out and shook my hand. It was only when I got to the slip that I realised Brendan had followed me . . . he was always following me, you know, and I was always walking away. But I didn't wait for him. I'd been stunned by the sight of the crowd on the walls.'

In 1913 Herbert's mother and father, uncle, two aunts, four nephews and three nieces had all come to the station in Keswick. His father had been speechless with pride. His mother had maintained the firm, distant look that had built India at the cost of immense social and cultural privation – her habitual look, in fact. They'd all shaken hands and Herbert had left to join the regiment.

Corporal Mackie jangled keys, held high like a lantern.

Herbert blinked, surprised that they'd already reached the school at Oostbeke. At the sound, Flanagan moved away from Herbert without another word. Obediently, he descended the steps towards the cellar, and Herbert found himself wanting to call out, but there was nothing to say. After securing the door, Mackie said, 'Begging your pardon, Sir, but why isn't Flanagan locked up with the other arseholes?'

'An incisive question, Corporal,' replied Herbert, his limbs heavy with rage. 'I imagine it's because within the week we're going to shoot him, and our CO thinks he deserves some privacy beforehand.'

'Of course, Sir.' Mackie saluted, content that he'd shown his disapproval.

He'd swagger about that within half an hour, thought Herbert. He'd tell his mates the officer had gone red in the face. The corporal marched off – he didn't know how to walk any more – and as he grew smaller, his arms swinging with magnificent ease, Herbert realised his question hadn't been answered. He still hadn't the faintest idea why Joseph Flanagan had joined the British Army.

3

Duggie Hammond was in the courtyard, walking in a circle, hands behind his back. Angus charged ahead and charged back again, his jaws slack, his limbs shaking. (The view of Tindall was that he had shellshock. He'd been brought to the front on a visit with General Lindsay. A 5.9 came out of the blue and took out the brass hat, leaving the dog behind. He'd been with Duggie ever since.) Herbert appraised the deranged animal with pity. It had stopped running and was staring at the ground as though it were a radio. The chickens stood well back.

'I received this communiqué from none other than the Assistant Adjutant General for discipline, or, more likely, a servant thereof.'

Duggie withdrew a folded sheet of paper from his tunic pocket and handed it to Herbert, who read the text out loud: '"The point helpfully raised on intention and drunkenness regarding the offence of desertion is being considered by my legal team. In the course of discussion on the subject it has been brought to my attention, quite rightly, that the cost of two field dressings ought to be deducted from any pay due to the convicted prisoner. Please make the necessary arrangements."'

Herbert folded the page back into a neat square and offered it to Duggie as though it lay upon a platter. Angus slumped exhausted on the ground, growling at the chickens.

'Herbert, do you know the species of this creature?'

He shook his head, utterly disinterested.

'He's an Irish Setter.'

Voices and footsteps approached. The seven other officers of the battalion had come to Duggie's billet for a nightcap. Over whisky, the discussion quickly turned to the unrest in Étaples. Apparently someone had been killed. An MP shot a Gordon Highlander by accident and the crowd went crazy. Despite the gravity of the subject, Herbert's mind was elsewhere. He was listening to that Gaelic music. The foreign music he'd heard in the reserve trenches the night he'd shot Quarters as he sank with a mule.

Chapter Twenty-Three

1

Sarah Osborne, great-great-granddaughter of General Sir Ralph Spencer Osborne VC DSO, commander of the Ninth Army between 1915 and 1918, lived with her father, David, in the family home purchased by the general shortly after the armistice. Then, as now, it was situated comfortably back from a quiet lane and surrounded by several acres of land rented out to local farmers. This much, and clear directions, Anselm learned from a village newsagent, having got lost on his way to tea at four. The main entrance was beneath a portico supported by two Greek columns. A fire crackled in the hall.

'For chatting and leaning upon,' said Sarah, stroking a velvet padded rail that framed the hearth. 'They're from the officers' mess of the Cambridgeshires. They became redundant after the MoD obliterated four hundred years of tradition by amalgamating three regiments with nothing in common save an acknowledgement that you can't reduce an army's size and increase its responsibilities at one and the same time.'

Sarah was in her early thirties, thought Anselm. Despite the pastoral calm of her surroundings, she had a windswept look. Her hair was unruly, thick with early strands of grey, held aside by a single wooden clip. When she spoke her face barely moved. Her gait was strangely delicate, as though she were avoiding broken glass on the carpet. Anselm followed her into the sitting room and was immediately struck by the panelling of rich dark oak – all culled, it transpired, from the mess in which several Osborne sons had learned the customs of war. Anselm sank into a wonderfully soft armchair of faded chestnut leather.

'My father's making the tea,' said Sarah, propped on the edge of her matching seat, one leg hooked elegantly behind the other. 'I understand you'd like to talk about the outcome of the Flanagan court martial?'

'Yes.'

'Can't *really* help, I'm afraid,' she said, apologetically. 'But I have a little something for you . . . something I found among Ralph's papers after I'd looked at the Flanagan file myself. But first, let's have some refreshment.'

The door had opened while Sarah was speaking. A balding, slight man in a shapeless suit bustled in pushing a clinking trolley laden with sandwiches and crockery. His high, dark eyebrows reversed the shape of his smiling mouth, giving his face a jolly appearance.

'You come in the wake of Kate Seymour,' said David, having introduced himself with a vigorous handshake. 'I understand you've met.' He placed a cup of tea on a side table near Anselm. 'Martin effected the introduction. Said she was a private researcher and, like you, wanted to trace the missing pieces in Joseph Flanagan's trial.' He fell back in an armchair. 'Frankly, we got the impression she was connected to the family and wouldn't say so.'

Which was hardly astonishing, he stressed. Often the relatives weren't told about the execution of a husband, father or son. It was just 'died of wounds' if they were told at all. They found out, though, when a pension was stopped; when there was no 'dead man's penny'. That's when the shame began, and a great silence without any commemoration.

While he spoke gently, using modest hand gestures – offering a plate; cake? More tea? – Anselm could feel the tenacity of the advocate in David's voice. He was an Osborne soldier, too. Anselm felt vaguely at risk.

'Sometimes a relative asks why granddad's name isn't on the memorial,' continued David. 'Questions are asked. The stitching gives way. They get a fresh perspective on the army that won the war.'

'Nine out of ten had their sentence commuted,' said Sarah, eyes closing.

'One in ten was shot,' corrected David. 'The weak were sent to the wall.'

The strong win wars, guessed Anselm.

There was a pause while father and daughter regarded each other across the divide of statistics and interpretation. In the hush, and not for the first time, Anselm tried to craft a ninth Beatitude: *Blessed are the strong for they* . . . He couldn't work out what might come next.

'We went to my study,' said Sarah, changing the subject. 'I dug out all my files for the period September to December nineteen seventeen. This included all Ralph's extant notes, letters and diaries, along with material sent to him or retained by him. We drew a complete blank. The name Flanagan does not occur, presumably because at the time Ralph had a war in mind, along with the lives of a hundred and fifty thousand men.'

Blessed are the strong, suggested Anselm, *for they are not yet weak.*

'Before she left,' began David, 'I wanted to help her . . . to try and loosen the grip of this tragedy on the family. I said that finding the missing papers wouldn't explain why Joseph Flanagan's sentence was confirmed. That he'd been a victim of a system that thought in straight, brutal lines.' He shrugged his dissatisfaction. 'All she said was that this trial was different . . . that it had a meaning. It's one of the worst things I've ever confronted. The wounded looking for *meaning* in the one place it cannot be found.'

Tea, sandwiches and cake don't go well with this kind of conversation, concluded Anselm. Any more than beer and crisps. When the trolley had been rolled to one side, he asked a question out of politeness.

'Why are you sure that Flanagan was shot? The file, to my mind, was ambiguous.'

'Two reasons,' said David. 'First, there was a degree of anxiety in the High Command about the effect of contemporaneous events on the troops.'

'There'd been a rebellion in Ireland in nineteen sixteen,' explained Sarah. 'And nineteen seventeen was a *bad* year: in spring the French were dazed by mutiny; in September some of our lot took to the streets of Étaples. Meanwhile, Third Ypres had to be won. Flanagan was tried and condemned in that climate.'

'And in that climate, I think the top brass were looking for an *example*,' resumed David, 'which brings me to the second reason. This was a time when the British attitude towards the Irish was often tainted by antipathy and—'

'Wasn't it Meredith who said that the Irish provided the English with her soldiers and generals?' quoted Sarah, wanting to dissociate herself from the coming argument.

David paid no heed to Meredith. He shrugged himself forward and said, on the edge of his seat, 'There seems to be a correlation between recruitment figures throughout the empire and death sentences passed on regiments from individual countries. For example, sixty-seven per cent were recruited in England and sixty-five per cent of death sentences were imposed on English regiments – and, in passing, I'd point out that almost half of those who were subsequently shot came from the working class north – but it's the pattern I'm stressing now.'

'And that pattern holds for other countries?' asked Anselm.

'Indeed it does,' replied David. 'For Scotland, Wales, Canada, Australia, South Africa, New Zealand . . .'

David paused and Anselm said, 'And Ireland?'

'That's the one exception to the rule. The Irish recruitment figure stood at two per cent, but the convicted Irishman was four times more likely to get a death sentence. That was Flanagan's real problem, as much as his conduct. He was born in the wrong place and he was tried by the wrong people at the wrong time.'

Anselm dabbed his mouth with a napkin, though his lips were dry.

'You won't find a shred of paper that reveals a deliberate policy,' said Sarah, wearily. 'Not an instruction, a memo, a letter, a memoir. Nothing.' She stood up and smoothed her dress. 'Father, would you like to see what I did find? It may not take you much closer to an understanding of Joseph Flanagan, but it will shed a little light on Herbert Moore.'

2

Sarah's study looked on to the undulating fields of Cambridgeshire. Anselm's attention, however, was with the rows of box files covering the life of General Osborne. Each was labelled with a year, beginning in 1860 through to 1953. For the period 1914–1918 there was an entire shelf for each year. Pebbles of various sizes, chunks of driftwood and shells covered the borders of Sarah's desk, surrounding a blue folder and a black ledger.

'I'm writing this biography for my father,' she said. 'He couldn't do it himself.'

'Why?'

'He was very close to its subject. Ralph lost his son in nineteen seventeen and David lost his father in nineteen forty-four. Both killed in action. Of course, with that first death, David had lost his grandfather, and with the second Ralph had lost a grandson. Unexpressed grief bound them together for the sixteen years they shared this house. Unexpressed because dying was a family tradition. We were prepared for it.' Anselm noticed that Sarah had almost left herself out of the reckoning, though the cost of war had determined the focus of her life. She was a military biographer. A regular visitor to the PRO. 'My father was the first to refuse the uniform,' she said, not quite sadly but with pity, 'and his rage and sadness have settled on the cause of those who were not prepared and who had no one to speak for them. We agree more than he admits, actually. Here, look at this.'

Sarah sat at her desk and opened the blue folder. She gave Anselm a memo from General Osborne to all three Divisional Commanders under his control. It was entitled 'Desertion and Drunkenness'.

'After Kate Seymour's visit, I read the Flanagan file for myself,' said Sarah. 'I then went back to my own records. This memo was written on the 10th September nineteen seventeen – the very day Ralph gave his recommendation to reduce Flanagan's death sentence to a term of imprisonment.'

While reading the text, Anselm wedged himself on to a sofa loaded with books. Strips of white paper hung out from the ends like so many tongues panting at his elbow. The general was concerned about a spate of recent cases in which drunkenness was the cause of absence from duty. He wrote:

> Intoxication is increasingly presenting itself as an excuse when a soldier appears unrepresented at a court martial. Please warn all ranks that such offenders will be liable on conviction to the full penalty for desertion.

'By implication,' resumed Sarah, 'Ralph was for commuting Flanagan's sentence, but then sent out a warning to say he'd be the last. And since Ralph was the most senior voice in the review process, there's every reason to suppose that his opinion carried weight.'

Anselm had read the warning. It was set out in the Adjutant and Quartermaster General's diary. On reflection it had saddened Anselm. Drunkenness must have been a means of escape from the hallucinations brought on by war, and even that route, at times, had to be blocked.

'Flanagan remains, as ever, elusive,' said Anselm, disingenuously.

'As does Captain Herbert Moore.'

She tidied the blue folder and opened the black ledger.

'Ralph kept a daily journal throughout the war, covering more personal matters,' she said. 'The entries are spare. For example, when his son died in August nineteen seventeen he simply wrote, "Bernard killed at St Julien. Twenty-two yrs seven m two d nine h. Am heart-broken." So he was not a man of many words. This is what he penned on fourteenth September – two weeks after the trial and four days after his recommendation on Flanagan. I've made a copy for you, but here is the original.'

Anselm took the ledger carefully and placed it on his knees. The General's handwriting was, of course, familiar, very small and perfectly legible. He read the passage identified by Sarah's finger.

> Woken up at 1.37 a.m. Herbert Moore wanted interview. Broke some regimental crockery long ago. Mended. (Served with father at Spion Kop.) Came on matter of conscience rather than law. Did what I could. Fitful.

'Whether this refers to Flanagan or not I don't know,' said Sarah, hands behind her head. 'Most personal war diaries are annoyingly cryptic because noting the detail was forbidden. But sometimes you can read between the lines . . . and I sense the conclusion of Flanagan's review process.'

Anselm wished David farewell and then joined Sarah between the pillars of the portico. A family's history added shadows of experience to her face, a generational mark from events she had not known, but which had touched her nonetheless. He sensed, correctly, that she wanted to say something, to state her case on the troubled question of military justice in action. After all, her great-great-grandfather had recommended the extreme sanction on several occasions. He was implicated in a process that had become, for some, a scandal. She, like her father, was an advocate.

'The problem with a morally necessary war is that morally unnecessary things happen,' she said, steeled to the reality of her own remark. 'No one is proud of that. But we have to remember, also, that the rank and file stared a senseless death straight in the face and went on, for love of king and country. On the day of any execution you care to mention, four hundred men were killed in action. We can't take anything away from their resolve.'

Anselm nodded, fumbling for his car keys. He agreed entirely. They did their duty, while others, for whatever reason – be it choice or illness – did not. But he had a squint of his own on to the past: some of those others had been *executed*; and defending them now, late in the day, did not prosecute the achievement of those who'd fallen nobly. It was a thought Anselm would keep to himself. Sarah didn't seem to accept that tragedies never compete for pole position. There needn't be a winner.

Chapter Twenty-Four

The Heavens Open

On the 13th September the preliminary bombardment opened up. Herbert looked from the mock battlefield to the savage sky over Ypres and the Salient. Even from this distance the noise was terrific, not through volume but depth. He tried to imagine the amount of ironware screaming through the air and the devastation it would unleash. Theoretically, the German defence zone was being ripped apart, inch by inch: wire, men and soil being thrown high into the air. According to Tomlinson, revealing another secret not to be shared with the Kaiser, the pounding would increase every day, building up to Zero hour on the 20th.

'It'll be bloody hell,' he disclosed, speaking exactly. 'Furthermore, twice daily, at fixed intervals, the artillery boys will rehearse the barrage scheme that will protect the advancing attack brigades.' And as if answering the cocky Australian officer who'd implied there would be no element of surprise, he added, 'Of course, Jerry'll know we're coming –' he paused for effect – 'but he'll be in no fit state to organise a welcome party.'

The thunder went on and on. The battle drill became tense, and voices were raised. There were no more jokes. Men crouched by their line of coloured tape knowing that soon it would all be real. That evening, the riot of crumping fell on the pitch, and the men played wildly, some awful force having entered their limbs. They sweated and grunted after the ball, and Elliot laughed hysterically. Pickles yelled at Flanagan to keep behind the back feet of his own defenders, but he kept running forward, off-side. And Herbert kept looking up at the sky, awed by the awful weight it was carrying.

The bellies of the Observation Balloons flashed with sallow light from the inferno on the ground. They were tethered over the entrance to Hell. What could they see?

In the darkness of his billet Herbert lay on his bed, listening to the haemorrhage of steel. Fear settled upon him, for what was to come. And he panicked for what he might leave behind, for he was no closer to understanding Joseph Flanagan. The Irishman was either detached from his circumstances or resigned to them: it was impossible to say which. Either way, he seemed indifferent to the fact that his sentence was under review and that a decision on his life would arrive without warning. The only way to explain such indifference was to entertain the unimaginable: that Flanagan was following a chosen path, fully appreciating the direction it would take.

Herbert, on the other hand, felt the increasing pressure keenly. He'd got nowhere in understanding the trial, and time was running out. And he'd got nowhere because Flanagan only spoke about his life *before* he joined the army. Everything after enlistment was vague, as if it hadn't really happened, or as if Flanagan hadn't been there. In rest moments during training, or on the way to the football field, Herbert had talked innocently of Étaples or Abeele and the tremendous bond between Irish lads in the army, but Flanagan had left the bait, in each case, completely untouched. On the other hand, when Herbert had asked him, again, why he'd left labouring to join the army, he got a comprehensive answer.

When Flanagan got to Tyneside he knocked on the door of Mr Drennan's friend: a fervent nationalist named Power who loathed England. Mr Power gave him a room in the attic and a job at a shipyard where he was foreman. Of a night, Flanagan would join the family at table. Talk turned frequently to the war and the men from the docks whose names had appeared on the casualty lists. Many of them were Irish. In a strange way, Flanagan was moved by these countrymen, away from their country, who'd died for another country. And it struck him that these people somehow or other fell outside the Drennan code of honour; that his old teacher, for all his revolutionary credentials, had, in fact, turned his back on a great struggle. He'd barely mentioned the war. Here, in Tyneside, that was inconceivable.

Shortly afterwards, Flanagan met Eamon O'Brien. He was a tall Kerry man with flaming red hair. Everyone called him High-Pockets. He was going to enlist, he said. This was a world war, he said. There were Turks involved. Germany was expansionist, he added, getting his mouth stuck on the length of the word. But he understood what it meant. And High-Pockets was going to do something about it. 'Fine, so' said Mr Power, when he told him, 'but I can't keep your job open.' To Mr Power's astonishment, Flanagan resigned too. There and then. And with High-Pockets and four lads from Kerry, all shipyard men, he went to a recruitment booth on Grey Street and joined the NLI.

Only it wasn't that simple . . . for Flanagan wasn't that simple. Herbert had listened, noting once more that characteristic, profound disobedience. Just as the islander had cut loose from his people's expectations, so had he cut loose from Mr Drennan's. Flanagan had become his own master, a rebel and a freeman; a soldier before his chosen Colours. But Herbert had also listened, wondering how events could unfold such that this man, of all men, would one day be tried for desertion? Flanagan had given no clues. He'd only mentioned the trial once, stunning Herbert by his abruptness. 'Sir,' he'd whispered, when Herbert had awarded a penalty against him, 'I hold no resentment against you.'

The guns thundered over Ypres and Herbert's stomach rolled. Fear was always a fresh emotion; it always brought a pure havoc to the mind and body. Holding himself tight, he closed his eyes. And there, plain as day, he saw Quarters, helpless and expectant. Herbert shot bolt upright, his chest pounding. The farm machinery seemed ready to pounce, the angled limbs spiked and sharp. After he'd calmed down, he lay slowly back, remembering that night in August when he'd seen Flanagan and Father Maguire huddled in the rain. They'd spoken Gaelic in hurried tones. And Flanagan had then gone to Étaples with Owen Doyle.

'What happened over there?' whispered Herbert. 'Why did you come back?'

Chapter Twenty-Five

Parting Words

1

Lisette crouched by Flanagan's chair, the candlelight bright in her eyes. They were alone now. Doyle was asleep upstairs in Louis' bed. A grandfather clock ticked in the corner, the heavy strikes sounding hollow in its box.

'Is it true?' she whispered. 'Will you stay?'

Exhaustion laid hold of Flanagan. He wanted to lie down for ever.

'Won't you run to me?' said Lisette, touching his hand.

Her skin was warm and Flanagan couldn't take his gaze off her nails. They were cut short for the serving and cleaning, though some were still split and ragged.

'I have to go,' he muttered, at last. 'The boys are waiting at Black Eye Corner.' He struggled with another explanation, because it was so obvious, but it was important. 'The war hasn't ended.'

Lisette folded herself over until her knuckles touched the floor. 'Don't join Louis, I beg you. There are plenty of other soldiers for the front. They don't need another one.'

Flanagan looked down upon the woman he'd never touched. When he'd first met her, he'd been deadened by the war. The very sight of her had drawn him back to the sensations of ordinary living. But it was because his sensibilities had recovered that his nerve snapped during the burials last spring, and again after the mines at Messines. He'd been defenceless. But, being exposed, important truths had slipped home; and they'd brought him here, on this night, with a purpose: a purpose that would save Lisette as much as Doyle. Slowly, Flanagan reached down towards the bunched black hair.

If you leave the land, Seosamh, death will claim you.

Meg had warned him in a dream. And she'd been right. Flanagan had taken a boat to the shattered place of trenches and broken roots like God's dead fingers. He closed his eyes and, in his mind, heard the crunch of seashells as he ran away from the black cove. He heard Lisette crying, refusing to rise off her knees.

Flanagan loved her. And he always had done, from the days when Feiritéar had put a phrasing on desire. No . . . from before then, when he'd first seen something frail in the sea's strength, when he'd watched the grasses shiver and mist rise off the rocks; when something violent in him had leapt out to touch what could not be touched. Somehow all these sensations had been gathered into Lisette, like the rain off the sea. He loved her.

A charred voice bounced off the cliffs behind Meg's cottage. *Seosamh, don't leave the land*. The terror had been a dream, that's all.

Flanagan's arm fell lower still, and one hand lightly touched Lisette's head. Her hair was soft, like the push of a breeze; and at that instant of touching, an anguish greater than any suffering he'd known entered Flanagan; and it seeped into the pure place prepared for loving.

'I have to go,' said Flanagan, harshly. He came to his feet. 'I'm expected at Black Eye Corner.'

Lisette rose, too, and brushed down her knees. Embarrassed, she took out a handkerchief from her sleeve and dabbed her face. 'You'll need to explain yourself.'

'Can I take some wine?'

Lisette entered the darkness beyond the sitting room and came back with three bottles in a cloth bag. 'Let them breathe for an hour beforehand.'

Flanagan went swiftly upstairs to the first floor bedroom where Doyle was sleeping, the room he'd known since he'd spent all his leave at Pap's. The sheets were bright in the darkness and smelled of soap. Flanagan sat on the edge of the mattress . . . and thought of Brendan at home . . . and Muiris downstairs, smoking his pipe in the corner, and Róisín sitting opposite, hands in her lap, dreaming, perhaps of the wonderful things Seosamh had seen. He touched Doyle's head as if he were his little brother, wondering if he should wake him to explain that he'd never intended to stay. His profile was just discernible against the pillow – the boyish side that had first roused his confidence. One arm lay on the blankets, the palm cupped as if to receive a hand-out. Flanagan left him be. He drew Doyle's army book from his breast pocket and put it on a washstand.

Lisette was waiting for him in the shadow of the stairwell. In silence, she led him through the kitchen to the back door. Flanagan stepped outside into the night. The rain had stopped and the sky seemed to throb. He turned around. She was on the other side of the frame, he knew, but he couldn't see her. It was as though she'd already gone. He struggled to manage the swell between his heart and his mouth.

'Watch the till,' he mumbled, 'The lad's a thief.'

The presence in the darkness didn't move.

Grief choked Flanagan and he stepped backwards.

'Goodbye, Seosamh,' came the gentle voice . . .

. . . the voice from the sea and the grass and the mist.

A voice that followed him through the rain . . . back to the station and on to another goods carriage; a voice that said 'Goodbye, Seosamh' again and again as he ran through the dawn, mile after mile from Abeele to God knows where, utterly lost. He was back in the shattered land. The abandoned land.

'The fields will die,' Meg had said in his dream.

2

Flanagan had acted with such conviction on meeting Doyle that he hadn't given any clear thought to his route back to the front. Like all people going in one direction, he'd thought all he had to do was turn around and retrace his steps. But that wasn't possible. He had to avoid the streams of wounded and dying, for he was one against their flow, now, straggling in daylight. Gathering his wits, he sought the position of the sun, to give him compass. A glimmering through the cloud and rain sent Flanagan northeast. He ran on lanes and across hedged fields, an eye to the light. This area had not been shelled but the earth around him steamed as if it had been poached: yellow scum clung to the edge of khaki pools and his feet slid through a pulp of grass and clay. Dripping cattle watched him from firmer ground.

'Goodbye, Seosamh,' murmured Lisette.

'I shall save the other glass for your homecoming,' snapped Mr Drennan, 'however bitter the grape might turn.'

'Death will claim you,' said Meg, whispering now.

A widow, a dreamer and a seer: two banshees and a Fenian: each, in their own way, intoning the one song. Their voices rose out of the mist and sucking of the mud.

In the mid-afternoon Flanagan saw a barn by the side of a road. Exhaustion wouldn't allow him to go any further. He stumbled through an open door and collapsed among dung and hay.

He woke with a start.

The gate had creaked. Flanagan just caught sight of a wrinkled face and a huge beret. Feet splashed through puddles, falling dull on reaching the grass.

With a pocket knife Flanagan quickly opened all three bottles of wine. And then he paused. A sense of ceremony gripped him, as if Mr Drennan had kicked open the door with that full second glass in one hand, and his own, empty, in the other, waiting to be filled.

''Tis a sacred drink, boy,' Flanagan recited and, slowly, like a ritual cleansing, he poured the wine over his head. It ran down his cheeks, cutting into his eyes. His lips were folded in, and he breathed through his nose. When the first bottle was empty he moved on to the second and then the third. The strong smell brought back the fishermen from Brittany, men who would have known the flats of Guérande where Lisette had heaped salt with a long wooden rake. At the sound of a horse's canter he put the bottle down and walked towards a kind of accomplishment.

Chapter Twenty-Six

On Parade

1

Shortly after lunchtime on the 14th September 1917, a signal from the legal boys at GHQ arrived on Duggie's desk. Herbert sank on to a stool. Chamberlayne stared over the top of his typewriter.

'I'll read out the relevant passage,' said the CO. '"The point raised on drunkenness and intention – that a drunken frolic may evince a lack of intention to evade duty in an otherwise reliable soldier – has no merit in this case. Flanagan did not absent himself because he was drunk but because he was sober. The episode with alcohol came after an absence of almost forty hours. This was implicitly accepted by Flanagan, though it was not formally brought out at the trial by the prosecutor. That officer might be reminded of his duty to adduce all relevant facts in a clear and comprehensible fashion. The review process should be concluded shortly." It is signed by a Staff Major of no fighting consequence.'

Chamberlayne began typing: slow, light taps with a finger held like a dipstick. He said, 'We go back into action in six days.'

The men would be warned the night before, hopefully when flushed with victory against the Lancashire Fusiliers, or enraged at having lost – either way emotionally prepared for the onslaught. How did Flanagan's fate fit into that schema? Would he be the example to buck up the men's resolve? Especially the new lot from Blighty, Canada, Australia, New Zealand . . . the four corners of the Dominion. They'd yet to find out what some men ran away from. The thought made Herbert tremble.

'It's in the hands of the Field Marshal, now,' said Duggie, putting on his cap. 'I need some fresh air. Edward, I'm expecting a call from Brigadier Pemberton at any moment. He's a natural teacher, and he'll want to satisfy himself that I understand the nature of "intention". Unfortunately, you can't find me.'

'Indeed I cannot.'

Duggie nodded at Herbert and Angus, and both subordinates fell into step.

Outside the air was heavy and Herbert began to sweat. As Tomlinson promised, the bombardment had been turned up every day. The volume had gradually increased, as had the tension in the camp. The men were brittle. Duggie, however, exuded a sort of professional nonchalance. He sauntered among other men's anxieties with a wink and the strike of a match over his pipe.

'Well,' said Duggie. 'Do you know why two Irishmen took a breather when they should have been giving Fritz a headache?'

Herbert had given up, wearied by thinking and his efforts to draw Flanagan out of himself. 'He's told me everything from his life on Inisdúr to the day of his recruitment. And that's where he's stopped. Nothing about Neuve Chapelle, Aubers Ridge, and the rest. Nothing about active service. Just more and more about his bloody island of rock and mist and dried out weed . . .'

The barrage suddenly jumped a grade and Angus whined. Herbert wanted to kick the dog. Fear was contagious. It had to be stamped down. A match popped and the CO lit his pipe.

'What the hell is Flanagan doing here?' asked Herbert.

'The same as you and I,' replied Duggie. 'He's doing his bit. Or he was.'

Herbert agreed with Duggie but there were other facets to Flanagan's motivation. He tried again. 'I sometimes wonder if it's really of Ireland that he speaks, or some inner world. He joined up for all the right reasons, but the most important impulse is an odyssey to a slip, away from three fields.'

Herbert kicked a stone and Angus ran after it, obedient to some half-remembered ritual. He brought it back, slobbering and defiant.

'People enlist for all sorts of reasons.' Duggie took a puff on his pipe. 'It's not always a rush to the Colours for England's sake, or Belgium's, for that matter. They run away from home, from prison, from an ordinary, boring life. But in the end initial motivations don't matter. War plunges everyone into a drama about good and evil. For once in our lives the choice becomes clear. The lines are drawn and we dig in. Sometimes when I'm very, very drunk I wonder if no-man's-land is our natural territory . . . the place we come to when we leave our childhood behind. It's the Blighty we've lost, it's the English meadow in our memory that's not really England. It's the world as it ought to be, and our life only makes sense in winning it back at any cost, if we redeem it from an invader.' He struck another match and tugged at the air. 'When I'm sober, it's back to basics. My satisfaction lies in that to the best of my limited ability I'm doing what I can to bring this ghastly war to an end. But the other stuff helps me through. Poor Flanagan: he's never been drunk, so he's never known the consolation of madness.'

They'd attained the abbey. The gate was half-open and Herbert saw the white door at the end of the flagged path. For a moment he wanted to go inside. Ignoring the impulse he moved on, drawn by a racket in the carpenter's barn. Fresh deliveries of timber were stacked high – inside and out the other side, visible through an open door on to a field of yellowing wheat. The saws were under way. Some extra hands had been brought in. They were measuring with a tape and ticking with a pencil while others took the marked wood to one of four benches where the lengths were cut to size. In the middle, arms folded, stood the master, lips pursed. Angus stared, shivering and uncomprehending.

Satisfied that he'd avoided Pemberton's telephone call, Duggie returned resolutely to base. As soon as Herbert, Duggie and Angus entered the room, however, it was clear that Chamberlayne was rattled. 'The Brigadier's been on the line,' he said. 'He was very sympathetic. Wants to see you immediately. This arrived ten minutes after you'd gone.' Chamberlayne held out another telegram.

Duggie read it in silence and folded the paper in four. 'Call a parade at five this evening,' he ordered, sharply. 'Herbert, take another long walk.'

2

Herbert did not take a long walk. He arrived at 4.50 p.m. as the men were being knocked into shape. He knew a lot of their faces now. This was the reconstituted NLI. They were going to support a major offensive on the Menin Road. The four Companies were formed up, each flanking a central square of well-stamped ground. With the other Company commanders, Herbert stood in the centre, hands behind his back, legs slightly apart. His eye sought out Flanagan. He was at the corner of a front row, placed there by Mackie, who stood to one side. At 4.58 p.m. Duggie arrived, followed by Chamberlayne and the Assistant Provost Marshal, a man called Hooper. They strode resolutely to the line of officers waiting on the middle ground.

The bombardment cracked on and on, like millions of plates shattering on a tile floor.

At 5.00 p.m., Duggie nodded at the RSM. Joyce straightened his neck and boomed, 'Private Flanagaaaaaaaaaan. One step forwaaaard.'

Flanagan obeyed, head erect, teeth visible.

Joyce took off Flanagan's cap and placed it under his arm in a single sweeping gesture, at once dignified and momentous.

Hooper held out a sheet of paper and began his recitation. 'On the first of September nineteen seventeen, four-eight-eight-eight Private Joseph Flanagan of this regiment was tried by Field General Court Martial at Oostbeke on a charge of desertion and found guilty.'

He stopped so that all the men could fix their eyes on the prisoner, and reflect. Far away, the barrage hammered and pumped iron, endless amounts of iron, into the trench systems beyond the Salient. Everyone listened, their nerves raw.

'The sentence of the Court was death.'

Hooper breathed in to raise his voice higher, to get above the shells. 'The Commander-in-Chief has confirmed the sentence and it will be carried out in Oostbeke tomorrow morning at five forty-five a.m., eleventh instant.'

The ranks moved as if a wind had been thrown off the hop frames. Heads swung left and right. Flanagan stared ahead, as he'd done at his trial. That grimace of a smile didn't change. Oh God, begged Herbert. Come down from heaven.

Blinking as if grit had struck him, Herbert watched a three-man escort march over to Flanagan's Company lines. The Islander was in a daze. He had to be positioned and pushed by Mackie as if he was drunk. Herbert couldn't watch any more. He glazed his eyes . . . and saw the white shutters on the chipped brick walls, the black and white tiles, the parquet flooring, and the rose wallpaper. He flung his head to one side, and saw something worse: the waxy yellow light behind a cellar vent a foot or so above the ground. When Herbert had calmed himself Duggie and Chamberlayne had gone, and the men had broken formation, released by the barked commands of the Sergeant-Majors. No one approached him. Except Joyce.

'Excuse me, Sir.' His voice was tight and his lips barely moved. The air shot through his nose.

'Yes, Joyce?'

'It's not your fault, Sir.' Air fired again like pistons out of synchronisation.

'Thank you.'

'Good day, Sir.'

'Yes . . . good day, Joyce.'

Herbert tracked the stamp of explosions. For the first time since he'd come to the Western Front, it was simply a racket in Belgium. A greater fear had taken hold of him.

3

Herbert did not eat that evening. He kept away from the officers' mess, knowing that the talk would be stiff and charged. They'd argue about the rights and wrongs of military punishments, of their need and their shame, of the Australians who didn't have the death penalty but who fought just as well. He'd heard it all before, but never, never on a subject so close to home. He felt stranded. There was one road in Oostbeke. In one direction lay the tents and huts, the men on every side. In the other, stood the abbey . . . he found his feet heading towards the open gate without a bolt or a lock. He pushed open the door and stepped into the smell of wax and incense. Almost stumbling, he hurried to the accusing space between the two carved statues: the man and the woman of wood: the place where he'd felt the disappointment of his parents. He looked at them again, first left and then right. There was no blame there at all. Their faces were kind and smooth, their eyes closed in confident supplication. He'd entered another kind of space altogether.

Herbert fell on his knees and a violent pleading broke from his mouth. 'God of the many things I cannot understand, please save him. Show yourself in this man's story. Please, I beg you, save him.'

Herbert had nothing else to say. Vaguely comforted, he left the abbey. At the end of the narrow corridor open to the sky he saw the figure of Father Maguire, hiding this side of the gate, his face pressed into the stone while he wept.

Chapter Twenty-Seven

1

'It was a disturbing visit,' said Anselm to the Prior. 'They quarrelled on every question of importance regarding the executions as a whole, yet each voice without the other would have been incomplete.'

They were sitting in the cloister on a ledge between two columns. The garth trapped that alluring stillness that had drawn men as varied as Herbert and Bede. Above, cloud streaked the sky like a half painted ceiling.

'This is where things stand,' said Anselm. He'd brought some structure to his research which gave an interpretation to the court martial. 'External factors crowd around the Flanagan file – political events in Ireland, the Ypres campaign, mutiny, eugenics, racism – and against those momentous problems, you'd think that Flanagan would be shot. But *internal* factors disperse their importance. Someone weeded the file, not because he was dead but – I think – to hide the fact that he was alive. Reading between the lines of General Osborne's diary, it seems that such an unlikely survival was thanks to Herbert's intervention.'

It was tempting to say more. To share his thoughts on the 'nine-on-ten, one-in-ten' mercy-brutality argument. To dwell a moment on the increased chances of receiving a death sentence if one was Irish. To ponder the dark universe behind the statistics. But upon such questions Anselm's mind had imploded. He'd found himself, appropriately, drawn away from the men of percentages to a man of flesh.

'Ever since Martin suggested that Flanagan was the stronger personality, as opposed to Doyle, I've been trying to conjure up the essence of the man. And there's something extraordinary to be seen, and it's plainly set out in the court's transcript. When giving his defence he talked of rain "coming off the sea after weeks of the gathering"; he said, "the land was part of the air" –' Anselm shook his head in astonishment – 'this is a *trial*. The man's fighting for his *life* . . . what does he say? "And cold I was and wet."' Anselm rubbed a thumb and finger as if feeling silk, or showing its unearthly cost. 'There's an exceptional *sensibility* to Joseph Flanagan. A frailty. And this is the man who, five months earlier, helped bury two thousand three hundred and fourteen English and German soldiers in four days. Try and picture it. Dragging bodies for hours on end . . . by the arms, by the legs . . . in April, the month of early sunshine. The experience must have affected him deeply, this poet who'd seen the land and sky join up and turn to water. Come June his nerves are wrecked by an explosion that removes not his friends, but his *enemy*.'

'You think April and June lead to the trial?' asked the Prior, already convinced. His arms were folded tight, his dark eyes trained on the rich grass and moss.

'I do,' replied Anselm, emphatically. 'The next time we know anything about Joseph Flanagan, he's a deserter. Only not in an ordinary sense. He's been to Étaples and back. And the evidence against him, without any reference to the trip, is like a *script*. I believe something profound happened to Flanagan in April and it came to a head in September when he met Doyle. But what did they say to each other? More to the point, what did *Doyle* say?'

Anselm and the Prior looked at each other helplessly. The trail into the past had come to an end on these, the most important questions of all. There was no way of finding out the answers. And there was nothing else that could be done to advance their understanding of the trial or Herbert's message.

'At times like this,' said the Prior, 'I always sit tight.'

Like Herbert in his Cortina, thought Anselm.

They'd swung their legs into the garth. Facing a new direction, they'd left behind the claims of Herbert, Joseph Flanagan and Owen Doyle. Released like boys, they dreamed up excruciating product labels for the jars that would shortly be filled: Honey from the Rock. The Baptist's Choice. The Promised Brand. While they laughed, freely, Anselm found his face growing stiff. He had a horrible feeling that the Prior might not be joking.

2

The Prior cornered Anselm while he was unloading crates of pears off a trolley outside Saint Hildegard's, the fruit-press shed. In all seriousness, he said, 'The Dew of Hermon . . .'

Anselm raised a hand. This sort of thing happened to Priors. They're responsible for the livelihood of a monastery. Between reading the Rule and the Fathers, they occasionally get visions of the shelves in Tesco. He was about to say something harsh when Benedict waved from the shed, pointed at Anselm and tapped his ear, which meant that Sylvester had transferred a telephone call from reception.

The voice took flight without introduction. 'My research, of necessity, takes me frequently to Saint Catherine's House in London – where the national indexes for births and deaths in England and Wales are helpfully stored. Many of my great-great-grandfather's comrades are in the lists and it's my painful duty to check basic details knowing that they are of marginal importance. In a moment of boredom I decided to enquire after one Owen Doyle.'

'Yes?'

'I rather got carried away. Have you got a pen to hand?'

Anselm gestured frantically at Jerome who, with Benedict, had just lugged a heaped crate towards the press. The former always carried an ink pen in his top pocket. It had been a gift from his father. 'Go ahead.'

'He was born on twenty-first January eighteen ninety-six.'

'Yes.'

'In the parish of Saint Stephen, Bolton, Lancashire.'

'Yes.'

'At the time of his birth, his family address was three-five-nine Leyland Park Avenue, of that town.'

Sarah paused while Anselm scribbled, repeating out loud what he'd just heard. Fruit thumped into the press like heavy rain on a roof.

'The father was named Colum, occupation mill worker, the mother was Alice, maiden name Lowther.'

'This is tremendous,' said Anselm, not quite sure what he was going to do with the information. But Doyle had been close to Flanagan. He was the absent presence at the trial.

'There's one hitch.'

'Oh?'

'Owen Doyle died on the twenty-fourth of August nineteen hundred and eight at the age of twelve years eight months.'

'What?'

'Cause of death tuberculosis,' continued Sarah in an even, reading voice, 'certified by Kenneth Spinks LMSSA. The father, Colum, was present at the death.'

Anselm slumped on to a stool. His brother monks, satisfied that he was all right, returned to their work, leaning on the limbs that lowered the press.

'I made a few phone calls,' continued Sarah, 'and people really are enormously helpful if you only ask the right question in the right way. Owen is buried in Blackburn Road Cemetery in the far left-hand corner as you enter the main gates. It's an iron cross among failing slabs of stone.'

Anselm noted the details, thinking hard, trying to link this development to Flanagan's secret crisis . . . and to Herbert.

'I'll send you a copy of the birth and death certificates,' said Sarah, 'though they're of little if any use. Whoever enlisted in nineteen fifteen was not baptised Owen in the parish of Saint Stephen.'

Watching Benedict and Jerome, heads bowed and pushing, Anselm fell into a kind of trance. The pressure fell inexorably on to the soft pears and juice tinkled into a vat. It was a wonderful sound, stirring some forgotten simplicity in his depths. Fountains had a similar effect. He listened, gratefully.

Part Four

Chapter Twenty-Eight

Preparations

Herbert drew back the gate and Father Maguire pressed his face further into the wall as if he'd been caught and didn't want to be identified – like a smoker behind the school sheds. When Herbert reached Duggie's billet he stepped into a kind of oven. It was as though fires had been laid in every corner, though in fact the grate was cold and the windows were open. It was a lovely, fading evening.

'. . . then we'll have to find somewhere else,' shouted Duggie at Chamberlayne.

Both men turned in Herbert's direction. Each was breathing heavily. Chamberlayne thrust out a document and stared at Herbert – his expression telling him that they were comrades; that what was unfolding they would handle as brothers. Herbert nearly sobbed at the gesture.

'A rider just brought it from Brigade.'

The Order had originated at Division level. Herbert quickly read it, starting after the preliminaries.

> The sentence will be carried out at 5.45 a.m. adjacent to the west walls of the monastery at OOSTBEKE facing the Divisional camp. The exact location should be two hundred yards from HUT 42.
>
> The following detail from the 8th (Service) Battalion, Northumberland Light Infantry will be selected tonight:
> Regimental Sergeant Major
> Provost Sergeant
> Escort: 1 NCO & 2 men
> Firing Party: 1 officer

1 Sergeant
12 men
Burial Party: 4 men

The NCO in charge of the escort should be able to identify Private FLANAGAN.

The firing party should be assembled at 4.15 a.m. in HUT 42 and confined thereto. The men need not be informed of the duty for which they are being detailed until 4.30 a.m. on the 14th instant.

All other necessary arrangements will be made by this office.

Please return Proceedings after promulgation.

Herbert's head fell back. Flanagan was to be shot by his own battalion. The Regimental Sergeant Major was Joyce. The men to be gathered in HUT 42 knew already what they were being detailed to perform. Why else were they expected to get up at 4.00 a.m. and wait in a shed?

'The Abbot won't let us use his walls,' said Duggie, trying to be calm. 'He won't let us do anything on the abbey's land. And it stretches for miles around.'

'But, Sir,' said Herbert, his mouth sticky, 'we can't do this, we can't ask Joyce—'

'Captain,' thundered Duggie, swinging around, 'we don't *ask* the RSM anything. We TELL him. Do you understand? This is the British Army. Not some Benevolent Society for the distribution of alms. We are at war, and this is *part* of war. It's a *nasty* part of how we WIN. One of the many, many nasty parts.' Duggie scratched viciously at the flea bites on his face. 'Look, I've done what I could . . . I've tried to get the lad out of the frying pan.' He sighed as if he'd reached the top of a hill. 'Pemberton blew my arse off. Said I should never have kicked up that nonsense about intention. Apparently, it's gone to the top and we can expect a directive on the subject – throughout the BEF.'

'Why shoot Flanagan, for God's sake?' asked Herbert. 'What does Brigade want?'

'What does Division want,' corrected Duggie. He looked at Herbert as if he were a little slow. 'They want to give morale a quick kick before we go back—'

'*Morale*,' said Herbert, bewildered. 'We lost eighty-five per cent of our men, and our morale needs a *kick*.'

'I know, I know.' Duggie was exhausted and hot. 'They mean an example. They mean no one can even think of stepping back. We have to take Passchendaele Ridge. Remember, Herbert, this lad took a quick vacation, even if we don't know why.' Again he scratched his face, his temper rising. 'It's not my job to understand *why*. Damn it. I've only made recommendations to mercy and they've all been heeded. I can't be that surprised if they ignore me for once. You know, Herbert . . . military law . . . Wellington's code, tarted up? Well, it may have been dreamed up for the Regulars and not the Volunteers, but most of 'em are volunteers or conscripts now. And they all have a pocket book with a warning in it, telling 'em what'll happen if they bugger off. Flanagan's got what he expected, believe me. He's less surprised than we are.'

Chamberlayne poured some whisky into three glasses and handed them round.

Duggie raised his portion as if he were a connoisseur checking its colour and said, 'Gentlemen, we have "an unpleasant duty to perform". That is the term of art. Now, let's get on with it.' He drained his glass and dropped on to a stool by the empty grate. 'Edward, send a chit to OC Companies. Tell them to supply four men each. Inform Father Maguire that he can attend Doyle through the night and to the moment of execution. Tell the RMO, Tindall, that he should join the detail to witness and confirm death and provide a certificate to that effect. I want to see Joyce, on his own, now.'

'Sir, you said Doyle,' observed Chamberlayne.

'Did I?' said Duggie. 'Slip of the tongue. I meant Flanagan, of course.'

Chamberlayne started typing, swiftly, with various fingers. His jaw was rigid and the dark rings around his eyes seemed to pulsate with shadow.

'God, where are we going to shoot him?' said Duggie, looking into his glass.

The problem with the camp was that it was utterly flat, like all the landscape around Ypres. Apart from the hop frames and a few patches of woodland there was nothing on the horizon. The land was a great table reaching to the coast. There were no quarries or farm walls – places to draw up a detail with 'an unpleasant duty to perform'.

In his mind, Herbert saw a scattering of mauve and yellow flowers at the mouth of a track. 'Sir,' he said, 'if you walk past the school for a mile or so, you come to a wood. It's fairly thick, but there's a wide path that leads to a clearing. A barn faces the entrance.'

Duggie tapped his teeth, thinking. 'Edward, give the Abbot a ring. Tell him if we can't do it beneath the trees we'll do it on the side of an open road.'

Chamberlayne instantly picked up the phone, dialled, waited and then spoke in fluent French to a Père Koopmans. When he'd put the phone down, he said, 'The Abbot wishes me to inform you that the woods are not his; that if they were he would forbid you entry; and that wherever we choose to shoot this man – in the light or in a shadow – it will be seen from on high and ring throughout eternity to our disgrace.'

'What did you say?' asked Duggie.

'I replied that I was most grateful, and that I feared he was right on both points.' With that, he started swiftly typing the chits for the company commanders. The speed, the sense of time having become vastly important, impressed itself upon Herbert. He began to shuffle on the spot, as if there was something he might do, only not knowing what; as if water had burst in an upstairs pipe and he didn't know where the stopcock was located. 'I'll inform Maguire and Tindall,' he said, and then chewed his bottom lip.

Duggie nodded, rasping his forehead and grinding his teeth. Herbert ran outside, past a sleeping general's dog, and had reached the courtyard gate when Duggie called him back. He'd opened the skin above one eyebrow and his whole face was red from the grating of his nails. 'Look at me,' he said.

Herbert dared not . . . he knew well enough the frown that revealed restraint and gentleness.

'Look at me, Herbert,' ordered the CO.

Herbert faced not the soldier but the man who might have been a teacher, the loved master of a public school, inflexible but yielding when least expected. 'This is not your fault. Flanagan was finished the moment he met Doyle.'

Chapter Twenty-Nine

In the Cellar

Flanagan was marched from the parade ground along the dusty road to the school at Oostbeke. He didn't know the guards on either side, or the NCO marching in front as if he was on full view to the Field Marshal himself. Each member of the escort had a fixed bayonet. Uncertainly, Flanagan descended the cellar steps. Corporal Mackie was waiting.

'Belt.' He pointed at the buckle. 'Remove it.'

Flanagan obeyed and Mackie slowly rolled it up.

'I've got no hard feelings against you,' he announced, completing the coil. 'You have my pity.'

The arched door banged shut and Flanagan was alone. He'd slept in the cellar for two weeks but now everything seemed different. The camp bed, the table, the two chairs. It was as though Flanagan had never seen them before. Arranged neatly on the table were some sheets of paper, a few envelopes, a pencil and a candle.

'What can I write?' he cried. His mind span. How could he find last words?

A waxen light seeped through two vents. He turned to the fragment of sky, the cusp of a cloud. He felt ill with shock – the same feeling he'd had when the bodies of a neighbour were washed up near Meg's cove. Two brothers. They'd gone out for the lobsters. The only warning was a lift in the waves, when it was too late to avoid the storm. That was Flanagan's first experience of unnatural death. The bodies had been black and bloated and slimy, like the lustrous weed around their feet.

'What's to be said?' he begged of himself.

He saw his father, eyes on the barley; his mother, dreaming of Boston; Brendan shouldering his first currach; Mr Drennan checking the wine beneath the slate. And he thought of what had brought him to this cellar, and why he would never see Inisdúr again. At once he dragged back the chair and picked up the pencil. It was sharp.

There was not sufficient light to see clearly, but Flanagan didn't look at the page. He didn't care if he left the tramlines. No, he looked ahead, feverish and concentrated, citing and writing the remembered line. *Ba thaise ná an fhearthainn do shódhantacht, Ba dhaingne ná an charraig do chrógacht.*

With wild capitals he then scribbled a plea in English. A strange notion had settled upon him as he'd trekked from Abeele across the steaming grassland to Elverdinghe; but now, at this stark moment, it seemed no longer strange but profoundly right and proper. When he'd finished the letter, he folded the paper in half, put in an envelope, and wrote on the outside: *Lisette.*

'Joseph, would you come into the parlour,' said Lisette, one afternoon.

This was only the second time that Flanagan had entered that room. As he passed through the corridor, following her steps, he sensed her openness to him and he feared her purpose. Taking a seat, he glanced around him: at the grandfather clock; the carved wardrobe with a brass lock; the roll-top writing desk; a book case jammed with tall volumes; the side table holding a decanter and small glasses housed in a glass box, all painted with golden lines; and beside it a photograph of a boy in an oval silver frame.

'My son,' said Lisette. 'Louis.'

Flanagan could see the ambience of the mother in his face: a long neck, a straight nose, that thick black hair; but the boy had low, level eyebrows, features perhaps drawn from the father's line. He was about Brendan's age.

'Where is he now?' asked Flanagan. She'd never spoken of him for long, save to say he was at the front, fighting for France and Brittany.

Lisette tied a bow with the black silk ribbon on the collar of her blouse. It had fallen open, showing her throat and the whiteness of her skin. Flanagan saw a vein; its winding course roused his blood. 'He's dead.'

Flanagan wanted to cross the room but his feet seemed nailed to the floorboards.

'I killed him.'

He stared at her, expectant and unbelieving.

'A few years after the photograph was taken he joined his battalion . . . at the age of fifteen,' she said, quietly. 'He went in the name of his father, to honour his memory. I could have stopped him but I didn't. Far from it. I encouraged him. With these hands I blessed him on the second of January nineteen fifteen.' She held them up as though they were ruined tools. 'Five months later, on the eighteenth of May, he fell at Artois.'

Lisette fiddled with the black ribbon, arranging it on her blouse. She sat upright, resuming the posture of reserve that they shared. But he knew that she was desperate to explain her own reticence, to tell Flanagan that in keeping back she was not rejecting him.

'I want you to know, Joseph,' she said, as if describing how the cooker worked, 'I cannot love again. It's not the war and what love might do to anyone I might meet; it's not even what I have done. It's what has become of me. My heart is like these wrung out hands. There is no life beating there. I've nothing left to give. So I look after all these boys who come back from the front. I wash the floors and clean the glasses and peel the potatoes and crack the eggs –' she lifted her hands helplessly – 'that's all that's left of me, Joseph.'

Flanagan never entered the parlour again, not until the night he came back with Owen Doyle. And when that lad was upstairs, fast asleep in Louis' bed, she'd knelt at Flanagan's feet and begged him to stay. She'd crossed that awful, fiery divide and called him Seosamh.

'Are you free now, Lisette?' whispered Flanagan to a summoned shape in the cellar. 'Are you free to love again?'

He looked to the vent. The edge of cloud had drifted away and the sky showed the first glamour of the night. Before the sun rises high I shall be dead, he thought.

Chapter Thirty

1

Anselm took a train to Bolton, surprised not so much that the Prior had required him to make the trip but that he asked him to leave the next morning. It revealed the pressure behind the Prior's calm acceptance of events. Anselm duly arrived at an Augustinian Friary where, warmly welcomed, he obtained a room, a local map and a telephone directory.

Anselm walked first to the cemetery at Blackburn Road where he discovered that, try as they might, people aren't always as helpful as they might think. After an hour of pacing between the neat graves, he found an angled black cross – but not in the far *left*-hand corner as reported to Sarah Osborne, but in the nearside *right*, rather close to the main gate. For several minutes he studied the little name plaque attached with a screw that recorded the deceased's particulars: Owen Doyle 1896–1908. The Prior had suggested, and Anselm agreed, that there were only two possible hypotheses.

'First, the dead boy was known to whoever assumed his identity – let's call him X – and the use of his name was a careful decision, or an impulse towards something personally significant; either way, not a random choice.'

That scenario, they both accepted, would be problematic: if X had been a friend of Doyle there would be no clue left behind to tie the two individuals together in the one document. If X had been a family member, similar difficulties would arise, because a search would have to cover all Doyles within the family tree, along with those holding a different surname: it would be a massive genealogical enquiry that might take years to execute.

'Second,' the Prior had said, 'the dead boy was *not* known to X.

But someone important to X, and bearing his surname, was buried nearby, and that is how X came across Doyle's name and grave in the first place.'

With these two hypotheses in mind – and banking on the second – Anselm noted the details engraved on eight tombstones, four on either side of Owen Doyle's resting place. He read them over in the breeze, the sound of traffic behind him, hoping that one of them had been close to X; that X had come here out of affection and respect; that his eye had caught on the tragically young age of Owen Doyle at the time of his death.

A further supposition shared by Anselm and his Prior was that X was a runaway. This young man had left the northwest of England for London, where he'd joined The Lambeth Rifles. If he simply wanted to run to the Colours under a pseudonym, for whatever reason, he could have done so just as easily with the local regiment, the Lancashire Fusiliers. But he hadn't. He'd gone south. On the basis that X was a fugitive of sorts, Anselm and the Prior made a further assumption: that somebody local to Bolton cared; that they'd kicked up some fuss and left behind a trace of their distress. Anselm's plan was to check the archives of the *Bolton Evening News* – a paper with a long history and widely read (according to a Friar born in the suburb of Astley Bridge). A call to the paper's reception sent Anselm to the Bolton Archives and Local Studies Service located in Le Mans Crescent where, to his enormous pleasure, he joined the twenty-first century. He'd expected bound volumes covered in dust. For the remainder of the day he examined Microfilm copies of the paper, checking for personal notices, his eye sharp for a 'Come Home All Is Forgiven' plea. Not one of the names on his list surfaced.

2

After breakfast the next day, Anselm followed his map, on foot, to 359 Leyland Park Avenue. With every step he thought the project increasingly hopeless, such that, by the time he knocked on the door, he was embarrassed. How would the occupier have any idea about the Doyles of the earlier twentieth century? The thought rather blanked his mind, and he stared at a young mother holding the wailing baby as if he'd lost his voice.

'Sorry, Father,' said the woman, clearing strands of blonde hair off her face. 'I don't go?'

'Pardon?'

'To church, I don't go.'

Anselm told her not to worry and that frequent attendance was sometimes a problem for him, too. He then said he felt an utter fool but would she by any chance know anything about the Doyle family who'd once lived in this house. She didn't. But there was an old woman in 459 who had a bomb shelter in her garden and she knew everything. Her name was Mrs Spencer.

'And she goes.'

'Sorry?'

'To church. She goes.'

Anselm went along the cobbled street, past neat terraced houses until he reached 459. A young man chewing gum pulled open the door. Having listened, he shouted over his shoulder, went back inside, shouted some more and then returned with a beckoning hand.

Mrs Spencer did indeed know everything. She sat in an armchair, a tartan blanket over her knees, describing all the families of her childhood. She'd been born upstairs and her husband had run the corner shop until he got the gout, though God knows, it wasn't from the good life. He'd loved tripe, grown his own radishes and stuck to a pint of mild on a Friday. Anselm stayed for roughly two hours without any detail coming forward that remotely touched on anyone called Doyle. It was only when Mrs Spencer said that everyone had gone to Saint Stephen's round the corner that a glimmer of light came from an unexpected quarter. School records. There was a slim chance that they'd been retained. Profuse with his gratitude, Anselm made his escape. He stepped out into the street and looked left and right, sensing a vanished universe, a whole history of memory spilling out of the door behind him.

When Anselm got back to the Friary, he rang up Saint Stephen's Primary School and made an appointment with the Head Teacher, a Mrs Holden. She was a local woman (she explained) and even if the available records were of no assistance, she might know of individuals Anselm might approach, or other places he might go. That evening, he sipped a glass of scotch and listened to a friar tell a very funny story about a priest who fell into an open grave. It seemed apposite, somehow.

3

Mrs Holden was what Dickens would have called an 'ample' woman. Small and compact in a brown skirt and yellow cardigan, she filled her clothes so the stitches had to work. Her face was cheerful, made up of soft lumps of flesh, well pressed together around an indomitable smile. Swirls of brown hair, perfectly groomed, suggested that very little indeed could ruffle her feathers. A jolt of a handshake told Anselm that this was a woman of efficiency, affection and inspiration. She led him through the foyer, past a display cabinet containing oddments from a bygone era – sepia photographs of Bolton's mills and mines, a pen, a watch, a book – and into her office. On the table was a selection of large, thin volumes, all open, all marked with slips of paper.

'Owen Doyle was a pupil here,' said Mrs Holden, her Lancashire vowels uncompromisingly flat. 'Attendance was not his strong point.' A finger touched the list of absences, week on week throughout 1904. She went deeper into the pile, to 1907. 'By the age of eleven, he's doing rather better, though there's still considerable room for improvement.'

The use of the present tense showed that Mrs Holden never lost hope.

'And he was dead from TB the following year,' said Anselm.

'Yes, these were hard times in the north, Father,' said Mrs Holden. 'Most of the parents crawled underground or stood over the cotton machines. You'll be familiar with the critique passed by Engels on the Manchester situation?'

'Vaguely,' replied Anselm, glad of teachers and their never-ending expectations.

Anselm asked if he could examine the registers on his own for a while. The headmistress left him to his research, quietly closing the door while summoning a child who'd run down the corridor. With his list of graves, Anselm checked the registers between 1903 and 1912. Several of the surnames occurred and he began noting their frequency, drawing up another list, gradually realising, to his irritation, that the entire project was doomed to failure. He'd hoped to find one particular name that stood out, establishing a potential link with Doyle. But he was awash. There were several McCarthys, Nolans, and Kellys . . . along with all the other names on Anselm's list. They were scattered all over his notebook. He stared at them, noting for the first time that most of them were Irish . . . that these were the immigrant families who'd left Ireland in the nineteenth century, searching for work, sending money back home. He tapped the names with his pencil, losing heart, thinking – hopefully to Mrs Holden's approval – of the Great Famine which, like Engels' critique, had not been a prominent feature in Anselm's education. Trying to salvage something worthwhile out of the previous hour and a half, he concluded that X was Irish.

That detail was more important than Anselm at first appreciated.

For it completely changed the complexion of the meeting that had taken place between Flanagan and Doyle in September 1917. Sensing the advance of a presentiment, Anselm carefully aligned his pencil in the middle of his notebook, not wanting to disturb the idea taking shape. Perhaps their association goes back much, much further. Could it be that the 'Doyle' of The Lambeth Rifles had hailed from the same part of Ireland as Flanagan?

Anselm stared at the children playing in the yard. Boys crowding together. Girls in smaller groups. Worlds apart, for the moment . . .

'Had Flanagan met Doyle before?' said Anselm, out loud. 'Possibly,' he replied, concluding that it didn't really matter. The meeting between the two men in no-man's-land could not have been planned in advance. It had to be a coincidence, because Flanagan had been *sent back* from Black Eye Corner with a wounded officer. There was no way his presence in the reserve trenches could have been foreseen.

Another possibility struck Anselm – the second hypothesis –

Flanagan and 'Doyle' weren't friends. They didn't know each other. But they were bound by a strong sense of Irish identity. Anselm sighed and turned to the window. Mrs Holden had corralled some boys and was wagging a finger. The girls were grouped, too, and loving the show. On a step to one side a little boy swung a hand bell and the children formed straggling lines according to their class. Within minutes desk lids banged, doors closed and Mrs Holden stood smiling at Anselm, her keen intellect interested to know if Anselm's trip had been worth the bother.

'Yes,' said Anselm, 'but not in the way I expected. I'd hoped to find a specific name linked to Owen Doyle, but instead I've found myself on the ground of his birth, and that has changed my outlook.'

They walked back to the foyer and Anselm paused at the display cabinet with the pictures of Industrial Bolton. In the centre was a photo of a strong-looking man, a headmaster of the school from the war years through to the twenties. Mr Anthony Lever. His ink pen and pocket watch were like relics, reminders of life before the flood of computers and the digital timepiece. Anselm's eye caught on the open book.

'*That* is a very interesting document,' said Mrs Holden.

'What is it?' asked Anselm, quietly dismayed. He'd started reading some of the entries, checking the age against the offence and the outcome.

'It's the Punishment Book. Offence and consequence are noted, just like daily attendance. Repeated infractions led to the cane. But if someone did something very serious, the entire school was obliged to witness the punishment. The boy – always a boy – was hit at the end of assembly after a short discourse on his misconduct. I once met an old man, a former pupil, who told me his trousers had been pulled down while he stood on the top step. He had to bend over while he was whacked. I misunderstood the point of the story, however. He wholly approved and went on to say that when they had the birch there was no thieving in Bolton.'

'Ah.'

'I've met other pupils who think differently. But all schools were like that back then – many far stricter than ours. The social expectation of conformity and duty was high, and rather simple. Everyone knew where they stood and what happened if you moved out of line.'

Anselm read some of the ages: eight, eleven . . . and the date on the page: February 1906. 'May I see it?'

Five minutes later Anselm was back in Mrs Holden's office. He was flushed with both excitement and compassion. Owen Doyle's name featured significantly between 1905 and 1907. And in that penultimate year before his death, so did someone else. The two were paired on no less than seven occasions for the same offence: dirty hands and nails.

Mrs Holden then checked once more the registers in which Owen Doyle's truancy had featured so significantly and there, sure enough, was the boy who, Anselm was quietly sure, had one day enlisted in The Lambeth Rifles using Doyle's name. He was called John Lindsay.

Anselm watched her industry from a very great distance. He gazed through and beyond her on to England's green and pleasant land. He thought of those many mills and the deep tunnels spreading for miles beneath the ground in search of coal. He thought of men and women who couldn't read or write, of bent heads, both English and Irish, their nationality lost in the sweat and the clatter and the grime. Labour was their nation state. And he thought of poor Owen Doyle, beaten with a stick because his parents hadn't checked his hands were clean before they went to work at four in the morning.

Chapter Thirty-One

Rebellion

1

Herbert ran to Oliver Tindall's billet, a barn cleared of animals and serving now as a surgery. The medic was lying on a camp bed, legs crossed, boots off, a newspaper held in the air like a shelter from the rain. An oil lamp on the floor sent light upwards on to the open pages. Packing cases of medical supplies lined the timber walls. Metal dishes glinted on a table covered by a white cloth.

'Oliver, there's an execution tomorrow, you know.'

'Yes. Flanagan.' He continued reading.

Herbert snatched the paper and hurled it across the room. 'He's one of ours, don't you appreciate that?'

Tindall sat up, baffled by Herbert's rage, embarrassed by the show of this type of feeling. 'Steady on, Moore, old fellow,' he said, swinging his legs around. 'The blighter did run off. Bloody hell, you sat on his court martial. I mean, I may not see the charge and parry and all that, but I see the consequences.' He paused and gathered his pride. 'You've not seen the RAP twenty minutes after the whistle . . . it's . . . it's –' indignation at Herbert's impudence burst open – 'a slaughterhouse. You lot carry on running, throwing things, pulling a trigger, stabbing and doing God knows what . . . on and on you go, but I stand *still*. I stand there while they bring the pieces back to me –' he stood up, his lips stretched tight, the cleft in his chin deep like a cut – 'I hold them in these miserable hands and their lives don't even drain away, there's nothing left . . . and I *stand* there . . . Do you hear me? . . . I stand there with cotton wool and a needle and scissors and all around me is this *screaming*: the screaming that you leave behind.' He glared at Herbert – an astonishingly different man who, seconds before, had been reading the paper – and bellowed, 'So don't *you* come in *here* and tell *me* that one of *ours* deserves my pity . . . not when he ran away.'

Herbert swayed on his feet, numbed by what he'd heard; wearied by his empathy. He looked at his own hands . . . and the finger that had pulled the trigger on Quarters. The haunted face stared out of the mud with beseeching eyes and Herbert almost collapsed. 'I'm sorry, Oliver,' he mumbled, sinking in a swoon. One hand gripped a chair back and he sat down. The face withdrew.

'So am I, old man.' The RMO spoke quietly, finding calm. 'This bloody war, I hate it. It's necessary, but I hate it. I spend my nights trying to link it all to some bigger purpose, to something beyond a battle . . . but the war won't end, I can't see the *end*.'

'Me neither,' said Herbert. His heart had raced but now it was falling back into line. 'Look, I didn't come to lecture you. Just to remind you that you're part of the detail . . . you appreciate that?'

'What?' Tindall picked up the newspaper.

'You attend the execution.'

'Do I?' He rolled up the paper into a tight tube. 'Doesn't someone from Division do that sort of thing?'

'I'm sorry, Oliver, it's you,' replied Herbert, despairing of the bureaucratic machine, its hit and miss efficiency. They should have shown the RMO the drill before sending him into action. 'You have to witness it, check that he's dead, and then write out a certificate for the file.'

'Dear God.' Oliver threw the paper on his bed and put the oil lamp on the table. He bent near the glass and raised the wick. 'Er . . . what happens if he's not?'

'Not what?'

'Dead.'

'You check and see.'

'How the hell would I know?'

'You do what doctors do.'

'Oh my God. Then what?'

'You tell the OC firing party. He takes care of any complications.'

'Yes, of course. Obvious really. Right-o. What time did Duggie say?'

'The where and the when are being revised as we speak,' said Herbert. 'Chamberlayne will let you know within the hour.'

Tindall nodded, lowering the lamp's wick a fraction. He closed one eye as if to be absolutely sure of the measurement. The light dipped with the loss of flame. 'Funny, isn't it; I've handled the RAP at harvest time but I still don't want to do this. Even though I feel nothing for the blighter, it's different, somehow.'

Herbert nodded. It was very different.

'You know, I always wanted to be a vet.'

'Yes. Goodnight, Oliver.'

'Just one thing, old man . . . none of this is your *fault*, you know. You've done your duty, that's all.'

Herbert left the medic and went in search of Father Maguire. He wasn't in his billet, or the abbey, so Herbert went back to Duggie's office. Somehow or other, all this charging around helped, as if the frenzy might, by some miracle, prevent the inevitable.

2

Chamberlayne was sitting on the edge of his desk, the telephone mouthpiece thrust against his mouth. He was listening, one foot tapping gently on the floor. Duggie sat with his legs crossed, one hand scratching a cheek. Quietly, he said, 'It's Brigade.'

'I'm afraid I can't make it any clearer,' said Chamberlayne, sympathetically. 'The Company Commanders refuse. All of them.'

Chamberlayne listened, nodding. 'I'd have thought various offences meet the bill: Mutiny, Disobedience, Scandalous Conduct—'

Pause.

'Murray, I've made a habit of never joking with intellectual subordinates; it causes untold complications, and now is not the time to make an exception. Let me try again. The officers of the eighth Battalion, Northumberland Light Infantry, refuse to organise a firing party, don't you understand? You're not going to arrest them all, are you?'

Pause.

'Good evening, Major. I'm terribly sorry but Lieutenant Colonel Hammond is engaged with Father Maguire, the Chaplain, and I'm most reluctant to interrupt their conversation. It's a spiritual matter, I believe.'

Pause.

'Indeed, Sir . . . of course, Sir . . . frequently, Sir . . . in those circumstances, might I be impertinent and offer some advice? I'm grateful, Sir. The problem is quite simple. Flanagan has been with our battalion since nineteen fifteen. He's been in action countless times. He's never taken home leave. He's one of the survivors, Sir. Good moral is not served, I respectfully suggest, by asking other veterans or the new boys to shoot him, even if – in the end – he did let down his own side.'

Pause.

'Disgraceful is the only word, Sir.'

Pause.

'Quite. You are wise, Sir. I suggest another regiment, Sir . . . I'll tell him directly, Sir . . . goodnight, Sir.'

Chamberlayne put the phone down and said, 'Major Ashcroft will handle the firing party. But we have to send the RMO. He says if the battalion hadn't been wiped out in August and we weren't due back in the line, he'd tell Pemberton immediately. As things stand, he'll let the matter drop.'

Duggie stood up, hands behind his back. He knew that his tolerance of dissent was a failure of leadership; that Pemberton would find out eventually; that his military career was probably over. 'Fine. And now, gentlemen, understand something.' His gaze jumped from Chamberlayne to Herbert and back again. 'This is my battalion. It is my pride. There is nothing else I can do for Flanagan. I've done too much already, you both know that. We must all, now, stand side by side. Flanagan will be shot tomorrow morning. We will then thrash the Lancashire Fusiliers. And we will then go back into the line and do whatever is required of us, at whatever cost.' Duggie's neck swelled with blood and his voice became spare. 'We will lead our men in the memory of those who've gone before. Flanagan may rank among them, as far as I'm concerned. Look to him in any way you like. But from now on he's an example.'

Chapter Thirty-Two

The Vigil Begins

1

Chamberlayne told Herbert that the Chaplain had gone to the cellar where Flanagan would spend his last night. On a practical note, a detail from D Company had checked out the woods referred to by Herbert. They'd followed the track and found a clearing open to the sky. A fence post had been procured from the carpenter and sunk into the ground. Unfortunately it kept falling over when leaned on, so a chair had been taken from the music depot and placed before it – rendering the timber quite useless, but, to quote Chamberlayne, an aesthetic quality had been retained that was wholly proper to the proceedings.

It was now 8.50 p.m. Herbert walked briskly towards the village school in Oostbeke. The land being so flat, his attention was drawn to the sky. A deep indigo announced the coming night, washed out in places and streaked above the trees with that fresh green found in young peas. It seemed wrong, the beauty of it, since the sky was polluted with steel. He passed the abbey and the closed-up barn and shortly nodded at the guard before the cellar steps. After the door had been unlocked Herbert entered a gloom lit by a candle.

Flanagan was sitting on a chair, his chin propped on one hand, the elbow resting on the knee like a pillar. The jaw was pushed to one side by the weight of his head. His eyes were closed, presenting a picture of resignation and powerlessness that Herbert could not bear to contemplate. He was like a king in the moments following his abdication. Herbert shook Father Maguire's hand, waiting for Flanagan's eyes to open, but they remained closed.

'I suppose I'd better go,' said Herbert to the Chaplain, all at once feeling his presence to be blindingly inappropriate. 'I'm sorry, I shouldn't have come. I just . . .'

Flanagan opened his eyes. 'No, stay, so.' He stood up and raised a hand in salute. Without a belt his trousers slipped right off his waist and he looked like a clown.

'Stop,' said Herbert, flinching.

He stepped further into the room. The walls were brick, like upstairs. The candle's flame threw the shadow back; it was like a quivering canopy over them all.

'I wish you'd got home by Christmas, Private,' said Herbert.

'Aye, me too.'

The three men were silent. Herbert sensed he'd brought the Army into the cell; that he represented its code, its requirements.

'You know, Sir, I joined without a noble thought in my head,' said Flanagan. He spoke to the system, wanting to have a last word, before its wheels rolled forward. 'I just came over with the lads. But I hadn't expected –' he shifted in his seat – 'this tearing up of the land, with us all floundering in the holes, in a fight without end.'

Herbert sighed a yes. Whenever Flanagan had spoken of 'the land' before, it was always in relation to Inisdúr. This was the first time he'd used that term when talking of the world beyond his island's shores.

Father Maguire strode behind Flanagan. Close-shaven with hair like silver wire, he had a stern reserve, save for something generous in the wide gestures of his arms. He placed two huge hands on the sides of the prisoner's shoulders and rubbed them as if the muscles had cramped and his palms were laced with ointment. 'You've done your part, my boy, so you have. You have a nobility none can see.'

Herbert realised that they were speaking English on his account. It humbled him, for their linguistic habitat was Gaelic. He'd heard them in the reserve trench beneath the rain; he'd listened to them squabble over the off-side rule.

'I want to ask you a question,' said Herbert. Apart from the chaplain's stool, there was nowhere to sit and he felt awkward, hovering with all his authority . . . his English weightiness. 'Why didn't you go home?' He spoke for the family whose names he'd heard, and the crowd who'd stood around the slip.

'Hah . . .' breathed Flanagan – Father Maguire kneaded the shoulders, pressing deep into the muscle beneath the uniform – 'I couldn't, sure, that was impossible.'

'But why?' pleaded Herbert, seeing a route of escape abandoned.

'If I'd as much as seen those three fields –' he gnawed a lip and his brow tightened – 'I'd never have come back to Flanders.'

'And no one would have been able to bring you . . . to this.' Herbert's strained face showed all he'd learned of the island. No one could have crossed from the mainland to bring Flanagan back to his unit. They'd have been stoned, like the taxman.

Flanagan nodded, and like a father the chaplain moved his warming hands on to the neck and head. 'But, you know, Sir, I wouldn't leave Major Dunne, the RSM or the new boys.'

'They know that, Joseph,' said Father Maguire, his hands gripping the shoulders again.

Herbert wanted to push down the walls, to bring fresh air into this darkening pit. Surely Muiris, Flanagan's father, the man who'd made the fields, or Róisín, a mother famed for her quilt work, surely one of them had fallen on their knees and begged him to return – in a letter or a message. He didn't know how to raise their names without wounding the man who'd never see them again.

'Since nineteen sixteen, it's been difficult for Irish soldiers,' said Father Maguire, his face dark, his spiky hair catching the candle's flare. 'There's been a rising, you know that.'

Herbert did, but it hadn't influenced his outlook on individual troops. He'd heard the odd remark from Staff Officers, functionaries away from the firing line, but not in the 8th. Staff Officers were full of that kind of thing: always in 'the know', like Tomlinson, and slightly aloof, hinting they were privy to the Field Marshal's current strategic view. The Irish battalions were first class, one gloved Colonel had said, but one has to watch the wind towards England. What had that meant? It was plain nonsense. A Captain from a cavalry regiment: 'The fact is, we're roast beef and Yorkshire pud and they're bacon and cabbage. You have to keep an eye on the kitchen.' More nonsense.

'Trust is the question,' said Father Maguire, 'here and in Ireland. Some dare not go home on leave.'

'Why?'

'It's possible they might be killed, for being in the British Army . . . on the mainland, at least. There's a place for them in London.'

Herbert hadn't known. No one had ever mentioned it to him. He looked down at the prisoner, understanding everything: Flanagan *didn't* go home because he knew he'd never come back; he *couldn't* go home, even if he wanted, because his world had turned off its axis. Flanagan had been trapped: by himself and by his people. And now *we* are going to shoot him. 'He's never taken home leave,' Chamberlayne had said to Major Ashcroft at Brigade. Where, then, had he gone? Herbert dared not ask . . . because it no longer mattered, nothing mattered. Flanagan's life was draining on to a cellar floor, like one of the wounded in the helpless arms of Oliver Tindall.

'If you'll excuse me,' Herbert said. He had to leave and yet he knew he could not keep away. 'May I return? Later?'

Father Maguire whispered something in Gaelic, a soft phrase that made Flanagan smile. 'The door is always open,' he said.

2

Herbert ran down the road towards the Divisional camp, not knowing where he was going or what he would do. But his mind searched for a lever, a switch, a spanner to throw at the cogs now moving, but there was nothing he could find. Flanagan was to be an Example. To the 8th. The whole Brigade. To the Division. To the Corps. To the Army. To the whole BEF. That was quite an honour. And no one would be watching, and no one would be remotely persuaded that they ought to fight that little bit harder.

Out of breath, Herbert came to the abbey. He pushed open the gate and passed through the white door at the end of the corridor. Staying at the back, he recovered his breath. Up there, near the little light, he'd prayed – for the first time in his life and with desperation. 'What can I do?' he said, helplessly. 'I still don't know why Flanagan went to Étaples. He went with someone from another battalion in another brigade, but he came back . . . because he wouldn't leave his comrades.'

Herbert looked right and left, to the statues of the men and women. Their heads were bowed in confident supplication despite the prevalence of tragedy. The scent of wax and fading incense seem to creep upon him, increasing its concentration. While it was soothing, Herbert felt a most suffocating responsibility for what was now unfolding. Major Ashcroft had been on to another regiment. There will have been a hell of a row, with the unfortunate CO finally wading in to give Duggie an earful. Meanwhile, a detail of sixteen soldiers will have been formed. Minutes before, any of those men were probably playing Brag or Pontoon. They, like Herbert, would now be marked for life by something quite different from the horrors of front-line fighting. Inner disgust swelled in Herbert's lungs. He quickly made for the door and the cool air of evening. If he was to do anything to save this man, the reason lay in the Étaples fiasco. It was now 10.20 p.m. He would have to go back to the cellar and ask Flanagan – beg him – in the name of Muiris and Róisín, to explain why he'd returned when Doyle had stayed away.

Chapter Thirty-Three

Muiris and Róisín

'Won't you tell him what you've done and why?' repeated Father Maguire in English. 'It's the only thing that remains to be done. You should release the man from his burden.'

'But then he'll be trapped,' said Flanagan. 'The CO will have to be told and then Lisette will be arrested . . . and maybe Doyle, if he's still there.'

'I assure you, Seosamh, *that* officer is not going to say anything to anyone. Come here, will you?'

Flanagan stood, one hand bunching the material at the front of his trousers. He dragged the chair a few feet towards the table and sat down again, leaning towards the candle. Father Maguire sat facing him. Between them, in the pool of light, was the letter for Lisette. The priest reached over with two hands, and Flanagan took them in his own. They gripped each other like in a game of strength.

'Have you written to your father?'

'No.'

'Your mother?'

'No, sure . . . how could I?'

The night before Flanagan left Inisdúr his father banged on the bedroom door. He was a big man, a man of authority, a man who knew every rock on the island. He was much respected. The mainland was unknown to him, save as a place that sent forth priests and doctors. He'd only ever rowed to another island – Inismin, where he'd met Róisín at a dance. The matchmaker had said it was perfect, for while Muiris could be obstinate like rock, Róisín had the strength of the sea.

'Here is what's yours by right, boy,' said Muiris, standing in the doorway. He held out the money promised after the argument when Seosamh had said his mind was made up. Towering by the door, Muiris was blocking the idea of any true departure.

Seosamh took the money . . . a thick wad of notes, more than he'd ever seen; he hadn't the faintest idea where his father had kept it. The paper was damp and the edges mouldy.

'Won't you stay?' asked his father, this bull of a man, weakened by something he dared not understand.

'I can't say any more,' mumbled Seosamh, feeling the chill in the money.

'Seosamh, we have three fields, our fields, your grandfather made one of them, I made the other . . . and we . . . we made the third. That one is ours.'

The seaweed had been dried on the flat rocks. They'd dragged it by cart up a track to the farm and spread out the black life-source, before descending to the cove, to haul out more weed for the drying and the dragging. They'd made endless trips, up and down, and then heaved up the sand, in sacks and with the cart. Always up, up, up, towards the flat space that captured the sun. In silence they'd raked and sifted and gently turned the growing soil. Often, when he'd woken in the morning, Seosamh had found his father carrying a rock to the field, for the wall yet to be built. A bowed man he'd been at such times, with a great stone on his shoulder.

'The fields are made,' Seosamh said.

But Muiris wanted another. For Brendan, who was listening from the corridor.

'And a man has no other needs, save a wife, a good woman, and my eye is open for you, boy.' Muiris had swelled with anticipation. 'The matchmaker has confidence.'

The Matchmaker. Old Tomás Ó Broin, a broker of fates over poitín. Seosamh hadn't appreciated that his father had made soundings.

'Are you not happy, son?' Muiris could be gentle, his big limbs incongruous with his lightness of tongue. He moved from the doorway and sat on Seosamh's bed. 'The farm, the fishing . . . is it not enough?'

Seosamh couldn't reply. He wanted his father to leave, to go back through the low door. He hated himself for rejecting this man who loved him. But their worlds were different. Seosamh wanted to cross the sea.

'If you don't talk to me, I can't help you.'

He'd said the same thing by the fire before their argument, quietly puffing his pipe, when Seosamh had said he wanted to walk for miles without sight of the sea. He may as well have spoken in English. How could Seosamh even begin to talk of Mr Drennan's map?

'Why labour on someone else's land?' pursued Muiris.

Seosamh unrolled the money. Some of the notes were stuck together. He'd have to dry them out carefully. 'It's not the labouring that's important.'

'Because there's things to be seen beyond three green fields?' added his father, like a man citing a learned poem he'd never understood. And yet, in that slight mockery, Seosamh discerned a refusal in his father: a refusal to look upon an unknown that had perhaps once attracted him.

'Yes.'

'It's that teacher, isn't it? This is Drennan's doing.'

'No,' shouted Seosamh, rising high, and angry, 'This is *my* doing.' He stabbed his chest with each word, and then his hands fell. He was penitent, but resolved to sin.

Until then, when left alone – for his father stooped beneath the door's beam and trod heavily away, striking the walls with his fists – he hadn't realised the great gulf between the rough and the smooth, between Muiris and Róisín.

Róisín's family were all from Inismin. Seosamh had many cousins and aunts over there, but one was just a name: Úna, Róisín's sister. No one mentioned her save to say, 'She's gone away'. Seosamh suspected a love story with the wrong kind of man, maybe a fling in Dublin that had turned sour. After the row by the fire, his father went out into the evening light and his mother leaned forward and gripped Seosamh's wrist. He flinched for the hand was strong from the sewing; on her lap was a quilt of russet, green and brown.

'Go, Seosamh,' she said with hushed urgency. 'Spread your wings, like Úna.'

Young Úna had gone to Boston, he learned; an act of rebellion for which there'd been no forgiveness. Seosamh looked out of the window at the bulk of his father.

'Go, my son, *go for me*,' she said, her face bright with excitement. 'And tell me what you see.'

So when Muiris had come with the money, his damp consent, and sat on the bed beneath a roof of spars, Seosamh had known all along that his mother had blessed his going; that he would leave for her, and for all the women who'd dared not step off the sand.

Father Maguire repeated his question. 'Have you written to your mother?'

'Sure, what would I say?' replied Flanagan helplessly.

He'd left Inisdúr with a sense of wonder, freed from the limitations of the island; he'd joined the army with High-Pockets, and entered a conflagration beyond his expectations. What could he tell his mother? The sights he'd seen? For all the wrong reasons, perhaps, his father had been right about the land; and so had Meg. And this was the soldier who'd met Lisette, another mother who'd blessed her son's going. And who would have him back.

Chapter Thirty-Four

Mrs Holden's brown leather shoes made a loud clip-clop down the shining lino of the corridor. Pupils stared at Anselm, shyly. Quite a few laughed and one of them opened the door that led to the foyer. Outside, Anselm following, Mrs Holden crossed a quiet road and rattled loose a bunch of keys from her handbag. Facing them was a tall building of forbidding brick. It had the feel of a foundry or a workhouse. The walls were high and blackened by the smog of another time. Several windows were covered with plywood above stone lintels like hard bottom lips.

'This is the old school,' said Mrs Holden, opening a padlock and letting a chain fall. 'It'll be demolished next year, and then we'll build a gym.' She pushed open a rusted gate and they stepped into the playground, a sloping expanse of ribbed concrete with patches of asphalt, claimed here and there by clumps of dandelion and strong wild grass.

'This is where John Lindsay learned the basics,' said Mrs Holden. 'Don't knock it too hard, Father. I think they did their best.'

'They' being the staff who'd carried an enormous responsibility: to instil the values of a parish, a nation and an empire. Clean hands, punctuality, hard work, counting, spelling, and Englishness. It must, indeed, have been difficult. The photographs in the display cabinet gave a glimpse into that world: hundreds of mill towers, tightly packed houses, women in clogs, men's faces blanked by coal, wide smiles for the camera; and, of course, the Punishment Book.

Mrs Holden rattled another key and opened a side door into the school. A long corridor stretched ahead with classrooms on either side. The ceiling was high, but not high enough to contain the rush of memory between the flaking walls. Anselm was entranced by the imagined hum, the fall of feet, the shaved heads . . .

Lindsay was the younger, following Doyle, the big lad. John and Owen. One looks up; the other looks down. They're bound as strong as blood. They run outside, with a kick to the door. They're off, before the Head catches them. They're always running and laughing . . . until Owen falls ill. He dies aged twelve and John looks up to an empty sky to mumble his name.

Walking down the corridor, past the half-open doors, Anselm told Mrs Holden the full explanation behind his visit to the parish of St Stephen, beginning with the encounter among the aspens. Her feet landed precisely, clip-clopping up stairs, along other corridors and past other doors. The entire building seemed to be listening and watching. Hundreds of tiny ears and wide eyes. They all remembered Doyle and Lindsay. Who could forget them?

Doyle died in 1908. Kenneth Spinks LMSSA said so. The father, Colum, had been present. But what had happened to little John Lindsay? For a while he keeps up appearances in the Punishment Book but by 1915 he's no longer a local boy. He's gone to London. He joins The Lambeth Rifles. But it's 'Owen Doyle' that's stamped on his tags, the one true friend he ever had, dead seven years earlier.

'He's in a right bit of bother, then,' said Mrs Holden, jingling for another key. 'Otherwise he'd have used his own name. Didn't want anyone to find him, did he?' She opened a large door, the old main entrance to the school, and said, 'The top step.'

The top step. The two boys had known it well.

For a moment, Anselm lost his bearings. He paused to catch hold of a sudden outpouring of pitying comprehension. Lindsay followed Owen Doyle even to the gates of hell, the top step at school; and when he got to Belgium he followed Joe Flanagan out of the fire. It's the same story, a lost boy forever being led. But you wouldn't have known. He'd got manly tattoos on each knuckle. He'd have been a bragger, more than likely. To hide the pit of insecurity and self-hatred that comes with misfortune, stunted talent and public humiliation.

Anselm went outside into the cold, on to the stage where the unruly and disobedient were admonished to change their ways. They'd been given every chance. The rules were on the notice board. The rest could do with a damn good warning.

'Each time it's two Irish lads against the world and all it can throw at them,' said Anselm, surveying the concrete, seeing the host of boys and girls neatly lined up, class by class with their teacher. Mr Lever had probably given a little speech.

'I don't want to break your stride, Father,' said Mrs Holden, kindly, 'but I don't think "Lindsay" is an Irish name.'

Not caring, or at least not registering the significance of the remark, Anselm looked to the new school and the sound of children at play. We are making progress, he thought, fierily. Things do get better. We don't beat or shoot those who fail. He watched the bobbing heads and listened to the cries.

And then, as if a friend had popped out of the crowd, Anselm recognised an important truth. He'd seen it once in his sleep, but it had vanished when he woke, leaving him reaching out to a sort of banging window.

'Mrs Holden,' he said, controlling his excitement, 'do you have a record of John Lindsay's date of birth?'

'It'll be in a register. Everything's in a register.'

Anselm all but led the way back to Mrs Holden's office. He walked quickly, wanting her to rush with the locks while he fanned the flames of a growing certainty. They passed through the foyer to more children's shyness and laughter, and moments later Mrs Holden opened a ledger from 1907, the year John Lindsay enrolled at St Stephen's Primary School. After some flipping of paper she pointed to the day, month and year, written in black ink.

They looked at each other, soberly understanding another facet to a boy's life. Anselm felt surprise, too, because Mrs Holden seemed deeply moved. And that moved Anselm. For this woman, like all great teachers, carried close to her heart the life and aspirations of a community, the open future of its children and the tragedies of its past.

Chapter Thirty-Five

The Nightingales Sang

1

Herbert pushed past the sentry at the top of the steps without even a nod of acknowledgement, as if his presence was an offence to his eye. He averted his head while the keys rattled in the lock. As soon as he entered the cellar, Flanagan stood up, clutching his trousers. He was bowed like a dog struck for having barked, his head low to one side.

'Please, please, don't stand for me, ever again,' said Herbert.

Father Maguire spoke low in Gaelic over the table. His arms lay flat, one on either side of the candle, reaching across to Flanagan's side. The priest rose and pointed at his chair: it was almost like an instruction to Herbert and he obeyed.

'Private,' said Herbert looking through the flame, 'there is something I must know.'

He wanted to call him Joseph but that simply wasn't possible – not because of their difference in rank, but because the executioner's lance-jacks don't call a victim by his Christian name; it offends the nature of their relationship. But Herbert spoke as a penitent.

'We both know that I condemned you.'

Flanagan's face was only partly visible because Herbert was hiding behind the brightness of the candle. But at the heart of the penumbra he could clearly see the closed lips, the uneven growth around the chin and cheeks.

'Please don't die without telling me what I've done,' he pleaded, covering his face with one hand. He'd meant to ask directly about

Étaples, but a deeper incomprehension had leapt from a dark, anxious place of Herbert's mind.

Father Maguire's footsteps sounded on the flags. He leaned over the table and drew the candle to one side, clearing the space between Herbert and Flanagan. His feet sounded again and he moved into the darkness of a corner.

Flanagan leaned on the table, arms folded. His head remained drooped and angled.

'I came to France with a bunch of Irish lads. They're all dead, now. I watched them go, one by one. High-Pockets O'Brien was the last. A tall fella. I found him sitting on a shell hole like a man reading a book. Then I saw he'd been halved at the waist. He looked a bit surprised, you know, as if to say, "Jasus, I've lost some height."' Flanagan licked his lips and cleared his throat. 'Yes, he was the last. And then, in the spring, we buried a field of men. English, Scots, Irish, Germans. We put their tags in baskets off a mule. A pannier. It was my job to count them. I moved them from one bag to the other. Two thousand three hundred and fourteen. Clink, clink, clink –' Flanagan moved a hand from left to right, his eyes wide with pain – 'and when I got to the end, and the bag was empty, I looked inside . . . and I knew that I was going to join the pile. That it was only a matter of time.'

Herbert, too, had lived for a long time with the expectation of dying. It was numbing. And, for many, ultimately depraving. The bouts of drinking and sex in the base camps were just so many last gasps, brutal outbursts from a desire to live. Since Herbert's upbringing discouraged any conduct that might produce embarrassment, he settled for depression in the Officers' Club. But he hadn't gone as far as Flanagan. The Irishman had crossed a line from expectation to a kind of certainty.

'And then, back in June, Sir, we were in the front line trenches, ready to fight for the Messines Ridge,' said Flanagan. 'It was three o'clock in the morning with a high moon. Major Dunne lay beside me and whispered, "Look ahead Flanagan –" his watch was in his hand – "you're about to see something wonderful, something beyond your imagination." We'd only just been told about the mines beneath the German front line. "Any second now . . ." said Mr Dunne. And do you know, Sir, then, at that moment . . . I heard nightingales singing in a wood. I heard a song. I stopped breathing to listen. It was like a sound from another world, real like this one, but only just out of reach. Surely someone's warned them, I thought. Surely they know . . . nothing can sing *like that* in a place *like this* . . . and then the ground began to tremble and shake, pitching like a boat between waves, and *whaaaaaa* . . .' Flanagan whispered the explosion, his hands rising from the surface of the table, his mouth gaping. '*Whaaaaaa* . . . the land lifted up. Do you remember it, Sir? The flame and the smoke and the wind? I'd never seen anything like it in my life. The land high in the sky, and then falling slowly back . . .' Flanagan's arms came down, till they were flat, one hand on top of the other. 'Later in the day, after we'd taken the Ridge, I looked into a crater the size of a lake without water. The clay was blue. Gas from the cordite was still rising from its veins and everywhere lay men with their eyes open, dead men with their limbs bent in strange angles, like clowns . . . bunkers the size of houses back home, upturned and split open . . . it was hell without demons or a devil . . . just smoke and grey uniforms and all these eyes wide open like moons.'

The men in Herbert's Company had been aghast with exhilaration. The war had to end, someone had said. Their own dead had been avenged. One spoke of planting a flag. The German front line had literally disappeared in a matter of seconds.

'That day, Sir, I discovered something else,' said Flanagan, head sinking slightly lower. 'The war has to be fought, I don't doubt that, Sir. I never have done. But it was the sight of the *land* torn up like that, and men who hadn't blinked lying among lumps of clay . . . I couldn't see them as enemies any more.' His confusion made him shift on the stool. 'If I was going to join them, I wanted my death to have a meaning.'

Flanagan couldn't finish. He joined his hands and Herbert almost grabbed them, to squeeze out the connection with Étaples.

'Tell him, Seosamh,' came Father Maguire's voice from the darkness. 'Go on, son.'

Flanagan for once looked at Herbert – as he'd done at his trial: with the tentative confidence of mutual understanding. 'After I left Mr Dunne with the RMO I was on my way back to Black Eye Corner when I came across one of The Lambeth Rifles. He was finished, Sir, couldn't stand up. He'd twice run off already and been sentenced to death. But this time he'd strayed into our lines. He'd easily have been picked up.'

Herbert frowned. He flushed hot. He'd been there, in the rain . . . when Flanagan had spoken to Father Maguire while some kid crouched weeping against the trench.

'You helped him escape?' said Herbert, in disbelief, his voice straining over a whisper.

'I did.'

'You took him to Étaples?'

'Yes.'

'So he'd avoid another court martial?'

Flanagan nodded.

'So *he* wouldn't be shot,' Herbert shouted.

Flanagan didn't respond.

'And then you came back . . . knowing that *you* . . .'

Bewildered, Herbert bent his own head to look up into Flanagan's face, but Flanagan's eyes were lowered. Squinting towards the darkness, Herbert tried to find Father Maguire, to understand what this wild story really meant because it still didn't make sense to him, but the priest was a vague shape within the shadow, a presence with arms folded tight.

'But why him?'

'Joseph, speak,' said the priest.

Herbert lost his patience. He kicked back his chair and stumbled towards Father Maguire. 'Tell me yourself,' he whispered. 'If there's the slightest chance I can help this soldier I need to know what happened and why.'

'You can't do anything,' said the priest.

'I'm not waiting until dawn to see you proven right.' His desperation made his whispering lower but harsh. Leaning forward, he felt the rasp of the priest's cheek. 'Please tell me what this death really means.'

* * *

By the time Herbert reached Chamberlayne's office it was midnight. The adjutant was clearly drunk though his speech remained as smooth as ever. He guessed that Army HQ was about an hour and half away and produced a map, identifying the location of a chateau outside a village. Twenty minutes later Herbert was galloping down a lane skirting more fields of hops, their frames high and crowded by foliage. The moon was bright as it had been at Messines. The stars flickered like phosphorescence in water. The entire landscape was like pewter with etchings of woods, low farmhouses and drowsy cattle.

General Osborne had helped the Moore family once before; hopefully he would do so again, and this time for a cause more worthy.

Chapter Thirty-Six

To Break a Vow?

Clasping his trousers, Flanagan shuffled to the bed. He lay down, weak from fear, wanting to vomit but having nothing to draw up from the pit in his stomach. He closed his eyes and wrapped both arms around himself. Ah, I would be held, he thought. I would have arms around me, now.

As a boy, his mother had stroked his hair at night, brushing it back off the forehead with her hand. She'd never spoken, they'd just watched each other in the darkness, the sound of the sea crashing on the rocks below, a wind whistling over the young fields that held the seed. Her warm hand, soft despite the farm work, had slowly smoothed his forehead and to this sacrament of touching he had fallen asleep. The sea's thunder had roused him in the morning and he'd always been surprised to find that he was alone. It had been a lesson: that one day this hand would be withdrawn, and he would meet the night as a man.

'Move over,' said Father Maguire.

Flanagan edged towards the wall. The priest lay down beside him.

'Give me your hand, son.'

They held hands. Father Maguire's touch wasn't as firm as usual. When he'd gripped Flanagan's shoulders he'd been a sculptor managing clay, but now he was tender, as if his strength had always been a bluff.

'You said nothing to Mr Moore of Lisette,' said the priest.

'No.'

'Would you like me to explain?'

'Yes.'

He thought of Lisette on her knees, begging him to stay. She had a brother who worked on the docks in Boulogne. Flanagan could have hidden in the cellar with Doyle and waited for a safe passage to England. But the boys had been waiting for him at Black Eye Corner.

'I'll go to Inisdúr,' said Father Maguire, his grip tightening.

'Thank you.' Flanagan thought of the rocks near Meg's cove. From the cliff top, on a misty day, you couldn't see the waves below. The ocean was like a basin of milk near the boil. 'Will the army tell them I was shot for desertion?'

'No. They'll say you died of wounds. Nothing more.'

'Good.'

Though Muiris and Róisín wouldn't give a second thought to the British or their laws, a shameful death would still crush them. They wouldn't pay their taxes, but they'd be mortified if dragged to court on a summons.

'What shall I say to them?' asked Father Maguire.

Flanagan thought for a long time. The candle was guttering. Bricks danced overhead, the meandering salt lines bright and unreal.

'Tell my father I've returned to the land, and my mother that I saw wonderful things beforehand . . . unimaginable things. That I heard a nightingale on a summer's evening. And tell Mr Drennan I died a rebel.'

It wasn't quite the protest the old Fenian would have dreamed of, but to his own mind Flanagan had made a stand nonetheless: in this place of chance and brutal uncertainties, he had chosen the manner of dying: and it had purpose; it had a meaning.

'Seosamh?'

'Yes?'

'Don't hold out any hope. There's nothing to be done. No one can help you now. I'm sorry to speak like this . . .'

'I know.'

'Mr Moore has lost his senses, and when he returns to them he'll understand what you've done.'

Lisette. Did Lisette understand why he'd come with Owen Doyle, of all people; why he'd brought him to her? He thought of the hair he'd only touched once. It had been so very soft. This was a longing the matchmaker well understood. It was his business. 'A man has need for a companion, Seosamh,' he'd said. 'Don't be carried away with books.' Beetle eyes, he had. 'There's flesh and there's paper.' A gambler he was, on horses and all four-footed things that crawled upon the earth. Flanagan hadn't known his father had made soundings, that the matchmaker had been to see the fields. When Flanagan had walked down to the slip, the barley had been lush with promise. Did Lisette understand? Did she understand that Flanagan had gambled the trial, and lost, but won in another way?

'Father?'

'Yes, son?'

'Will you ask Mr Moore to visit Lisette? I think he can explain to her why I came back; and maybe she can explain why I ran away. Would you do that for me, so?'

'That I will.'

Outside boots fell hard on the flags, coming closer. A lone marcher came ahead. The sentry stamped his foot. A rifle butt struck the ground. Orders were spoken with brittle authority. Keys rattled.

'Father?'

'Yes?'

'I'm frightened.'

The priest's grip was so tight that Flanagan's knuckles crunched.

'They're early,' said Father Maguire, thickly.

Both men swung around on the bed and stood up as the door banged open. The candle flickered, casting light upon an officer. His Sam Browne belt glistened. A cap's nib covered the forehead and the eyes were black.

'Flanagan, out.' It was Captain Chamberlayne's voice. 'I have no intention of using this firearm,' he observed, holding a Webley & Scott with two fingers as though it were wet and sticky, 'but I shall happily despatch you if you behave in a manner remotely unbecoming a member of the eighth Battalion. The same stipulation applies to you, Father, though I appreciate yours is a Divisional appointment. Either way, is that understood?'

Flanagan flung a look to Father Maguire but he, too, was baffled.

'I said, OUT,' repeated the Captain, leaning against the wall, eyes lifted high.

Flanagan walked up the steps, his left hand gripping his trousers. At the top the sentry moved to one side, his rifle lowered, the bayonet blade dull in the moonlight.

'He's more windy than I am, Flanagan,' said the Captain by his ear, 'so I wouldn't scare him if I were you. Stop right there.'

Flanagan's eyes rapidly became accustomed to the night. The moon was high and nearby cloud shone with the same silver radiance. Ahead of him stood a line of men shoulder to shoulder . . . none with a helmet or cap. His heart beat viciously and the muscle in his bladder fluttered. 'Can I relieve myself?'

'Absolutely,' said the Captain. 'Take your time . . . in fact, I think I might join you.'

After a short trip into a shadow Flanagan was back before the sentry with the lowered bayonet. Captain Chamberlayne appeared at his side, pistol once more held between two fingers. He swayed slightly and said, 'Private, the men here gathered represent the interests of your battalion. They are the proud remnants of your section. With others they will play the Lancashire Fusiliers, but they will do so in your name. Now they wish to receive your handshake.'

Each of the men who'd waited near Black Eye Corner for Flanagan's return came forward and took his hand: Stan Gibbons, 'Pickles' Pickering, Tommy Nugent, 'Chips' Hudson, and the RSM, Francis Joyce. Mr Chamberlayne handed round cigarettes and then his lighter scraped, the flame revealing each face.

'Have your got your head around the off-side rule yet, Joe?' asked Pickles.

'Sure, it's a crazy notion,' pouted Flanagan. 'Ruins the game's flow.'

The banter ground to a halt. No one else could speak. They stood huddled and awkward, blowing smoke, tiny red lights whipping through the darkness.

'Listen, Joe,' muttered Joyce, 'none of us think you left your mates. We don't know what you did, but you were never a slacker, and never a deserter.'

The rest added their strong agreement, thumping Flanagan's shoulder, shoving his back, the rough gestures of desperate friendship.

'You went off-side, mate,' quipped Stan.

They laughed and Captain Chamberlayne nodded at the RSM. The men shook Flanagan's hand again and, before he could think of anything to express the scale of his emotion, they were dark shapes heading away from the school.

'I know you've made a vow of some kind,' said the Captain, 'but this may ease things in the hours to come.' He reached into his jacket and pulled out a bottle of whisky. 'Start drinking at half past four. That's not advice. It's an order.'

Flanagan took the bottle by the neck. 'Thank you, Sir,' he muttered. Not that far away he could just make out the road cutting through the flat fields towards the abbey. Joyce and the others were a bulk of huddled shadow upon it, crawling towards the camp; but another shape moved, opposite the school gates; a figure stepped out from behind a wall. Whoever it was didn't budge another inch. He just watched.

'Sir, would you pass on a message to Mr Hammond?' said Flanagan.

'Yes. What is it?'

'Tell him there are lots of Flanagans in the army.'

Turning his back to the silver sky and the moon and the range of stars, Flanagan descended the steps. When the cellar door had been locked shut Flanagan could just hear the Captain addressing Corporal Mackie. 'Remember what I said. This didn't happen. I may be drunk, but the RSM and his boys are sober, and they can be very nasty this side of no-man's-land.'

Father Maguire tipped the candle to drain the wax and the flame spread along the wick, lifting the light. Flanagan, feeling unsteady and bewildered, sat down on his side of the table. They each looked at the bottle between them: 'Old Orkney'. An officer's brand.

'Well, now,' said the priest, his mind made up, but seeking permission. 'Do we break our vow?'

Flanagan heard a crashing in his mind as Mr Drennan clattered down the steps to kick down the door. He imagined an almighty scuffle with the sentry, and the Fenian rising victorious with the keys held high. 'Now is the time, boy,' the phantom said. 'You have brought the pink lands to their knees, now drink to their everlasting destitution.'

'No,' said Flanagan, no longer frightened – at least not in the same way. 'I leave it to Mr Moore.'

Chapter Thirty-Seven

Pity the Disordered Mind

Army HQ was located behind ornamental gates and at the end of a sweeping drive: a manorial dwelling with several weathervanes black against the night-blue sky. They were all pointing in different directions. Sentries positioned at both the gates and by the huge front door checked Herbert's name and purpose, the last refusing him entry until a Colonel in full uniform appeared, bustling with importance and exhaustion in equal measure. On hearing Herbert's demand he refused to disturb the army commander, be he known to the family or not. Instead he woke up the senior staff officer, a Major General, who eventually stood before Herbert resplendent in burgundy slippers and a capacious dressing gown, the hairs on his legs standing proud as if they were scared of the body from which they grew. Rousing him had not been a wise move.

'What the bloody hell do you think you're doing?'

'It is a matter of the utmost urgency, Sir.'

'Damn your urgency. Your appearance is a disgrace.' His greying hair stood on end too.

'Sir?'

'Your boots . . . your buttons . . .' He couldn't speak any more because of his indignation. 'What rabble do you come from? Which regiment—'

'It's all right, Lionel,' said a voice with studied patience. 'Send him up.'

Standing at the top of a magnificent staircase, blocked by his outraged staff officer, was the General himself, one hand on the balustrade. He, like the Colonel at the door, was still in uniform, though the jacket was open revealing his braces – a deplorable state of affairs that would have broken Lionel had he turned round to honour his master's voice. Instead he glowered at Herbert's cuffs and collar, snorted, and marched through a pair of double doors held open by a mute Captain who closed his eyes as the wind swept past.

'Take a seat,' said General Osborne, closing his office door and pointing towards a hearth lit by a fire burned low. 'It's safe now, the lion is back in his den.'

Herbert had met his army commander several times, but only two occasions stood out as important now: the first was at Sandhurst before receiving his commission, the second was at Keswick when his parents had decided to show Colonel Maude what they were made of. The General hadn't changed in the slightest since that last encounter. His lower jaw seemed slightly advanced, suggesting a constitutional determination; the pencil moustache highlighted an uneven mouth; hair parted in the centre showed precision as his crowning trait.

'You said your errand is of an urgent character?'

'Yes, Sir.'

The furnishings were limited to the essentials: a desk with a black ledger in the middle; a large oval dining table covered with Intelligence Reports; another desk to the right of the General's, occupied by a typewriter; and a variety of chairs, closely arranged by the fireplace, into one of which Herbert slumped while the General poured them both a large glass of whisky.

'Your father is well?' said General Osborne.

'I hope so, Sir.'

'Your mother?'

'She too, I hope, is well.'

'You've been back to see them?'

'No, Sir. I won't go home until the war is over.'

The General handed him the glass, but drew back just as Herbert was about to take it. 'I think you ought to visit them. The winning is not immediately in view.'

Herbert gulped the whisky and the General sat directly facing him, legs crossed.

'How can I help you?' General Osborne's face barely moved. The effect was of a man wholly concentrating on a decision made or yet to be made, all other impulses subordinate to the mental processes involved; no gesture was wasted; his gaze was both calculating and assured. In his mid-fifties, he was much the same age as Herbert's father, though the regiment had only held on to one of them.

'Sir, I sat on a court martial,' said Herbert, leaning forward in his seat. 'The man was found guilty and condemned to death. The sentence was confirmed and he will be shot in three hours. I think this is a mistake.'

General Osborne made no movement – either to stop or continue the argument – so Herbert pressed on.

'Sir, I have got to know this man. He is a dreamer. A man of susceptibility. I believe he's been rattled by what he saw at Messines last June. He was very shaken by the other side's casualties. And now it's as though he's lost his wits while apparently remaining sane.'

The General permitted himself a trace of a smile and instantly Herbert knew that he was thinking of Lionel. But his eyes were grave and unfeeling, his intellect locked on to Herbert's submission. 'You are speaking of the Irishman?'

'Yes, Sir.'

'He talks of the island he comes from as though it were a land of make-believe, somewhere his mind has run to, away from the ghastly realities of front-line duty. He's mesmerising to listen to and somehow he dredges your own memory, stirring your own sense of loss, whatever it might be, and he brings you back to what you'd rather forget –' all this was true; it had caused Herbert pain, and on that account he'd cut short every conversation, wanting to know more, but scared that Flanagan would undermine his own resolve – 'but I've come to think, Sir, that he's not fully responsible for his actions – not then, not now, not any more.'

'This is the soldier who may or may not have gone to Étaples with another Irishman?' The General looked at Herbert's glass, and Herbert noticed that it was empty – he had no recollection of having tasted anything, though his throat was burning.

'Yes, Sir, and that is the point, Sir; this Irishman, Flanagan, is no deserter. He *did* go to Étaples with a kinsman. But he was *not* avoiding any special duty. He was fulfilling another kind of obligation –' the General took Herbert's glass – 'a duty recognised by a disordered mind, Sir.'

The General poured Herbert a larger whisky than last time. His own stood untouched on a graceful three-legged table.

'Sir,' said Herbert, 'Flanagan took someone to Étaples who'd twice been condemned by an FGCM and spared the ultimate sanction.'

The General produced a handkerchief from his pocket, saying, 'Yes, and twice I'd recommended that he be shot.'

'Sir, that other soldier was not a *man*.'

'Really?' The tone was even, not mocking.

'No, sir, he was a *boy*. Someone who should never have put on a uniform.'

General Osborne's face remained expressionless for a very long time. Revealing nothing of his thinking, he said, 'Was this Flanagan medically examined?'

'Not that I'm aware of, Sir.'

'You say you got to know him? That you spoke with him about his island?'

'Yes, Sir, I did,' replied Herbert, not daring to show any eagerness.

'In your judgement,' asked the General, reaching for his glass, 'would it have made any difference to the trial if he had been so examined?'

Herbert didn't want to reply: because it would involve him closing the one door that had just begun to open. But the truth was, an examination by Tindall back then would have achieved nothing. Just like an examination now would not change the direction of the machine moving towards Flanagan. All that Tindall would conclude was that his patient was completely sane, as normal as any other man in the regiment. But in that, he would have been wrong. Blinking rapidly, his mouth aflame, Herbert acknowledged that he, himself, was the man who'd lost his senses . . . along with Duggie, Chamberlayne, Joyce, Elliot and the Major General in his pyjamas. Flanagan had recovered his wits. His was not a make-believe world. It was the world no one else dare look upon or think about – ironically what they were fighting for, what each side was fighting for, shorn of someone else's imperialism and, what did that ranting teacher call it? The politics of tenure?

'No, Sir,' said Herbert. His throat burned and again he saw an empty glass in his hand. 'There is nothing medically wrong with Flanagan. He was in complete control of all his faculties.'

'He is sane, then?'

'Yes, Sir, he is completely sane.' It sounded like an unforgivable offence. The world had turned upside down and Herbert's mind reeled. We will shoot a man at dawn for having rushed headlong towards his humanity; for having reclaimed it from the barbarity of war and the monstrous scale of killing. 'But he took a boy out of the war, if that is madness.'

General Osborne had still not tasted a drop of whisky. He held the glass more like a prop in a serious drama, a gentleman who'd never taste the real stuff for fear he might fluff his lines. 'Why have you come to me?'

'Because you are a man who gives unworthy men a second chance.'

Chapter Thirty-Eight

Father Andrew, the Prior, called the meeting because he believed strongly in communal discernment when resolving a problem. Sometimes, in Larkwood's life, these gatherings simply traversed the obvious (to the irritation of all) but at others, a breakthrough would take place, often through the surprising contribution of someone judged insensitive to the matter in hand. And so a week after Anselm's return from Bolton, the Prior invited Sarah and David Osborne to Larkwood. He wanted them to be present when Martin Reid shared the outcome of his research into the background of John Lindsay. They were also members of the loose community that had gathered around the trial of Joseph Flanagan.

For the meeting Anselm prepared a fresh dossier. All the participants were given a copy and brought to the large parlour. There were two bottles of water on the table but no glasses, an unfortunate Gilbertine touch to what might have been a fairly impressive performance. Anselm brought with him the *Manual of Military Law* as a kind of relic, conscious that no one was likely to open the cover.

The Prior thanked everyone for attending. 'I seek your patience and your help,' he said, eyebrows bristling, his gaze roving and kind. 'We've come to an understanding of the past. Perhaps it is flawed. If so, correct us. We don't know what step to take next. If you can, guide us.' He raised a hand to Anselm.

Anselm began towards the middle of the story.

He began with the first certainties of the matter: Joseph Flanagan had left his section at or about midnight on the 26th of August escorting a wounded officer. By 1.45 a.m. he'd reached the Regimental Aid Post and by 2.00 a.m. he'd set off on the return journey.

Anselm unrolled the map showing the Ypres Salient and the disposition of the British troops. 'We also know that a soldier named Doyle, a private in The Lambeth Rifles, was with his unit immediately behind the Northumberland Light Infantry, and that he and his comrades were due to follow through the assault when the order was given. Doyle, however, lost both his nerve and his senses, seemingly at the last minute. He was noted to be absent at roughly one a.m. I say lost his senses because he didn't run backwards and neither did he head sideways . . . he went *ahead*, drifting – I imagine – directly into the return path of Flanagan.' Anselm pointed to an imagined spot, somewhere between the British front line and Black Eye Corner. 'I picture a very frightened and disorientated individual, not least because this runaway had nowhere left to go. He was, I imagine, just waiting to be caught.'

Whatever the nature of that meeting, at 3.49 a.m. Doyle was registered as injured at the NLI Aid Post – the place Flanagan had left an hour and half earlier with two field dressings. 'One of the important questions is what was said at this accidental meeting. I'll return to that in a moment, but now, I think, we should hear something about the person Flanagan met: Owen Doyle, or, to be precise, John Lindsay. He was born in nineteen hundred and one. Would you please turn to page thirty-two in the bundle.'

Everyone did.

'These are entries taken from a Punishment Book.'

The key date was August 1908, Anselm said, when Owen Doyle died from TB. Before then Lindsay's offending was broadly limited to comportment and cleanliness; afterwards he graduated to theft and all manner of insolence. 'Here, aged seven onwards, we no longer have a scamp but a very angry boy. We next hear about him in the courts.' And with that cue, Anselm left the narrative in Martin's hands.

The Military Specialist began a quick preamble, explaining that upon Anselm's call with the name of Lindsay, he'd checked the borstal records and found a mine of information. Much of it had been faxed through and formed part of the bundle. His refined enunciation gave strong contrast to the Prior's Glaswegian brogue.

'John Lindsay's criminal record lacks variety and imagination,' said Martin, as though he was assessing a cadet for promotion, 'but the boy can't be faulted for application or perseverance. Almost without exception it is shopbreaking and theft. He did the same butcher's four times, on the last occasion being apprehended by the proprietor who'd been waiting with a meat cleaver. Lindsay was, I suspect, incompetent. He probably stole from himself and smiled with half his face for having got away with it.'

Martin took out a reproduced photograph from a folder and held it up. 'This was taken in nineteen fifteen after he received a three-year custodial sentence from a court in Bolton.'

It was, Anselm agreed, a face that could try to deceive itself: one eyebrow rose while the other was level; he was old while still a youth. The black hair was smooth, the forehead marked and rough.

'Lindsay, however, did not serve that period of detention,' continued Martin. 'He escaped from the court and was never seen again. Interestingly, the borstal authorities guessed correctly. The file contains a note to the effect that Lindsay, like so many others, had probably enlisted under a false name. We now know that he joined the army in London at the end of that year, on December twenty-ninth, giving his age as eighteen.'

'When he was, in fact, fourteen,' added Sarah. She'd carried out the calculation as soon as Anselm revealed Lindsay's date of birth. Like a tutor marking an essay, she'd written the number in a margin and circled it twice.

'Which itself is interesting,' began David, addressing the Prior. 'Conscription came into force in January nineteen sixteen. Underage enlistment would have been very difficult after that date, because a birth certificate was required and the National Register was used by the authorities to summon the flower of England.' Turning to Anselm, he said, 'This Lindsay dashed for cover and made it just in time. But from then on, he was in serious trouble. As far as the army was concerned his age was that given on attestation.'

A general discussion broke out. But Sarah did not contribute.

Sitting beside Anselm, she'd discreetly opened the *Manual of Military Law*. The cover was only half raised so Anselm couldn't see what had caught her interest.

Surely Lindsay could have revealed his true age, argued the Prior. He'd need someone to vouch for him back home, replied Martin. No point, added David. The War Office wrote various orders to weed out the young, but there were *tens of thousands* of boy soldiers. It was an open secret. Martin agreed, tentatively observing that they grew easily into the job. According to the records they were good at it, too. Top class snipers. Adapted easily to trench conditions . . .

. . . and all the while Sarah stared at something in the Manual. She let the cover fall and then looked at the ceiling, pursuing her thoughts.

'. . . I don't justify it,' Martin stressed to David, very calmly, 'but one has to look at the time from its time and against the demands of the time. The point is, Lindsay never revealed his true age at either court martial. You can't blame the army if they didn't know.'

The Prior called the meeting to order with a gentle patting of the table. He'd felt the growing heat. He knew that frayed tempers simply frayed judgement, and friendships. 'How old was John Lindsay, then, at the time he met Joseph Flanagan in no-man's-land?'

'Sixteen,' replied Martin.

'And he would have been shot, if caught?'

'Without much doubt,' said Martin after a short delay.

The Prior joined his fingertips, elbows on the table, a characteristic gesture somewhere between prayer and thinking.

'This, then, is the boy that Joseph Flanagan took to Étaples. I believe that young Lindsay had told Flanagan his age, and that he'd twice been condemned, seeking no help but just a measure of understanding. Only, of course, he didn't know what sort of man was listening to him.' He knotted his fingers and laid his chin on his thumbs. 'Anselm . . . what do you think he was like?'

Uncertainly, because it is always difficult to talk of inner journeys, even ones that are not your own, Anselm sketched out Flanagan's possible route: a gradual . . . weakening, or maybe an *awakening* . . . that had begun with the burial of the dead in the spring and ended with the chance meeting with Lindsay. 'In June he goes back into the line and immediately suffers a kind of relapse. To his superiors it's "nerves" again but I wonder if Flanagan simply *saw* things differently. Faced with what was once familiar, he shivers – for it is no longer the same thing in his eyes. But, oddly, he has not, in fact, lost his courage: remember, having got to Étaples, he came back to the battle from which he'd apparently run away. The only explanation, then, is that Flanagan chose to save Lindsay, and returned to face the probable consequences . . . the very consequences that would have finished off Lindsay once and for all.'

No one spoke.

'The June reference is interesting,' volunteered David, not wishing to break the hush. He leafed through the bundle and then, for a moment, he read quietly. 'Yes, here we are. Page twenty-six. This is Flanagan's Battalion War Diary. He was at Messines. The greatest man-made explosion in history took place at ten past three in the morning on the seventh of June.'

Tunnellers, he explained, had placed twenty-odd mines beneath the German positions, in all about a million tons of high explosive Ammonal. When they were simultaneously detonated Elgar heard the explosion in his Sussex garden. 'It must have been *apocalyptic*.'

Anselm vaguely remembered some phrases from Flanagan's defence at his trial. He opened his own bundle and, without introduction, read out the passage noted by Major Glanville, the court's president, who would presently meet his own death. '"It was terrible dark, raining like it did back home, when a load comes off the sea, after weeks of the gathering. The sky and the waves would join up, so, and then for days it would pour, or rather everything returned to water. The land was part of the air."'

The land was part of the air. Anselm repeated the phrase to himself several times, as he had done since that first, surprised reading at the national archives. The April burials had turned out to be a tilling of the inner soil. But at Messines, Flanagan had seen something very different: he had seen the innocence of his infancy rise into the air; and when it came down again, he was an utterly changed man; and a man resolved.

'I think there is greatness here,' said the Prior, letting his smouldering gaze move around the room. 'Joseph Flanagan saved a boy's life and when he faced a trial for his own, he said nothing.'

David was thinking hard, one hand against his balding head. With a glance at his daughter he said, 'I think there's an additional perspective, and it must have been apparent to Flanagan at the time, if not anyone else.' He spoke deliberately, faintly nodding at each person around the table. 'This is the story of an Irishman who saved an English boy from the British Army.'

The only sound in the parlour came from the woods close to the monastery. Anselm looked into the blue and green shadows, not quite hearing the singing of the birds. 'And yet,' he said, 'Doyle was to die while Flanagan survived.'

In a gathering-in voice, a final voice, a strong voice that submitted itself to those who listened, the Prior said, 'Has anything been left unsaid? Have we misunderstood any matter of importance?'

Silence and a shaking of heads united everyone present.

'Does anyone have an idea of the step we might take next?' The Prior's eyes were sharp with hope.

Doubt passed remorselessly from Martin to David. They lifted empty hands and apologised, for the Prior had a way of asking questions that made you want to have an answer.

'I have a suggestion,' said Sarah.

She had been a restrained presence throughout the entire meeting. She'd read the bundle closely enough, but with a subtle dissatisfaction, as if something else ought to be there. And she'd let the spat on boy soldiers run between Martin and her father without contributing a single remark. It was a grave subject, and one that ought to have attracted her attention. Anselm's conclusion was that her mind had raced ahead to what might be done, and, having seen nothing, she'd become impatient to leave. He'd been quite wrong.

'Why not ask this fellow?'

She opened the *Manual of Military Law* and took out the letter that had been found in Herbert's breast pocket.

'Harold Shaw of The Lambeth Rifles.'

Sarah passed the envelope to the Prior.

'The address gives the man's unit,' she explained. 'Harold Shaw was in the same crowd as John Lindsay. But this letter ended up in the possession of Herbert Moore, of the eighth Service Battalion NLI. I'd find out why, if I were you.'

Chapter Thirty-Nine

Dawn Breaks

When Herbert tethered his horse to the railings of the school at Oostbeke, Flanagan's three-man escort had already arrived. They stood, head-bowed, with the sentry. Burning cigarettes danced like fireflies round their mouths. One of them scuffed a boot back and forth upon the ground. Behind them the building loomed large and black, darker because the sky carried the faint allure of morning. Some stars remained, their presence weak like lanterns on the bows of parting ships.

Herbert spoke loudly by the door as the sentry fumbled for his keys. He did not want to alarm Flanagan, though he must have heard the escort arrive, the strike of matches and their low conversation. The door closed and Herbert looked towards the bed, wondering what to say.

Flanagan and Father Maguire were lying side by side on the narrow bed, hand in hand, the priest's bulk hanging over the edge, one arm touching the floor as if he were dead. They were reciting something in Gaelic, their voices low and measured, a soft pulse sounding with the strange words. Herbert was quite sure that it was the Lord's Prayer. He fell to his knees and searched for the phrases he'd uttered as a child in Keswick when they hadn't especially mattered. *Thy will be done, on earth as it is in heaven*. Dear God, what words, what a longing. That something good and pure might prevail here, in this damp cellar; that there was another kingdom beyond no-man's-land, beyond the shattered stumps and the wet clay. The two men said 'Amen'. Neither of them turned to face Herbert. They lay in silence, a silence so charged that it almost sent Herbert reeling through the door behind him.

What was he to say? He'd ridden through the night rehearsing a conversation in another kind of cellar, a General's vault.

'Let me speak as a soldier,' said the man who wouldn't taste his whisky; whose decisions would be tempered. 'I've sent many boys home, when their age has been proved; but this boy – if boy he was – has chosen to remain a man to the army, and he abandoned his regiment. Don't you see, what Flanagan has done is another capital offence? I could never have recommended mercy if I had known what you now tell me.'

Herbert looked at his empty glass, longing for it to be refilled.

'Now, let me speak as a man,' said the soldier. 'On the day Flanagan lost his nerve, if that's what happened, I sent a thousand men to their deaths for an objective they cannot possibly visualise with confidence. They went obediently and on trust. In six days from now, upon my orders, those who survived – and many more – will support the attack on the Menin Road. The casualty figures should be here by early evening. You ask me to stop due military procedure to save a man who ought to have been alongside those others who placed their trust in me? I can't do that – in their name. A sacrifice claims them both.' He swished the whisky and drank some while it span. 'It's not August nineteen fourteen any more, Herbert. Or September. It's a different war, for you and for me.'

'Yes, Sir.'

Ah, that September. That was the month when Herbert had failed. Constance and Ernest had berated Maude, who couldn't tie his laces; and they'd concealed their disappointment; but they'd also found Whitelands in Northumberland. The Keswick gentry had, by and large, been of the Maude frame of mind and they hadn't kept it to themselves.

The General walked Herbert out of his office and down the great staircase. They both slowed at the gate to the lion's den. Lightly, he said, 'Were you at Sandhurst with my son, Bernard?'

'No, Sir.'

'I'd have sworn you were the same vintage.'

'No, Sir.'

'You know . . .' The General's face coloured with emotion, but his features remained in place. 'Bernard won't be coming home either.'

Footsteps in the Oostbeke school playground sounded behind the cellar door. Boots struck the steps. The lock turned. Scrambling to his feet, Herbert put both hands against the door, as if to stop its swing. Weak and powerless, he moved aside at the first sensation of pressure. He turned to face the man he'd condemned. Flanagan was on his knees with the hands of the priest upon his head. The prisoner rose, holding his trousers, and he spoke calmly in Gaelic. While Herbert couldn't understand a word, the sound was majestic. A thump struck his heart with longing: to understand so very foreign a man . . . his way of talking, his way of *seeing* the world: the rain gathering off the sea; the veins in the clay. He moaned as the NCO said, 'Come on, now, lad.'

As Flanagan came level with Herbert he said, 'Goodbye, Sir.'

Herbert nodded.

'I never did quite work out the rules of football, did I, Sir?'

'No, Private, you didn't.'

'Sir –' Flanagan came up short and the NCO's hand appeared on his shoulder forcing him forward – 'This was my choice, Sir; there's meaning to it, Sir . . . for me . . .'

Herbert stared, as though for the first time, into Flanagan's face. His eyes were a sharp blue, his skin pale with faint freckles of bleached orange congregating on the nose; the forehead clear, as if a careless hand had just pushed back the hair. He did not blink; there was no fear behind the iris, no storm upon the distant sea. Herbert dropped his gaze.

'I'm sorry, Sir,' said the NCO. Herbert saw the two stripes on the sleeve, but couldn't look any higher. 'Can't linger, Sir, you appreciate that, Sir. Can't have a hitch, can we now.' He shadowed Flanagan up the steps and Herbert followed. 'Whoaaa, steady you go, lad.'

The sky was clean of all other lights save the rinse of morning. Another of those unpredictable pauses in the bombardment had taken place. And instead a strange rush of sound came from the woods over a mile away . . . birds were singing. The firing party organised by Major Ashcroft at Brigade would be standing nearby, thought Herbert, his eyes smarting; they'd be gathered somewhere out of view to the road and the path that led to the post and the chair. Tindall, who should have been a vet, was among them. They were all smoking in silence, listening to this din rising from the trees.

The escort formed up: Flanagan flanked by two guards; ahead the Corporal; behind Father Maguire. Boots rang out on the flags and the walk began. Unthinking, Herbert tracked them: across the yard, to the gate, on to the road, and then a right turn, on towards the low shoulder of trees. The road was perfectly straight, heading away from the camp. Against the low skyline Herbert saw the rifles at the shoulders, the barrels black against the early morning light. Overcome with unhappiness, remorse and protest, Herbert's eyes blurred. In the fields on either side, larks had joined the song. He tore at his battle dress, wanting to get at his chest, to bring out the pain. All he could do was listen to this fresh sound, so much worse than shell-fire, and follow the steady march towards the break of day.

And between the guards shuffled Flanagan, one arm swinging free, the other raised as he clutched his trousers.

Chapter Forty

The Walk to the Slip

Flanagan stared ahead at the low line of trees. Larks were singing at his side, and ahead in the woods. Far off the guns thundered beyond Ypres. A sliver of bright light beckoned above the wheat field. It was like the blade of morning, seen on the sea from Inisdúr. Flanagan walked down to the slip once more, summoning the faces of his island people. The blue woven cloth on the men; the brown shawls on the women. Róisín was standing at the window, fiery and proud of her boy's rebellion; Muiris was alone, facing the fields of lush barley. He wouldn't let his eyes see a mast or sail on the hooker. Brendan was hiding somewhere, crying.

The birds' singing grew louder than the guns. The woods grew taller. The sliver of light lost its sharpness. On they marched. Panic lay crouching in the remaining darkness, but he was not frightened.

Meg's voice was weak now. *If you leave the land, Seosamh, death will claim you.* Sure, it had been a bad dream, that's all. It was a gorgeous cove, where she lived: a beach of small stones and shells swung beneath the cliffs, and birds floated high, circling her cottage. She threw them scraps when they swooped low, their beaks open, their eyes bright. She lived off fish and bread baked beneath peat.

At the entrance to the woods, the escort slowed. The guard on Flanagan's left leaned into him, forcing a right turn towards a path. Small flowers, their colour indistinct, speckled the entrance. Branches hung low like rafters in the cottages back home. Muiris had used spars from boats wrecked upon the rocks. Sailors had cut names into the timber, along with dates. As a boy, Flanagan had stood on a chair and followed the scored letters with his finger, wondering who they all might be, and where they'd lived their days. They were all women.

A hundred yards ahead was a clearing. The green of the leaves was brighter, the grass thick and trampled. All Flanagan's senses seemed to flare with violent activity. All at once he suffered a kind of attack: from the scent of bruised ferns and nettles; the taste of the dew on the air; the crazed, hidden chattering of the birds; the colours bleeding into one another. He moaned and almost recoiled from this sudden, glorious opening out of the world. It was like a first and final disclosure: a showing of something that had always been there to be taken away within an instant.

I'll drink this one now, said Mr Drennan. *The other I shall save for your homecoming, however bitter the grape might turn.*

Upon entering the trodden space, Flanagan saw to his right a section of men with their backs turned, lined up in two ranks of six. They faced the woods, heads down, hands by their sides. Laid on the ground behind them in a neat line were their rifles, breeches closed. An officer stood at attention, a swagger stick under his arm. His boots were shining. All at once Flanagan felt the presence of panic, but it kept still, rounded its shoulders like a cat watching its prey. Flanagan's muscles tensed, his teeth bared and he began to wheeze. Hands grabbed each elbow and brought him stumbling to a chair before a pale wooden post. Straw had been laid on the ground.

'Sit down, mate,' said a Sergeant.

Flanagan obeyed. Immediately Father Maguire blocked his view of the firing party. The priest placed a strong hand on Flanagan's neck and drew him hard into his shoulder. Other hands gripped Flanagan's wrists and forced them behind the chair. Rope burned his skin. A voice muttered something about the knot being loose.

'This day you enter the kingdom prepared for the just,' whispered the priest ferociously, as he was drawn away. His eyes were ablaze with passion and faith and rage.

When Flanagan had reached the crowd at the slip, he'd turned to see Brendan . . . he'd come out of hiding to follow him. He'd come to handle the currach that would take Flanagan to the hooker at anchor. They'd hardly spoken as he pulled the oars. At the boat's side, they'd shaken hands like men.

'God, I never knew my own brother,' moaned Flanagan, remembering those blue-green eyes, and the boy's tears. He'd never made the field. He'd left no message with Father Maguire for Brendan . . . it was too late . . . the priest was out of reach . . .

'Sit right up, lad,' said the Sergeant. He had a thick moustache that covered his top lip. His rough hands pushed Flanagan's head against the post. 'There you are, now.' Dangling off one arm was an old gas mask, the round eyepieces large and black. The rope tightened on Flanagan's wrists and there was more whispering about the knot. The same hands tied his feet to the chair.

The only soldier Flanagan recognised was the RMO, Mr Tindall. He was beside Father Maguire, his face twitching. Abruptly he marched to the officer with the swagger stick and began a hushed conversation. After a moment, the officer shook his head and patted his jacket pockets. He then strode among the ranks asking a question. Most shook their heads. One nodded and produced an envelope from his battledress. He handed it to the officer and promptly vomited. All the while, the sergeant stood close to the chair, one hand on Flanagan's shoulder. The gas mask swung off his arm, the round black eyes staring at the hay.

Had the grape turned bitter? Flanagan asked himself.

The vomiting soldier leaned forward, one hand on a knee. He coughed and spat and wiped his mouth on his sleeve. Panic crouched lower in Flanagan's guts, ready to pounce. To one side, he glimpsed four men and a stretcher. They, too, had their faces turned away. The only person who looked at him was Father Maguire.

I left the slip for this. Hysteria shook Flanagan's limbs and his hair went stiff: everything he'd said to Mr Moore – the journey from the spring burials to this chair – was an islander's tale. It was a mist over the shells on Meg's cove.

Chapter Forty-One

Tracking down Harold Shaw proved a complicated affair for reasons Anselm could not have foreseen. An enquiry placed with the Royal British Legion brought him into contact with a Mrs Watson. A week later she rang Larkwood to say that Mr Shaw was indeed a member, and had been active in the Legion all his life. He was now in a retirement home and she proposed to visit him to canvass the possibility of an interview with Anselm. Four days later another call came through. It transpired that Mr Shaw had never spoken about 'the incident' to his family. He had no intention of doing so now, but would speak to a monk in private on the understanding that the discussion remained a secret.

The incident. The phrase carried the heavy weight of understatement. It reminded Anselm of all those other English garden remarks, all neat and trimmed, a way of keeping an appearance for the greater good. With growing apprehension, Anselm drove through the crowded streets of Tooting Bec, South London, and parked in the forecourt of the Birches Nursing Home. At Mr Shaw's insistence, the interview was to take place in his bedroom.

The old soldier wore a suit and all his medals for the occasion. From his chair, he bowed with his head, as if Anselm were a dignitary, and then patted the seat beside him. The room was brightly coloured and all the furnishings were new. Photographs of children in silver frames crowded a model of the *Mayflower* on a dresser.

'You have the envelope?' he asked.

Anselm nodded

'May I see it?'

His face was milk-white. All his hair had gone, save for a few strands tinged with copper. He held his head back as if he was trying to read a page held up to him. Large glasses magnified watery blue eyes. With a shaking hand he took the envelope from Anselm and stared at it.

'This is between us, then, Father?'

'It is,' said Anselm.

'You want to know what this means?' He held up the envelope, his eyes vivid with emotion.

'Yes, if I may.' Anselm felt very much out of his depth, but that this was a conversation Mr Shaw had wanted all his life.

The order came through late on the 14th September 1917, he explained. He was a private aged eighteen in The Lambeth Rifles. His Company Sergeant Major came into his billet and read out four names. Shaw's was one of them. Special detail, he said. He didn't look very happy, so everyone thought it must be a trip back to the front to carry ammunition. The four men joined eight others in the village square where a bus rolled up and took them a mile or so down the road to Oostbeke, right by the Division HQ. They were driven another mile out of the camp, past an abbey to some woods, and housed in a nearby barn. The animals had been put into a field and clean straw laid on the floor.

'This staff officer turns up,' said Mr Shaw. 'And he says he's very sorry but we've been picked for a nasty job. Orders is orders, for him and for us, he said. We were going to shoot a deserter at first light. Well, we almost fell over. I mean, we'd just come out of the line. Half our mates were dead. The last thing we felt like was a "special duty" . . . that's what the Brass Hats called anything that was especially unpleasant. Now let me tell you something, Father –' the old man took Anselm's wrist and squeezed it, but the strength had gone – 'before that night, if you'd asked me would I pull the trigger, I'd have said, "Yes." We was all volunteers, we had our pride, we wouldn't stop the fight and we wouldn't give in. And when I heard of these others who'd hopped it and got shot, well, frankly, I felt nothing. It was war. And there had to be discipline. But that night, when the officer told me I'd be in the front line of six . . . well, I wasn't so sure any more.'

The staff officer said the firing party needed a rehearsal. So young Shaw and his eleven comrades – six of them from the same ten-man section – were lined up in two rows of six. 'The rifles were left on the ground. We were told they'd be mixed up while our backs were turned and a blank inserted into one of 'em. Well, everyone knew that was a waste of time. You can tell a live round from the kick, you see. But it was a small comfort, I suppose. Anyway, nothing was to be said out loud. At a signal we'd all turn around, pick up a weapon and aim. The OC firing party – our captain, Mr Crane – would drop his handkerchief, and then . . . bang. But you know, Father, a handkerchief takes a long time to hit the ground. When are you meant to fire? When he lets go, or when it lands? I didn't say anything, of course. I mean, I was just a kid, and these officers knew what they were doing, but in the dry run, there was a string of clicks . . . not one of us pulled the trigger at the same time.'

The firing party spent the night in that barn. No one slept. They'd smoked, talking intermittently of the poor blighter who was writing his letters and, hopefully, getting well drunk. Someone had said, 'Not likely'. He'd met the lad. Didn't touch a drop. A teetotaller.

'Did you know his name?' asked Anselm. Dread had been settling upon him. And he'd remembered the censored page of a War Diary.

'Joseph Flanagan.'

Too soon, Mr Crane turned up. By the look of him, he hadn't slept either. His cheeks were flushed and he spoke through the side of his mouth, as though to hide the smell of his breath. Outside, in the field, watched by some cows, they formed up in twos, ready for the short march to the other side of the woods.

A light knock sounded at the door. Moments later, a nurse laid a tray of tea and biscuits on the table. Alone once more, Anselm poured from the pot and heaped the sugar for them both. Father Andrew's great message to his monks was to know when to speak and when to be silent. Here, there was no need to discern.

'It was still dark,' said Mr Shaw. 'I'll never forget it . . . but the birds were singing. And I don't mean tweet-tweet. It was one hell of a racket. We stood there, in this clearing, just listening to them. I looked ahead from my line of six, wondering if they'd ever stop.

After a few minutes I peeped over my shoulder – it was getting light now – and I saw this empty chair, an ordinary common-or-garden chair, sitting among a heap of straw.'

The rifles were laid on the ground. Mr Crane shuffled them. The breeches snapped into position. Then the escort arrived. Mr Shaw, facing the woods again, could see nothing of the prisoner; he could only hear the movement of feet as they took him to the chair.

'My stomach was turning like I was on the boat home. And then I heard Mr Crane whispering, asking if anyone had a gun cloth or a letter. I found out afterwards the medic had forgotten to bring a marker for the heart . . . hadn't known it was his job.'

Mr Shaw sipped his tea as though it were too hot, though Anselm had been generous with the milk. He put the rattling saucer on the table and he turned away, his face towards the window. The grounds of the Birches were very pleasant. A brochure at reception said that they boasted a rich selection of mature trees and variegated shrubs. Anselm, however, looked at the arm raised in the air, and the hand holding an envelope.

'That was the last time I held this thing in my hand.'

Chapter Forty-Two

A Handkerchief

Herbert crossed a field and entered the woods, stepping carefully through the undergrowth towards the clearing. He avoided the track because he did not want to be seen. Reaching the trees' perimeter, he knelt, hiding behind a large trunk gripped by ivy. In front he could see a soldier, hands on his knees, vomiting. Behind him and the firing party, only twenty steps or so away, he saw Flanagan tied to a chair. The light had gathered force. A sergeant placed a gas mask over Flanagan's head, the glass eyes facing the opposite direction. Tindall hovered nearby while the strings were tied. Then he leaned forward and attached a white square of paper over the left breast. He fiddled for a while, making sure it was secure.

Herbert closed his eyes. He had only prayed once in his life – and that was the day before – when he'd begged that this man's life be spared. Could hope reach this far, into this clearing? He'd once heard of a man to be shot in the prison at Poperinghe. Apparently the squad was lined up and were ready to fire when a rider turned up with an order commuting the sentence. Someone had made representations to the Commander-in-Chief and the man was spared. Had General Osborne thought longer about Herbert's plea? He strained his ears, willing the sound of a gallop on the road from Oostbeke. Prayers rushed into his mouth and he listened to his whispering like a man at the door of someone else's heart.

The OC firing party spoke quietly. 'Turn.'

The men obeyed and picked up rifles laid on the ground. The front six knelt; the back six remained standing.

They aimed. All the barrels wavered like poles in the wind. Herbert stopped breathing. There was no sound in his mind or heart, or out there in the clearing open to the sky. Hope had fled. His prayers were over. A hush, so very like that of the sanctuary, entered the space surrounded by the trees. Herbert looked through the branches at one hand holding a pocket watch and the other a spotted handkerchief, held high for all to see.

Chapter Forty-Three

The Wine beneath the Slate

Flanagan couldn't breathe easily. The canvas of the mask was close to his mouth. It billowed like a diaphragm, in and out, matching the panic in his lungs. Any second now there'd be a crash. Terror pumped into his mind. For an instant, time dragged . . .

For a staggeringly sharp and clear moment, he heard himself. It was a voice made up of all the good he'd ever known, however disguised its appearance: his mother by his bed, his father in the field, Mr Drennan on defiance, Meg's wail for the land, High-Pockets on Expansionism . . . Father Maguire, Lieutenant Colonel Hammond, Lisette, and more. None of them could be identified because it was Flanagan's voice now, and this voice spoke in a fantastic flash of speed and accuracy: the grape had not turned bitter; he'd taken a boy out of the war who would have been shot; he'd brought him to a woman who'd sent her son away, a woman who would not let herself love again, a woman who would have punished herself for ever had she not received the chance to make a gesture of reparation. He'd seen all this in the rain, listening to Doyle's pathetic tale. Though it would not be Flanagan, this woman would love again; and the boy in Louis' bed would grow to be a good man. All this was a blazing certainty. The wine he'd never tasted was sweet. This was Flanagan's reward. The voice crashed upon his soul and in the shuddering aftermath time broke loose.

Flanagan couldn't breathe. The canvas had been sucked into his mouth. Something flared. At the same instant, a wall seemed to smash into his chest. It threw him upwards as lightly as a feather beaten from a pillow. Down he came in the air, sweeping left, sweeping right, slowly falling to the earth. His landing was so soft he hardly felt it.

Chapter Forty-Four

'When the body flopped forward, the medic walked over, you know, to check whether he was actually dead,' said Mr Shaw. 'He wasn't a very decisive man because he stared down for a while as if he didn't know what to do. Then the OC took out his pistol . . . I turned away, but I heard that shot. I've heard it many times since, down these long years. You don't forget anything. Nothing. Not a sound, not a smell. We were marched off, back to the barn, where the medic gave us some rum. He wasn't very happy, I can tell you. No one could speak. Everyone looked at the ground. It was covered in hay – this is where they'd got it from, for putting round the chair. We stood on it, drinking rum, hardly able to move. Lots of the lads said afterwards – long afterwards – that they'd felt the weaker kick, that they were lucky ones who'd got the blank. I said so too. I even began to believe it after a while.'

Mr Shaw's face was concealed behind his hand as he leaned towards Anselm. He shook his head continuously as he spoke.

'I don't know whether I hit him, Father. The gun was uncommonly heavy and I could hardly hold it straight. Neither could anyone else. I didn't even look. I pulled the trigger and . . . well, you've seen the envelope: no one hit the mark.'

The ordinary motion between Anselm's heart and mind, the manoeuvring of emotion and thinking, came to a standstill. He was like a winded man who no longer cared to breathe. For Mr Shaw, the moment was alive once more, with the awful freshness of a new calamity. He was crying with the tears of the young man who'd had to turn away.

Anselm reached over and held his hand.

'Mr Shaw, I know nothing of wars and what it does to men, and what men have to do,' said Anselm, very quietly. 'But when the world turns upside down, and you have to do things you'd never do when it's the right way up . . . well, there's no blame. You must not accuse yourself any more.'

The old soldier gently shook his head. 'For the rest of the war, you know, I tried to get shot. I walked upright into no-man's-land. I ran at the bunkers, I went straight for the machine guns . . . and I got these –' he pointed to his chest and the array of medals – 'I wanted to die for my part in the killing. But I kept surviving. And as for the execution . . . well, it served no purpose. We didn't need that kind of encouragement. And what of the lad? From what I heard he'd been with his regiment since 'fifteen. He'd seen the Somme. And yet we shot him. I'm told he polished the regiment's silver before he was strapped to that chair. He was a volunteer, you know.'

Anselm closed his eyes, begging for words, but nothing came. The soldier cried and cried, and Anselm gazed out on to the birches, the yew and the oaks. The lawns were neat and bordered by flowerbeds covered with mulch and bark. A gardener leaned on a rake. And this poor man beside me shot Joseph Flanagan.

Mr Shaw dropped his hand and dried his face on a pressed handkerchief.

His wife of sixty-three years had passed away and he'd never told her of that early morning on the 15th September. He had three sons and two daughters. All of them were married, and they all had children. They'd all done projects at school. They'd all taken his medals into the classroom. He'd even lent one teacher his bayonet. The British Legion had been his friend and family. And to none of these – not one – had he spoken of that unforgettable day, his sharpest and most enduring memory of the war.

'You know, Father, I've felt like some kind of murderer all my life. There's no escaping the killing. You're left with what you've done. But for a very long time I was angry with the Army, for what they did. They picked us, you know. They were punishing us as well.'

'In what way?'

Mr Shaw asked for some more tea, though it was cold. He ate a biscuit, the crumbs falling on his regimental tie. The gardener's rake scraped gently on the grass.

'There's ten men to a section, see? And in my section was a lad my age who was always in trouble with the Sergeant, the Lieutenant, the Colonel, everyone. He'd twice deserted. On the third occasion, he wasn't found. It was the best thing that happened to the unit. He should never have been in the army – it was obvious to us lot, but they wouldn't let him go. Said he was fifteen but no one believed him. But when he finally got away, who did they ask to shoot a deserter, a couple of weeks later? Us lot, The Lambeth Rifles. Most of the firing party was taken from this lad's section, and there were a thousand men to choose from. That order must have come from on high because our CO was very upset about it. They were sending us a message, even though most of our company lay dead on Pilckem Ridge.' He sipped his tea, leaning forward over the saucer. 'Owen Doyle he was called.'

I've held his tags in my hands, thought Anselm. Herbert had *worn* them . . . Herbert, who'd helped put Flanagan on that chair . . .

'. . . the fact is, you see, he was one of our own,' continued Mr Shaw. 'And even though he was a deserter, we wouldn't have wanted him tried and shot. But do you know what happened? The lad was killed in a bombardment. You escape a firing squad and then something hits you out of the sky. That's war for you, Father.'

Fresh emotion disfigured the old man's face: agony, indignation, confusion, compassion; they all belonged to a youth from 1917 but were raw once more, decades later in a nursing home. Anselm had to say something. He had to reach out to that youth who'd never forgiven himself.

'Mr Shaw, I can be very rude if necessary,' said Anselm.

The old man looked at Anselm, head lifted back to get his focus right.

'I have listened to all kinds of misconduct, but until today I've never met anyone who accused themselves so wrongly.'

The old soldier squeezed Anselm's wrist with affection and pity, saying, 'You were right, Father, you don't know what war is like. Thank God, that's what I say. It brutalises a man. And though the peace comes, you remain brutalised. You bury it from shame, but it's always there. And the remorse is all you have to show that you're still a human being.'

It was not quite a reproof. But Mr Shaw had showed him the true weight of a veteran's burden. It wasn't all about minnies and trench foot and bloated rats. The men who'd marched every November to the cenotaph had carried stories that didn't quite fall into step. There's a romance to hardship and patriotic suffering, but the idea of a concealed self-disgust that won't abate . . . well, it ruins the ending. It takes away the jubilation of winning; it gives sorrow a seat beside remembrance. It darkens a life.

'Let there be shame, and remorse, then,' replied Anselm, feeling an enormous privilege for having met this man. 'But let there be peace of heart, also.'

As if it were a deal, the old soldier shook Anselm's hand.

The gardener had put away his rake, and the light had begun to fade.

Mr Shaw leaned back, hands folded on his chest in a habitual gesture of contentment. He talked fondly about his wife, Nora, who'd been a nurse at a Casualty Clearing Station. They'd fallen in love as he recovered, he said. She'd changed his dressings. Brought him this and that. He'd given her a right old run around. When he was much better she pushed him here and she pushed him there. It was only as the conversation progressed that Anselm realised Mr Shaw had no legs. A coal-box had hit him and his pals in the summer of 1918. Above-knee amputations had been carried out in the field. He should have died but he didn't, thanks to the doctors. And Nora, who told him he was still a man. Anselm smiled at photographs of his children, and their children, and their children. In many of them Mr Shaw was seated, his heavy medals pulling his dark suit out of shape.

The nurse who had made the tea led Anselm to the front door, singing the praises of their oldest resident. He was a sprightly soul, wasn't he? Full of fun. Cheered up the place when it rained.

Chapter Forty-Five

Who Did We Bury?

1

Herbert's arms were wrapped around a tree, his face pressed against the ivy. He watched the firing party about turn and head back down the track, followed by Tindall, his face ashen. Four men emerged from the trees on the far side of the clearing. Two of them were carrying a stretcher, the other two had spades. Huddled around the chair, they loosed the knots at the feet and hands and the body slumped on to Father Maguire, who laid it gently on the straw. One of the soldiers cut off the gas mask and threw it aside. The chaplain then knelt with a purple stole around his neck, his thumb turning in a silver pot of ointment. Slowly he marked Flanagan's forehead while the OC Firing Party stared down at his boots.

Herbert stepped into the clearing and approached the group around the body.

'I'll do the formalities,' he said quietly.

The officer didn't raise his head. Under his breath he just said, 'Five forty-six a.m.' With a turn of the heel he marched away from the splattered chair and the heap on the wet straw. Father Maguire rose at once, looked at the body for a long moment, and then went after the firing party. Even in this place of utter abandonment, thought Herbert, awed, the chaplain remains anxious for the living.

Under the gaze of the burial party, Herbert knelt down, his hands open on his thighs. Blurring his eyes, he fixed his attention slightly to one side, using peripheral vision to guide his hands. Mechanically, he unhooked the envelope flap from the chest pocket. Faltering and feeling dizzy, he reached towards the neck and felt for the identity discs. He pulled the cord free from the shirt and raised his gaze, staring savagely at the rich green of the woods. After a few gentle tugs – excruciating because Herbert felt the weight of Flanagan's head – the tags came free. In a trouser pocket he found three small shells.

Stumbling backwards, he let the burial party get to work. Two of them put the body on the stretcher and moved it a few yards away while the others piled up the straw with their feet. The NCO in charge, a Corporal, struck a match and tossed it on the pile. The flames rose quickly, black smoke rising high out of the clearing. It woke Herbert to the moment: the birds were singing. He had no recollection of them having stopped or having started again. Lowering his gaze, he fell into an anaesthetic trance: the chair kept its shape while the fire raged. It was as though it refused to burn, or could not be burnt. Flames licked up the legs and ran along the back struts. The wood blackened and the varnish boiled. But the chair kept its shape. Of a sudden, the Corporal brought a spade crashing down on to its spine. The blaze made a gust of success and Herbert covered his face.

Herbert hadn't noticed that the other three soldiers were marking out a plot on the ground. They were planning to dig a hole right there in the middle of the clearing, at the site of execution.

'What are you doing?'

The three Privates looked at each other uncertainly. 'We're going to bury him, Sir.'

'Not here,' replied Herbert hotly. 'There's a cemetery down the road, and a church. Dear God, man, where's your humanity?'

The Corporal came over, opening a sheet of paper. 'Sorry, Sir, orders is orders.' He started to read. '"Retrieve mask. Burn straw and chair. Grave to be four yards distant. Depth—'

'To hell with your orders,' snapped Herbert, snatching the paper and tossing it on to the fire. 'Tell whoever wrote this that I wouldn't allow it.'

'But he's a Major, Sir.'

'I don't care if he's the angel Gabriel.'

'Where do we put him then, Sir?' asked the Corporal. He was unshaven. Stubble covered his face up to his eyes. His breath stank of rum. The other three stared with their mouths open, not from surprise but as if they were dumb beasts. These weren't the funny grave diggers who turned up in school plays. They were haunted men.

Herbert looked around. The gas mask glared at him from the trampled grass. This place is contaminated, thought Herbert. It has been fouled. 'In the trees,' said Herbert sharply.

'I beg your pardon, Sir?'

'Among the trees.'

'But trees have roots.'

'Yes, they do, Corporal. Cut through them. And go deep . . . very deep into the land. Is that clear?'

'Well, yes, Sir.'

The Corporal drew his men away for a smoke while Herbert went back into the woods. He found a place between three different trees that vied for the light. There he sat on the ground and waited for Father Maguire. Leaning back, eyes closed, he noticed that the bells of the abbey were ringing. A single toll that sounded over the wheat fields.

2

Chamberlayne may have been sober by late morning but the consequent hangover was very much in evidence. When Herbert told him Brigade hadn't provided a cross, despite their manufacture in the thousands on site, nor consecrated ground, he reached for the phone intent upon another conversation with Ashcroft at Brigade, and a swipe at Murray who would probably answer the call. Herbert, however, disconnected the line with a tap of his fingers on the stand. 'It's better this way,' he said. 'Don't ask me why, but Flanagan would prefer the anonymity of a forest.'

Herbert drew up a chair to the corner of Chamberlayne's desk and borrowed his ink pen. Without hesitating he began to endorse the Army Form A3. The anaesthesia induced through watching a chair among flames was still effective. Herbert could feel nothing. He wrote a legal-sounding phrase to the effect that the sentence had been carried out at 5.46 a.m., adding, 'without a snag'. The burial party had cursed him quietly as they'd hacked at the thick roots and the tight soil.

As Herbert returned the pen to its tray, Tindall kicked open the door. He stamped across the room clutching a piece of paper.

'No one told me I had to provide the target.' His face was contorted with accusation.

Chamberlayne glared back at the RMO, his fists clenched and white.

'Here's the bloody certificate.' Tindall threw it on to the desk. The final sentence read: 'Death was not instantaneous.' The 'not' underlined three times.

Chamberlayne picked up the chit as though it were a stray sock. 'Do you have to be so precise, doctor?'

'It's what happened.'

Chamberlayne crumpled the certificate into a ball and threw it into a bin at his feet. 'Try again, I suggest.'

'No, I bloody well won't.'

The door smashed shut and Chamberlayne looked wearily at Herbert. Together they listened to Tindall's angry retreat. Someone must have stopped him because he suddenly yelled out, 'You're normal, man. Get back to your Section. You're just bloody NORMAL. Like me. So get used to it.'

Chamberlayne held out a languid hand and said, 'Can I have the tags, please? This wretched business isn't quite over yet.'

Herbert drew them out, catching sight of the name as they swung towards Chamberlayne. 'Hang on a moment.' He drew them back and stared at the stamp on the disc: 6890 Pte Owen Doyle. 'What's Flanagan doing with these?' he whispered.

It was obvious really, thought Herbert, sinking inside himself: they'd swapped identities. Doyle was still on the run. If the Military Police stopped him, he'd say he was Flanagan: he had the tags to prove it. Herbert gazed ahead, feeling a shudder of sadness and grief.

No one was looking for Flanagan any more. He'd returned to almost certain death, banking on a drinking defence, never really believing it would help him. He'd worn Doyle's discs because he'd taken Doyle's place.

Chamberlayne reached over and read the name. 'He's the one who should have been shot.' He sighed as if an opportunity had been lost. 'Wishful thinking. It's the only way to survive, that's what I say.' He gulped some water. 'I'll need them anyway.'

'No,' replied Herbert firmly. 'I want them.'

'So do I. They go to the grave people.'

The exchange with Tindall had sharpened Chamberlayne's temper and he, too, was distressed. He was seeking another fight.

'But they're not Flanagan's,' said Herbert, his limbs taut, his neck lowering in an animal posture of readiness.

Chamberlayne's eyes roamed around, seeking a weaker target. He picked up the Form A3 and read out Herbert's endorsement on the execution. He looked further up the page, back two weeks to Glanville's entry of 'DEATH'. Purposefully – and to Herbert's complete amazement – he crumpled the paper into a tight ball and threw it in the bin along with Tindall's death certificate. 'A cat among the pigeons, as my father used to say.'

'What are you doing?'

'More wishful thinking, old son,' replied Chamberlayne, reaching for the glass of water, his eyelids dark and swollen. 'When this file gets to the Judge Advocate General's office, all they'll see is what should have happened: the recommendation of General Osborne: a reprieve: some bloody mercy among the havoc of retribution. And on that note, I think I'll have another drink. Hair of the dog and all that. Care to join me?'

Chamberlayne drained his glass and then poured them each a large tot of rum. Then, like an afterthought, he added, 'I've a confession to make, Herbert.'

'Yes?'

'I've got a cushy job at Division. It's pure nepotism and it's shameful. My brother pulled a string.' He drank deeply. 'I can't take much more of this war. We shoot people for that, you know.'

3

Herbert left Chamberlayne to his paperwork. Walking to his billet, he put Doyle's tags around his neck, conscious that they would confuse matters if he was found dead in the weeks to come. But that was not a consideration that remotely troubled him. He'd kept the letter, too, being absolutely certain that Harold Shaw, the poor kid who'd handed it over, would not be anxious to get it back. The three shells were like boulders in his pocket.

There is no grieving in the army. Let loose, it is a species of sentimentality that weakens the moral fibre of a unit. In an officer it would further demonstrate a want of good upbringing. One gets on with one's duty. So the morning was spent rehearsing for the coming battle, and the afternoon was devoted to the usual round of drill, bayonet practice, musketry and marching. Only the football practice was cancelled. Throughout, the sky carried unimaginable quantities of pots and pans, as Joyce called the barrage. The men were used to it now.

When evening came, Herbert withdrew once more from the society of his brother officers, each of whom was eager to know what had happened in the clearing at dawn. Had the poor blighter been scared? Did he have to be carried? What about the firing party? These questions he'd deflected, hiding the violence of his emotions, for these were the men with whom he would shortly fight and probably die. One might as well fall as friends. So Herbert sat alone in the gathering gloom of his billet, among the spikes and claws of farm machinery whose function he could not understand. A single window looked on to the road that led to Oostbeke. And, black against the loaded sky, Herbert saw the lumbering figure of Father Maguire. In one hand the priest held a bottle.

The chaplain sat at the makeshift table. It was made of planks laid across two petrol canisters.

'Well,' snapped the priest, resolved. 'Will you help me break my vow?'

He pointed to a stool on the other side, as if it was time for men to be men.

Herbert took his place while reading the label: Old Orkney. Chamberlayne's preferred tipple, though the night's squalid duty had driven him to rum.

'No thanks, Father,' replied Herbert, 'I've got enough on my conscience.'

The priest looked very disappointed. 'You keep it, then.' The stern reserve had weakened; even the short, wiry hair seemed soft. 'Joseph asked me to give you this.' He placed an envelope on the planks.

'Who's Lisette,' asked Herbert, recoiling inside himself.

'A widow in Étaples. She's hiding Owen Doyle as we speak.'

Herbert reached for the Old Orkney and pulled out the cork. He poured a large measure into a tin mug and then put the bottle out of reach on the floor. 'I shouldn't really know that.'

'No,' replied the priest, 'any more than you should know that I marked the boy injured before they went to Étaples.'

'Why did you do that, Father?' Herbert was not reproving; he was simply weary, utterly worn out by the sight of good people being forced to do what was wrong for another kind of right.

'Because Joseph would have gone anyway,' replied the priest. 'Because I thought it might buy the time. Because I hoped, with time, he'd get back, and live.'

They were bound together: two men sharing their culpability in a necessary crime. The priest had sent him on his way; the officer had imposed the penalty when he got back. Neither of them could avoid what they'd done. Ah, dear God, thought Herbert. Who among us is ever free?

'Joseph would like you to explain to Lisette why he did not stay with her, why he returned to the battalion.'

Herbert felt a thump inside his temples. 'Me? But I sent him into that clearing.'

The priest nodded. He had nothing to add, nothing to help him on his way. But I don't really know, cried Herbert in his mind. He wouldn't desert his comrades: that was one answer. But it only scratched the surface. He'd saved a kid, yes. But even that description wasn't sufficient. Flanagan had walked willingly towards his death. And however much the war had dehumanised him, Herbert had not reached that stage of freedom. Flanagan had taken one step beyond the hostilities, into a different landscape that only he could see, that to Tindall was a mirage caused by a jingling of the nerves. But Flanagan had glimpsed the peace. He'd seen bodies without regard to nationality, the land without boundaries. Perhaps the world without its history. Herbert couldn't fathom the man. 'Who did we bury this morning?'

Father Maguire leaned his elbows on a plank and rested his chin on one hand. Eyeing the bottle on the floor he said, 'A lad from Inisdúr.'

The chaplain spoke as if he'd never heard of him, or the strange island that gave him birth.

Chapter Forty-Six

Anselm drove away from the Birches Nursing Home, and Mr Shaw, in a torpor that seemed to absorb the light in his mind. He could not feel or think anything. By late evening he was roaming along quiet Suffolk lanes, passing through unfamiliar villages, his eyes alert for the solemn memorials he'd long ago ceased to notice. They were everywhere, usually in a market square or at the confluence of important roads. Some had three or four tiny wooden crosses on a bottom step, grouped together as though for comfort or company. Anselm saw them all as if for the first time. Abruptly he parked in a silent street of a village he did not know before a monument he'd almost missed.

There was no central focus for the community. A few old weavers' cottages and shops were stretched out along the road with a few tight lanes meandering between gable ends. It was a place to pass through rather than linger, the mullioned windows seemed to say. But on the way out, set back from the road within a low box hedge, Anselm had seen a tall granite cross and a small bunch of paper poppies in a jam jar.

Wrapped in his monk's rough cloak, Anselm stood in silence reading the inscriptions on the plinth. There were nine names in all for the Great War of 1914–1918, though he hadn't seen as many houses in the village. Strong Suffolk names, conjuring up slow and steady men. Farmers, perhaps, because grain and beet fields rose gently behind the cross towards the skyline. Or weavers, from up the road. Anselm looked around, as if for help. Behind him was a half-timbered cottage with shell-pink plaster between the beams. There was an old well surrounded by fuchsias and, in the distance, a restored windmill gently turned its arms. They creaked across the century. This was the England those Suffolk men had fought and died for, as well as the mills and mines they'd never seen in Lancashire. As Sarah Osborne had said, they'd ploughed on for God, king, country, empire, justice, freedom, and for their waiting families. And here in a village whose name escaped Anselm's notice, four men from the same home had not returned.

Reading over the names of these nine noble men, it suddenly struck Anselm as inappropriate that Harold Shaw would never be commemorated in stone. He deserved an inscription for public memory. As did all those who'd fought and survived. But with Mr Shaw, along with three or four thousand others, there was a rough edge to their determination, and it required compassion rather than memorial, for there could be no public remembrance. They had been obliged to shoot one of their own and live in the aftermath . . . which was, in Mr Shaw's case, the question he'd whispered to Anselm out of the blue, when they'd been talking happily of cheeky grandchildren and declining standards at school: 'Why didn't I shoot wide, Father? That's the rub, then and now. Why didn't I shoot two inches wide?'

Martin had been right, thought Anselm, driving aimlessly between wild hedges, past the warming lights of low houses. He'd said that Flanagan's trial had taken place in an interlude – or some such phrase – during the battle for Passchendaele. Thousands of men had died, and thousands more were about to die. Between these two apocalyptic harvests, one man had sat in a schoolroom at Oostbeke, his life in the balance. This had been Joseph Flanagan's moment. Martin didn't think that he'd survived. And neither, for different reasons, did David Osborne. Both of them had been right. But everyone had been so utterly wrong: Joseph Flanagan had made a very different kind of sacrifice known only to himself. Herbert had probably learned of its scale in the early hours of the morning, when it was too late, and when an eighteen-year-old Harold Shaw was waiting in a barn near a copse of trees.

Instinct took Anselm along certain lanes, guiding him towards the familiar shambles of rooftops belonging to Larkwood Priory, the place where Herbert had come to rest in his own aftermath. A place he had helped to build. Twinkling lights from the corridor lit up a row of rounded windows. A single steeple pierced the night sky, releasing a faint shower of stars over St Leonard's Field, the bluebell walk, and the lake with a statue of Our Lady at its centre. Looking at it now, Anselm knew with depth and certainty that while Larkwood was Herbert's lasting memorial, it belonged also to Joseph Flanagan: the man whose name would never lie among the great fallen. Upon leaving Mr Shaw, Anselm had sat in his parked car and checked the Battalion War Diary for the early morning of the 15th September 1917. There was no reference to the execution. It had been business as usual. Drill for all Companies. Musketry. A cancelled football practice. Flanagan wasn't even there for the attention of a thin-skinned censor.

At the gatehouse, Anselm left the engine running while he manhandled the gate. As he leaned against the ironwork, he thought: Who had come and wept near Herbert's grave? Edward Chamberlayne, the only survivor of the trial? Anselm couldn't think of anyone else. But why had Herbert called him Flanagan? The old man had kept back from the cemetery of white crosses and trees, his face hidden by a thick white beard; he'd been dressed out of season in a heavy jacket woven from wonderful greens and blues. He'd almost vanished into nature. Kate Seymour had been disenchanted but he'd been broken.

The questions and impressions tailed Anselm into the chapel like stray cats crying out for attention. No sooner had he sat down than they fled, scared off by the appearance of someone else in Anselm's mind: Owen Doyle. The photograph had been a stark image, and Anselm saw it now in the darkness. The scarred forehead. The raised eyebrow. He'd been old yet young. And he'd come back to the front where his commanding officer had turned a blind eye to his absence . . . that's what must have happened. What was the point of sending Doyle to another common-or-garden chair? The regiment had already been punished. Twelve men like Harold Shaw had just been sentenced to a lifetime's remorse.

Unable to pray, Anselm simply waited for the memories of the day to fall away like so many autumn leaves. As they tumbled down, a feeling very like grief welled up from his depths. His image of Herbert had changed. It was no longer simple or clean. Like a betrayal, he acknowledged the disappointment on Kate Seymour's face and his compassion for the unknown man was roused to flame. In his spirit, he reached up to a kind of wintry heaven, his heart's eye on the monumental sacrifice of Joseph Flanagan. He'd saved Owen Doyle who, two weeks later, would die near Glencorse Wood.

Part Five

Chapter Forty-Seven

Farewell to Arms

1

There'd been a promotion at Division, so there was an opening for a man with soft hands, explained Chamberlayne. They'd sent a Brigade Major to check that his nails were cleaned and trimmed before confirming the appointment. His self-mockery was bitter and sincere. He pursued the theme while packing his things into a crate for vegetables.

'A going-away present,' said Herbert, plonking the Old Orkney on the table.

Chamberlayne picked it up and read the label. 'Where did you get this from?'

'Father Maguire.'

'The teetotaller?'

Herbert nodded.

Chamberlayne put the bottle in his crate. 'To he who gives,' he said solemnly, 'much will be given. Isn't that how it goes?'

'Something like that.'

Detailed orders had come through from Division. At midnight on the 19th instant the 8NLI would join sixty-five thousand men from eighteen brigades for an assault at the Gheluvelt Plateau. The rehearsals were over: it was time for the show. They'd be alongside the East Yorkshires, Glanville's lot – who, incidentally, had caught a sniper's eye two days back. Stood up after breakfast and got a clip around the ear. The weather reports had also been leaked to Duggie. Rain was expected. This was hardly a secret. Clouds had been banking.

The 8th was heading back to the mud and the mist and the screeching iron. The preparations had ended just when the sky turned black. It would be last August all over again.

'I'm glad you're out of it, Edward.'

Chamberlayne didn't reply.

'Perhaps after the war we can meet up in Piccadilly and have a dreadful time.' Herbert didn't resent the string-pulling. These things happened in the army, as he well knew. And he didn't share Chamberlayne's scorn for the staff away from the line. General Osborne could hardly lead the charge with Lionel taking up the rear. Someone had to hang back and think through the aggressive gestures of an army, to make it a battle and not a brawl.

'If I ever get back to England,' said Chamberlayne, 'I shall be taking a package boat to Canada. I have an uncle in British Columbia. He makes a fortune watching strapping fellows cut down trees that he bought for a song. I've been led to believe he needs a man of talent rather than application. It is a long way from Piccadilly. They call it the New World. I might even change my name. I'll send you some syrup. They bleed the stuff from trees, would you believe that?'

Flanagan's execution lay between them like a swinging chain. The details had been promulgated that morning throughout the Army, though everyone at Oostbeke already knew. The men had taken it badly, nonetheless, and while few had cold-shouldered Herbert – that was Duggie's achievement – they were bitter, to officers in general and to the administrators to whom Chamberlayne would shortly become a colleague. All this spleen had spilled into the football match to be played that afternoon. They were going to win back some pride. It was horrendous. The men would enter the line with as much guts and determination as ever, whether Flanagan had been spared or not. But his death had made all the difference to a game of footy. Did they appreciate that, in the lion's den at GHQ? Did they realise that Flanagan's death just might secure the Lambton Cup for the 8NLI? Chamberlayne would; and he'd bring the insight with him.

'You'll watch the match before you go?' asked Herbert.

'Oh yes. It's going to be a right old ding-dong.' He tossed a diary into the crate. 'I'm told half the Lancashire boys are Irish and they're out for blood. Behold the mystery of the British Regimental system –' he held out his hands in mock astonishment – 'it's why, small as we are, we've conquered half the world; it's why we're so bloody good at what we do. We set brother against brother, father against son. You can't beat a family who fights like that. They're all out to show they're better than their own kin. The enemy is neither here nor there.'

Chamberlayne dropped his crate of belongings on to the floor. The only remaining objects on his desk were the telephone, the typewriter and the Flanagan file, waiting to be sent up to Brigade.

'Did Tindall provide another death certificate?' asked Herbert.

'Did he hell.'

'And the original?'

'It stays in the bin, with a few other truths.'

Herbert was amused by Chamberlayne's complete indifference to the *modus operandi* of the administrative machine he was going to join. They'd kick him out just as surely as they had at Oxford. And he would bow at the door, ever so slightly higher than the authority to which he was a servant.

'You know, Herbert,' said Chamberlayne, thumbs tucked into his belt. 'I'm no different to Doyle.'

'Neither am I.'

'Spare me the team spirit in my hour of honesty. I'm being serious. The only difference between him and me is that I will get away with it. I may even get a medal for neat writing. They'll catch him eventually.'

And they very well might, despite the support of Lisette Papinau. The military police were everywhere. Especially in Étaples: it was right by a base training camp. All it would take was an informer – decent and law-abiding, he meant no pejorative overtones – and the boy would be brought back to his unit and sent winging in Flanagan's direction.

'Do you remember Doyle's number?' asked Chamberlayne, without much confidence.

Herbert did, although he'd made no effort to learn it. 'Six-eight-nine-zero.'

All at once Chamberlayne flopped into a chair and reached for the telephone. 'I'll just make one last call to Brigade.'

Pause.

'Murray? Good morning. This is the eighth Battalion NLI. We've just had word that one of The Lambeth Rifles has bought it.'

Pause.

'Six-eight-nine-zero Private Owen Doyle.'

Pause.

'Haven't the faintest idea. Didn't ask and I don't care. Someone checked his tags. I'm just doing the decent thing.'

Pause.

'A shell, I presume. There wasn't much left.'

Pause.

Chamberlayne looked at the receiver as if it had just belched in his ear. He thought for a long moment and then said, very clearly, 'Northwest of Glencorse Wood.'

Pause.

'Sorry, old son, no can do. The idiot buried both tags in lieu of the body. A sort of hamster ritual in the garden of war. Hadn't quite grasped their intended purpose. A slow sort. You don't have them at Brigade.'

Pause.

'Murray, nothing is complicated. It's as simple as falling off a log. Just inform my opposite number in The Lambeth Rifles and send a note to Division. They'll tell the grave people.'

Chamberlayne popped the telephone back on its hook. 'That should slow the hunters down.'

Herbert's mouth had fallen open. 'What have you just done?'

'Completed what Flanagan began. It's the price of my own escape. Now I can go to Canada and watch those trees fall without a bomb in sight and without the slightest stain on my conscience.'

2

Herbert collected his travel pass from Duggie. In his pocket was the letter from Flanagan to Lisette. He'd been given leave to visit Étaples, though he had to be back sharpish for the move to the front on the 18th. They stood awkwardly in the yard. Yet again the execution linked two men with weighty arms, a hand on each of their shoulders.

'Of course, you'll miss the match.'

'Yes, Sir.'

'The Lancashires haven't a chance. The men could eat nails.'

'Pity they can't bite, Sir. But it's a sensible rule.'

The dog with glassy eyes lay by a wall, its tongue hanging out like a tie from the bottom of a jumper. Hens with red necks strutted back and forth, their chests inflated with pomp and wrath. Since entering this yard, Herbert had never looked at the RSM in quite the same way.

'Remember what I said,' counselled Duggie, 'none of this was your fault.'

'No, Sir.'

Duggie swung his arms behind his back, the hands slapping as they met. 'Please pass on to this lady my sincere condolences.' The gesture was a familiar one: that was how he spoke to the men when sending them towards the green line, knowing many would not return. He understood that this woman's war would never end.

'Of course, Sir. And thank you, Sir.'

Duggie sniffed a sardonic laugh. 'What for?'

'Your care of the regiment, Sir. And of me.'

'Go on, clear off.'

Duggie held out his hand and Herbert seized it with sudden affection. 'Goodbye, Sir.'

Should I tell him that I will not come back? Does he know that I no longer belong beside men like him? That I belong with Flanagan? Does he see the terror in my own eyes, that I am lost again, as I was when I came upon Quarters, and that I feel like another Doyle? Back then, Herbert couldn't tell north from south. But now the hand on the moral compass had popped off its spool. And if that wasn't enough, Herbert felt a most awful weariness: from the killing and the responsibility of having killed . . . from the churned up fields, and the endless rumpled cloth, the grey among the brown and blue. He couldn't go on. He looked squarely at his CO and he saw there a savage recognition. Duggie knew these ghosts, and he was trusting Herbert to drive them out, to drown them in Étaples.

'Bring me back a stick of rock, will you?'

He spoke to Herbert's reclaimed honour and Herbert saluted, facing disgrace once more, only this time beyond repair.

'It's not a French tradition, Sir.'

Herbert's hand fell. He could not conceive of a return. The men would be betrayed, yes, but he had never deserved them. The sight of Flanagan dumped on the straw had broken Herbert's resolve. You can't lead men in that condition. Herbert left his CO with the shell-shocked dog and the hens, wondering if the Commander-in-Chief appreciated that shooting your own only helped the other side.

3

Father Maguire sat at the improvised table in Herbert's billet. He'd brought directions to the home of Madame Lisette Papinau. There was another matter, he mumbled. During the night, Flanagan had asked the priest to translate into English something he'd written in his one letter. It had spilled out in Gaelic.

'A strange citation, in a way,' said the priest, looking around, Herbert suspected, for the forbidden bottle. 'It's just two lines from a lament by Feiritéar, a man at home as much in England as in Ireland. He made his choice when his back was to the wall.'

Herbert understood him to mean that the same might be said of Flanagan, that soldier and poet shared the same spirit of Irish identity.

'It's odd, but the first line applies to her, and the second applies to him,' said the priest. 'They're joined in the one lambent phrase. Maybe I'm just a romantic old fool, but that's what I thought.'

Herbert couldn't bear to read them. He took the folded paper and put it with the letter in his jacket pocket. As he struggled with the button, he felt the Chaplain's compassion upon him, as heavy as the hand he'd once placed on his neck – long ago it seemed, a world away – when he'd collapsed into the reserve trench, his arm torn and bleeding from the wire.

'Mr Moore,' said the Chaplain, 'I will go to Flanagan's people. I'll tell them everything: what their son did. Let that be an end for you.' He became gruff. 'The execution was not your fault. For Joseph's sake, there's no room for guilt. Yours or anyone else's.'

Herbert thought he might hit the next person who said that. It was a refrain haunting him, like the face of Quarters in the mud. Instead he held out his hand, as Duggie had done to him.

'Thank you, Father. For your example and comradeship.'

The priest shrugged his broad shoulders, showing his helplessness before his responsibilities, but his determination to plod on. Perhaps it was his remaining innocence that blinded him to Herbert's intentions. Perhaps the priest could only see the billet of a soldier who'd be coming back – slightly disarranged with shaving implements laid neatly on a serviette. He didn't know that three small shells were heavy in Herbert's pocket.

Beneath low cloud and a sense of rain, Herbert began his desertion, taking the same route as Flanagan. At Abeele he caught a train to Étaples and then followed the rights and lefts to an *estaminet* off a main street.

For a long time Herbert stood on the opposite side of the road, just looking at the frontage. The woodwork was painted a deep marine blue. Large frosted windows were etched with geometric designs that revealed nothing of the interior. Two small vent windows revealed a cellar. Across the top, painted in gold lettering, schoolbook style, was a brief statement of tenure: 'Chez Madame Papinau'. And above this panel were three windows, two of which had their curtains drawn. It took a while before Herbert noticed that the third framed a face that was intent upon him. She had the most beautiful countenance he'd ever seen, though one hand covered her mouth.

Chapter Forty-Eight

1

Anselm received the insight almost simultaneously to the sting of a bee.

He'd just finished harvesting the honey crop. Not thinking about what he was doing, he'd been letting his attention shift and start. One moment it was on Edward Chamberlayne and his abrupt disappearance from the country he'd served; the next it was on Joseph Flanagan and the elegiac quality of his life, the movement from spring, to summer to autumn. Then it shifted to the names on the war memorial, those nine lives without season. All the while Herbert seemed to be standing at Anselm's shoulder, seeking forgiveness. Anselm had just moved on, heavily, to the recollection of Mr Shaw – his joyfulness, his acceptance of suffering, his two walking sticks, each scratched with the initials of his grandchildren – when he felt a sharp stab upon the wrist. It had come with the shock of an unforeseen reprimand, the unjust kind that endures into maturity.

Anselm winced . . . and then his mind saw something very clearly indeed.

Harold Shaw never mentioned seeing 'Owen Doyle' again. And yet they'd been in the same Section, the same Platoon, and the same Company. The same Regiment.

Leaving his bees and jars, Anselm walked briskly to his cell, an intellectual aggression settling upon him while the poison inflamed his skin. He threw back the door and opened his bundle of documents, moving instantly to the War Diary entries for the 8th (Service) Battalion, Northumberland Light Infantry. Satisfied, he then checked a memo copied from the Doyle file. His intuitions confirmed, he almost ran to the calefactory and rang the Public Record Office.

'I'll explain later, Martin,' he said after some rushed courtesies, 'but could you please look up the War Diary of The Lambeth Rifles, and fax me every entry for September nineteen seventeen?'

Back in his cell, Anselm flicked through one of his books on the battle for Passchendaele, finally stopping when he found a diagram of the Army troop dispositions for the attack on Menin Road. He'd wanted to check which unit was near Glencorse Wood but he hadn't anticipated what he now saw. He stared at the diagram . . . this *meant* something . . . and he couldn't quite grasp it . . . but his mind was leaping onward . . .

Half an hour later Anselm guided the glossy paper out of the fax machine, almost pulling it ahead of the print mechanism. He read the entries slowly, his finger checking off each day. When he'd finished, he lowered himself on to a stool, barely conscious of his surroundings. He arranged the material in his mind, laying the facts into position. Shortly Anselm saw a picture whose wild shape and vibrant colour he could never have imagined. When he was quite calm and altogether sure of his judgement he dialled the Prior's extension.

'I think there's something you ought to know about John Lindsay,' he said, casually.

They met in the parlour where Anselm and the Prior had received Martin Reid and the Osborne family.

On the table was the map of the Ypres Salient. Beside it, laid out like torn pages from a book, were the faxed entries from The Lambeth Rifles' War Diary. Anselm read out a selection of each day's events, beginning on the 1st September – 'Divine Service held in the village, lecture to senior officers, route march, Company training . . .' – and stopping on the 18th, when he disclosed the fact implicit to every activity. 'The Lambeth Rifles were *out of the line*. They were preparing for the attack on the Menin Road. They didn't go into action until the twentieth.'

The Prior nodded ponderously. He drew back a chair, showing neither comprehension nor growing intuition. But he asked the key question.

'When was Doyle reported dead?'

Anselm had the place marked in his bundle of documents. 'On the sixteenth . . . the day following Joseph Flanagan's execution, and three days before The Lambeth Rifles set off for their designated areas. And from whom do you think the report originated? Unfortunately there's no name, but the unit is cited: the eighth Service Battalion, Northumberland Light Infantry. But they, too, were out of the line.'

'Which means an official in the NLI sent a memo about a casualty he couldn't know about . . . and which couldn't have happened.'

'Precisely,' replied Anselm. 'And that memo is just the opening shot in a savage but . . . *stylish* protest.'

Anselm pointed to the map. He'd marked in red ink the dispositions of the Army that was ready to attack the Menin Road, broken down into Corps, Divisions, and Brigades. Anselm's finger hovered to the northwest of a copse of trees near the entrenchments of 1 Anzac Corps.

'Whoever sent that message from the Northumberland Light Infantry wanted to make a point. And I'm now fairly certain that it was the same person who weeded the Flanagan file. He said Doyle died northwest of Glencorse Wood. That part of the line was held by the *Australians*. They're the only part of the BEF who *didn't* have the death penalty. This is an attack on military capital punishment . . . in one, sweeping sentence. If anyone within the administration had bothered to check the detail they'd have seen that Doyle could not have been a fatal casualty . . . and that would have led them back to the Étaples material and the link with Flanagan, whose file carried its own message: the leading recommendation in the queue was for *clemency*, which is precisely what should have happened and didn't. The actual decision of the Commander-in-Chief had been removed . . . thrown away. Along with the death certificate. It's as though this critic was saying to the Army, in the name of the regiment, "We *refuse* to accept this man's death."'

A mixture of sobriety and approval had gradually transformed the Prior's features. He was, of course, glancing impatiently ahead, to the identity of the man who'd come to Larkwood, and who remained out of reach, but Anselm hadn't quite finished his appraisal.

'First and foremost, however,' he said, admiring the economy and ingenuity of the unknown critic, his poise and insolence, 'this shredding of paper and memo-sending is not just a protest, it is an act of calculated subversion: by reporting Doyle killed in action he set him free . . . right under the noses of the administration, because they should have known that Doyle *couldn't* have died among the Australians . . . and *wouldn't* have done, if he'd been, say, a Queensland boy. But of course, they never looked. That's why the boy finally got away. He was as good as dead to the army.'

The Prior sighed and put on his glasses again. 'You're right, Anselm. But if we didn't understand the papers, neither have we understood the people. It makes sense now. Kate Seymour allowed Martin Reid and the Osborne family to believe she was related to Flanagan because she was protecting the dignity of John Lindsay. He lives, as Herbert anticipated, with enduring guilt and shame. Who wouldn't? Like Mr Shaw, he carries a unique kind of burden.'

He drew a hand across the bristles on his head, closing his eyes tight as though he were very tired. 'We now know the meaning of the trial; we know what Herbert wanted to say, and we know who is waiting to hear it. His tags are in our keeping.'

But the contact address had been mislaid by a dear old man who represented all that was good in Larkwood, along with its folly. A matchless Gatekeeper. This fond thought was shared by Anselm and the Prior. Their eye contact, however, betrayed a recognition that the resulting state of affairs was almost hopeless.

But only almost. With the Prior hopelessness was often rapidly converted into buoyancy and clear-thinking. Folding his arms, eyes smouldering like a forest fire, he began talking as if he were addressing the community at Chapter. Tracing Mr Lindsay through conventional means was a massive task, he conceded. It required professional skills that Larkwood did not possess. The simplest solution – in fact the only option left open – was to follow John Lindsay's movements after September 1917. He almost certainly returned to England, either during the war or afterwards and had, of course, a ready means of permanent concealment: he would be coming back as *John Lindsay*, not Owen Doyle.

'And Mr Lindsay had never joined the army,' said Anselm, understanding the Prior's line of thought.

'And he'd never been tried by Field General Court Martial.'

So the military suspended sentences lay buried with Doyle near Glencorse Wood . . . while the three-year borstal sentence from 1915 remained very much alive. Wasn't this their best chance? argued the Prior, knitting his hands. Could it be that the court system had eventually caught up with Lindsay? Martin Reid may have examined the borstal files but he didn't go beyond 1915 because that was the year Lindsay had joined the army.

'I think you should go back to the national archives and trawl any penal records held after nineteen eighteen,' concluded the Prior. 'I'm confident you're going to pick up his trail fairly easily.'

'Why?' Anselm didn't share his optimism in the least.

'Because John Lindsay first left his mark in life upon a school punishment book. He was a prolific offender before and during the war. He can't have a turned a new leaf that easily.'

2

Martin listened to Anselm's exposition with unconcealed admiration. That John Lindsay had survived was, he agreed, 'the meaning of the trial', to use Kate Seymour's phrase. Finding him, however, was another matter, and it was plain from his tone that he shared Anselm's lack of confidence. His own reluctant view was that—

Anselm for a brief moment lost his bearings. He leaned on the calefactory wall, reliving that first accidental meeting by Herbert's grave. *This was no ordinary trial, Father,* she'd whispered with sudden feeling . . . as though hiding her thoughts from the old man who wouldn't draw near. She'd looked down on Herbert's cross from a wounded place inside herself, and said, *I'd hoped he would explain it to me . . . and bring an old man some peace before he died*. Anselm tried to penetrate that plea, knowing what he'd subsequently learned. Floundering, he gripped a terrible probability: the old man could not begin to comprehend what Joseph Flanagan had done for him; and it needed Herbert, who became a monk, to place revealing words upon it, healing words . . .

'. . . so, you see,' said Martin, 'I didn't research the borstal records after nineteen fifteen because any subsequent action regarding Lindsay's sentence for shopbreaking would have reactivated the file.'

'Ah,' said Anselm, disorientated, as if he'd just surfaced out of nowhere in someone's swimming pool.

'Of course, Lindsay may have attracted later custodial sentences for other offences—'

'I was just going to say that.'

'—but most records are kept at the *prisons* themselves . . .' Martin stalled portentously – 'and, frankly, I doubt if any of the registers kept from the twenties have been placed on a data base.'

'Which means that I'd have to check the vaults of every prison in the United Kingdom?' asked Anselm, moored to the conversation now. 'Turning pages in ledgers?'

'Precisely.'

When someone wants to hold out hope, they often say all sorts of nonsense – anything to cushion the impact of disappointment which will, ultimately, have its day. And with such a tone of confidence and helpfulness, Martin said he'd check the available records at the PRO. 'We've got some . . . not many . . . but you never know.'

Anselm went back to his hives, rather like a witness might revisit the *locus in quo* of a complex accident. He sat on his bench between Augustine and Thérèse. Slowly, he walked out of the clearing and into the shade of the aspens, approaching Herbert's grave by stealth. With the freshness of the enactment, he listened again to Kate Seymour's words, and he looked at the man with the wide cap and the wild, white beard. Something at the back of his mind told him a greater truth had presented itself that day, but that even now he lacked the vision to see it.

Chapter Forty-Nine

A Matter of Example

1

The *estaminet* sparkled with all kinds of glass: flat, round and tinted. Green and yellow bottles stood in rows on a back wall counter beneath shelves covered in upturned glasses. A vast mirror multiplied their number and the depth of the room. Pictures covered the remaining walls: of boats and bays, a packed harbour, buildings of timber and stone leaning into one another, a walled town with a great gate, men and women in large flat hats working with rakes by the sea.

Herbert sat at a polished wooden table opposite Madame Lisette Papinau. Unable to face her directly, he let his eyes rest on a vague spot over her shoulder. But all he could see was the woman whose face had been framed by the window, the beautiful woman who'd opened the door in silence and drawn back his chair in welcome, surmising why he had come.

'Joseph is dead?' she asked.

Her self-possession was so complete, her tone of voice so measured, that his compassion was out of place. She wanted a clinical reply.

'He was executed by a firing squad yesterday morning at five forty-six a.m.'

'Where?'

Herbert still couldn't look at Madame Papinau. But neither could he escape what he'd already seen: rich black hair wound into a bun at the back of the head; a spotless white blouse with loose cuffs, like a buccaneer's, the laces tied into neat bows; a black silk band held the collar high, covering her throat.

'Oostbeke.' He sensed a brutal requirement for greater detail. 'A road leads out of the village past an abbey and a school. After a mile there is a wood. A track on the right leads to a clearing . . . I was there. The singing of birds is all I want to bring you from that place.'

'Thank you.'

A hint of flowers captured the room, though Herbert couldn't see any blooms.

'He was buried with dignity among the roots of great, living trees. There is no other marker.'

Now that he'd managed to say what had happened, Herbert brought his eyes into focus and saw a door that led, presumably, to Madame Papinau's living quarters. It was slightly ajar. And in this place of cold precision, even a door left open was incongruous. Owen Doyle was on the other side, listening. Herbert was sure. The certainty gave him the confidence to finally look upon Madame Papinau. In complete silence he reached over and placed three small shells in her cupped hand.

'Joseph asked me to give you this letter.'

He passed the envelope across the table. Madame Papinau took out the single sheet of paper and opened it. Her eyes swam but no tears fell. Herbert could see the writing through the paper; it crossed the lines in a wild diagonal. Very little had been written but Madame Papinau read it over and again, her face gathering into a frown – not because of the sharpness of moment: the handling of a dead man's final words – but because she was completely taken aback by what she read. The hand holding the letter dropped and she closed her eyes in thought, like someone trying to hear a very distant sound. Thus occupied, she slowly folded the paper and put it back in the envelope. After a long moment, she looked at Herbert as if she'd emerged from the dark, and said, weakly, 'He wrote something I don't understand.'

Herbert gave her Father Maguire's translation.

'"Softer than rain your innocence,"' she read, quietly, '"Unyielding as rock your firmness."'

With a gesture of slight impatience she put the paper with the letter, as if it were important but irrelevant to her confusion. To comfort her, Herbert said, 'I'm told the first line applies to you, and the second to Joseph,' but Madame Papinau was still adrift.

'That's not what I meant,' she said. 'He wrote something else.'

Abruptly, with tears running free, she offered Herbert coffee and then disappeared through the door that had been left ajar. A tap ran in the distance. Crockery fell to the floor and smashed. Herbert listened to the sound of a pan and brush, determined to be honest with this woman; to tell her of his own decision. Ten minutes later she returned with a tray, her face flushed from being rinsed and dried too roughly. Once again, the door had been left ajar.

'There is something I have to tell you, Madame,' said Herbert.

Madame Papinau poured coffee from a pewter pot into two small cups.

'Joseph asked me to come here, but I'm the criminal.' Herbert placed his arms on his knees, bringing his face close to the edge of the table. 'I condemned him to death.'

He waited for something to strike his head; he lived out an imaginary attack, accepting each blow as he was beaten on to the red and white polished tiles. But there was no sound or movement. Emotion welled up from his depths. Guilt, weariness and self-loathing burned him like the whisky at General Osborne's. He pulled at his collar as though Madame Papinau's thumbs were pressing hard on his throat.

'He knew that I had done this,' Herbert managed to say, 'and yet he asked me to come here, to explain why he couldn't stay, to tell you why he'd gone back . . . and I don't know; I don't understand anything any more – not what he did, not what I did . . . nothing.' He coughed but got no relief from that imagined grip. His windpipe seemed to have twisted. 'I will not go back. I'm not part of the army that did this to him . . . or to me.'

Herbert longed to feel a blow, to see his own blood spurt hot on to the table. But it was as though Madame Papinau had quietly left the room. Not sure that she was there, he glanced up. Her eyes were wide, as when she'd read Flanagan's letter. There was no rage or blame whatsoever. Only a vast compassion . . . something predatory and more frightful than the sympathy of Father Maguire. Seeing her face and her hungry eyes, he said, 'I'm sorry . . . I'm so sorry . . .' and flushed with self-hatred he cried, not wanting to bring his own cheap remorse into this cold palace of glass.

'In early nineteen fifteen,' said Madame Papinau, quietly, 'I condemned a boy to death. There was no court. He'd done nothing wrong. But I sent him away from home to die. And do you know why I did it? For France, yes. And to buy the respect of my neighbours. Because everyone else's son had put on a uniform. I don't condemn you . . . not with these hands –' she held them up as if they didn't quite belong to her – hands that blessed her own son's going.

Herbert drew a sleeve across his cheeks and looked aside at the frosted window. Shapes passed against the light, people who would have this war end, who bore with its awful, relentless consequences.

'I don't think Joseph sent you here to explain why he went back,' said Madame Papinau. 'I knew already. I'd always understood. He sent you here so that I could say something more important.'

Herbert wiped his eyes again, attentive and exhausted.

'Please listen to me,' said Madame Papinau very clearly. 'I once said something to my son when I shouldn't have done so, when it was wrong; but now I say it because I must, because it is right: you have to stay with your comrades. You cannot stay here, or anywhere else; you *must* go back.'

She was uncompromising and supremely confident. 'If you don't, Joseph's return means nothing; his death means nothing. You have to continue . . . step on step, and I *know* how appalling it is, I see and hear the boys when they come here night after night . . . but you, like them, have to maintain the pace, putting one foot in front of the other until the guns stop –' she held up her hands at the word – 'and when they do finally stop, well . . . then you can go home, and I'll find a way of honouring the memory of Joseph.'

2

Herbert squeezed himself on to the troop train that had brought regiment after regiment to Abeele. There he joined a convoy of reinforcements heading to Oostbeke, all prepared to support the eighteen brigades that would attack the Gheluvelt Plateau. He'd left a great weight behind at the *estaminet* in Étaples, without any discharge of responsibility. The release occurred at a very deep level, and Herbert couldn't quite understand what had happened. But he'd not been condemned by someone who had the power and authority to do it. And in opening the door on to the street he'd found himself light-headed and eager to see Duggie and Joyce and the boys. And even Elliot who would never forgive him. Above all, he'd hoped to catch Chamberlayne, just to enjoy any last minute dig at the pedantry of the administration.

Herbert's billet was, of course, as he'd left it: mild to moderate disarray but with a tidy shaving kit. Outside the clouds above Flanagan's woods – the name just appeared in his mind – were darker and lower. A mist rose off the fields and the road out of Oostbeke seemed to vanish in the air. Herbert walked resolutely towards the abbey spire and the school, though these markers in his life were not his destination. He went instead to his battalion's makeshift HQ, quite sure that he would continue along that misty road and die in the next few days. That he'd join good old Glanville who'd been clipped around the ear. But at least the mess in his life had been broadly cleared up. And his parents would be proud.

'Glad to see you,' said Duggie. There was just a trace of relief in his voice. He sat astraddle a chair, cleaning his revolver with a cloth. His hair, like that of all the men, had been shaved off in preparation for the battle. 'Edward has gone and taken the dog with him. He thinks the level of medical care for nervous disorders is likely to increase with sophistication the further he gets away from the front line. He really is a disgrace and I shall miss him. And the dog, I suppose.'

Duggie held the barrel towards the light, one eye closed. 'You missed the worst football match in regimental history. We won six-nil.'

'What's wrong with that?'

'The Fusiliers scored four own-goals on our behalf. The other two were accidental, though Joyce thinks otherwise.'

Herbert couldn't imagine such a rout.

'The Irish lads gave us the Lambton Cup,' said Duggie. 'I've never seen such self-sacrifice and inter-battalion unity.'

Herbert settled himself down at Chamberlayne's empty desk. He fiddled with an abandoned pencil. 'I forgot to pass on your sympathies.'

'Don't worry.' He span the chamber, listening for scrapes or clicks. His face was still red from the lice bites and the scratches of his nails. 'What did she say?'

'That we all have to carry on to the end, through sunshine and rain.'

Duggie snapped the chamber into place and pulled the trigger several times watching the smooth rotations. 'She said that?'

'Yes, Sir.'

Duggie paused to think, divining, perhaps, what had transpired in Étaples. Busy again with his cloth, he said, 'Maybe Flanagan died as an example after all.'

'I agree, Sir,' replied Herbert. Wanting to make an admission of sorts, he added, 'For me, at least.'

After being shorn that evening, Herbert retired to his billet but he couldn't sleep. And not simply because the regiment would pull out of Oostbeke the next morning, or even because of Lisette Papinau's haunting face. No, he'd left something else undone. Just as he'd forgotten to pass on Duggie's sympathies, he'd left the *estaminet* forgetting to throw some words towards that gap between the door and its jamb. Everyone had been reciting them to Herbert, but it had occurred to him with a flash while listening to Madame Papinau that the person who needed to hear them most was Owen Doyle. 'This is not your fault,' he said to the darkness of his billet. 'There's no room for guilt. If Flanagan's death means anything, you of all people have to live a long and happy life.'

Chapter Fifty

1

When Anselm answered the telephone in Saint Hildegard's there was a note of suppressed jubilation in Martin's voice. His self-reproach was too severe, revealing both his high professional standards and his humility.

'. . . so I was completely wrong and your Prior was absolutely right,' he said, finally. 'I checked the borstal files and I confess to being entirely self-satisfied. There was nothing there. I hadn't the slightest intention of pursuing the matter any further. But then I half wondered if the *probation* people had ever had any contact with Lindsay . . . and that the files had not been linked up afterwards. And there it was. Under my nose, so to speak, only – of course – one never looks there.'

The reason for the separation of records highlighted what had come to pass. And peculiar it was, too. The entire affair was laid out in a detailed report prepared by the probation officer who'd been assigned to the case: Mr Gerald Slater. On the 19th February 1923 John Lindsay had presented himself to the officer on duty in Bow Street Police Station, London. He identified himself as an absconder from a three-year sentence for shop-breaking, imposed by a court in Bolton in 1915. He was duly charged with a cluster of further offences, including the assault of the policeman from whose custody he'd escaped eight years previously. The case came for plea and review of sentence before a judge in the Bailey and Middlesex Sessions, who confessed himself to be pleasantly bemused by the defendant's conduct. His surprise was all the greater because guilty pleas were entered in relation to charges unsupported by any evidence, save for the account volunteered by the defendant himself. The learned judge was further impressed by the defendant's offer of monetary compensation to a family butcher situate at and known as Albert Powick's of 149 Baxendale Street – the one victim in respect of whom the defendant had a clear and undisturbed recollection. As a token punishment that reflected the gravity of his previous conduct, the judge confined Mr Lindsay to Wandsworth Prison for a period of five days. And this explained how the borstal file was left 'incomplete', said Martin: that system only dealt with boys up to their legal majority – aged twenty-one – and Lindsay was now twenty-three. The Wandsworth episode therefore floated free from the existing borstal paperwork, probably through oversight, given the lightness of the sentence.

'How very interesting,' said Anselm. 'Lindsay presents himself years later to answer for his past, but says nothing about the more serious matter of two prison sentences imposed by military courts during the war.'

'Exactly,' replied Martin, 'and they amounted to fifteen years hard labour. Lindsay was holding his hands up, but not for everything. But there is something else . . . something even more interesting in the report of Mr Slater.'

'Yes?'

'Mr Lindsay had come all the way from Étaples to submit himself to the law of England, and once his sentence was complete it was to Étaples that he intended to return – to a café where he lived and worked, and in which he had an interest.'

'An *interest*?'

'Yes. Lindsay had built a life in France.'

'Did Mr Slater record the address?'

'He did. During the war it was known as Pap's. Several diaries refer to the place. Ranks only, no officers. And it seems that once he'd completed his sentence at Wandsworth, he went back to France and stayed there.'

'Why stayed?'

'Because Lindsay's name is nowhere to be seen in the British military lists for the Second World War. He didn't serve and he wasn't a conscientious objector. In short, it seems that after young John

Lindsay left England in nineteen fifteen he never came back, except to face an old punishment. More precisely, after he left Ypres and travelled the sixty-odd miles to Étaples, that's where he stayed – at least until early nineteen twenty-three. And somehow, I don't think he moved again. He'd arrived at something like home.'

2

The Prior showed no gratification on having guessed where John Lindsay might next leave his mark. Instead he observed with a smile that he'd been completely wrong in his reasons. The recidivist offender was nowhere to be seen. Whatever happened between 1917 and 1923, Lindsay was a changed man. He'd found work. He'd earned money and saved up the necessary funds to compensate at least one victim of his criminal behaviour. The coming back to England was only explicable as an act of self-imposed rehabilitation, for the sentence served no purpose whatsoever, save in Lindsay's mind. So the Prior was not especially pleased. He was, in fact, troubled.

Anselm and the Prior followed the banks of the Lark where it ran between the Old Abbey walls and the orchard in St Leonard's Field. Larkwood's flock searched the grass for windfalls, several raising their heads to contemplate what may be a mystery for the thinking sheep: their masters were dressed remarkably like themselves: a bulk of white with some black bits here and there.

'Given what you witnessed in the cemetery,' the Prior said, 'and given what Kate Seymour revealed to you, John Lindsay is not in fact a man at peace with his past. It's an awful thought, Anselm, but has he punished himself continuously since nineteen seventeen . . . for the death of Joseph Flanagan?'

It was possible.

Anselm had met this kind of self-hatred before and it was unforgettable. No doubt the Prior had, too. People can harm themselves and all who approach them because they won't or can't allow themselves to hear a message that places love over the law which condemned them. It's a kind of integrity that ultimately saps away their life. Mr Lindsay exemplified something so very human and so very tragic: the greater one's sense of guilt, the harder it is to forgive oneself, to live completely freed from past debts.

The Lark raced between its failing banks. Anselm stopped to check the shoring with his foot, nudging the rotting timber, and remembering Mr Shaw. He had not closed his eye to what he had done, and yet . . . the names scratched on his sticks revealed the nature of the pilgrim: he was a man who had loved much, and was much loved. Where did Lindsay stand between these extremes of visionary peace and blind torment?

'What now?' asked Anselm. 'How do we find Mr Lindsay? The café must have changed hands years back.'

Interesting as Martin's discovery might be, 1923 was a long time ago. France was a big place: if John Lindsay had stayed there, he'd probably moved. Few people stay in the same spot for decades. And he could easily have come back to England any time after 1945.

'Call Les Ramiers.'

'Why?' Anselm couldn't see the point. And he couldn't imagine what he'd say.

'It is a silent presence in this entire affair,' replied the Prior. 'No reference is made to the community in any of the papers you obtained. And yet, this is the monastery to which Herbert returned after the war, and he never left it, save to come here. Mr Shaw was driven past its spire on his way to the barn. The execution site is only a mile from its walls. I simply don't believe that John Lindsay – this strangely reformed payer of past debts – could live nearby and never come to the place where Joseph Flanagan was executed. And if he did go there . . . well, maybe those walls of ours provided a refuge from things no man can understand. Isn't that what a monastery is for?'

Anselm made the call after lunch. He wasn't quite sure how to frame the question without sounding foolish. When Père Sébastien, the Prior of Les Ramiers, came to the phone, Anselm said the bare minimum, which was all that was necessary.

The Prior had been right again; and this time for all the right reasons.

Chapter Fifty-One

In Memoriam

1

Herbert did, of course, march up the misty road that vanished into the air, but he did not die – not in the following days, during the attack on the Menin Road (though Joyce did), nor in the following month (early October) when the 8th supported the Anzacs at Broodseinde – when Elliot said, 'Excuse me, Sir,' extinguished a cigarette on his boot and shot himself in the head. It was the dreadful fulfilment of a promise made long ago, when he'd stood in front of a flare gun.

No one on the ground knew the full cost but most of the Gheluvelt Plateau was eventually secured. All they had to do was press on. German morale had to collapse. It was a matter of certainty. That was the word from Intelligence. So the 8th, like the rest, kept the faith. And still Herbert did not die, not even in late October during the hail of rain and metal, when his Company drowned in shell holes that filled with water as they were made, or were shot in the mud like Quarters, or were simply blown off the earth, like Stan Gibbons, 'Pickles' Pickering, Tommy Nugent and 'Chips' Hudson. Herbert lived, though his pistol and rifle were jammed with mud, though his ammunition was covered in slime. He crawled into battle, up to his elbows in a kind of putty that clung to his skin and clothing. He lived, though strafed, and pounded by rain and debris; he kept moving forward, his hands finding a shattered root, a house brick, or the soft corruption of the dead.

The Canadians took Passchendaele in November. That was where the blood-letting slowed to a drip. When Duggie took the battalion out of the line, it was down to half its strength. At the command level, all the new OC Companies who'd come to Oostbeke were dead. By a hideous irony, there was no one left to punish for the refusal to organise Flanagan's execution. Expcept for Duggie. The whole debacle hardly seemed important now. Chamberlayne paid a visit to the rest camp. He didn't have any jokes left. He said that, according to one report, there was no chance of holding the Passchendaele Ridge if there was an organised counter-attack. Apparently ninety thousand men had simply disappeared – no bodies, no tags, nothing. Altogether, casualties were over two hundred and fifty thousand. 'What now?' asked Duggie. A new show, further south: an attack at Cambrai. 'Blimey, it just goes on and on,' said Duggie. And the dog? Not very well. Keeps slobbering in public.

'What's my replacement like?' asked Chamberlayne with something like envy.

'Dead,' replied Duggie. 'In life he was a stickler. When an enquiry came from London, he told me you must have thrown half of Flanagan's file in the bin. The paperwork was a complete mess, he said. I didn't believe him for one moment.'

Herbert lived through another mess in the spring of 1918. A massive German offensive was launched across a fifty-mile front. The expected but unthinkable decision was made: Passchendaele was to be abandoned. So was Messines. And the Salient itself. And so, in a daze of obedience, all the ground bought in blood between July and November was ditched in three days. They fell right back to the canal this side of Ypres. '"A coherent and defendable position,"' cited Chamberlayne on another day out. He'd made notes while the strategists thrashed out a plan. 'Why didn't we think of that?' moaned Duggie. Of course, he wasn't surprised at the move. No one who knew Ypres was surprised. It was obvious: a Salient is *always* a death trap. As Chamberlayne mounted his horse, he confirmed a rumour flying through the officers' mess: this withdrawal to the canal had been first suggested by a general way back in 1915, for all the same reasons, but no one had listened . . . he'd got the sack. The Salient. God, what a place. What did we defend it for? Almost everyone Herbert could remember lay buried out there.

The 8th was topped up, as and when, with fresh faces. They held the new line with distinction as Jerry made his last, violent roar. Herbert was mentioned in Despatches. There was talk of an MC for some other act of soldiery, but he didn't get it. He lived, right up to the armistice in November 1918 and the return of the regiment to England, though Herbert missed the boat. And throughout, around his neck, hung the identity tags of 6890 Owen Doyle.

2

Herbert's failure to stay with his unit constituted an act of desertion, but he was quite sure that Duggie would not convene a Court of Inquiry, or refer the matter to Evans, the new Brigadier. (Pemberton had been killed by a burst of shrapnel at Polygon Wood.) They said goodbye in Étaples, of all places. Herbert then retraced his steps to Oostbeke where the Divisional Camp was being gradually dismantled. The outline of the mock-battlefield where the Menin Road attack had been rehearsed could still be made out. The coloured tape markers had been left flapping on the ground. Herbert walked among them thinking, strangely, of Elliot, the one soldier who'd never forgiven him. The fields were terribly bare and dry, and a cold wind whistled through the hop frames. Looking around him, Herbert began to weep with a quite awful sound like laughter. He could not contain himself. The loneliness of the land was in his soul. His shoulders heaved with an immeasurable sorrow and all the dead men he'd known seemed to turn round in his memory and ask, 'What's up, Sir?'

Throughout the unspeakable horrors of the Flanders campaign, Herbert's attention had frequently returned to a sound in his memory – the singing of the monks in a language he could not understand. In the early evening, drawn by that remembrance, Herbert knocked on the guesthouse door of Les Ramiers. He was still dressed in his uniform and Doyle's identity tags were still around his neck. No one asked any questions, though he'd expected a fairly gentle interrogation on his background and why he was still in Flanders. The

Guestmaster, it transpired, was a chatterbox on English Rugby League, with a particular interest in the fortunes of the Wigan team. He led Herbert to a room overlooking the road that ran towards the school. A note on the wall told visitors that the maximum stay was a week. Seeing Herbert's consternation, the Guestmaster explained that everyone had a tendency to run away from things they ought to face. The monastery, he promised, was not that kind of refuge. The peace and quiet wore off after you'd lived with yourself for a while. And other people, he added, darkly. It was ultimately a school for prayer, he said. With that thought, he withdrew. Alone, Herbert sat at the window, his eyes on the low bank of trees and the pink light in the greater distance. With a stab of feeling like homesickness, he remembered gazing at the sea from his hotel room in Boulogne, when he couldn't write to Quarters' mother, when he'd written instead to Mrs Brewitt; that period of simple suffering – almost innocent it seemed, now – before he'd been called back to sit on a court martial. 'Third officer required.' As he'd stared at the sea then, Herbert now gazed upon the woods beyond Oostbeke. Between those two obscene executions the whole world had spun off its axis.

On the sixth day, when ambling around the enclosure, Herbert saw a monk by a compost heap. His head was almost perfectly round and with his thick round glasses he seemed to be a phenomenon of where humanity met mathematics. He raked leaves on to a pile and then prodded them with a long stick. There were no flames to be seen, though smoke rose in sudden gusts. Herbert joined him and for a long time they just watched the heat in the mulch. Though they did not speak, a kind of mutual confidence grew between them, and Herbert said, with feeling, 'Father, what do you do here?'

The monk gave the leaves a stir and they crackled quietly. 'We tend a fire that won't go out.'

They fell silent again. The monk pushed his stick deep into the pile, letting the air in. 'Captain, may I ask you a question?'

The mention of his rank told Herbert that the community must have talked about him. For a moment, he was unnerved. 'Yes, of course.'

'Are you a tormented man?' The gardener's face was very still and all the rounder for that.

'I am,' replied Herbert, bowed and broken.

'Have courage,' he murmured. 'Approach the darkness in your heart, a darkness that needs more than enlightenment.'

Part of Herbert's consciousness, a remnant of who he once was, almost fainted at the words. The impact of the whole war on him was summed up in that phrase. He'd seen the annihilation of a civilisation. He'd lost faith in its past and its future. He simply could not articulate the desolation he felt: there was no possible connection between the world he'd known as a boy and the one he must face as a man. He looked elsewhere now, hungry for something permanent; another land whose sound he once heard behind a white door.

Before leaving the next morning, Herbert went to the chapel where he'd once prayed for Flanagan's release; and where – to call a spade a spade – his prayer had not been answered. He sat between the two statues, those guardians of the sanctuary, and realised – well ahead of any informed intention or even the evocation of a desire – that one day he would join these silent men.

3

While mulling over the words of the gardener, Herbert taught English in a small school near Poperinghe. The thought of travelling any great distance from Les Ramiers destabilised him. He had become a loiterer, neither in the world nor of it. But, inevitably, letters from home urged Herbert's return: his parents were troubled at his self-imposed exile. And so in June 1919 Herbert crunched up the gravel path to Whitelands. He paused to look over the treetops – for the house was high on a bank – and he could see lush green fields dotted with sheep, and the Coquet winding towards the purple moor-grass of the Cheviots. It was an enchanting vista; but it was no longer home, if it ever had been.

Constance and Ernest threw a party. Friends came from near and far, including Keswick. When everyone had gathered in the dining room, Herbert's mother handed him a gift: a typed, bound volume of all the letters he'd sent home since 1915. Everybody clapped while Herbert flicked through the pages: 'The rations came up on limbers . . .' '. . . the wooden huts were stamped F. J. Lewis of Alnwick'; 'No-man's-land is just covered with litter . . .'; 'The Lambton Cup is ours!' Herbert's eyes blurred and he toasted dear, absent friends. He could find no other phrase.

Throughout the meal, Herbert was like a man deep within a pool of water, listening to voices from high above the surface. There was such a gulf between what he'd seen and done, and what anyone who wasn't there could reasonably imagine, that he could barely speak. His participation in the slaughter separated him not just from ordinary people, but from history, his understanding of the past, the very culture that had brought about the conflict. He felt adrift in a cold place, haunted by millions of faces. And he thought of the monk prodding a pile of burning leaves. While the cheese plate was being passed around the table, Herbert announced that he would shortly return to Belgium, resolved to become a monk.

The considered view of many was that Constance and Ernest's son had shellshock. And that, thought Herbert, was a fitting memorial.

4

Those at the monastery charged with discerning a vocation were more lukewarm than pleased. They hummed and hawed and suggested he work off the idea, as if he might be slightly drunk. But he kept coming back, drawn by the rhythm of life; its focus on something beyond the matter in hand. Finally, the novice master suggested he meet the Prior to discuss his intentions. There, by the compost heap, he was introduced to Père Lucien Koopmans. Herbert had met him once before. He was the gardener with the rake; the monk who'd no doubt ordered that the bells be rung after Joseph Flanagan had been shot.

Over the following months, the Gilbertines slowly but judiciously opened their doors to him. However, the more they did so, the more

Herbert realised that he could not go on, that he'd been deceiving himself and the community. He packed his bags and told the novice master that he belonged in England. That evening Père Lucien asked to see him where they'd first spoken together, by the compost heap. After a long, awful silence, Herbert began to shake.

'I condemned Joseph Flanagan to death,' he finally whispered.

'I know,' he replied.

Father Maguire had told Père Lucien long ago. Nothing more needed to be said.

Abruptly Herbert blurted out another name. 'Quarters . . . Jimmy Tetlow . . . he was a fisherman from North Shields . . . I said I'd meet him on the Green Line.'

Digging his nails into the scar on his arm, he spoke of the mud and the drowning of a beast and the hesitation – the long, unending hesitation – before he pulled the trigger. And he spoke of the other dead he'd seen: the blank faces from all corners of the world.

Père Lucien didn't reply until Herbert had stopped shuddering, until his breathing was completely normal. Quietly, but with the force of a prophet, he said, 'Herbert, you are forgiven. But you have wounds that will never heal. They are part of your loving. Use the suffering, your immense suffering, to heal others.'

Within the hour, Herbert had unpacked his bags.

Herbert frequently pondered upon these words. With a new kind of freedom, greater than anything he'd known in his life, he ran to his chosen future, tripped occasionally by those who knew the territory and what it meant to live there. But his progress was relentless: he moved into the guesthouse until, on a sharp November morning in 1920, Herbert was captured by the stillness of a cloister garth.

Herbert's entrance into monastic life, at one level, owed something to Flanagan's talk about 'the land'. It was as though the enclosure wall marked out a plot of ground, part of humanity's shattered expectations, and gave it back to God. This land could never be the same again, never simply ordinary. It was a sign for everyone, of another possibility beyond all walls: a new, restored creation. And as if in tribute to the dead soldier, Herbert's first significant act as a novice was to make a contribution to Gilbertine cartography. He suggested an English name for the bank of trees a mile beyond the school: Flanagan's Wood. It was adopted by everyone at Les Ramiers. And everyone understood its meaning. While Herbert immortalised the location, he didn't dare venture along the road out of the village, let alone enter the clearing.

That changed in 1922.

Herbert was on his hands and knees, one of six monks digging potatoes in a field. Looking up he saw Madame Lisette Papinau on the road that led out of Oostbeke. She walked past him without a glance but he recognised her profile instantly. Her black hair was tightly braided. In her arms was a sack that she held across her chest. A long blue dress reached to her ankles.

Herbert scrambled from the field and shadowed her progress, keeping well back. When she reached the wood Herbert panicked. He did not want to go down the track; nor did he want to meet her, especially in *there* . . . but now she was out of sight, so Herbert cut through the trees, intending to hide but watch. He moved slowly, not wanting a branch to snap and give him away. It was so very like the morning of the execution, when he'd crept upon the firing party. The ferns were thick and the branches low and charged with leaves. He saw her blue dress through the foliage. She was in the centre of the clearing. Slowing, he tiptoed behind a tree, as he'd done when a soldier. Again he was present to that moment, but also to the one unfolding before him: the two events occurred at the same time: the drop of the handkerchief, and the fall of Lisette Papinau to her knees.

She opened her sack and took out a trowel. Slowly, she untied the braid so that her hair fell loose and thick around her shoulders. Then she began to dig, leaning forward. Her hair tumbled over and touched the ground. It was like a pall and Herbert could not see her face. A strong desire moved his hands: he wanted to touch her and a terrible awkwardness made him blench, for this impulse was new to him, and came out of his growing identity: he wanted to bless her. Boldly, with humility, he raised both his hands.

When the hole was finished, Madame Papinau reached once more into the sack. She took out a small bush and planted it. Rising, she brushed her knees clean with her hands and compacted the soil with her feet. Stepping back, she looked not at the place where the chair had survived in the flames, but all around, high into the branches. After a short while she braided her hair, picked up the sack and left the clearing.

Herbert stayed alone in the woods until the bells rang for Vespers. When the pealing found a regular strike, singing over the fields, he stepped into the open and approached the memorial to Joseph Flanagan. It was a mulberry, that most English of trees, and a symbol of lost love.

Chapter Fifty-Two

1

Anselm thanked the Prior of Les Ramiers warmly for his help and put the phone down. He then walked rapidly to Father Andrew's study, beginning his account even before the door had clipped shut behind him.

John Lindsay *was* known to Les Ramiers and he *did* run a café in Étaples – or he used to, for the management had passed to his family upon his retirement. He'd been a regular visitor to Les Ramiers for about twenty years. Of late he'd always been accompanied by one of his children or grandchildren. They were a very private family and volunteered nothing of their purpose in coming, though their routine suggested a ritual of some importance. Each year they arrived on the evening of 14th September in time for Compline. Mr Lindsay rose very early – something like five in the morning – and went out somewhere, regardless of the weather. He was back for Lauds at seven. After lunch the family left, and Les Ramiers didn't see them again until Compline a year later. An interesting family, Père Sébastien had said. Spoke together in English and French with relatives in both countries and further afield.

It was obvious to both Anselm and the Prior that John Lindsay's habit was to make a pilgrimage to the woods where Flanagan was shot on the date of the execution.

'Go to Les Ramiers on the fourteenth,' decided the Prior. 'That is the place for you to approach him with Herbert's message and *these*.'

He held up the tags and for a moment they both watched them swing. Time was about to lose its momentum and its control over the ordering of events. They knew that when Mr Lindsay reached out to take them back his youth would reappear, as frightened and desperate as ever.

The period of waiting was peculiarly charged for Anselm. He fulfilled his monastic duties mindful that, long ago, these mild September days had been an interregnum between two very different kingdoms, one of life and one of death. The thousands of names for the many, many monuments had not yet been determined. And he was about to meet someone who'd been smuggled out of the reckoning.

'So where is it now?' asked Bede, in the cloister, 'Barbados?'

Anselm stared back from that forgotten September and simply waved goodbye. He took the train to Folkestone, the ferry to Boulogne and a coach to Poperinghe, where a taciturn monk drove him the remaining twelve kilometres to Les Ramiers. Throughout the journey Anselm felt a subdued presence at his side: this was the route Herbert had taken long ago when he'd first left England in a uniform. At the end of Compline Anselm sang the Salve Regina with his brothers in the nave, wondering where Herbert had once stood, acutely aware that among the handful of guests were an old man and a woman. They sat at the very back, close together, apart from the others, hidden by shadows.

2

Anselm's alarm went off at 4.30 a.m. He washed and dressed and then waited among a scattering of fruit trees planted not far from the guesthouse. At 5.30 a.m. two dark shapes appeared on the top step. Both were well wrapped to meet the cold of the morning. Mist came from their mouths as they whispered to each other. Arm-in-arm they descended the short stairs, left the enclosure and began walking along the main road out of the village. After a few minutes Anselm followed them.

The man and woman were about a hundred yards ahead, etched black against the first indications of the dawn. Anselm slowed, his senses sharply tuned . . . larks were singing in the fields on either side; and ahead, from a low line of trees, came yet more birdsong.

It was like a secret festival, gathering voice with the coming of the light.

They came to a school with quaint shutters, slowing for a moment before moving on. At a copse – the copse described by Mr Shaw – the man and woman turned on to a path and vanished from Anselm's sight. When he reached the same spot, he paused, struck by the speckling of flowers. Looking up, he made a soft gasp.

The track was flanked by aspens, oaks and chestnuts. But straight ahead grew a glorious, tangled Mulberry tree . . . all on its own, its roots sunk deep into the middle of a clearing. And like pilgrims before a shrine Mr Lindsay stood motionless before its branches, the woman at his side. The birds' song had become a riot. Anselm couldn't move a hair. He watched and prayed knowing that, in 1917, at roughly this moment, Harold Shaw had fished out an envelope from his mother, and that shortly afterwards Joseph Flanagan had been shot among the secrecy of the trees.

When Mr Lindsay and the woman turned to leave, Anselm remained where he was, waiting at the mouth of the track. The morning light had given colour and depth to the woods. He could see the two guests clearly now. And they saw him. But Anselm was the more astonished . . . because he'd never seen either of them before.

When they came level, Mr Lindsay said, in French, 'Now you know my secret, Father.' He held out his hand warmly, his eyes assured, his manner calm. 'You're new here, aren't you?'

Anselm drew out the tags from his pocket, gripping them tight as if he might squeeze some guidance from Herbert. 'I'm a monk from England,' he said. 'I live in the monastery where Herbert Moore spent sixty years after he condemned Joseph Flanagan to death.'

His words stunned Mr Lindsay. He placed a hand on Anselm's shoulder, not for need of support but out of . . . what was it? Anselm knew it was *pity*. The old man's head fell low. He remained like that, quite still, as if he were back before the mulberry tree.

For a man of advanced years, Mr Lindsay – like Sylvester – possessed remarkable good health. And like Sylvester, he seemed ageless and had a certain childlike quality. His ears were pink, his face lightly tanned. One eyebrow rose higher than the other, suggesting more mischief than surprise. Looking up he said, 'I do hope he lived a happy life?'

'He did,' replied Anselm.

'And without any guilt.'

Anselm's failure to reply immediately unsettled Mr Lindsay, so he hastily explained that Father Moore had founded Larkwood, had been an inspiration to many, but had secretly longed to meet the boy saved by Joseph Flanagan. 'And he wished upon you what you have wished for him.'

Mr Lindsay's mouth fell open, and he looked to the young woman by his side to share the wonder of this strange happening. She was in her early twenties. A hood covered her head and, within it, thick black hair framed an oval face. Fine black eyebrows arched to a low fringe. She was shy but her silence was heavy and protecting.

'Father Moore wanted you to have these –' Anselm held out the tags – 'and it's why I came to Les Ramiers to find you.'

'These are mine,' he whispered. 'This is who I was.' He fumbled behind his tie, opening two shirt buttons. He reached inside and tugged out another cord and other discs. Holding them up for Anselm, he said, 'four-eight-eight-eight Pte Joseph Flanagan. We swapped tags . . . because he knew no one would be looking for him . . . ever.'

3

After Lauds, Anselm joined Mr Lindsay and Sabine, his granddaughter, for breakfast. Given the circumstances, Anselm secured a room in the monastery by the kitchens, where they would be guaranteed privacy and bounty.

Anselm and the Prior at Larkwood had pretty much misunderstood every detail of importance. John Lindsay had not led a tormented life at all: he'd married, had four children, seen numerous grandchildren arrive and attended more weddings and christenings than he could accurately calculate. He was a happy man. That said, it had taken him fifty years before he could step into that clearing where

Flanagan had died. 'My only remaining desire is to visit Inisdúr, where he was born. He spoke of it all the time to Lisette. But that can never happen. It's part of the price.'

The brother in charge of the kitchens nudged open the door with his foot and laid a platter of meats and cheese on the table. A novice followed with fresh bread and a bowl of fruit. Another monk brought hot steaming coffee.

The plan had always been that Mr Lindsay would catch a boat from Boulogne when Madame Papinau's cousin had secured a passage to England. But the day following Herbert Moore's visit to the *estaminet*, she asked him to stay. Not for a few weeks, but for good. Étaples could become his home, she said. He could work here, in the kitchens. The war would end one day. He wouldn't have to hide for ever. Mr Lindsay didn't have to think for long. He had no life in England, just a borstal sentence, if he was caught. 'But I don't speak French,' he stammered. 'I'll teach you,' she promised. And she did – without a single formal lesson. She just stopped speaking English.

'She never married again,' said Mr Lindsay, his face soft with affection, 'though she changed. When I first came she was a cold and brittle woman, for all her kindness. But she grew warm, over the years. One day she asked me to call her Maminette. It was only after her death that I found this letter. Joseph wrote it to her in his cell, hours before he was shot. She kept it in a drawer by her bed.' Mr Lindsay drew an envelope from his inner jacket pocket. 'I bring it with me every year. It's as though she comes with me to see him.'

Written on the front was one word: Lisette. Anselm opened the single sheet of paper inside. There was a Gaelic phrase he didn't understand – making it sacred and secret. Written underneath it, rising across the lines, was a sort of desperate afterthought, a plea that went to the heart of Flanagan's purpose, as if he hadn't quite realised it himself until afterwards:

> Keep hold of the boy for a while. Teach him what you would have taught your son.

'I first heard about Louis, her son, on the day Mr Moore delivered the letter,' said Mr Lindsay, taking it back. 'I was listening at the door as they talked. She'd sent Louis off to the war, as Mr Moore had sent Joseph off to the cellar. Both of them were killed. I think my life changed when I heard that confession, because she then sent Mr Moore back to his regiment – and he would have stayed in Étaples, believe you me.'

Sabine poured the coffee. She evidently knew everything. It was part of her identity. Her own life blood flowed from an execution. There was a blush to her skin as though she felt what Lisette had felt – along with Joseph and the old man around whom these events had turned. Anselm thought she might cry but the door swung open and the novice brought in a rattling tray of jams arranged around a single pot of English marmalade.

For over a year Mr Lindsay lived like a prisoner, hiding in the house and never going out, except at night and only into a small walled garden at the rear of the premises. After ten minutes he was back in the cellar. During the day he remained in the kitchen peeling potatoes and in the evening he sat in the parlour listening to Lisette. She made him repeat words and phrases until her ear was pleased, though he didn't know what he'd been saying. And ever so slowly a new world opened out before him – one that he could never have imagined. He began to speak in a language that was, for him, pure. He'd never sworn in it. He'd never robbed anyone with it. None of these sounds had ever been heard in a court or a borstal. By the time the war ended, he was dreaming in French. He walked on to the streets of Étaples a different man.

'When I was twenty-two, Maminette had a shock for me.' Mr Lindsay checked the jams. 'She said I was a grown man, now, and I should go back to England and serve my sentence. I knew she was right. What I'd done – who I'd been – hung round my neck. So I did my time. And I've never looked back.'

'But what of "Doyle's" two prisons sentences?' asked Anselm. 'Weren't they around your neck, too?'

'Oh no,' said Mr Lindsay, both eyebrows raised high. 'They were around Joseph's. If I'd claimed those back, he would have died for nothing.' He opened a jar marked Reine-Claude. 'But it's one of the reasons I could never return to England. I was a deserter – I still am; it remains with me – and I didn't deserve what the others had fought and died for. There were plenty of boys my age who stuck it out, and I ran away.'

He screwed the lid back on to the pot, not having taken any jam. And without Anselm having to ask, he talked of his parents, that rascal Owen Doyle, and a butcher called Albert Powick. Sabine took up the story, as if she'd been there, and Anselm listened as from a distance, as he'd done in the woods, his eyes on a mulberry tree.

The next morning Père Sébastien, the Prior of Les Ramiers, drove Anselm to Poperinghe, where he took the coach to Boulogne and the ferry to Folkestone. On the train home he mused on sundry peculiarities: he'd come to the battlefields of Flanders without visiting a single war cemetery; his sole pilgrimage had been to the site of an execution; a copse of trees was known locally as Flanagan's Woods, but no one knew why; and John Lindsay, a man whose only unfulfilled desire was to visit Inisdúr, had never heard of Kate Seymour.

Chapter Fifty-Three

Time to go Home

Herbert went back to Flanagan's Woods frequently with a watering can, for he feared for the life of the tree. Lisette Papinau never came to Oostbeke again – at least not to Herbert's knowledge. He'd waited on the anniversary of the shooting, wondering if she might again walk solemnly along the road between the school house and the trees, but it never happened. From this he deduced that her life had moved on; that she had left her memorial, just as surely as Owen Doyle had left her, and moved on also – back to England and an open future.

Over the years Herbert grew in understanding. Of himself; and why he had come to Les Ramiers and why he would stay. His first painful lesson was the discovery that for much of his life he'd lived outside himself, reacting to the multiplicity of events, be they mundane or harrowing. In the silence of the monastery or out working in the fields, he gradually noticed – with a new kind of terror – that within himself he was quite hollow, and probably always had been. Without a jab from the outside, he was nothing. He had no depth . . . none at least that he was aware of. Reluctantly, fearfully, Herbert began the journey inward, the voyage that cannot be put into words or explained but only lived. And he made another discovery: a richness of existence, intrinsic to his identity and true for all humanity, whose depth was beyond the reach of any calamity.

Herbert never tried to articulate the confidence that grew within him, but he noticed that the closer he came to his final vows, the less he felt he had a 'vocation', in the sense of an Office, or something he had *to do*. He had simply set about becoming *himself*. Monk and man were one. The steady rhythm of life at Les Ramiers had disclosed something basic to his humanity: he hungered for something within reach and out of his reach; he looked to a Beyond that was near and yet far; he sensed another place over the burning leaves, a green Kingdom behind so many broken windows. Without wanting to study the anatomy of association too closely, Herbert obscurely linked this inner landscape with the memory of Joseph Flanagan's sacrifice, and the island of his birth, where the land and the sea were one.

In the spring of 1924 Père Lucien asked to see Herbert in the vegetable garden. The Prior was attaching wire and posts to make a raspberry patch, despite the designation of the location.

'You are due to take your final vows next year?' said Père Lucien, his round face uncharacteristically sad.

'Yes, if you think it fit,' replied Herbert.

The Prior wrapped wire around a post. 'A few months ago I received a letter from Les Moineaux in Burgundy. They're setting up a new foundation in England. Suffolk. The Order is being asked for volunteers.'

'No, Father, please,' said Herbert, his heart suddenly void. 'I want to stay here, this is my home.'

The Prior stretched the wire to the next post and wrapped it tight. 'It's also been a refuge, hasn't it?'

Herbert didn't want to admit that Père Lucien was right. In a flash of painful foreshortening, Herbert was back as a soldier by a pile of raked leaves.

'I think it's time for you to go home, Herbert.' The Prior waddled back to the first post and unravelled some more wire off a spool. 'Take your final vows in a new monastery. You'll lay its roots with your example. Maybe something great will grow.'

That was the end of the conversation, for Gilbertines don't say that much, unless they work in the guesthouse; and Herbert recalled his first night at Les Ramiers – suddenly precious now – when he'd read the maximum stay was for a week, when he'd been warned that you can never escape into a cloister.

Chapter Fifty-Four

The community at Larkwood gathered in the Chapter Room before Compline. A candle burned on a central stand. Each of the monks drifted to their seat built into the circular wall of stone. Everyone was present, save Sylvester. After a brief prayer the Prior gave a summary of all that was known about Joseph Flanagan and his trial. He then invited Anselm to take the floor. 'This is the story Herbert never heard of the man he'd always wanted to meet.'

Anselm stood up, his arms hidden in opposing sleeves.

John Lindsay did not have an auspicious start in life. His father was probably a merchant seaman from Liverpool. Relationships were fluid and always bruising for Peggy, his mother. She was found dead on Hornby docks. John ran off, leaving his four siblings to a workhouse or an orphanage, he never did find out. Aged six, he would easily have been swallowed by the primitive care system of the time, only he met Owen Doyle playing by a railway shunting in Bolton. Owen, five years his elder, brought John home to his dumbfounded mother and father. Though born in Lancashire, both parents were from Irish families who'd migrated during the Great Hunger of the previous century. Nine other children shared the four rooms where they lived. They found a corner for John and, in that tight but warm space, he became Owen's shadow. At school they gave Mr Lever, the headmaster, a run for his money, though he grudgingly liked them both. Occasionally, on a Sunday after mass, he'd buy them sweets if their shoes were shiny and their nails were clean.

Perhaps all might have gone well for John. Maybe he'd have landed a warehouse job and married one of Owen's lively sisters. But Owen's eyes turned red and swollen, his skin became pale, and he coughed up blood into a rusted bucket. He died of TB. And so did an infant sister. That was when John first began to rebel against life: not after the death of his mother at the hands of some brutal man, but after the slow, tortured decline of the boy who'd saved him; when he learned that what you value most is only as strong as India paper. He started petty thieving; and fighting. Mr Lever, the headmaster, tried to talk him round, as did a priest, but there was a thrill in the disobedience, in the anxiety of adults, in being a disappointment to good people. When he got older Big Mr Doyle gave him a hiding with the belt from his trousers. But that didn't work. In truth, the family couldn't look after him. They were grieving themselves, for other children had died; and poverty can hamper loving. John stopped irritating the police and began, instead, to seriously upset them. They gave him a hiding, too.

'This is the boy who ran from court and joined the army in nineteen fifteen,' said Anselm. 'Within a year he'd twice been sentenced to death. But on his third approach he met Joseph Flanagan in no-man's-land. It was a moment, I suspect, more powerful for Flanagan than Lindsay. There and then, while a battle raged, he took the boy to a widow in Étaples whose own teenage son had been taken by the war. And for that unwarranted leave of absence, Joseph Flanagan was eventually tied to a chair and shot. Part of Herbert's story, and one he could never tell, was that he helped put that chair in place. He was obedient to the law and the circumstances of war but he nonetheless carried a burden of responsibility for the rest of his life. That is what Herbert felt, I am sure. And I'm also sure that he only discovered afterwards what Joseph Flanagan had actually done and why. He desperately tried to change the direction of the tide, but he couldn't. The tragedy among other tragedies is that the knowing beforehand would have made no difference: Joseph Flanagan had committed a capital crime at a capital moment.'

Anselm's eye fell on Sylvester's empty seat and a rush of sympathy made him want to quit the room and find the old fellow. To tell him that Herbert's silence on these, the most important experiences of his life, was not a species of rejection, not a lack of trust, just the inevitable outcome of a moral and emotional battering no man could recount without breaking down, perhaps permanently.

'There are two journeys of great importance that now took place,' resumed Anselm, after clearing his throat and his mind for the task in hand. 'Herbert's, to Larkwood as a man restored to himself, and that of John Lindsay – who owed his life, yet again, to someone he'd met by chance. As for Herbert, he set out with Doyle's tags around his neck. He never removed them. No one can know what happened during his passage save that, at its end, he came to define Larkwood's ambience. Now, while *we know* that John Lindsay followed a similar path towards fulfilment, *Herbert* remained in the dark. He had no way of knowing, because after leaving Étaples he had no contact with either the boy or his adoptive mother, Lisette Papinau. And he worried that Joseph Flanagan's sacrifice had been wasted by a life of remorse. Thankfully, he was wrong. There was no healing message to deliver, because John Lindsay had been nurtured to the harmony of light and dark by a woman who'd known both in equal measure, Lisette Papinau. If you like, everything Herbert had hoped for had come to pass.'

Anselm paused, recognising a question in many of the faces fixed upon him. Involuntarily, he glanced again at Sylvester's empty chair. 'The problem, as you are well aware, is that someone *did* come to Larkwood. Kate Seymour: a relative or friend to someone who *is* tormented; a man to whom Herbert never gave a glancing thought. And I have no idea who it might be.'

Anselm had finished. He sat down feeling weary, blood beating gently against his ears. He was exhausted by what he'd had to say; by his own long journey through scraps of paper to the wavering voice of Mr Shaw, through so much submission to suffering, only to reach this moment of confusion. He let his gaze rest on the guttering candle, unable to restrain the flood of names and imagined faces.

'It's fairly obvious, isn't it?' came Bede's voice.

Anselm snapped into the present.

Bede's stern eyes were upon him. Swiftly, Larkwood's archivist scanned the Chapter Room as if looking for support. No one made a sound. 'The family thrown aside by military justice was Joseph

Flanagan's. What about them? They've probably hidden their loss for half a century.'

Anselm felt like he'd been thumped from behind. He looked over to Bede and nodded, remembering the vehemence of David Osborne. 'You're right.'

'Did the army write to his parents?' continued Bede, again addressing Anselm. 'They might have done, but if so, the details would have been vague – something to hide what had really happened. "We beg to report that your son died from wounds. I remain, Sir, Madam, your obedient servant." Some nonsense like that. No precise location, maybe no date. If Joseph Flanagan's name vanished from all military records after nineteen seventeen, no member of the family would—'

'Bede is absolutely right,' insisted Anselm, turning to the Prior. 'There's no memorial save a tree among trees – the family would never know what had happened to their son. They wouldn't be able to find out. And that is precisely what has happened.'

The community were of one mind: whatever Kate Seymour's connection to the old man might be, they shared a secrecy of purpose entirely consistent with embarrassment or a sense of dishonour, however ill-founded. And that fact alone made tracing them a delicate enterprise because their privacy could not be compromised by a rudimentary public appeal.

'Let's sleep on it,' said the Prior, finally. 'I've never yet solved a problem the day it surfaced.'

With another prayer he drew the meeting to a close and extinguished the candle between his thumb and a finger. The community processed out of the Chapter Room, through the dark cloister and into the church for Compline. There, leaning on his stall like an exile, was Sylvester. Though he knew the words by heart, the Gatekeeper leafed through the pages of his Psalter as if he'd never seen it before.

Anselm slept badly, trying to think of schemes that would lead him to Joseph Flanagan's family. When he woke for Lauds he was as lost as the night before. Throwing his habit over his pyjamas, he glanced across his cell and froze. On the ground, inches away from the narrow gap beneath the door, was a small square of white card. He picked it up and read the embossed writing several times.

Dr Kate Seymour, Ph.D, was a forensic anthropologist based at the University of Galway. How she came to have an interest in Joseph Flanagan was the main question but Anselm was distracted by another. Who had knelt outside his cell during the night? He suspected Bede, who'd spoken wisely at the moment Anselm had confessed to defeat.

Chapter Fifty-Five

Where the Lark Runs

1

Herbert and ten other monks walked the eight miles from Sudbury Station along a country lane to the Old Abbey Ruin and a seventeenth-century manor that had been donated for the new foundation. The Benedictines had built the place in the thirteen hundreds and it had thrived until forced closure during the Reformation, when the abbey was quarried for local housing, and a manor built for Henry VIII's trumpeter. The property had passed through several hands until its ramshackle condition prompted abandonment. Such was the information sent to Les Ramiers, along with a citation from the earliest known manuscript reference to the site and its occupants: *hic monachi pacati habitant ubi manat alauda*: monks dwell in peace where the Lark runs.

Herbert stood at the large broken gates, his feet sore. On his back was everything he possessed. His brother monks were from Britain, France, Belgium and Germany, oddly enough the Christian countries at the heart of the conflagration that had destroyed empires and changed the face of the modern world. No map could chart the difference. There were too many dead. Our innocence has gone, as Duggie put it. Herbert gazed at the ruin ahead: tall arches covered in creeper, a worn night-stair leading to the open sky, a tumbling manor with red and pink tiles in disarray. Père Lucien at Les Ramiers had not seen this place; and he could not possibly fathom the delicate configuration of things that might move a man's heart. But he'd been profoundly right about Herbert's. I, too, can dwell here in peace, he thought.

Quite how it came to pass no one knew. The monks began restoring the building, sleeping in old army tents from different armies, and praying in the room of least leaks. In place of a bell they hung a plank between two ropes and struck it with a spade. Perhaps that strange sound had drawn the attention of passers-by, who'd then spoken of what they'd seen. Whatever the explanation, the monks gradually found themselves with other companions. People of faith and no faith, of all denominations and no denomination, began to help the silent monks in their work. Some came with a tent of their own and remained for months. Artisans worked for nothing, learning the blunt sign language that joined the community together. In the evenings, when tools were downed, all other sounds seemed curiously loud after the racket of the day. Herbert waited for that time with impatience. He liked to walk beside the stream, listening to the land: the rush of water and the jubilant song of larks hiding in the fields.

Despite their years, Herbert's parents joined the motley crowd. For a week at a time they, too, came to help. Ernest scratched his thick whiskers while deploring the shoddy work done since his last inspection. Constance laid out long trestle tables, covering them with fabulous needlepoint lace, family heirlooms from Bruges and Alençon. Her sandwiches and cakes, once the talk of the 22nd Lancers, became the fare of men without a nation-state. This couple from a bygone age were adored by everyone. They even saluted Ernest on his rounds.

'Herbert,' said Constance, nervously, on a day of parting. 'There's something I've wanted to say for a *very* long time.'

She twisted a cane umbrella between her gloved hands.

'A long time ago your father and I made a very wrong decision. And it affected you deeply.'

Herbert thought of Colonel Maude and the High-Ups of the regiment. Inside, he felt a burst of remembered humiliation.

Like someone stepping honourably under a train, Constance said, 'When you refused to go to Stonyhurst we sent you to the local school.'

'Pardon?'

'Please, Herbert. You know *very well* what I'm referring to. We wouldn't let you change your mind, even though you were quite miserable. You see –' she blushed, tapping a shoe with the umbrella's point – 'we thought it would be character-building to make you stand by a decision. I'm so very sorry for my harshness. So is your father. We were frightfully silly back then.'

If only she knew, thought Herbert. If only she knew of the decisions I've made and had to live with. Not even Stonyhurst could have prepared me for the pulling of a trigger . . . for when he'd said 'Guilty' and 'Death', banking on someone else's mercy. Herbert never wished to be once again in the consuming presence of Colonel Maude, but he did now: that his commanding officer might hear his mother confess to a great wrong; that the Lancers might learn how innocent she was, even after all these years.

When the restoration work on the monastery was almost complete, someone came up with the outlandish idea of erecting a statue of Our Lady right in the middle of a secluded lake behind a shoulder of trees. So one evening Herbert and the Prior, an experienced monk from Les Moineaux, went to take a long look at this hidden eye on to heaven. After gazing at the reflections for a long time, the Prior nudged Herbert's arm and deftly signed, 'Where are we?' He meant: 'What are we going to call this school for sane living, run by the not so sane?'

Herbert listened intently to the music in the trees. Then he was drawn elsewhere, to another sound, first heard on a dark road out of Oostbeke when the dawn silvered some nameless trees. He tried a few clumsy manoeuvres with his fingers. Eventually he whispered, 'Larkwood.'

2

One of the more talkative helpers – a whisperer and nudger – was called Sylvester. He came to help with the thatching of a barn and never left. He became a novice in 1925, the year of Herbert's solemn profession. With tousled blond hair and bright blue eyes, he was, at twenty-two, a lively presence: a practical joker (using a plumb line as a trip wire) who was always late for everything. He had to be dragged out of bed in the morning and hauled away from the table after meals. Despite hours of instruction he never mastered the sign language – even though it had been devised to accommodate the slower medieval mind and had worked smoothly for centuries without need of alteration. He took to whistling, pointing and winking. During recreation, when the monks talked freely, he occasionally pressed Herbert for stories of the war.

Sylvester had wanted to join up but he was only eleven in 1914. He'd been frustrated, because plenty of boys only a few years older than himself had enlisted. They got a spread in the paper. Time and again there was an article about a fifteen-year-old in the trenches, bravely fighting for King and Country. His father, a skilled thatcher, would slam the paper shut every time he saw the photo of some young hero – not because he thought it a disgrace, but because he was ashamed. A back injury had rendered him unfit to serve in uniform. Despite the growing casualty lists and the drawn blinds in the streets, he tried several times to get past the army doctors, but they always turned him away. He was eventually banned from the premises. So Sylvester, eager to please his father, had joined the scouts. He'd even met Baden-Powell, the man who'd stood firm during the siege of Mafeking. And Herbert, ten years his senior, and a veteran, listened to Sylvester's ardour for England with a deep melancholy. He shared it, still.

However, something in Sylvester's questioning unsettled Herbert. Despite knowing many war widows, and former soldiers – both injured and apparently 'normal' – the young man didn't seem to appreciate what it had been like in France and Flanders. Which, perhaps, was not so surprising. In order to survive, most soldiers had bottled up their experiences, or changed their way of talking, to make it credible, to bring it properly dressed into decent society. It was the same for Herbert. He said nothing to his brother monks, but he was still haunted by the face of Quarters; he still had to steel himself to watch those eyes vanish in a spurt of mud. And he still saw Elliot at Broodseinde with the cigarette in his hand, just before he stubbed it on his boot. Herbert had been right beside him. And, of course, there was Joseph Flanagan, his breath beating against a canvas gas mask. None of these moments dimmed. They formed such an intense presence of intimate memory that he could not speak of them. To do so would be like talking while someone died in his hands. Certain tragedies require silence as an epitaph – at least for the participants. And consequently, it was with some alarm that Herbert sensed in Sylvester the birth of a new romanticism, an excitement not dissimilar to that which preceded the war.

And so one evening Herbert went to the lake where Sylvester was working. A railway official had donated some sleepers to the community and the young monk had spent weeks sinking them into the ground in unusual places, creating benches for those who wandered while they prayed. One such was by the lake, and so it was here that Herbert met Sylvester and led him away, to a copse of aspen trees. There, beneath the shivering leaves, he talked simply about sacrifice and shame; about Joseph Flanagan's execution and Herbert's breaking of regimental crockery.

Colonel Maude would have been proud of him.

Chapter Fifty-Six

1

Anselm sat by a murmuring fire near a hotel window that looked on to the beach of Brandon Bay. A strong wind swept off the Atlantic, tugging at a line of trees crouched like men with their collars turned up. Beyond the white crests, concealed by the mist, was Inisdúr. Sitting beside him, dressed in jeans, Wellingtons and a thick woollen jumper, her hair tied in a rough, reddish knot, was Kate Seymour, the only niece of Seosamh Ó Flannagáin. Her father was Brendan, Seosamh's only brother.

This friendship of immediate significance; this meeting, a preamble for what would happen that evening; this strange anticipation of something good: all these swift developments had been driven by a kind of relentless inevitability. It was a final ordering of events, the doing of what ought to be done. After Anselm had rung Kate to explain the meaning of the trial, she had told Brendan; and he had wanted to meet John Lindsay, who, in his turn, had wanted to come to Inisdúr. 'Want' was not the right word. This was a new experience, of yearning, demand and obedience to history. There was no term for it.

'This is not just a gathering,' Kate had stressed. 'My father's going to hold a *leanúint* . . . it's an island custom. It means "following". On Inisdúr, when someone died, the body was laid on a table. The family kept watch . . . to follow the dead to their awakening. Throughout the night anyone could visit to speak a word of memory. Then they'd leave. Only the family saw the sun rise upon the body. Then the burial took place. It's one ceremony from dark to light.'

And so Anselm had come to follow Seosamh Ó Flannagáin to his awakening. He'd come in Herbert's name.

* * *

Anselm gazed across the ruffled fields that drifted without boundary on to the sand. To the south, heavy clouds were banked like grey mountains sinking into the sea. Cattle mooched by the surf.

'The Ó Flannagáins left Inisdúr during the "great evacuation" of nineteen fifty-four,' said Kate. She had a natural smile that vanished when she spoke. Tiny lines gathered round her mouth, seeming to show sudden seriousness. 'We were, in fact, the very last to leave.'

Her grandmother, Róisín, refused to move. Brendan literally carried her down the slip to the waiting boat and a new life on the mainland, with a house provided by the Land Board. She never recovered from the displacement and would stare out to sea, when the island was in view. 'Muiris is still there,' she often whimpered. 'We left him behind.' He'd died thirty years previously.

For Kate's parents, Brendan and Myriam, this subsidised existence was almost equally disorientating. They'd lived off the land. Now they lived off the State. It was an incomprehensible state of affairs: they got something for nothing. Brendan set up a shop near Brandon harbour, to serve the fishing boats, and Myriam knitted sweaters for the men – like the one Kate was wearing now – and socks. Once they could make ends meet, they found a house of their own and cut themselves free from those heavy grants.

For Kate, aged twelve, the leaving was the foundation of her future.

Inisdúr had been a dying world. Hence the 'great evacuation'. All the young men and women, bar 'the loyal' few, had gone – to the factories, the wages and the electric lights. There'd only been four other children in the school, where old Mr Drennan, the teacher, had long ago abandoned any pretence to structured education. He'd romped through poetry that caught his mood, taught them wild songs, or lambasted the air itself on the sins of Collins and De Valera. His thumping obsessions had all been way above their little heads. Kate had thought him an injured man; a man of strange and private rituals . . . for as long as anyone could remember, he'd kept a glass of wine-vinegar beneath a writing slate. He'd kept a map facing the wall.

On the mainland, however, all that changed for Kate. With conventional though less interesting teachers, she flourished. Another world of limitless possibilities opened. She duly chased some of them to ground, beginning at the gates of Trinity College, Dublin, and ending at the University of Philadelphia. She returned to Ireland a forensic anthropologist, two words her parents couldn't begin to pronounce or understand, and a career they found vaguely deviant: the scientific examination of human remains.

'We never spoke of Inisdúr at home,' said Kate. The sprinkling of freckles on her nose and cheeks were a stronger characteristic than Anselm remembered. They showed emotion through a slight increase in colour. 'For my parents it was a kind of grief. For me it was part of my escape. Even Gaelic seemed a retrograde language, a way of speaking for a world that no longer existed. For a long while I wouldn't speak it, except at home where it was the means of intimacy. On leaving the farm, the currachs and a whole *craft* of living, the island was cut loose from me, and it drifted free into the Atlantic and almost disappeared . . . except that I knew my father went back . . . frequently.' For a fleeting moment the faint smile returned. 'He'd stay out there, all alone, for a week at a time. Year after year he crossed over. I thought it was because he missed the sounds of his infancy. In one way, I was right. In another, I was wrong. Very wrong.'

Kate had just come back from Bosnia where she'd been helping UN investigators prepare forensic evidence for prosecutions at The Hague. Exhausted by her work, she'd returned to a very different manner of trial – a third and possibly final separation from her husband of sixteen years. She went home to Brandon Bay to ponder the meaning of divorce. And then, one fine morning, when a mist had cleared off the sea, she decided to go back to that simplest of places, where the Matchmaker would have been brought to book for getting it so badly wrong.

'I walked up the slip towards the farm,' said Kate. She'd planned to camp out for a few days in the house. 'But when I got there, I saw a beautiful, tended field.'

'A field?' repeated Anselm.

'Yes. Only I'd never seen it before. The surrounding wall was typical Inisdúr . . . huge rocks and small stones laid to an inimitable pattern, created through a deep attachment to the land. It was in perfect condition. Not a single boulder had slipped out of place. When I got back to the mainland, I'd barely walked through the door when my father said, much too quietly, "It's Seosamh's Field."'

Kate had never heard of Seosamh in her life.

'Now, come meet my father,' she said, rising. 'He'll tell you what else was hidden from me and this mainland life.'

They walked south along the beach through a tearing wind, their feet crunching upon a vast scattering of blue and pink shells. Ahead, beneath clouds that seemed to suck up the distant hills, was Kate's childhood home, a white cottage on a promontory. Small flags fluttered on a crowd of mast heads, their main lines tinkling like millions of tiny bells. The Ó Flannagáins had left Inisdúr but they'd never got further than the harbour where they'd landed.

2

All the furnishings in the small sitting room huddled together. Even the walls seemed to lean in towards the plump armchairs, the low table and another murmuring fire. Heavy condensation ran down the windows. The walls were bare and whitewash clean. Roughly cut timbers like spars ran across a dipped ceiling.

'You'll have tea,' ordered Brendan. 'And bread to build your strength. We don't give stone in this house.'

Despite his age, he was an imposing man and filled his chair completely. His thick beard grew high on weathered cheeks. The blue-green jacket carried the warmth of the hills, his hazy blue eyes the immeasurable distance of the sea. He regarded Anselm closely, weighing him up. He wasn't altogether sure.

Myriam laid bread and butter on the table, poured tea from the pot and then slipped out. An island way, thought Anselm. He'd barely seen her. But she, too, had a strong presence: in slow, decisive movements, with that firm hand of welcome. He'd seen delicacy, too, in the pale skin sprinkled with freckles; like Kate, who sat close to her father like a protecting angel.

The men from Inisdúr needed no invitation to speak, no preamble to set the scene. Brendan simply started talking, his aching eyes on the fire, a remembered island fire. He chose his words carefully, as if there was no rush, as if he was building one of those strange walls to a pattern no one could summon in their dreams.

'I was twelve years of age when Seosamh stepped on that boat and off the memory of the land,' he said. 'With these arms I rowed him to the lee. From then on, his name was only ever whispered. And spoken once out loud.'

He nodded solemnly at his daughter and then returned his gaze to the low flames. Rituals ran within his blood. They were a way of understanding experience. Each person had their place, including the educated Kate. At the nod, she went out of the room and came back with an envelope. Anselm took out a flimsy sheet of paper, folded in two. Dated 18th September 1917, it was more distressing to handle than anything he'd touched on this, his long journey to a sharing of bread, not stone.

Dear Mr and Mrs Flanagan,
You will no doubt have heard from persons in Authority as to the unfortunate manner of your son's death. He was held in great esteem by his comrades. None of us believed he was a deserter. I hope it is of some consolation when I tell you that he rests now in a place of considerable beauty, among trees untouched by war.
If there is ever anything I can do to be of assistance, please remember, Sir, Madam, that I remain,
Your humble and obedient servant,
RSM Francis P. Joyce, 8th (Service) Btn. NLI.

Feeling a swell of tears, Anselm put the letter on the table, grateful that it was his place to listen.

'My mother and father didn't utter a word for a week,' said Brendan. 'We hadn't known Seosamh had joined the ranks of the British Army. Now we knew he'd been executed by them. We didn't know why. We didn't know where. And we didn't have his *body*.'

Brendan let the last word escape through his breath so quietly that Anselm shivered. It was as though Seosamh's flesh – all human flesh – was intrinsically holy and had to be handled with fear and reverence. But Seosamh's had been heaped on straw . . .

'My father slowly died,' resumed Brendan, still looking towards that island fire. 'He worked the fields but there was no will left in him, no desire. The passion that had made them, that had brought up the weed and sand, had gone. He willed himself to death. We buried him two years later. As for my mother –' emotion came heavy upon Brendan's face, he thrust out his jaw in silent pain; mastering himself through inner violence, he continued – 'she'd always wanted to leave the island, to travel to Boston, that mysterious place of opportunity and enchantment, to find her sister, Úna . . . but after Seosamh's death she wouldn't even go to Inismín. She was cursed. Cursed because she looked upon devils and would not turn away.'

Anselm wholly understood Brendan's meaning. He meant regret and remorse, and their tormenting, mesmerising power.

'For the next thirty-six years she never mentioned Seosamh, though I knew she thought of him every day. And then we left the island. She was to die within nine months. There was no illness to come, no accident. She made a decision, like my father. That was when she spoke of Seosamh once again, though she didn't utter his name.'

Brendan took his eyes off the hearth. Leaning forward, he compressed all his age and remembrance into one, alarming expression, fixed on Anselm. 'Before she went to bed to start the dying, she said, "Brendan, bring your brother home. Hold the Following. And bury him on Inisdúr."'

Brendan relaxed, releasing Anselm from his stare. Possessed by the same force that had mesmerised his mother, he turned inward, a massive physical presence, somehow absent.

Kate explained that Brendan tried to find out why Seosamh had been condemned and where he'd been buried. He wrote to the army and government offices in Dublin and London. No one could tell him anything, save that the trial papers had been retained in the War Office archives. A Whitehall official observed that the Army Act was quite clear on the issue: such papers could only be released to the subject of the court martial; and since that person had not made the application, the matter could not be taken any further.

Only a dead man could ask to read the transcript of his life's undoing, thought Anselm, marvelling at the poise of the legal mind; thinking of the blocked road left for those who'd loved a man found wanting.

On that basis, resumed Kate, all capital court martial files were closed to public inspection for seventy-five years. But then she came back from Bosnia and found Seosamh's Field, and the name of an uncle whose papers had just been released at the Public Record Office in London.

'And as soon as I opened the file,' said Kate – after her father had stepped outside, wanting air. He'd sunk away, into his beard, his clothes, the sea – 'I realised that this was no ordinary trial . . . that something had happened between Seosamh and Owen Doyle. The situation was laughable. Here I was, a specialist in reading bones, and I couldn't understand the fragments left behind by my own uncle –' she joined her hands earnestly, dishevelled by feeling – 'we are so very grateful to you. For finding Seosamh; and the *wonderful* meaning of his life . . . it drove out whatever feeling we had against Father Moore.'

Brendan was large against the misted window. A gale was lifting against him, cleaning out his mind. He was preparing for the Following, when darkness would give way to light, when he could be released from the grip of demons.

3

Anselm struggled back along the beach towards his hotel, hardly noticing the cold, colossal roar from the sea. He was thinking of Brendan, who'd never told Kate about his brother, who'd made a field to his memory; and of Kate who'd gone to the national archives, unable to confide in Martin Reid, or, later, Sarah Osborne. Father and daughter were tracked by the shadows of Muiris and Róisín. A deep privacy covered them both like a shroud. Unable to make sense of the trial papers, they'd gone on a pilgrimage to Étaples, Elverdinghe, Ypres and Oostbeke. A display on the Gilbertines at Les Ramiers had caught Kate's eye. She'd read the name of Herbert Moore. And a brief reference to Larkwood had brought Brendan to the edge of a copse of trees where, remembering the words of Francis P. Joyce, RSM, he'd wept. Maybe Seosamh was laid in such a place, he'd thought. A beautiful place untouched by war. He'd never know.

'The Following begins at nightfall, Father,' Kate had repeated, having shown him the chosen room, a parlour facing the sea. She'd given him the time, too, but had then slipped back to the language of the island, where commitments were judged by the placement of the sun. 'At first light, we go to Inisdúr. Would you find a reading, please? Something for this long-awaited moment?'

In the peace of his room, to the rattle of windows, Anselm opened his pocket bible at the Apocalypse, that book on the wrath of the lamb. He quickly turned the pages, his eyes sharp for two words. Like a bird of prey, he flew into an abysm of thunder, over burning lakes of sulphur, beneath a moon red as blood. Finally he found what he was looking for: the gifts bestowed on the Victor as he enters the Kingdom of Heaven: manna and stone.

This was the passage that Herbert would have chosen, Anselm was sure.

Chapter Fifty-Seven

Nothing Happens by Accident

Herbert had been at Larkwood over fifty years when he met a prowling lawyer called Anselm.

Years previously, in the sixties, a green Cortina had been found crashed into the enclosure wall. The owner couldn't be traced so the police gave it to Herbert on the express understanding that he never drove it off the monastery grounds, because he had no licence. In time it became a sort of wheelchair, and Herbert enjoyed trundling here and there, whenever he wanted to be on his own.

On one of those warm November days where summer and winter meet to confuse any sorting of the seasons, Herbert drove to the very extent of Larkwood's boundary. Taking a lane too sharply, he skidded into a ditch. The instantaneous terror roused by the scraping and final thud was altogether exhilarating. Herbert whistled and tapped the steering wheel with satisfaction. He caught his breath and looked out of the window. It was a lovely afternoon. Oaks and chestnuts were shedding their modesty. You could almost hear them fall. Herbert started laughing, because he was stuck: an old leaf among other old leaves. A knocking by his ear made him turn towards an enquiring face. He had light brown hair, tired eyes, and he looked far too serious. Herbert wound down the window and quipped, 'Do you want a lift?'

The young man smiled woodenly and disappeared into the woods. He came back with a large branch. After jamming it under the back wheels he issued authoritative instructions on what Herbert had to do. 'Father, accelerate gently, and I will push.'

Maybe part of becoming old is that you don't listen very well.

For whatever reason, out of excitement or playful desperation, Herbert pressed the pedal to the floor. Mud sprayed high and the car swivelled as if it wanted to get deeper into the ditch. With some jolting and jamming, more instructions, and some gentleness this time, the car slid back on to the lane. When Herbert turned in gratitude to the voice at the window, he almost cried out. The young man's face was splattered . . . and for an horrific instant Herbert saw Quarters looking back, desperate and terrified, out of the swamp at Ypres . . . the banks of the Zenderbeek had collapsed, shells soared and crashed on Passchendaele, the mule sank, its mouth open, the tongue hideously long and blue. 'Hop in,' Herbert chimed, to bluff his panic. 'I'll take you back.'

But Herbert couldn't stop his hands shaking. He locked them tight on to the steering wheel, while the old Cortina just stayed put in the middle of the lane. To calm himself he asked endless questions, while the young man wiped clean his face and hands on a handkerchief. Gradually Herbert found his footing in the present, and he began to hear the answers. 'Bix Beiderbecke . . . it's hard to say, Teddy Wilson or Art Tatum . . . the incomparable Maxine Sullivan . . . London . . . Gray's Inn . . . Criminal Law . . .'

Herbert's saviour was a barrister, dear God.

'The Lord wasn't that fond of lawyers,' he said with a groan. 'Law and love . . . it's not always a happy marriage.'

Herbert couldn't think of what to say next; and he wished he'd kept his mouth shut, for while it reflected his own experience the remark was, if anything, a touch rude. But he was a tough nut, this prowler, and he fought his corner.

'Might I suggest something?' he began, all lawyerly. 'Love without the law would be licentious and the law without love would be ruthless.'

Herbert could almost hear the fellow sit down in court with a flourish and a bang, and for a moment Herbert was left blinking at the trees, unable to reply. He couldn't quite keep pace with his breath. He snatched for air . . . and his eyes smarted: in the darkest place of his memory his old mind discerned a strange light.

Herbert had been the ruthless hand of the law, he'd always known that; but he saw something else, now: of all the lives Herbert's hand might have touched out there on the Western Front, of all the many broken men who'd been condemned by the savagery of a wartime dispensation, Herbert had touched . . . love. Rough justice had met a saving mercy. Herbert's participation in a monstrous crime had been part of that mystery. In Joseph Flanagan, Herbert's ruthlessness had been purified.

He glanced sideways at the young man, whose name he did not know, grateful for this precious, accidental gift given in the autumn of his life . . . while copper leaves fell from the oaks and chestnuts he'd planted in 1925. He'd received a word of mercy, from a man who looked so terribly like Quarters.

'What do you do here?' asked the prowler, suddenly. 'At the monastery, I mean.'

Herbert gave a slight start. He'd asked the same question, in much the same way. He, too, had crept around an enclosure. With an old longing, he said, 'We tend a fire that won't go out.'

The young man frowned, not satisfied by half, but inside Herbert smiled. This fellow wasn't simply curious. He'd spoken out of a longing, a homesickness . . . a kind of hidden misery. The answer he sought would only come to him in the living: he would, one day, knock on Larkwood's door.

'I'm Herbert,' he said, to celebrate the moment.

'And I'm Anselm.'

After a shaking of hands, neither one truly understanding the other, Herbert gave the ignition a savage turn, randomly pressed the pedals with his dancing feet. With a bang they were off, birds leaping deranged from the trees. He cut through a field to the Priory, sliding like he used to as a boy, feet in socks along a corridor. The wheels span frantically but the old Cortina levelled out on a gentle slope, and it easily made the road, finding traction on a collapsed fence. Herbert drove slowly to the car park, quietly exultant.

'What would you have done if I hadn't turned up?' asked Anselm, again lawyerly.

Herbert sensed the eyes of a jury upon him, and a reproving, worldly judge. But he looked, instead, to his puzzled interrogator, the prowler who'd unwittingly brought the light with him.

'Nothing happens by accident,' he replied, rattling free the keys.

Herbert stayed in his Cortina, watching Anselm walk away with his hands behind his back, a young man slightly lost, though not as lost as he imagined. As the unhappy lawyer stepped through the guest-house door, Herbert felt a completely new type of fear, alluring in a way, possibly exciting, but frightening all the same.

He realised that he'd just given to that young man all the wisdom he possessed: it wasn't much but it was all Herbert had to give: on an understanding of accidents and faithfulness. And, speaking for himself, after today there was nothing left to receive.

Yes, thought Herbert, I'm frightened because soon I will die.

Chapter Fifty-Eight

1

Anselm lifted the latch on to the Following of Seosamh Ó Flannagáin. He gently opened the door and stepped inside. When his eyes had become accustomed to the obscurity he saw six chairs arranged within arm's length around a long table. At one end sat Brendan, a hand spread upon each knee. At the other, facing him, sat John Lindsay, head bowed. Kate and Sabine were side by side along one length. Anselm joined Myriam on the other. The circle was complete. Three men and three women. Three blood relatives mingled with three strangers.

Myriam struck a match and lit two candles, one at either end of the table. Flickering light fell upon a wonderful covering, a fabric of purple and orange and blue and gold. A Joseph's cloak of many impossible colours, woven, Anselm was sure, by Róisín. The space between the two flames was agonisingly bare. It was the length of a man. In the centre, upon the vibrant cloth, very small and just catching the light, were two discs, one red, one green.

'Now is the time of memory,' announced Brendan with a gruff whisper. He'd trimmed his beard, giving it shape and a kind of bristling softness. His short white hair was thin, parted cleanly, like a boy's. 'Speak if moved.'

The darkness was strong and bore down from the rafters. Outside, the wind had drawn back. Soft exhalations upon the harbour made the pennants lightly flap and the main lines clink. The smell of oil and salt filled the room.

'I was for ever following you,' began Brendan after an age, his voice both strong and weak. 'Did you know, brother?'

All eyes rested on the long, burdened table.

'Of a night time I followed you, often enough, to the teacher's door, and listened to that other learning. Of the pink lands and another tongue. Did you know, Seosamh?'

Brendan paused, swelling his chest.

'I heard my mother's voice that night, when she gave you her secret blessing. When she told you to fly, boy, and bring back wonderful tales from far away places.'

Anselm shrank into the folds of his habit.

'I stood at the door when my father begged you to stay, when he said there was one more field to be made. I heard that, Seosamh, did you know? Well, I made it, brother . . . in your name, with these hands.'

Anselm's prickling eyes found the two stamped tags, the remains of an executed man on a robe for an island king: name, number and religion.

'I followed you to the slip. I rowed you away from the crowd. Did you think of me afterwards, as I thought of you?'

Brendan stared ahead, as he might have done when the boat pulled away from Inisdúr. It was a hungry stare, and helpless. And unbearable to witness, because there was nothing else to be said. This was the moment when friends and neighbours should have raised their own voices of remembrance – old people who'd once been young in that crowd. But they'd passed on themselves. Myriam had never met Seosamh. Neither had Kate. There was no one left. Anselm closed his eyes, reaching wildly for prayers or hymns, anything at all to drive back this encroaching emptiness . . . but then John Lindsay's voice broke the silence.

'I followed you, too,' he said, head still bowed. 'I followed you out of hell. You saved my life when it was least worth saving –' his shoulders sank, and his voice all but faded away – 'you took my place.'

There was no other sound, save the clink of the mast head lines and that faint fluttering of tiny flags. When John Lindsay looked up, his face crushed and unrecognisable, Brendan rose, huge in the gloom.

'When Seosamh took your place,' he said, eyes on the woven cloth, 'you became my brother.'

* * *

Despite the tradition of an all-night vigil, Myriam invited the weary to sleep, to be fresh for the crossing at sunrise. Anselm had no idea how long he stayed. He seemed to have entered a floating universe where time did not run, where the darkness had a pulse and the real world was itself a memory. When he got up to leave, only Brendan and John remained, kinsmen at either end of a table: near to one another, yet so very far apart.

Anselm had no recollection of sleeping. He lay on his bed, eyes upon the depth of night, committing to memory the passage he'd chosen from the Apocalypse. The sea was astoundingly silent, more a breathing presence. When a sliver of morning touched the horizon he went outside into a vast, growing murmur. He could see nothing, just the jagged outline of bent trees. But something was out there, greater than the bay, greater than the black sky. At the appointed hour, Kate came to meet him. She arrived as when he'd first seen her: in a long black coat, her thick auburn hair gathered tight, her face pale.

In a faint light that picked out the gathering of decks, cabins and wrapped sails, Anselm and his five companions stepped off the harbour into a small fishing boat. The pilot, a short wiry man with face wrinkles like scars, nodded to each of them in silence, doffing a rumpled woollen cap.

2

Anselm leaned on the prow, his cowl pulled tight around his face. Occasionally waves slapped on the fore timbers, sending a spray on to the deck. They were heading into a luminous vapour that neither rested on the sea nor rose from it. He could see nothing distinct, just the lines of foam like cut string. But then . . . vague dark rocks like smudges of black ink appeared in the mist. A hint of brown and green glowed with the rising sun, but then faded into grey, subsiding into the water where it joined the air. Collapsed gable ends, still white, flashed briefly. A rocky wall straggled into the sky as if it were built on nothing . . . but as they entered the haze a field took substance, grounding the stones. Quilted cloud lay upon a hillside with fallen houses spaced like broken ribs. Waves thundered on to a scree heaped at the base of a spectacular cliff. Sea birds circled on the breeze, their long wings held wide and still.

So this is Inisdúr, thought Anselm, the one place on earth where the land and the sea are one.

The pilot knew his route like Anselm knew Larkwood. One arm hung loosely on the wheel as he guided them through stacks and part-submerged tables of granite. Rounding a headland, they entered a cove where the water became calm, changing colour from blue-grey to green. Without seeming to look at what he was doing, the pilot moored along a stone wharf built against the rock. The wharf followed the cove, losing height until it met a small beach fronting steps that led to a track.

Seosamh came that way, thought Anselm, his eyes following the path that wound up a gentle incline to the brow of a low hill. This is the route we will take.

Anselm was right. As the dawn grew stronger, Brendan and John led the way. From some natural sense of correctness everyone else kept some distance behind them. Side by side, the family elders began their pilgrimage. Each of them had a stick, but they leaned more on each other, pausing at intervals to dredge up strength. They passed half-standing walls and gaping doorways, the stony vestiges of a long-forgotten life. Finally Kate and Sabine helped them, and Anselm took the arm of Myriam. They moved as one gathered assembly, bound together in a relentless, dogged march to a place of stunning tranquillity.

The farm of Muiris and Róisín Ó Flannagáin lay within the arms of a natural embankment, unprotected from the sounds of the sea but free from the wind. Waves hammered the rocks with rousing violence, but here, in the hollow, a breeze seemed to saunter round the hillside. A low cottage hugged the land. The roof was roughly intact but the windows had perished long ago. A timber door hung aslant. Beyond, the farm's walls lay in tumbled ruin . . . except one.

Brendan and Kate unfastened a wooden gate to a circular field.

Like hesitant intruders, unsure of their bearings, everyone walked towards the centre, looked around in bewilderment.

Angular stones, smooth boulders, rough rocks, pebbles . . . every kind of unyielding substance . . . had been brought together and balanced, miraculously. This wall should fall, thought Anselm, sensing the frailty. But it won't, because of the paradox of true strength. The great depended upon the small. It was perfect. A scraping sound made him swing around.

Brendan was on his knees. His wide cap hid his head and face so Anselm only saw the activity of his fingers: he was tearing at the land that he'd made. It was an overwhelming sight. Without a word, he forced his nails into the soil; he pulled at the roots of grass; he opened up the darkness in the ground. When a small hole had been fashioned, Kate and Myriam helped him to his feet. Brendan leaned between them, exhausted, his hands cut and shaking.

The morning had grown stronger now. Colours were deepening. Anselm could make out the delicate yellow of lichen on the wall. It was like lace, but no one could have invented the pattern, or made it. A soft clink came from his side.

John had taken Seosamh's identity tags out of his coat pocket. He held them up for a long time, so long that Anselm thought he was back in that beating darkness of the parlour . . . only now there was a growing tide of light. The wind carried the distant clamour of birds around the cliffs. Bending forward, Sabine's arm around him, John lowered the red and green discs into the land. Then Brendan sank once more to his knees.

'"If anyone has ears to hear, let him listen,"' recited Anselm, his voice loud. '"To anyone who is victorious I will give the hidden manna. And I will give him a white stone, and on it will be a new name, known only to him who receives it."'

Thus the righteous enter into glory, thought Anselm, looking beyond the wall, the salt-bitten fields, and into a very distant mist, the mist out of which Inisdúr had appeared, a mysterious mist that would come to reclaim it.

3

Kate lightly tugged Anselm's sleeve and whispered, 'Let me show you something.'

They left the others at the farm, to refreshments that had been brought up the day before. The compact rooms had been swept clean so there was a sense of homeliness and of Róisín's welcome; and an echo of Muiris, who had built the place with his father.

'Don't turn around until I say so,' said Kate.

Anselm followed his guide along a sandy path that ran along the embankment. Kate moved quickly, following an old expertise. This was still her island. She knew its moods and temper. And she knew its anatomy, for she left the path and drew Anselm upon a ravaged slope covered in scattered rocks. The land became steep. Against the sky, rising from the ground like the arched back of a whale, was Kate's objective, an outcrop of granite. She stood upon it like a conqueror, her auburn hair loose and flying in the wind. She was a girl again, the girl who'd fled the island but had come back to find it anew. When Anselm clambered on his hands and knees to her side, she said, 'Now you can look.'

Out of breath, he turned and gazed below, to the place he'd come from.

Dawn had died. The day had woken. The Following was over.

All around, as far as the eye could see, were the pastel shades of Róisín's weaving. The colours were almost transparent, and would have crumbled if a mortal hand could touch them. It was a landscape of frightening delicacy. But standing out, shockingly bright, was Seosamh's Field. The green was lush, with livid shadows and a blue bruising that shifted with the whims of the breeze. It was like a graveyard without graves. A memorial without a monument. It was simply and majestically alive.

Anselm breathed in slowly until his chest ached. He called upon Herbert to witness this verdure, along with Major Glanville, Lieutenant Oakley, Regimental Sergeant Major Joyce, Private Elliot, Captain Sheridan, all those involved in the review process, Harold Shaw and his eleven nameless companions . . . Lisette Papinau, John Lindsay . . . and the strangely powerful presence of a man hardly mentioned in the trial papers – a Chaplain who'd been present at the beginning and end of Seosamh's adventure into dying: Father Maguire. Anselm threw back his head and soared on the savage, joyous lift of the wind.

'The island belongs to Seosamh, now,' said Kate, from far, far below.

Epilogue

When Anselm came down from that island Sinai he was a different man, changed by what he'd seen. Perhaps the greatest transformation, though, was that of Kate Seymour. Up there, sitting on that exposed outcrop, arms around her knees, hair scattered by the wind, she made a decision. The name on the white stone of her baptism had been scripted in Gaelic: C-á-i-t. She'd renounced it, discreetly, on entering Trinity College, Dublin. It was part of the turning away from Inisdúr towards a modern life, an up-to-date life, away – she'd come to realise in these past months – from the secret grief of Róisín and her desperate attachment to the fields. The person who now came down to the wharf with Anselm was Cáit Ó Flannagáin. 'I just might introduce my husband to another woman,' she'd joked, seriously.

Anselm knew enough about mountain visions to be very cautious when he got to the bottom. Things were never quite as clear. Doubt often settled in. It required faith to abide by simple insights. This wariness was almost anticipatory, almost prophetic. And he sensed the approach of its fulfilment when, on a cold December morning, he saw Sylvester picking his way between the white crosses and aspens, coming towards the hives.

'Hail, Keeper of the Gate,' said Anselm, meeting him at the edge of the clearing, 'welcome to the communion of saints.'

They sat on the pew and the old man folded his arms tight. The hood of his cloak hid most of his face. Anselm could only see a pointed nose.

'I'm sorry about the address,' muttered Sylvester.

'No matter,' replied Anselm. 'Losing it helped everyone in the end.'

'I didn't lose it.'

Anselm leaned back, lifting his eyes to the branches spread like fingers across the pale sky. Now is the time of awakening, he thought. Now is the time when the secret thoughts of all will be laid bare. This is the Following of Herbert Moore.

'I've known about the execution of Joseph Flanagan since nineteen twenty-five,' said Sylvester. 'When young Kate Seymour came with her questions, I didn't know who she was . . . and I thought her true interest lay long before the court martial of nineteen seventeen. You see, Anselm, that's not where Herbert's story begins.'

The Gatekeeper drew back his cowl and passed a bony hand across his angular cranium. Strong blue veins crawled above large ears towards white fluff. 'I feared for him, and I feared for you.' He turned, bringing his watery eyes on to Anselm. 'I didn't want to see her disappointment on your face.' Lowering his head, he added, sadly, 'But I've seen it . . . even if you try to hide it from yourself.'

'When I was a novice, back in nineteen twenty-five, Herbert suggested we have a chat,' began Sylvester after a long pause. 'In those days we didn't talk very much, but on this occasion we used no hand signs. You see, I'd been asking for stories of the war, so he thought he'd tell me one. We came to those trees over there –' he pointed towards the aspens – 'back then, no one had died, so no one had been buried. It was just a copse. And Herbert and I stood among these thin trees and he said, "Now I'm going to tell you about sacrifice and shame." I don't know why he picked this spot, but it was as though we stood among witnesses. And this is what he told me.'

Herbert's military career began in May 1914 as a second lieutenant with the 22nd Lancers, explained Sylvester. Archduke Franz Ferdinand of Austria was shot in the June and by August Herbert was with the British Expeditionary Force in France. They were outnumbered and driven back from Mons. Amongst all that chaos, Herbert's unit took part in a vital rearguard action at Le Cateau. The objective was to buy time while the army made its retreat. Unfortunately, Herbert joined the withdrawal a fraction too soon.

'He was on the edge of a cornfield,' said Sylvester, one hand on his neck. 'Men to his right, front and left were shot, all in a split second, caught in a spray of machine-gun fire. Herbert didn't even decide to move. He found himself crawling away and then running. And once he'd gone a few hundred yards, he couldn't come back. It was too late. He'd left his men. That was the thing. And he was an officer.

'Herbert calmed himself and quickly rejoined what was left of his Company, but it was too late. A sergeant had seen him run. He was arrested at St Quentin, court-martialled for cowardice and cashiered.

'There was a quite dreadful ceremony afterwards involving every officer in the battalion, and one Private, its newest recruit.' With one hand Sylvester made motions in the air as if he held a knife. 'The Private cut off his badges and buttons – anything that showed rank or a connection with the regiment – and then, starting with the lowest rank, all the officers turned around in silence, showing him their backs, finishing with the Commanding Officer. Without giving a salute, the Private marched away, leaving the door open. Herbert then walked outside alone, forever an outsider. The family were so devastated by the cashiering that they sold their home and moved out of the area. The Moores had lived in Cumberland for two hundred years.

'Herbert had nothing to do with what happened next. He wasn't even consulted. But the family were well connected. And they weren't going to accept the verdict or the sentence without a fight. As far as they were concerned, the court martial should never have taken place: Herbert had only been commissioned for three and a half months and he'd gone missing for a very short time. It was unnecessary, they said. So they wrote a few letters to people of influence. A London barrister who did a lot of work for the government looked at the papers. "How can you run away from a retreat?" he said. A General close to the family concurred. So a petition was drawn up. For the King.' Sylvester paused, as if to give the monarch time to think. 'Herbert received a pardon and was quietly commissioned into another regiment. It was as though nothing had happened.

'But for Herbert it was a momentous conclusion. He felt he'd been saved in the wrong way and for the wrong reasons. And then one day he had to judge a man for what he'd done himself . . . only, of course, Joseph Flanagan hadn't done anything of the kind. He'd been innocent, whereas Herbert had been guilty. That was why he wore young Doyle's tags all his life. He'd felt he was no different. He'd escaped, only he didn't deserve it.

'That's what Herbert told me, over there.' Sylvester raised a bony hand, gesturing towards the crowded aspens. 'We were silent for a long while . . . and then I noticed he was crying. I told him that was all over . . . that even Moses had killed a man, with the hands that would receive the Law . . . but he became distraught, as I'd never seen him before, or saw him since. And do you know, Anselm, I sensed there was . . . something else . . . unrelated to Joseph Flanagan or his own shame.'

'Did you ask him what it was?' whispered Anselm, feeling the anguish of that breaking down in Sylvester's frail voice, sensing it in the awful stillness of the trees that had witnessed Herbert's only public collapse.

'No, no, no,' said the Gatekeeper, shaking his head, 'that would have been impossible . . . and wrong. From that day onwards, though, I often thought about it. And I came to think this: there were two profound experiences at the centre of Herbert's life, each the opposite of the other. The first was Joseph Flanagan, whose sacrifice transformed him. The second, this other . . . well, I can only guess . . . but I believe it was a brutal memory of war, something that bound him to all that was heartbreaking and meaningless. It could have transformed him, too, but it didn't. That, Anselm, is the magnitude of Herbert's faith. He'd looked into the abyss and still believed . . .'

The Gatekeeper stood up and started checking his pockets with the look of confusion that settled upon him whenever the phone rang. Finally he took out a small strip of leather and two drawing pins, enclosing them in a shaking hand. For the first time since Anselm had known Sylvester, the old fellow seemed charged with a quite particular authority. His lines of age brought a lifetime of profound solitude and silence into his trembling voice.

'I said I feared for you,' he began, 'but I feared for Herbert, too. He was a wonderful man. He cared for everyone he met, as though he was meant to meet them. He understood joy and sorrow, accepting both without clinging to the one or complaining about the other. He never once condemned a man or a woman in my hearing. He lived as if every moment were his last, investing it with love and meaning. And as I've got older I've looked as much to the saints I've known as to the names upon the calendar.' He glanced around the hives, nodding at each of them as though from long acquaintance. 'Anselm, do you think Herbert might join their number, if only here in this remote place seen by none but you?'

Anselm took the leather strip. Written upon it was Herbert's name in unsurpassable copperplate. With the drawing pins he attached it to the bench, in the centre of the backrest.

Anselm didn't know what to say. But it was a Gilbertine habit not to reply immediately; to keep counsel for a while. He sat down, watching Sylvester leave the aspens and find the trail back to the monastery.

This was the end of Herbert's Following, he thought; and the beginning of my awakening. It was a numbing experience, permitting the clear-sightedness that comes with vulnerability. He now profoundly understood Larkwood's inspiration: triumph out of failure, forgiveness over condemnation, light from dark. And whatever Herbert had done or failed to do at the outset of his great journey, he'd ended his life a shining, transparent man. And it was at this point, in a stranded car, when neither of them was going anywhere, that Herbert gave to Anselm two small gifts – an understanding of accidents and of fidelity to the flame. He saw once more his lined, simple face: a love greater than himself had burned there, and brightly. Quite suddenly, Anselm felt a flush of gratitude – for all the good that had come his way ever since he'd opened his eyes on the puzzle of living, the wanting to do it well, and the recognition that it was an art to be learned, sometimes painfully. Running through the trees and crosses, he called out to the old man who'd first met Herbert Moore at a ruin by a stream.

The sky was hard and bright. It was cold, and the pink and russet tiles of the monastery sparkled with frost. Small birds floated round the bell tower.

'Take me back to Larkwood, Watchman,' said Anselm, putting his arm round Sylvester. 'I want to go home.'

Acknowledgements

For steadfast guidance and support I extend my warmest thanks to Ursula Mackenzie and Joanne Dickinson at Little, Brown, and to Araminta Whitley and Lucy Cowie at LAW. On Gaelic translation and orthography, I am indebted to the kind and generous assistance of Diarmuid Ó Giolláin at University College Cork. Various staff members of the Public Records Office were enormously helpful and I thank them for their professionalism and defining courtesy. A special word of gratitude goes to my friend Lucy Crawley who made available to me the diary of her grandfather, Major Leslie Peppiatt MC. His testimony, modestly written, exemplifies the astonishing forbearance and courage of the men who fought in the Great War. I hope something of his and their nobility has found its way into the pages of this novel. No book is written without the extensive collaboration of one's family, the partnership that makes withdrawal to write a possibility. For this and so much more, I thank Anne and our three children. As always, we are grateful to the communities at Bec near whom we have the privilege to live and work.

The statistical anomaly regarding death sentences passed on Irish soldiers during the First World War, cited in the text, was taken from *Worthless Men: Race, eugenics and the death penalty in the British Army during the First World War*, by Gerard Oram, (Francis Boutle, 1998). I doubt if anyone can touch upon the subject of Field General Courts Martial during the First World War without recourse to the work of J. Putkowski & Julian Sykes, G. Oram, and C. Corns & J. Hughes-Wilson. I am indebted to them all.

Author's Note

As the narrative makes clear, once Third Ypres was underway operations came to a halt on the 28th August and did not recommence until the 20th of September. During this period the weather was, as one commentator puts it, 'mercifully dry'. On either side of these dates, during the fighting, it poured with rain. It is into this haunting time of reprieve that I have situated the trial of Joseph Flanagan.

This novel is not about FGCMs in general. It does not imply a comprehensive critique of First World War executions from any perspective, be that historical, legal, or moral. Rather, one might say, it is a parable of how a man found meaning in death, and how another – on seeing that – found faith in life. And it is about a fictional trial that cannot be compared with any genuine case. That said, the details surrounding Flanagan's FGCM and his subsequent execution are drawn from myriad real events, gathered from memoirs, reports, published research, Battalion War Diaries, Adjutant and Quartermaster General War Diaries, and the original transcripts of the trials held at the PRO. As a matter of history, then, one might fairly say that Flanagan's experience of military justice was not out of the ordinary. Men and youths regularly appeared before a court without representation. On the other side of the table, notwithstanding best intentions, the court's members were not always qualified to handle evidence or procedure. Trials could be swift. A death sentence would be passed if a man had absented himself from an important duty (the troops had been frequently warned that this was the case). The review procedure involved not just an evaluation of the evidence and the state of discipline in the relevant unit, but also the weighing of a man's life by its worth – always militarily, and sometimes socially. Personal circumstances don't seem to have carried much weight. The transcripts carry the heavy marks of coloured crayon and the reader can almost hear the thinking of that analyst from a very different time. Chaplains tried to give a meaning to the dawn. Alcohol could be a last refuge. Twice a monastery was the site of an execution. Less ordinary (perhaps) but nonetheless true details are these: on at least one occasion, chits were sent to the OC Companies of a battalion requiring them to organise a firing party, and they all refused; a man did drive through the night to plead, unsuccessfully, for the life of a condemned soldier; another did die in a gas mask; and a handkerchief did fall as a signal to the firing party. There can, perhaps, be little that is more painful to read than these last confessions. That is what they read like, to me.

To such happenings Herbert Moore is a kind of witness, as he is to the entire battle for Passchendaele; a single voice for the reader to hear and follow throughout the summer and autumn of 1917. Consequently, his battalion does not track the movement or experience of any unit that actually fought for the Salient or saw it surrendered. The numeration relating to Army, Corp, Division, Brigade, and Battalion is fictitious, as are the titles of key regiments and the numbers of individual soldiers (save 4888, which belonged to my grandfather, a Lancashire Fusilier during the Soudan Campaign).

The Gilbertines were an English monastic order that did not survive the Reformation. References in the text to 'The Rule' are to that of Saint Benedict.

One matter of geography: there are no islands facing Brandon Bay on the west coast of Ireland: Inisdúr and Inismín are inventions.

The following is not a bibliography, but the interested reader will be greatly assisted (as I was) by the following references:

On First World War executions:

Public Records Office: WO 71/387-1027 (trials which ended in execution), WO 93/49 (Summary of Capital Trials), WO 213/1-34 (Courts Martial Registers, FGCM).

Shot at Dawn, J. Putkowski & J. Sykes (Leo Cooper, 1989, New & Revised Edition, 1992)

Blindfold and Alone, C. Corns & J. Hughes-Wilson (Cassell, 2001)

Military Executions during World War 1, G. Oram (Palgrave Macmillan, 2003)

Worthless Men, Race, eugenics and death penalty in the British Army during the First World War, G. Oram (Francis Boutle, 1998)

The Thin Yellow Line, William Moore (Leo Cooper, 1974)

Military Law in WW1, G. R. Rubin (RUSI Journal, vol 143, no 1, February 1998)

On the Battle for Passchendaele:

They Called it Passchendaele, Lyn Macdonald (Macmillan, 1978)

Passchendaele, The Untold Story, R. Prior & Trevor Wilson (Yale University Press, 1996)

Ypres, 1917, Norman Gladden (William Kimber, 1967)

On Boy Soldiers:

Boy Soldiers of the Great War, Richard van Emden (Headline, 2005)

Memoirs:

From the Somme to the Armistice, the Memoirs of Captain Stormont-Gibbs (William Kimber, 1986)

Soldier from the War Returning, Charles Carrington (Hutchinson, 1965)

A Passionate Prodigality, Guy Chapman (Leatherhead, 1990)

The Men I Killed, A Selection From The Writings of General F.P. Crozier (Athol Books, 2002))

Poor Bloody Infantry, Bernard Martin (John Murray, 1987)

Chaplains:

The Great War as I saw It, Canon F.G. Scott (Clarke & Stuart, 1934)

'Happy Days' in France and Flanders, Father Benedict Williamson (Harding and Moore, 1921)

Merry in God, A Life of Father William Doyle SJ (Longmans, Green and Co, 1939)

Novels:

The Secret Battle, A.P. Herbert, (Methuen, 1919)

Her Privates We, Frederic Manning (first unexpurgated version 1930, Serpent's Tail, 1999)

Generally:

Imperial War Museum Book of the Western Front, Malcolm Brown (BCA, 1993)

Forgotten Voices of the Great War, Max Arthur (Ebury Press, 2002)

Tommy, The British Soldier on the Western Front 1914 -1918, Richard Holmes (Harper Perennial, 2005)

Call to Arms, The British Army 1914 – 1918, Charles Messenger (Weidenfeld & Nicholson, 2005)

Forgotten Victory, The First World War: Myths and Realities, Gary Sheffield (Headline, 2001)